Sautee Shadows

Book One of the Georgia Gold Series

Denise Weimer

Sautee Shadows

Book One of the Georgia Gold Series

Denise Weimer

Canterbury House Publishing

www.canterburyhousepublishing.com

Vilas, North Carolina

Canterbury House Publishing

www. canterburyhousepublishing. com

Copyright © 2013 Denise Weimer
All rights reserved under International and Pan-American Copyright Conventions.

Book Design by Tracy Arendt
Cover Art by John Kollock

Library of Congress Cataloging-in-Publication Data

Weimer, Denise.
  Sautee shadows / by Denise Weimer.
     p. cm. -- (Georgia gold series ; bk. 1)
  ISBN 978-0-9829054-8-7
  1. Families--Georgia--Fiction. 2. Georgia--History--1775-1865--Fiction.
I. Title.

  PS3623.E4323S28 2013
  813'.6--dc23

2012032211

First Edition: April 2013

For information about permission to reproduce selections from this book write to:

Permissions
Canterbury House Publishing, Ltd.
225 Ira Harmon Rd.
Vilas, NC 28692

With thanks to my husband Wayne,
for all the times you encouraged me to not give up.

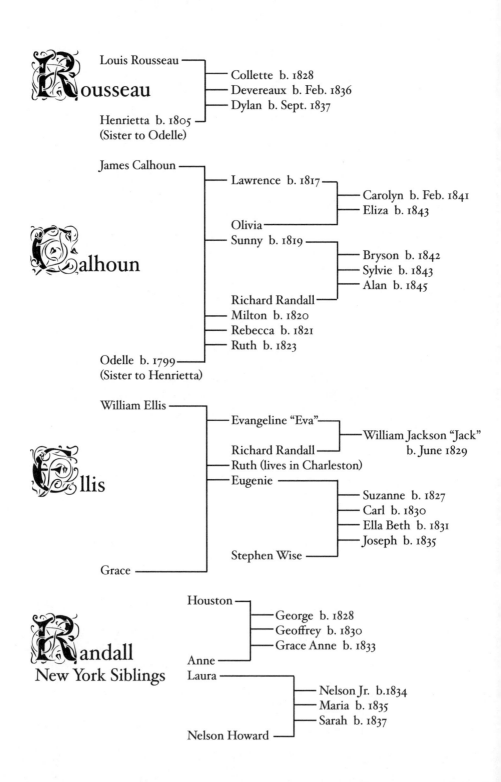

Rousseau

Louis Rousseau ─┐
├─ Collette b. 1828
├─ Devereaux b. Feb. 1836
├─ Dylan b. Sept. 1837
Henrietta b. 1805 ─┘
(Sister to Odelle)

Calhoun

James Calhoun ─┐
├─ Lawrence b. 1817 ─┐
│   ├─ Carolyn b. Feb. 1841
│   └─ Eliza b. 1843
Olivia ─┘
├─ Sunny b. 1819 ─┐
│   ├─ Bryson b. 1842
│   ├─ Sylvie b. 1843
│   └─ Alan b. 1845
Richard Randall ─┘
├─ Milton b. 1820
├─ Rebecca b. 1821
├─ Ruth b. 1823
Odelle b. 1799 ─┘
(Sister to Henrietta)

Ellis

William Ellis ─┐
├─ Evangeline "Eva" ─┐
│   └─ William Jackson "Jack"
│   b. June 1829
Richard Randall ─┘
├─ Ruth (lives in Charleston)
├─ Eugenie ─┐
│   ├─ Suzanne b. 1827
│   ├─ Carl b. 1830
│   ├─ Ella Beth b. 1831
│   └─ Joseph b. 1835
Stephen Wise ─┘
Grace ─┘

Randall
New York Siblings

Houston ─┐
├─ George b. 1828
├─ Geoffrey b. 1830
├─ Grace Anne b. 1833
Anne ─┘
Laura ─┐
├─ Nelson Jr. b. 1834
├─ Maria b. 1835
├─ Sarah b. 1837
Nelson Howard ─┘

FOREWORD

My personal trip back to Habersham County of the mid-1800s started with a private tour of a summer home of that period, perfectly preserved in every detail, and with the letters and diaries of that family. To the gentleman who offered this glimpse into his ancestors' lives – and who also lent me my initial stack of books and the skill of his historical editing – I owe boundless thanks. Thank you, Mr. John Kollock.

Mr. Kollock's cover artwork depicts a typical-style Cherokee cabin resting in the Sautee Valley in the vicinity of Lynch Mountain, with a view of Tray Mountain.

Most of the places, people and events in *Sautee Shadows* actually existed – apart from the main characters, of course. I sought to drop my characters into a very realistic time and place, and I hope you enjoy the journey with them. Find out what happens to Mahala, Jack, Carolyn, Dev and Dylan as the country spirals towards The War Between the States in Book Two of The Georgia Gold Series, *The Gray Divide!*

PROLOGUE

He wrote the words with the steady hand of one who already knew what he wanted to say. Testing, adjusting, so that each sentence was just right, he had framed the note in his head as his horse made swift passage home on the Unicoi Road this afternoon. It was important to state things accurately and delicately ... just in case. Of course as soon as he retrieved Kawani from the neighbors' farm he'd tell her everything. Why hadn't he before? But he could no longer delay, not with the permanency of his father's rejection, not with the threats mounting from all sides. Every rustle of the spring branches, every shadow produced by the clouds scuttling over the moon tonight had raised the hair on the back of his neck. He couldn't shake the impending sense of doom that had steadily built over the past few months. In his mind's eye, Michael saw again the screaming newspaper headlines about the Cherokee removal and the look on Rex's face when he'd lunged across the table at him. Hate everywhere.

Maybe it was the gold that made him paranoid. Recently he'd come very close to cursing its existence. But he couldn't do that ... not when it was going to buy peace for him, Kawani, and their child. Soon they would live in happy seclusion on the farm he'd just purchased, and the world could go to pieces around them.

Tucking the deed into his lock box, Michael closed the lid and slid it into the hidey-hole next to the fireplace. He still had a few hours before he had to sleep. He went to the barn to get packing crates. He'd be out of here before dawn.

A sound in the yard made him pause. His gaze ran along the fence line to the road. Nothing. But he remembered the drifter who had plagued Kawani and rethought his timetable. Would the Emmitts think he was crazy if he showed up past midnight to drag his wife out of bed, to a farm they hadn't even yet settled?

Michael packed quickly, only the essentials. He could come back for the rest. Suddenly he froze. He heard the unmistakable sound of a horse outside. This time of night, that could only mean trouble. He reached for his hunting rifle ...

CHAPTER ONE

October 1835
Off the Southeastern U.S. Coast

As the topsail schooner *Eastern Star* plied the Atlantic on her southward voyage, the air grew noticeably warmer. So much so that Evangeline Randall shed the fine woolen pelerine that matched her dress. The boy standing on the poop deck didn't notice. Clad in a practical dark green skeleton suit, he was gazing up at the sharply raking masts, entranced by the billowing spread of white canvas, the square topsail arching like a proud banner. He had spent all the time he could on deck since leaving New York and was no less awed now than he had been upon first boarding the clipper. To him, she seemed enormous. And fast.

Almost as if reading his mind, his father chose that moment to shout a contradiction. "She's gaining on us!"

Evangeline and Jack both turned to look at the tall man holding a bronze spyglass. His frock coat flapped about his strong frame as he gestured them to his side. "Come see!"

When they joined him, Richard Randall gave the glass first to his wife, then to his six-year-old son, helping secure the lens in front of the child's wide green eye. Sure enough, William Jackson – called Jack by all, save his father when Jack was in trouble — saw that the ship they'd spotted earlier on the horizon was now much closer. A thin column of gray trailed in the air behind her.

"But Father, where are all her sails?" Jack asked in astonishment.

"She goes on steam," Richard answered with a glow in his eye. "The future of transportation, Son, both at sea and on land. And we're going to be part of it."

"How, Sir?"

"By providing the iron the ships and railroads will need."

"All of it?"

Richard and Eva both laughed gaily. "Not all, Jack," Richard answered, "but as much as we can."

Jack smiled as his parents briefly parted with social custom to slip an arm around each other. He thought he had never seen his mother as beautiful as she was now, with her cheeks rosy and the wind whipping tendrils of her dark hair out from under her bonnet. The closer they drew to Savannah, city of her girlhood, the more radiant she became. He felt a little better, contemplating that.

Eva noticed his thoughtful expression and led him over to a bench. As she drew him down close beside her, she asked, "You do understand why we are moving to Georgia, don't you, Jack?"

"So that Father can work with Grandfather Ellis."

"Yes, and what will they be doing?"

Jack frowned in concentration. His father had explained it all, but it had seemed very complicated. "Sending ships with cotton to England?"

"That's right, Jack. There are men in New York making lots of money by shipping Georgia cotton to England. With Father's friend Mr. Collins helping us build fast ships like this one, our family will send the cotton directly to England from Savannah and bring back things people in Georgia need."

Jack's attention was distracted as his new hero, the slender young first officer, Jeremy Northrup, approached. Officer Northrup always smiled when he saw Jack. And while he was always busy, he had often explained his duties while he worked. Now he stood a respectful distance away but had obviously overheard Evangeline Randall speaking with her son.

Ever courteous, Evangeline smiled up at the fair-haired sailor. "Officer Northrup," she acknowledged.

Thus invited to enter the conversation, Jeremy added, "Did you know, Jack, that *Eastern Star* is the first ship Mr. Robert Collins built for your father and grandfather? This is her maiden voyage."

"Yes, Sir," Jack answered proudly.

"The next one will have more cargo space for all those cotton bales, but *Eastern Star* was built for speed."

"And she's about to be lapped," Richard, who had turned to again look out over the rudder, observed wryly. "I think 'the next one' may need to be steam-powered."

Jeremy Northrup gazed at the oncoming vessel with his mouth compressed into a flat line of displeasure. "That would be one of the New York and Charleston Steam Packet Company's, perhaps transporting troops bound for Florida. I saw her on the list scheduled to leave New York just after us. I hate to see the day a beautiful ship like *Eastern Star* eats the wake of such vessels."

"I should have known. Charles Morgan is following me even to Savannah," Richard groaned.

Jack had heard his father speak often of the man Richard viewed as a competitor, even though Morgan was a decade older. The iron and shipping magnate had begun as a grocery clerk in New York City and by age twenty had been owner of a ship chandlery. Richard frequently predicted it would not be long before Morgan bought out his New York and Charleston partners. The entrepreneur also owned the prosperous Morgan Iron Works. Morgan's foundry was nearer the city than Jack's father's, which was located in Ulster County.

"Will we lose you to the China trade, Officer Northrup?" Eva asked Jeremy.

"Oh, I'll stay with Captain Inglis for a while," the young man responded carefully. "But I admit the idea of turning a quick dollar sailing for exotic climes has its charm."

None of this interested Jack now. At the mention of Florida, he had hopped up and ran to the rail to watch the passing ship. "They're going to fight real Indians?" he asked.

"Yes, Sir, the Seminoles under Osceola," Officer Northrup replied.

"But why?"

"Well, the Seminoles don't want to leave their home there in Florida."

"If it's their home, why are we making them leave?"

An uncomfortable silence fell. Jack saw Officer Northrup glance at his mother.

"That's a good question with a complicated answer, Jack. Many Indian tribes are being relocated west. Let's plan to talk about it later," she said. "For now, why don't you come back and sit beside me. There's so much I have yet to tell you about Savannah and our family there."

Jack shot a parting glance at the steamer. The decks which he had half expected to see lined with soldiers in bright uniforms — like his toy wooden soldiers in a crate below decks — were virtually empty. The United States flag ruffled silently at the vessel's rear as the ship steamed slowly past into the distance.

Eva patted the seat next to her. As Jack rejoined her, Officer Northrup excused himself to go talk with Richard. For the next hour, as she sliced an apple and handed the pieces to Jack, Eva Randall spoke of "home." It was not home to Jack, though, who thought longingly of his uncles and aunts in New York City. It had been especially hard to say goodbye to his cousins George and Geoffrey. His mother's words created a knot of apprehension in his stomach.

She talked about how Savannah had been founded in 1733 by James Oglethorpe, who had created a militia. Each of the original four districts of militia had a square on which to train — now Johnson, Wright, Ellis and St. James. The city had grown up around these beautiful squares.

The Ellis family worshipped at Christ Church, the city's oldest church. "The first pastor there was the Rev. Dr. Henry Herbert, chaplain on the ship Ann, which brought the first colonists," his mother said. "Some day you may learn about other great men who have preached there, like John Wesley and George Whitefield."

Eva also told him the old families of Savannah had prospered over the years. Many had built rice and cotton plantations on outlying islands and riverfront property.

"And Savannah is now Georgia's busiest port, second only to Charleston on the Southeastern coast," she added with a hint of pride.

But what Jack wondered about was if those Savannah people would accept him.

His mother seemed to sense his concern. "I know you'll miss your New York cousins, but the family down here will love you. You don't remember them. On our last visit you were only three. But in no time it will seem like you've known them forever. Aunt Ruth lives in Charleston now, but Aunt Eugenie can't wait for us to arrive. I told you Carl is just your age, so see? And your grandparents — well, if I know them, they'll be waiting on the docks!"

"Will they talk like you, Mother?" Jack had always loved his mother's manner of speech. By its very softness it had stood out among the voices of the people up North.

Eva laughed gently. "A little bit. Maybe slower. I've lost some of my accent since I married your father and moved North. You'll probably find everything is a little slower in Savannah."

Jack pursed his lips. That didn't sound good.

His mother gave him a little shake. "It's wonderful, I promise. The people are so kind, even the ones you don't know. And the weather! So warm you can play outside all year long!"

"No snow?"

A flicker of consternation, alien to Eva Randall's sweet face, passed briefly across her features. Then she smiled kindly and drew her little Jack into her embrace. She ruffled his thick, straight dark brown hair.

"It will be all right," she whispered. "It's a beautiful city, and this is a glorious new beginning for us."

Jack wanted to ask why they needed a glorious new beginning when he had been perfectly content in New York. But his mother didn't like his contrary side, and he adored her so much he usually avoided upsetting her. She had always been pleasant, quiet and respectful of her husband, but ever since she and his father had begun to speak of moving to Savannah, Jack had seen something new on her face: hope. She had bloomed like a rose, and now she was as happy and enthusiastic as a girl. So he snuggled into her soft, floral-scented embrace and soaked up her optimism.

By the time his father called them to the starboard side of the ship, Jack was feeling better. Richard's words stirred Jack's innate sense of adventure.

"Come see! The Carolina coast!"

There it was indeed. When they had left New York, it had been a crisp autumn day, and the hills had been splashed with bright colors. But this coastline, robed fully in lush green, reflected the sultry Southern climate.

The ship became a bustle of activity. Sailors who before had lounged near the scuttlebutt or polished the brightwork jumped into motion as orders were shouted. *Eastern Star* slowed and turned into the mouth of the Savannah River.

Eva jumped and grabbed her husband's arm in an uncharacteristic show of excitement. She pointed to an island crowned by a low fortification. "Oh, there's Cockspur Island! It's so good to see it again — like an old friend. Eugenie told me Robert Lee worked on Fort Pulaski right after he graduated from the military academy. He's great friends with Jack Mackay, Mary Low's uncle. Did you know he courted her mother Eliza?"

Richard's eyes twinkled. "I think you told me something of that nature on our last visit."

"Oh, yes, I forgot."

"It's good to see you so happy, my dear."

"And you, Richard? Are you happy?"

"How could I not be? I'm about to start a shipping empire and invest in a new railroad."

Jack, who had sidled up to his parents, knew his father was speaking of the Central of Georgia. The ground breaking would occur in Savannah before the year waned. Before that time, Richard hoped to convince the directors to use Randall iron for its construction, instead of importing the metal from England.

Eva playfully smacked her spouse's arm. "Oh, you know I'm not speaking of business. It was such a big decision to leave your family, and give the management of the foundry over to your brother. I'm inquiring of your heart."

"How can it be anything but content when I see you like this?" Richard smiled warmly, intimately, at Eva. "I have my family right here. I have all I need, and much more. God has greatly blessed us."

Unexpectedly, Eva blushed. "You're right. He has ... more than you know. And ... you have more family here than you know, too."

Jack looked at his mother, wondering at her sudden shy but flushed demeanor. His father, too, waited for her explanation.

"I was going to wait to tell you, but, well, now seems the perfect time. Our new child will be born in Savannah."

"What?!" Richard barked, joy blazing across his features. Then he made an effort to control his voice. "Why didn't you tell me?"

"If I had told you sooner you would have fussed about this whole voyage, now, wouldn't you?"

"You bet I would have!"

"Well, then. You see everything's fine." Eva caught sight of Jack's perplexed little face. She bent down to gaze into his bright green eyes. "You understand, don't you, Son? You're to have a little brother or sister."

He nodded. It was almost too much to comprehend at once. But he knew how badly his mother wanted a baby, had seen her wistful looks as she held Aunt Laura's baby, Nelson Jr. So he put on a smile.

"You're happy, aren't you, Jack?"

"Oh, yes, Ma'am."

His mother put an arm around him and whispered, "You'll always be my first child, and I'll always love you just as much as I do now, or more."

Then his smile was genuine. The moment was complete.

Still basking in the glow of Eva's announcement, they turned their attention to the passing scenery. Richard kept laughing in a dazed manner, repeating "I can't believe it!" and whispering questions in his wife's ear. Distractedly he handed the expensive spy glass to Jack when the boy saw a massive brigantine anchored in the river. Captain Inglis, who was passing, explained that the ship's draft was too deep to reach the city proper, so she had to be unloaded by smaller boats called lighters. Jack watched the activity until they were past.

Then he gazed at the river banks, which were thick with waxy green leaves. His mother told him about the evergreen holly cassena, azalea bushes which flowered in the spring and summer, the feathery mimosa, fragrant tea olive and the hedges of bright green pittosporum. Jack could hardly comprehend that these leaves stayed green all year round. It was all so different from the autumn foliage at home, which would soon drop to reveal the bare branches of the hardwoods.

"Does all of Georgia have these trees?" he asked.

"No." His mother laughed. "The coastal climate is different. In North Georgia there are mountains. It's cool and there are lots of fall colors."

Jack thought that sounded like a nice place.

"Look! I can see the spire of the City Exchange!" Eva exclaimed. "There's the wharf, Jack."

"Yes, look at all the ships!"

While not nearly as busy as New York harbor, a variety of vessels bellied up to the docks of the little city, evidence of thriving trade. Richard pointed out the large-hulled, heavily-sparred packet ships which carried regular shipments of mail and currency, small fore-and-aft one-masted sloops used for inshore fishing, coastal schooners much like *Eastern Star*, and even a steamer or two.

"I bet that's the *John Randolph* that Eugenie wrote of," Eva said. "Remember, Richard, I told you Gazaway Lamar imported the iron plates and frames from England, and they built her at John Cant's shipyard?"

"Yes, she was launched last year, right?"

"That's right."

"Hmm. We'll have to see what we can do about that."

"Already sizing up your competitors, dear?" Eva asked teasingly.

"But of course. I'll grow lonely without Charles Morgan."

They all laughed as the boatswain's bright whistle notes signaled lowering the sails. They were docking at their appointed place on the wharf. The anchor was dropped, its rope as thick as Jack's body. Jack's parents' Irish servants hurried from the lower deck to the family's cabins to collect their trunks. The crates of furniture and household goods would be unloaded later, just before the ornate Randall wrought ironwork was brought out of the ship's hold to meet the ever-growing demands of the city's builders.

"Are we going to our new house now?" Jack wanted to know.

"No, dear. We'll stay with Grandfather and Grandmother Ellis on St. James Square* until we have a chance to move in our things. Then we'll get settled on Wright Square across from the courthouse and just down from your grandparents and Aunt Eugenie."

"We can go see the house tomorrow, though, and you can pick out your room," Richard added.

Jack nodded, satisfied.

As the gangplank was dropped, his mother gave him a quick once-over, straightening his cap and the black silk tie at his neck. A sudden anxiety had seized her. She took hold of his hand and followed Richard to the exit. All the sailors went from swarthy to swain in her presence. Captain Inglis bowed gallantly over her hand, and First Officer Northrup gave Jack's hand a gentleman's shake.

"I hope to see you again, Sir," Jack said.

Jeremy laughed. "Likewise," he replied. Shaking his head, he caught Eva's eye and added in a whisper which Jack overheard, "So grown up for his age!"

Jack flushed proudly.

* Telfair Square was named St. James Square until 1883.

Richard made arrangements to return later with his father-in-law and go over the ship, then took his wife's arm.

Halfway down the gangplank, Eva stopped. Jack almost ran into her, which would have upset his now-very-doting father very much. "Father!" she cried.

Hurrying as much as the descent would allow, Eva rushed down into the arms of a slender man with a mustache and salt-and-pepper hair. He buried her in a bear hug.

"You're here! You are here!" she said.

"I brought the family coach with instructions to speed you straight to the house to your mother, who is beside herself with eagerness." The man who was Jack's grandfather turned to shake hands with his taller son-in-law, then knelt to meet Jack. Behind wire-rimmed spectacles, fine lines creased around brown eyes as the older man smiled. Jack felt he would like his grandfather.

"My, how tall you are for six! You probably don't remember me. I'm William Ellis, your grandfather."

Hesitantly Jack stuck out a hand. Grandfather Ellis pumped it enthusiastically.

"Your mother tells me you love ships. You'll have to come to my office with me. It's very near here. I can see the wharf from my window."

"Oh, I'd like that, Sir!"

"Very good. Do you think I could have a hug?"

Jack nodded and put his arms around the gentleman's neck. He smelled of wool and cologne. His collar was starched and stiff. His mother laughed, a sound like tiny bells ringing.

Grandfather led them to the big, handsome family coach. It was so warm outside the top was back. He helped them get settled inside while he told the servants a wagon would be along momentarily for them and the trunks. Then they left behind the wharf with all its noise and bustle. They turned on Bull Street directly in front of the three-story Exchange Building, which William Ellis told them was used for everything from parties and shows to a place for dignitaries to be received or to lie in state — dead, he explained unwillingly to the curious Jack. Then they passed Johnson Square, where he pointed out Christ Church.

"I thought we'd go down to Wright Square so you could see your house," William added. "Then we'll cut across to St. James."

"What a wonderful idea," Eva agreed.

"The streets here are so wide and sandy," Richard commented. "I never can get over how quiet it makes the traffic."

"There's the house – the old Whiteberry place," Grandfather Ellis announced.

Jack stared at the edifice indicated. He couldn't help what burst forth. "It's pink!"

The adults laughed at the boyish horror in his voice. "It's stucco over brick," said his mother, "and unlike the typical Savannah gray brick, it's unique.* I like it. It's very stylish here on the coast to live in such a house. No one will make fun. I'm so glad you could secure it, Father. I love the Regency architecture. Thank you for your efforts on our behalf."

"You're quite welcome. It will be my pleasure to see my oldest daughter's family settled so near."

"Can we go inside?" Jack's feet itched to run up a flight of the curving twin staircases to the front door.

"Not today, dear," said Eva with a sigh. Her dreamy look indicated that she was already mentally hanging drapes at the front windows.

"Is our new courthouse not handsome?" asked Grandfather Ellis, as he gestured across the street to a huge white building with columns on the front and side. "It's the new Greek Revival design, completed not five years ago."

"Yes, indeed," said Richard. "It won't be a hardship to look at every day."

A few moments later the carriage halted before a Federal style home nestled welcomingly among the live oaks and palm trees. The oaks were draped with a gray substance that Eva told Jack was Spanish moss.

"Here we are," said William Ellis, stepping out and helping Eva alight. Then he lifted Jack to the ground with a smile. "Time to meet your grandmother."

After another annoying episode of fussing and fixing, they made their way to the porch. The sound of a small dog's yapping suddenly came from within. William paused.

"I forgot to mention, your sister is here. She would not be put off until dinner."

At that moment the door opened as if of its own accord. Jack stared open-mouthed at the figure framed there. The man was not only one of the tallest he had ever seen, he had the darkest skin. He was clothed all in white and on his head was a red silk turban. His face was a perfect mask of dignity as he said in a deep voice, "Welcome home, Mrs. Randall."

"Thank you, Saleem."

Jack's mother seemed as nonplussed by the dark giant as the giant did by the fierce ball of tawny fur skittering about his feet.

---

* A nod to Savannah's one-of-a-kind "Pink House."

"Hush, Pixie," hissed a petite lady with very puffy sleeves. She hurriedly scooped up the dog and came forward, smiling broadly. Jack could see a resemblance to his mother in this woman's features, though he felt sure not even a relative could imitate Eva's beauty. He watched as the two women embraced, then he was introduced to his Aunt Eugenie. He gave the perfunctory bow.

"Isn't he cute, Eva?"

Something about this unfamiliar aunt thinking him cute was faintly annoying. Maybe it had to do with the low growl the Maltese in her arms was uttering.

As the party moved inside, another lady emerged from a side door. Grace Ellis tearfully hugged her daughter, son-in-law and grandson. Jack found his face examined, his height again exclaimed over, and his resemblance to his father declared before being pulled into a second embrace. He didn't mind too much. He felt the woman's unconditional acceptance and while she wasn't and could never be Grandmother Randall, she would do.

"Come, come into the parlor. Jack must meet his cousins!" Aunt Eugenie declared.

"Yes," Grandmother Ellis agreed. "I've waited a tea tray ... with your favorite cranberry scones, Eva."

"Have you any sandwiches, hopefully of the non-cucumber variety?" Richard asked.

Grace shot him an amused, indulgent smile. "Yes, Richard, just for you I have chicken salad. It will tide you over until dinner."

"Good, after we eat we can go back to the wharf," Grandfather Ellis declared. "I can't wait for Richard to take me over the *Eastern Star*."

As they entered the parlor, three children rose from the sofa and looked for all the world like little soldiers at attention. Or maybe it was more like the three wise men, for Jack saw that each child held a small gift. They were dressed immaculately, the girls in blue dresses with kid slippers and embroidered stockings, the boy in tapering trousers which matched his leg-of-mutton-sleeved jacket. Its buttons strained at the waist, for he was round and short, with curly brown hair. His sisters, by contrast, were fair and tall. All three stared at him with open curiosity. Jack stared back, wondering if the presents were for him.

That question was settled directly, when his mother was asked to sit on the settee. While Grandmother Ellis oversaw the pouring of tea, Aunt Eugenie introduced her children, each of whom came forward in turn, made a bow, and handed their aunt a gift. Jack felt as if he were watching a very strange performance indeed.

Four-year-old Ella Beth was the youngest. With her blonde curls bouncing, she affected a charming curtsy. Then, after presenting a rose, she snuggled right up to Jack's mother.

"Oh, how lovely," said Evangeline. "Our roses at home — I mean, in New York — are long gone. And how lovely *you* are."

Jack felt a stirring of envy and thought the new baby perhaps should be another boy.

Carl's gift was a box of chocolates, which he looked at so wistfully Evangeline offered him one.

"No, no!" cried Aunt Eugenie, shooing her son away.

Suzanne of the pinched face, eight, stood by as her aunt unwrapped her present, looking, Jack thought, as if she smelled a disagreeable odor. But she did smile when Eva lifted a heavy brass key from its box. "For your new house. Welcome back to Savannah, Aunt Eva," she proclaimed.

Eva seemed greatly moved by the little ceremony. She hugged Suzanne and had her sit on her other side as the tea tray was finally produced. Jack resigned himself to a chair in the corner, where he made himself content, if not with the too-sweet tea, with the refreshments. With a full stomach it was easier to agree with his mother's declarations of how happy she was to be here.

Tea over, the men took themselves back off to the riverfront, declining Jack's offer to accompany them.

"I think you've had quite enough excitement for one day," Eva told him. "Our trunks have arrived by now. We can take a nap and freshen up before dinner."

"But I'm not tired!"

Grandmother Ellis surveyed her daughter. "You do look a little worn, dear. Perhaps you'd rest better in the quiet, with Jack and the children playing down here."

"Well ..."

Jack glanced from his mother to the trio of cousins, unsure which fate he preferred. Unexpectedly, Suzanne piped up. "We could play charades," she offered.

"See there, it's settled," Eugenie said, with a proud glance at her eldest. "I'll come up to help you unpack a bit."

Eugenie grabbed her sister's arm, as if afraid Eva might disappear if she let her out of her sight.

"Well, I do have news to tell both of you," Eva admitted. Over her shoulder she told Jack she'd be in the first room on the right upstairs, and directed her son to be good and have fun. Moments later the children heard shrieks and gasps coming from the women in the hall. Jack noticed his cousins staring at him again.

"I'm to have a baby brother or sister," he told them in a lame voice.

"Well, it's about time," Suzanne replied. "I have three, and my mother is younger. Baby Joseph is napping now."

Jack thought of several mean things to say, but he held his tongue as he knew his mother would have him do. He already felt he did not like this girl, cousin or not.

"So it's to be charades?" he said.

"You talk funny," Ella Beth observed.

"That's because he's a Yankee," Carl told her.

Jack wasn't quite sure if he knew what a Yankee was, but he knew when he had been insulted. "I am not!" he cried, feeling hot inside.

"Well, you're half Yankee, anyway," Suzanne conceded, and before her cousin could decide whether those were sufficient fighting words, she added, "So, I'll go first."

She stood imperiously in front of the fireplace while the younger children sat Indian-style on the carpet. Jack quickly assessed that Ella Beth was a bit young for the game, and Carl must be a little slow. Since Suzanne was older, she nearly always guessed his subject more quickly, but Jack kept pace with her for a good half an hour.

Finally Ella Beth moaned, "I'm tired of charades!"

"I have an idea," Jack said. "Let's play 'pinch, no smiling.'" He looked at Suzanne. He thought how much he'd like to pinch her nose, hard. Then she would no longer look like she was smelling something foul. The thought made him chuckle.

"What's so funny?" she asked suspiciously.

"Nothing."

"I don't know about that game. It's silly."

"Yeah, well, you just think you won't win. That's all right. We can play without you."

"I didn't say I wouldn't play."

"Well, come on, then."

"What shall we use as forfeits?" asked Carl. "Let's put them on the table. I can use my marbles." He dug in his pocket.

Ella Beth took the ribbons from her hair. Suzanne sacrificed her bracelet, and Jack laid down his ivory-handled pocket knife. Then they all sat in a circle. Jack was actually glad he and Suzanne didn't have to pinch each other's noses because he was fairly certain neither one of them would ever smile and they'd be locked in that awkward position until their parents put them to bed. However, he found he had a soft spot for little Ella Beth. She looked so funny and fierce with her face screwed up in an effort at self-control that he laughed before he caught himself.

Overjoyed, she grabbed his knife.

"Hey, don't open that!" he cried.

She jumped up and down. "Jack must pay! Jack must pay!" she sang. "If you want it back you have to hop all over the room on one foot and bawk like a chicken."

"Oh, all right."

Loathe to look so foolish in front of the others, Jack decided he would go to the extreme and be as crazy as possible. He began to bawk, peck and crow, flapping his arms like wings as he hopped like a one-legged fowl. His cousins erupted into wild laughter. He was making so much noise that the ball of fur returned, yipping ferociously. As the annoying animal entered, Jack looked to make sure he didn't hop on it, lost his balance, and went sprawling, taking a potted palm with him.

As if in a slow nightmare, he saw the palm branches slap a slender vase stand on the room's periphery, on which was perched a regal porcelain vase hand-painted with elaborate flowers. It fell, catching the arm of the wingchair in just the wrong way. The vase's handle splintered from its body as it hit the hardwood floor.

All the children gasped.

"Mother's vase from the Imperial Glass Factory! All the way from St. Petersburg!" cried Carl.

At that moment a glimpse of white alerted Jack to the abrupt entrance of the black giant. He glanced at the thunderous face. The whites of the man's eyes flashed under the red turban.

"What have you done?" the man growled.

"Exactly what you'd expect from a Yankee!" Suzanne declared.

Face hot with shame, Jack scrambled to his feet and did the only thing he could think of when surrounded by hostile enemies. He fled up the stairs as fast as he could go to the first door on the right.

Inside, his mother sat up on the bed, blinking her sleepy eyes in disorientation as Jack flung himself sobbing onto her skirts.

"What — whatever is the matter, dear? Are you hurt?" she asked him in alarm.

"I wanna go home! I wanna go back to New York! I hate it here! It's not fall when it's fall and the trees have big spider webs in them and people talk different and there are big mean black servants! And my cousins are mean, too. Especially Suzanne." Jack poured it all out in a rush, then gulped for air.

Eva sat on the edge of the bed and pulled Jack into a sitting position beside her. "What happened?" she asked. "Tell me everything."

Dolefully Jack related the events of the last hour, reluctantly admitting to breaking the vase, but finishing with the crowning accusation: "And Suzanne kept calling me a Yankee."

"As if that excuses you breaking the vase," his mother said in a low tone.

"It was that stupid dog's fault!"

"*Jack.*"

He glanced at her. Her severe expression started the tears easing out again. "I'm sorry, Mother. It's just that it's all so awful."

"I see I should not have left you. I underestimated what a big change this would be for you," Eva said, almost as if to herself. "You're so young … but I should have known." She returned her full attention to her son. "You know what you'll have to do. You'll go down and take responsibility and apologize to Aunt Eugenie. Perhaps the vase can be fixed."

"Oh, Mother, oh, no! She'll hate me, just like the others."

"She will not. But even if she were to, no son of mine would cower in his room afraid to own up to his misdoing."

"Yes, Ma'am," Jack said tragically.

"Look at me," Eva demanded. She lifted his chin. "Don't you for one second ever be ashamed of who you are. Yes, you're half Northerner and half Southerner, but both halves come from the best of families. Each side brings something special to who you are. Why do you think Grandfather Ellis wanted your father to move down here so badly? Not just because of me, I promise you. Because your father's smart. He's successful and well-connected. And me … do you think I hung my head in shame when I lived in New York? No, Sir. I held it proudly and never let anyone make me feel less as a daughter of Georgia. Do you understand, Jack?"

"Yes, Ma'am," he said slowly. "But Mother, I don't know if I can ever like it here."

Evangeline smiled gently. "You just might be surprised how much it will grow on you."

"I don't know about that."

"Do you love *me*, Jack?"

"Oh, yes, more than anything."

"Then you've got to love the South, even if it's only deep down, just a bit. Because it's so much a part of who I am."

"Well, when I think of it that way, I might can stand it," Jack admitted grudgingly.

His mother smirked and poked his chest. "It's part of you, too, whether you know it or not yet."

Jack made a face and acted as if he'd brush himself off, like he was a tree getting rid of that strange Spanish moss. Evangeline laughed and embraced him, almost fiercely.

"I love you," she said. "Always remember that. And God loves you, too. He can help us through any hard thing … like confessing a broken vase to Aunt Eugenie. Come, I'll go with you."

Eva stood him up, straightened his clothes, and washed his face at the basin. Then, with his hand in hers, she led the way downstairs.

CHAPTER TWO

April 1837
Sautee Valley, Georgia

ichael Franklin stood shin-deep in Sautee Creek, shoveling loads of sand and gravel into his wooden sluice box. Water rushed through a 15-foot flume, sweeping away the soil while more promising sediment collected on the sluice's "riffles," wooden strips nailed crosswise along the bottom of the box. The only sounds apart from the scrape of his shovel, the plunk of creek-bottom sand, and his labored breathing were the gurgling of the creek and occasional birdsong in the nearby trees.

Michael paused, taking a minute to wipe his face and look around with satisfaction. The leaves on nearby Lynch Mountain were putting out. Their bright, fresh green provided a heart-lifting contrast to the dogwoods and pink wood azaleas. Sautee Creek rushed happily towards its joining with the Chattahoochee, just down from the Indian mounds in neighboring Nacoochee valley. It was a beautiful scene.

Yes, he had done the right thing. Clarkesville could not be considered a large town by anyone's standards, but as the only son of the owner of Franklin Hotel on the square, Michael had constantly been pushed into the public light. Having to interact with guests and locals all day, every day, had slowly worn him down. He knew what his parents couldn't understand: that he was a man meant for the quiet life, for communing with nature.

Lowering a board at the head of the flume, Michael stopped the flow of water into the sluice box. As the sediment inside had time to dry, he'd get a better idea of what he had, but he couldn't resist a quick peek. He gave the box a shake. Removing a glove, he stirred around in the debris with a finger.

Sure enough, there it was. The glint of gold flakes in the noonday sun. And something more, too. A small nugget, the size of his pinky nail, the second he'd found in the last two weeks. Michael couldn't stop a grin from blazing across his face.

The funny thing was, he hadn't really cared if he found much gold or not. Oh, sure, the tales of miners staying at the hotel who had struck it big had caught his fancy. The fact that every Tom, Dick and Harry was heading for

Auraria or investing in a gold mining company had only served to increase his restlessness. But really, the gold rush had only provided an excuse.

And Rex Clarke had provided the opportunity.

Michael put the nugget into his leather pouch and waded over to the shore for a little break. He sat down on a log, unplugging his canteen and thinking back to the day he'd walked into the room Rex was renting at the hotel to discover a half dozen men deep into a haze of smoke — and a game of poker.

He'd already known Rex to be a gambler, and at only seventeen, the widowed doctor's son had already managed to establish a reputation as something of a womanizer, too. Rex loved to arrange horse races and shooting matches on his father's property just north of town where their new home, The Highlands, was under construction. But a poker game in the Franklin Hotel was a different thing entirely. Gambling with cards, dice or on billiards was illegal in Habersham County.

"What do you think you're doing?" Michael had cried, aghast. "You'll have the law down on not just you but on me, too, for gaming!"

"Oh, simmer down," Rex had said, waving a whiskey decanter at him. "Come have a drink."

But the other players had started to mumble amongst themselves and pack up their cards.

"Hey, where are you goin'?" Rex had slurred.

The oldest of the group had spoken up. "Are you kidding? We don't want to be arrested if he decides to go for the sheriff."

"Aw, he's not going for the sheriff, are you, Michael? Michael's an old friend. Hey — all right, then. Next time," Rex had conceded as the chips were shoved in his direction. When the door finally closed on the last man, he had turned to Michael with fire in his eyes. "Now what did you have to go and do that for? Since when are you so straight-laced?"

But Michael knew Rex and his father needed the rooms his family let them. And eventually out of his silence had come Rex's agreement for Michael to mine the Clarke land lottery lot in Sautee ... plus ready cash for mining equipment and supplies to repair the abandoned Cherokee cabin and stable thereon. In return, Michael was to pay Rex one-fourth of any profits, a fairly common arrangement.

Michael shook his head, amazed that Rex had not mined the property himself before now. It was true that most gold finds had been from the Nacoochee Valley and west towards Auraria and Dahlonega. But truly Michael thought that Rex was probably just too lazy.

And while Michael had at first thought of the venture as a chance to test his newfound manhood — a temporary reprieve from an undesirable path in life — the first glint of gold had whispered of true freedom.

Swallowing another gulp of water, Michael's gaze caught a movement on the creek bank, just up from where he sat. There was a flash of blue. Michael couldn't believe his eyes. A girl clad in a blue linen dress was emerging from the trees on the path that led to his cabin. And not just any girl: an Indian girl, her black hair, tied back with a ribbon, shining in the sun, her skin a tawny brown. Michael could easily imagine her in the native dress which the Cherokee had long ago abandoned in one of many attempts to Anglicize.

His surprise caused him to rise from the log. She instantly spotted him, and her face — which was quite lovely, he noticed — quickly went from placid to alarmed. She made a move as if to flee. Somehow the gesture made Michael intensely want her to stay. Inexplicably, he felt a connection, like he did to this land. She looked as natural here as he felt.

"No, wait," he urged her. "I won't hurt you."

She glanced back over her shoulder, uncertain.

He took a step toward her, placing a hand on his chest. "I'm — Michael. You are ...?"

"Kawani."

"Kawani. That's a beautiful name. What does it mean?"

Her eyes turned playful. Clearly she recognized he was desperate to keep her attention. "What does 'Michael' mean?" she threw back cheerfully. When he drew in one corner of his mouth in an expression of annoyance, she took pity on him. "It means month of the flower moon — the month of my birth, April."

A woman's worried voice sounded suddenly from up the path. "Kawani?"

"There are more of you? What are you doing here?" Michael asked.

"I can ask you the same thing." The girl's gaze flickered curiously over Michael's sluice box.

"I think that's pretty obvious."

"Yes, but a sluice box? Miners have advanced to digging tunnels and dredging the river with diving bells where we live."

"Kawani!"

"Here, Mother!"

Kawani made an impatient face as an older Cherokee woman broke into the clearing. Upon sight of Michael, the woman immediately tensed and hurried to put an arm around her daughter. To his ever-increasing surprise, a tall, statuesque man, Kawani's father, he guessed, was right behind her. Michael's expression congealed. He thought of the knife tucked securely in his boot.

"All right," he said roughly, "I have the permission of the property owner to mine this land, and papers to prove it. So I ask again, what are *you* doing here? It's not exactly natural nowdays to see Cherokee in these parts."

The man stepped forward, his hands lowered before him in a gesture of peace. "I am Henry Cornsilk from just outside Auraria. My wife, Sally, and my youngest daughter, Kawani. I bring my clan's hides and wild honey in my wagon to sell to families in Habersham. This farm was the place my wife and I started our family before the land was ceded. A friend who just passed through these parts brought word the cabin was long vacant. Sally — she wanted to see it again. I told her maybe we spend a few nights here and ride out during the day. I see we were misinformed."

Michael considered. Satisfied, he nodded. "I've been here over a month. Before that, the Clarkes — the owners — had a neighbor, Ben Emmitt, keep an eye on the place. Make sure no one was mining unlawfully, stuff like that. I'm Michael Franklin." He stuck out his hand, which Henry Cornsilk cautiously shook. "But surely you noticed signs of occupation."

"Yes. We had just seen your horse in the stable when my wife noticed Kawani had wandered off. She is forever too curious, putting herself in danger," he said, casting a stern eye upon his offspring.

"I assure you, she wasn't in danger." When Henry's quelling look turned upon him, Michael quickly added, "This time, anyway. From me. I mean — she wasn't in any danger from *me*."

A giggle from Kawani caused Michael to glance at her again.

He was still staring, trying to figure out why he wanted so much to know more about her, when Henry said, "We will go now. I'm sorry. I did not know how things stood here."

Sally Cornsilk began to turn their daughter away from the creek. It was not only the girl's leaving, but the poignant sadness in the mother's eyes, that caught at Michael's heartstrings.

"Wait," he said. When the family turned back to him, surprised, he went on, "You've come so far. There are no good accommodations near here, and it can hardly be comfortable sleeping in a wagon. Your original plan was a good one. I'm a bachelor out for a bit of adventure, and I don't mind sleeping in the stable a few days. Why don't you stay in the house while you sell your goods to the farmers and miners in the area?"

"You'd do that?" Sally looked aghast, albeit with a flicker of eagerness, but her husband looked downright suspicious.

"Yes, why would you do that? For strangers — Cherokees?"

Michael gave a half-shrug. "Dunno. Guess if this was my home, I never would have left willingly, either, and I'd give my eyeteeth to stay here another night."

The effect of his words was amazing. Henry's face relaxed and he met Michael's eye with a look that communicated respect and unexpected kinship.

"It is as you say," he admitted. "Thank you, Michael Franklin."

"The house is open. Take whatever of your things that you need to inside. Once I clean out the sluice box, I'll be up to move a few items out to the stable."

Sally gave a gratifying half-muffled sob of joy at the prospect. Before Henry shooed the chattering women up the path, Michael shot over his shoulder as he turned back to the creek, "Of course I am hoping for some good home-cooked meals out of the bargain."

"I give you home-cooked," Sally spoke up joyfully. "So much home-cooked you can't eat it all."

"All right, then."

I'm crazy, Michael told himself as he stared at the glinting sediment in his sluice box. *A trusting fool. These people could kill me in my sleep and take everything I have.*

But something in his gut told him he was a good judge of character. It was the memory of Kawani's bewitching black eyes, and not anxiety about securing his possessions, that made him hurry about his task.

The evening meal that night and the conversation around the fire became typical of what followed for the next week. Michael could see that sentimental memories of the snug, windowless cabin with its squared door jamb and stone fireplace — typical Cherokee construction — made the Cornsilks relaxed. Kawani and her mother had made potato soup and bean bread using a combination of staples in the cabin cupboard and supplies they had brought in their wagon. Sally appeared gratified by Michael's obvious delight in the dinner. She smiled and nodded at his praise and gathered the dishes for washing. Whether she did not speak English well or merely did not like to speak much at all, Michael could not tell.

No such handicap afflicted Henry Cornsilk, though. He propped his feet up in front of the fire, a strong brown hand cradling his tin coffee cup, and spoke of the downright frightened reception he had received from most whites in the area.

"I was here when the chestnut was plentiful, when wolves howled in the forest at night, and when a man had to be afraid for his livestock or his life because the panther would leap down from the tree above," he said, "and yet these farmers and miners look at us as if we were *didanvdo* — spirit — some strange thing they never saw before. Maybe they think we lead a caravan to reclaim our lands in these valleys of our ancestors." Henry chuckled mirthlessly. "As if we could. Instead, I fear the efforts of John Ross on our behalf have only served to give our people false hope. The legal victories we have had before your Supreme Court are meaningless. President Jackson has allowed those hungry for land and gold to do as they will."

Michael nodded. "I have been aware of the abuses your people have suffered – Ross arrested, the newspaper office burned at New Echota, Joseph Vann's house taken away as if he had no rights whatsoever. But this is the first time I have spoken of these happenings with — well, an actual Cherokee." Michael grinned sheepishly.

A ghost of a smile flickered on Henry's face, and he nodded. "And this may be the last time, too. The treaty party that signed at New Echota two Decembers ago was not truly representative of my people, but the government will enforce the paper. Petitions and court cases are futile. I have seen the lust of gold in the eyes of the white men. I've seen how many there are — more men than land. Like those already taken west from this area by the mixed-blood James Wofford, we, too, will have to go."

"That is not what I want," Michael stressed. "That's not what many white men want."

"I know. Good men like Senators Webster and Clay have done much to aid us. But the inevitable will come."

"The treaty deadline is almost a year away," Michael said hopefully. "Perhaps a miracle will occur."

"You believe in miracles, Michael Franklin? The white missionary to our people tell us of such things."

Michael was aware that the women had finished the dishes. While Sally put fresh blankets on the bed, he felt Kawani's presence near. She had drawn up a chair, listening quietly. He answered carefully, "I'd like to."

Henry nodded thoughtfully. "You do not have the lust for gold in your eyes, yet I see you with the sluice box at the creek," he observed.

Michael found himself uncomfortably telling about his background and the plans his parents had carved out for him which until recently had seemed so inevitable with three younger sisters who would eventually move away.

"I don't want the town life. A quiet spot in the beauty of this valley would suit me much better," he said.

Kawani had edged closer. She offered him a smile that took his breath away. He was basking in what he supposed such a look implied coming as it did right on the heels of his words when she gave him a nudge and he realized she was holding out a popcorn popper.

31

"Put it near the fire, Michael Franklin," she said softly. "A bedtime snack."

"Oh! All right. Sounds good."

Soon the cheerful popping of kernels and the fresh corn smell filled the snug cabin. Sally joined them. As they munched popcorn, Henry told of past councils and festivals when his family, of the Wolf Clan, had joined the six other clans at the Cherokee capital, New Echota. Michael was fascinated with his descriptions of Indian games, farming methods and social rituals. While Henry was fully knowledgeable about the native spirituality of his people, he, like many others, had apparently embraced much of the white missionaries' teachings of Christianity.

Each morning for over a week Henry took the wagon out, returning for a sharing of food and culture each night. At first, as Michael had expected, he took the women with him. Then one day Sally and Kawani stayed behind. Sally wore a holstered knife at her back while she washed clothes at the creek. Michael had no doubt she knew how to use the weapon well.

Kawani aided her mother until the garments were all spread on the nearby bushes to dry, then she came to watch Michael. After a few minutes the girl grew bored. With her skirts tied up she frolicked in the creek, her black hair hanging loose about her slim waist.

Michael was having a hard enough time keeping his eyes on the sluice box when she let a sheet of cold water fly in his direction.

"Hey!" he cried. Turning, he saw she had done it deliberately. Not only that, she was skipping mischievously toward him again. "Oh, no, you don't!"

He flung the contents of his shovel just far enough to keep her at bay.

"You work too hard, looking for all that gold," she taunted. "You look too serious."

"I'm serious about choosing my own future," he replied.

"I hope it has a little fun in it!" Kawani scooped up water with both hands and managed to catch him right in the face as he was bending for another shovelful of creek bottom.

"You little minx!"

As Kawani fled giggling, Michael started after her, stomping his boots hard to splash as much as possible. He wasn't sure what he intended to do if he caught her. But one look at Sally's alert, frozen expression as she watched from where she sat, back rigid, on the creek bank, stopped him. He sure didn't want that wicked steel blade waved in his face.

"Just go on now," he said instead, and turned back to his sluice box.

Out of the corner of his eye, he saw Sally take Kawani's arm and hurry her toward the house. Sally was talking rapidly, and not in English. Oops.

Two days later Henry announced over dinner that he had concluded his business in Sautee-Nacoochee. The next morning the Cornsilks would return to Lumpkin County.

Rather than linger by the fire as had been his habit, Michael excused himself to the stable. The thought of this being his last night on a pallet of straw brought him no joy, only an amazing sense of loneliness. Always the odd bird in his own family, he realized he had enjoyed the warmth of fellowship the Cornsilks had provided. And there was more, though it was premature and certainly foolish.

He slipped out to the fence where Kawani brought the scraps each evening. There he sat on a stump until he heard her light tread and saw her pleasing form framed against the orange evening light. This would be the first time they had spoken alone. He rose awkwardly, hoping he wouldn't scare her.

"Kawani." Michael spoke her name softly, tentatively, as she caught sight of him and paused. "I would speak to you."

Glancing back over her shoulder at the cabin, she decided it was near enough and came on to the fence. "Yes, Michael Franklin?" she said, tossing scraps from the pot into the gathering shadows. "If you speak quickly, they will think I have only stopped at the privy. If you take any longer they will come looking."

Michael nodded his understanding and got right to the point. "I'm trailing the gold up the creek. You've seen me gradually moving the sluice box. The past two days I worked the feeder creek. Where it empties into Sautee, the gold content dropped way off." A trace of excitement crept into his voice. "But farther up, it picked back up again."

Kawani looked askance at him.

"I think there's a big deposit in the hillside where the stream issues. I'm going to start digging a tunnel tomorrow. If I'm right, before long I'll have enough gold to buy some land. Your father was right, Kawani. I'm not a greedy man. All I want is a peaceful life. I want to try farming. I'm going to ask Rex Clarke about buying this land. But I need a helpmate, a companion, and to be honest, Kawani — I'm hoping that might be you. I know it's soon, but I have feelings for you. Of course ... maybe you don't return them. Maybe there's someone else."

"No," she said softly, her eyes as wide and luminous as a doe's in the fading light.

"No, what? You don't have feelings for me, or there's no one else?"

"There's no one else. But ... why would you want a Cherokee wife? You could have most any white girl in these parts, especially once you have all that gold." Curiously, she studied his sandy hair, blue eyes, and straight, narrow nose, assessing him inside and out. Many women considered him handsome, but Kawani seemed to look deeper within.

"Why not? Like you said, there's no one else. You're the first girl I can see living with. I think you'd bring some fun into my life." He grinned, recalling her words of two days prior. He also realized what he'd wanted to do in the stream: grab her and place a sound kiss on those full berry lips. He continued a little unsteadily, "And at the same time, you seem unafraid of work. I think you'd know what to do on a farm."

She nodded. "Yes. I would like that life with you, Michael Franklin."

Surprise and pleasure at her honesty washed over him. "Then, in a couple of months I can bring the gold to Auraria to have it made into bars. If you'll tell me where you live I'll come speak to your parents. In the meantime, perhaps you can make them aware of your feelings."

"You're that sure you'll have so much gold?"

"I'm sure I'll have *something*. Even if it's not as much as I'd hoped, I'll come for you, Kawani."

Kawani rapidly gave him directions to the Cornsilk farm, concluding with, "I'll be waiting for you, Michael Franklin."

"Do you think you could drop the last name?"

"Yes — Michael." Awkwardly she paused. Then before he knew what was happening she leaned in and pressed her lips to his. He reacted, drawing her in with a strong arm, savoring the sweet nearness. But the gesture caused her to drop the pot. A second later she broke the embrace and bent to retrieve the item. In that moment — in the glimpse of her flustered face — Michael realized how young she was. A tender possessiveness swelled within him.

"We won't be apart for long, Kawani," he said.

The girl nodded before dashing off to the cabin. Michael stood in the cool April dusk a few minutes, smiling to himself, before retiring to his pallet in the stable and sweet dreams of a Cherokee maiden.

CHAPTER THREE

August 1837
Clarkesville, Georgia

A cloud of dust rose from the porch of the Franklin Hotel as Martha Franklin's broom whisked away the trackings left by the day's customers. The heat was considerable, and the exercise had left her plump form decidedly damp. She raised an apron to blot at her flushed face, pausing for a moment to survey the scene.

She always appreciated the panoramic view commanded by the square. Today the mountains were hazy in the humid, red-orange glow of the summer evening. Yonah's distinctive leaning, rocky peak made her think of her son. Martha's already round lips drew into a sort of pout. Maybe she wouldn't be out here sweating like a slave for all the world to see if her thankless son had not left all the work to his father and four women. The Franklins prided themselves on running their own hotel, but Martha was starting to think about hiring someone. The family's two slaves, Zed and his wife Maddie, were both worked to capacity in their domains of stable and kitchen, respectively. And it was too hard to get a decent day's work out of three teenage daughters, all of whom were chiefly interested in appearing attractive and well-bred to the wealthy lowcountry guests. Not that that was a bad thing, acknowledged Martha. But now Charles' nephew Leon, there was a boy who knew the importance of advancing the family reputation. If he had been born in Michael's shoes, he would have counted himself blessed and happily done his duty. She didn't like him much, but perhaps she'd speak to her husband again about allowing Leon to run the front desk. It would free up Charles for so many other tasks.

Still, she had a mother's heart, Martha did. She did love her only boy, and she permitted herself a small smile as she thought of him mining in that lovely valley. What boy didn't need to sow his wild oats? He'd be back soon enough when the adventure wore off, and in the meantime, it might be for the best that he was away from that no account Rex Clarke.

Martha breathed deeply of the low-hanging tang of smoke in the air, accompanied by the ring of the anvil from a blacksmith's forge. With three of them in town, the daylight hours were so filled with their clinking that she scarcely noticed any more. One by one lawyers and clerks issued from the arched main door of the square brick courthouse. Some stragglers gathered at the public well, with a few horses still tied to the hitching posts nearby.

The western view was dominated by the Habersham House, now silhouetted by the setting sun. From its front door there suddenly issued a couple, quite weighted down with trunks and parcels, but obviously in a hurry. When Martha realized that a few more of their determined strides would bring them to her porch, she hastened to put away the broom and smooth her natural side curls.

She greeted them at the front door with a smile. "Good evenin', folks," she said. "What can I do for you?"

The rotund man puffed, "You can give us a room for the night. That is, so long as no one here is a-plannin' on killin' themselves today."

"W-what?"

"Yes, Ma'am, that's just what Lewis Levy tried to do. Went and drank a bunch of brandy and strung himself up upstairs. Somebody found him an' cut him down in time, and there he lies now, downstairs, for all the world to see! My wife was quite scandalized."

The missus waved her handkerchief in front of her own wide-eyed face. "And who wouldn't be?" she added breathlessly.

"Indeed," murmured Martha.

Before she could invite the refugees inside, the florid man continued indignantly, "Then to top it all off, that fancy Englishman from the stagecoach, Featherstonhaugh, came down looking for supper and said he found the two sisters in a brawl. One of them recognized him and put a paltry meal before him, not enough to entice *me* to stay, no, Ma'am! I can't imagine why Featherston-whatever would, either, unless it's just to get some more notes down about the place in that little notebook of his."

"Well, I assure you we have a hearty stew on the fire and our famous biscuits and honey," Martha told them, holding open the door. "I am only sorry you received such a poor impression of our town — and that it might be circulated due to the English guest. Mr. Levy has fallen on hard times."

As she passed, the new guest whispered, "They say not only creditors but a wife jealous and suspicious of her own sister — thus the fight."

"Mmm, who knows," was all Martha would concede. She didn't like people talking about her family, so she tried hard to avoid gossiping about others. "My husband, Charles Franklin, is at the main desk and we'll be happy to situate you for the meal and the night."

Martha was to hope her own disinclination to meddling would bear fruit among her neighbors sooner than she could have imagined. She had just turned to follow the newcomers inside when the sound of an approaching wagon made her pause. The vehicle stopped right in front of the inn, and to her acute amazement, it was her own son who jumped down.

"Michael!" she cried in joyous surprise.

"Hello, Mama!"

But then, what was this? A woman with him? Martha stood frozen as her son handed down his female companion, whose head was covered with a scarf. Then the woman looked up, the gesture faintly uncertain, and Martha gasped softly. An Indian! And a full-blood. For while the features were indeed lovely, there was no sign of white ancestry whatsoever in them.

"Who is this, Michael?" Martha asked as the two approached.

"This is Kawani ... my wife."

The words fell in Martha's heart like heavy stones in a pond.

"I know it's a surprise. We were only just married last month. I met Kawani in the valley, and when I took my gold to Auraria to the refining lab, I asked her parents for her hand. I have to go back when the new mint in Dahlonega opens, but I just couldn't wait. Mama, I've decided — we've decided —" drawing the woman to his side — "to farm in the valley. I've come to town to bring Rex his share of the gold and to convince him to sell me some property."

"And, of course, to meet you," added the young woman hesitantly.

Martha gave her an automatic stiff smile. But inside her head was reeling. Had her son completely lost his mind? Marrying an Indian? Farming? What would his father say? At the thought of Charles, Martha's stomach turned to jelly. Her husband could be a hard man — a very hard man — when crossed. And this was so crossing Martha felt dizzy.

Michael sensed her inner chaos and reached out to touch her arm. "I know this is all very sudden, Mama. I'm sorry to shock you. But for the first time in my life, I feel peace. I'm happy."

And what, you weren't before? she wanted to ask. *What did we do to make you so unhappy that you had to run away and change everything about your life?*

She didn't speak her accusations, but she did pull away, and unsmiling, said, "Come in."

In the foyer, the Indian girl lowered her scarf, clasping her leather satchel. She gazed in awed silence at the Persian rug and wide pine staircase with its red runner. Before any customers caught sight of her, Martha hurried them through a door and into the family's rooms. Thankfully Charles had gone with the guests to get them settled and was thus spared a public introduction to his new daughter-in-law.

As soon as the girl was corralled, Martha turned to her son. "You said you have business with Rex Clarke? He's in now. Perhaps you'd best see to him before your father comes for his supper. I can serve Kawani some lemonade."

"Oh, yes," Michael said, immediately catching onto the wisdom of her plan. There was an almost imperceptible tightening of his features. "That is a good idea. I'll be back in soon as I can, Kawani. Just stay here."

The girl turned her cheek up for Michael's kiss, seemingly forgetting Martha for the moment. She even jested, "As though I'd go running out into the unfamiliar street."

Michael chuckled and Martha was startled to see the flash of love on her son's face. Kawani seated in the parlor, Martha went to fetch the lemonade. When Martha handed her the glass, Kawani stuck a finger in, poking at the floating lemon and the ice cubes.

"Ice," she said appreciatively, cocking her head as if relishing the tinkling sound coming from within her glass.

"We serve some wealthy and influential people. We must have all the amenities," Martha said. Her voice sounded stiff again. With an effort at breeziness, she continued. "Tell me how you and Michael met."

Minutes later, Martha digested the story but felt no better.

Then Kawani said with a soft directness surprising in one so young, "You do not approve of me. It's all right. I expected as much."

Martha's eyes widened. "I — do not know what to think. I'm sorry ... I really must get the table set for dinner."

With no further ado, Martha rose and hurried into the pantry. She steadied herself there a moment. Then she put out the butter and jam and checked the temperature of the biscuits in the warming oven. Quickly Martha set the table, taking peeks into the parlor as she did.

Kawani sat quietly on the settée. Thus framed, she made a strange figure indeed, with her calico dress and ribbon-tied hair. The lemonade gone, Kawani did not rise to look around as most fidgety girls would have done — Martha's own, to be sure. Martha gave a little prayer of thankfulness that the three of them were passing the evening with the Trippes at the colonel's home on Jefferson Street. No, the Cherokee girl stayed right in place, satchel at her feet, but her eyes studied everything with slow, intentional curiosity, especially Martha's prized gilded mirror with its fancy inlaid swags and bell flowers. The girl recognized quality. Well, she had chosen Michael, hadn't she?

In spite of herself, Martha felt a slight softening.

But look at the time! Charles! Should he come barreling in in search of supper and find this person seated in his parlor, Martha shuddered to imagine the results. He must be warned. Excusing herself, and feeling a little guilty for not showing Michael's bride to her son's old room where she could freshen up, Martha re-entered the lobby.

She was relieved to spot her husband at the desk, his head, crowned by thinning sandy-silver hair, bent over the hotel register. Martha headed for him, but at that moment the front door opened. Leon Franklin, son of Charles' brother Thomas, entered. He looked for all the world more like Charles' son than Thomas'. The twenty-year-old even had his uncle's straight, rather large nose, though he lacked Charles' other strong facial features to balance it. At the moment Leon was burdened down with bags of flour, but Martha was so dismayed at her nephew's untimely appearance that she did not offer to help him. In fact, she could barely muster a greeting in response to his bright smile.

"Aunt Martha, hello! Here are the bags of flour that my father sent over from the store, Uncle Charles. We can't have you running out before the breakfast biscuits are made." Leon hefted his load right over to the desk and dropped the bags on the floor with a floury flourish that made Martha cringe. "Say, that sure looks like the horse Michael bought off Rex Clarke I just saw Zed leading around to the stable. Couldn't be, though, right?"

"I'd hardly think so," Charles chuckled. "Thank you, son."

Martha didn't miss the way Leon drew himself up at the word, spoken in an unusually friendly tone. She thought the subject of her errant son best discussed behind closed doors. "When you are free, Mr. Franklin, I would speak with you."

Charles was jotting another note in the register, not paying attention to her. "I'm free enough, Martha. It's only Leon. Speak on."

When Martha hesitated, Leon took note. He didn't miss much, that was for sure. "He's not here, is he? Michael?" His color had deepened.

Charles quickly looked up.

"He's — yes," Martha admitted. "He's home for a visit."

"What? Well, where is he?" her husband demanded.

"He's gone to see Mr. Clarke. He'll be along shortly."

"It's about time," Charles said emphatically. "I guess the gold has petered out and he's finally realizing where the real treasure is at."

"Is he not going back, then?" Leon wanted to know.

Before Martha could respond to either of them, Charles burst out, "Why don't you join us for dinner, Leon, and you can hear all about it. No doubt Michael will appreciate an audience for the telling of his adventures. I'll just take these to Maddie in the kitchen ..."

Had they not heard anything she had been trying to say? Honestly, men were great lumps sometimes. Martha put a hand on her husband's arm as he bent to lift a flour sack. "I'm not so sure that's a good idea," she said nervously.

"Why not?"

"Michael is not alone. He's brought a woman ... a wife."

"A wife?!" both men echoed in perfect, shocked unison.

"Even now she is waiting in our parlor. I wanted to warn you, because —"

At that moment, as if she were in the midst of a very bad dream, Martha heard the door to the family's living quarters open.

"Mrs. Franklin?" asked a very small voice.

Martha didn't have to turn around. She could picture with crystal clarity the young Cherokee woman emerging behind her, as easily as she could see the faces of both men she faced drain of all color, then turn blazing crimson.

Kawani stared into the flames on the hearth before her, reliving the awful moments that had followed her stepping out of that door in the Franklin Hotel. These months later, she could still see the looks of horror on the faces of the men, as though she were the Wog itself, that legendary creature native to Georgia that supposedly terrorized settlers in their beds.

"This — *this* is the wife?" Michael's father had thundered.

Before a public spectacle could be made, a flustered Martha had shooed them all back into the family's home. There the Franklins had proceeded to discuss Kawani and her marriage as though she were not even present. She had stood drenched from head to toe with an alien sense of shame. Not even Michael's arrival had helped to bolster her innate sense of identity. He had argued bravely for their love and his right as his own man to make his own choices, but his father's rejection had been complete.

Charles' bitter words still rang in Kawani's ears. "Have you no concept of what this family has worked years to accomplish? I left Athens a desk clerk. My brother and I came here to better ourselves. Now we are upstanding businessmen *trying* to attract the respect of the wealthiest families in Georgia. What do you think your Indian wife will do to our image? There is a line — and you have crossed it. I *will not* recognize this marriage. And if you persist in it, I will not recognize *you*."

The slender, bird-faced Leon had urged his cousin to annul the union. At the time, Kawani had not understood what he meant. But now she did, and a tentacle of fear snaked through her. At the time Michael had scathingly refused, rushing his wife out into the night, to make the long wagon journey home over Unicoi Road, himself in seething silence and Kawani in silent tears. At dawn he had declared, "We'll be fine alone. We don't need them."

But now, Kawani wondered. What if, as time wore on, Michael changed his mind? What if they *couldn't* make a living, *couldn't* find land to farm — and his devotion turned to disdain? What if, one day, Michael looked at her the same way his father had?

Unconsciously, Kawani placed a hand on her rounding abdomen, as if to protect the child within. With the gesture, her ball of yarn rolled off her lap and onto the rug.

Nancy Emmitt noticed and bent her own swollen frame to retrieve the yarn from the foot of her rocker. "What's the matter, Kawani?" she asked, handing it back. "You look worried. Surely you're not thinking of Michael's parents again?"

In her reverie Kawani had forgotten where she was, at the home of her friend and neighbor while Michael made the trip to the new mint in Dahlonega. She had tried to convince him to take her along, but in her condition Michael would not hear of it. Sitting here now, Kawani had even tuned out the boys playing on the rug — tow-headed Sam, three, and little Jacob, still in his diapers. He had crawled after the yarn ball with delight and now sat looking up at Kawani with a frustrated expression as she clasped the object of his desire.

"Oh, here," she told him, handing him the yarn. "It's not like I can keep my mind on anything, anyway. You are right, Mrs. Emmitt. I was thinking about the Franklins."

Jacob tried to get his jaws around the ball, only to spit it out, smacking and looking as if he'd sucked a lemon. The women laughed. Nancy reached down to wipe the fibers from his lips.

"See?" she said. "Go back to your blocks." Then, turning serious, she told Kawani, "You know so much worry is not good for the babe. And I've told you a hundred times, please call me Nancy."

Kawani nodded. Even though at thirty-two Nancy Emmitt was nearly twice her age, the woman seemed more youthful and carefree than Kawani. During the past months, she had become a true friend — the only friend Kawani had.

"But you are not without worry yourself," Kawani reminded her. "How do you remain so calm?"

Nancy placed a hand on her own stomach, considerably larger than Kawani's with her fourth child a month more advanced in pregnancy than her younger friend. The doctor in Clarkesville had told her the child had been conceived far too soon after Jacob's birth. His dire announcement had seemed on target, for Nancy had experienced spotting and had often remarked that the child's movements seemed weak and erratic. But now a peaceful smile lit her face.

"Every day — sometimes many times a day — I commit my worries to the Lord. I pray for you, too, Kawani."

"I thank you," Kawani said stiffly. She thought of her parents. It didn't seem to her that her father's prayers were doing much good, for their family or the Cherokee people.

"Will Michael ask Mr. Clarke again about buying the lot?"

"Yes. He waits and hopes that when there is no more gold Mr. Clarke will change his mind. I don't understand why he wouldn't sell to us back in August. Michael agreed to continue to pay one-fourth of any gold mined."

"He knows Michael is not greedy. He was probably afraid Michael would stop mining if he owned the land and got busy farming."

"I suppose," Kawani agreed. "But it is hard to feel settled until we can own the land we live on. Michael is keeping an ear out for other parcels for sale, but ..."

"But you'd much rather own your family's old farm?"

"Yes. It gives them great comfort that I am there ... especially my mother."

At that moment the cabin door opened to admit Nancy's oldest son Seth. His arms were full of wood. He was followed by the big, bulky form of his father, Ben. A current of December wind chilled the women and children gathered around the hearth.

"Look who I found wandering around outside!" Ben declared.

As her handsome husband stepped into the door frame, Kawani squealed with joy. She jumped to her feet as quickly as her expanding girth would allow and flung herself into Michael's open arms. She was aware of the smiles of their neighbors as she snuggled into him, breathing the scent of cold and horse and leather, and his own unique scent — the scent of her life, she thought.

"Are you surprised?" he asked. "I told you I would be back before Christmas!"

"I am just so, so happy," she said, and felt relieved that he seemed just as glad to see her. She should not have doubted him. Michael was good and true, the bond between them strong. It was just his absence that made her melancholy. Realizing suddenly that her eagerness for Michael's return might be misinterpreted by their dear neighbors, Kawani hastened to add, "But the Emmitts have taken good care of me."

"That I see!"

"Care of her, indeed!" Nancy exclaimed. "It's she who has taken care of us. The children will miss her so."

Unloading his wood by the fireplace, Ben Emmitt added, "Well, there's no need to rush off. There's a bitter wind, and it's late. Might as well spend the night."

Michael knew Kawani had been sleeping on Seth's pallet. "No, no, we wouldn't impose any further on you good people. Please forgive me if I'm eager to wisk my wife back to our own home. I've missed her."

"Won't you at least have a piece of shoo-fly pie while Kawani gathers her things?" Nancy asked.

"Oh, that I will!" Michael eagerly agreed.

Minutes later, Kawani was ready, but considering how much she looked forward to lying that night in her husband's embrace, she felt a surprising reluctance to leave the warm Franklin home. Ben was a somewhat stoic man, but Nancy and the children had lavished more love on her than she had ever known save from her own family. They were good, God-fearing people. They had been among the sixty-one families who had come to this valley from Burke and Rutherford counties of North Carolina in 1822. When Kawani had commented once on Nancy's refined drawl, Nancy had shared that like the English Stovalls who had settled on nearby Blue Creek, the Emmitt roots — and faith — went back to Virginia's earliest settlers. Also like many of their neighbors, the Emmitts attended the Methodist Church in Nacoochee.

Kawani caught Nancy in a close embrace. "Thank you — for everything," she said softly. "I hope there will come a time when I can pay you back."

"I think not of payback," said Nancy, "merely, friendship."

Outside, Michael helped Kawani mount, then swung up behind her. Tied to the back of the horse was another mare bearing the packs of Michael's supplies and — Kawani guessed, knowing her husband's mistrust of banks — a goodly share of cash and gold as well. Part of her relief upon seeing him had been gratefulness that he had not been set upon by wild-eyed miners-turned-robbers. The country was crawling with such ruffians.

"Remember you promised to return on Christmas Day so that Kawani can try a traditional holiday meal," Nancy called.

"It would be our great delight," Michael agreed.

"Only if I can come early enough to help you cook," Kawani added.

"God go with you!"

The ride home was not a long one. Snuggled up in front of her husband, Kawani found it pleasant, with the silvery light of an almost-full moon dancing on the creek and the shadowy mountains looming up all around.

The first thing she asked about were her parents. Michael said that they were all well, including her married brothers and sisters, and the family of her clan. "I've brought a letter for you from your father, written just yesterday. He said it was very important that you take his words to heart. You can read it as soon as we get home."

Michael proceeded to tell her about the amazing machinery at the Dahlonega mint.

"I'm so glad that the legislature agreed to build it," he said. "Being gone this long was too long already. I can't imagine having to make a trip to Savannah and only getting two-thirds of the estimated value of the gold, then waiting months for the value to be fixed by the Philadelphia mint. Or using a private minter like Templeton Reid in Gainesville — who, it turns out, was including almost five percent silver in his ten-dollar pieces."

"He tricked people?"

"Naw, I think he just didn't know what he was doing."

"So, you got a good price for the gold, Michael?" Kawani asked.

"A very good price."

"Are we rich then?" Kawani turned to gaze at him with wide eyes. She cared little for such things, and left all material decisions to him. It was enough that he loved her and took care of her.

Michael affectionately flicked her nose with a gloved thumb. His breath became a white cloud on the frosty night as he replied, "Rich enough to buy any piece of land we want to." He grinned in a satisfied manner that made her smile, too. "In January I'll go back to Clarkesville to pay Rex again, and I'll be more persuasive this time about the land."

When they arrived at the homestead, Kawani carried their personal items inside and lit a couple of candles while Michael took care of the horses. She was struggling to feed a reluctant fire when he came in. He shooed her to bed and piled covers on top of her.

"In Cherokee homes, the men never do such things," she protested.

"You have a white husband, and he is very interested in taking care of his pregnant wife," he replied. He shoved an envelope into her hand and set a candle down beside the bed. "Read your letter while I get this fire going."

A wave of love for him so intense that tears came to her eyes washed over Kawani. God must be with them, as Nancy had said, to have given them to each other. She blinked away the moisture and tore open the envelope eagerly. Her father's familiar writing, rendered in Sequoyah's alphabet for her people, boldly filled the page. She read:

December 20, 1837
Dearest Daughter,

Your mother and I send greetings. You will be eager to know that we are well. We have enjoyed this time with your husband, and though we understand the reason you could not visit and are filled with great joy at the thought of a grandchild, we missed you, our child of the flower moon.

But our words to you must bear truth, as they did to Michael. I would not be as Sequoyah described so many whites, whose words are like the talking leaves that dry up and blow away. I fear for our people. The American General Wool, who is in charge of the Cherokee situation, is sympathetic and encouraged us to remove to the West on our own. Since few have done so — mostly those of the treaty party who agreed to sell our land — I expect the government will force the rest of us to leave. According to the treaty deadline, this will happen soon after your birth month, and it may not occur peacefully. I expect there will be much grief.

Why have we stayed then, you may ask. In your heart you know the answer, my child. You feel the rightness in your soul as you wake each morning and see the sun rise over the hills that were your father's fathers. We will not leave willingly. We would rather go in tears, under the white man's gun. This is right. We will hold the integrity of our people until our last breath. And if we can, we will not go at all, but will flee into the mountains.

Michael has placed some money in the bank nearby and has left his spoken and written word that I can withdraw it. I will do so only if the need is dire. If that should happen, he said we can come to you. But we can only stay for a time. You must not worry about us ... only pray for us.

Your mother and I feel satisfied that we have done right by you. Many nights we laid awake and discussed our fears — the quick nature of your love, your youth, and what sort of man this Michael Franklin of yours might really prove. Then he came to us bearing the traditional gift of venison, and we had to decide quickly whether your mother and brother would stand with you before the minister. Even when he covered you both with the white wedding blanket, we prayed that we had made the right choice in blessing your union.

Now we see your husband's heart. He is a good man. We know peace that even if we must leave, as Michael's wife, you will remain where you belong.

With our love,
Henry and Sally Cornsilk

As Michael slipped into bed beside her, the cabin at last growing warm, Kawani was again wiping silent tears from her eyes. Extinguishing the candle, Michael whispered, "Your father's letter has made you sad."

"Yes. His words make all that may happen to my people seem so — real."

"It is real, my love. I saw much unrest between the whites and the Cherokees in the gold country. I spoke positively of the new mint, but unfortunately many settlers have taken its construction as the government's stamp of approval on their future there."

"My father spoke of going into hiding should the Cherokee be forced out. But where would they go?" Kawani's voice quavered.

Michael drew her against him, sharing his warmth, his protective embrace. "I don't know," he sighed. "I don't know."

"Will I ever see them again?"

Kawani's question hung in the air, for her husband had no answer.

Two weeks later, Kawani sat before the fire shucking the last of the autumn corn. A pot of venison stew simmered over the flames. As she had cut up the carrots and potatoes she had thought with a smile about the garden she would plant on the sunny side of the cabin this year. There would be not only corn, beans and pumpkins — the traditional, life-sustaining "three sisters" of her people — but English peas, tomatoes, cucumbers, squash, radishes, melons, and sweet potatoes. She had learned so much from Nancy Emmitt ... not only how to plant and tend vegetables and fruits common to a white woman's garden, but how to prepare them as well. Michael had been delighted with her cooking experiments, even when the dishes did not always turn out as expertly as Nancy's.

Thoughts of the Emmitts caused Kawani to recall the Christmas Day recently spent in the family's home. It had been nothing short of wonderful. Nancy had decorated the cabin with pungent pine and holly. There had been meat pies, wild turkey and stuffing, roasted nuts and plum pudding. She had even presented to Kawani a small book wrapped in brown paper and tied with a red ribbon — a Bible, for Kawani to practice her English reading, Nancy said. And she had asked Michael to read to them the Christmas story. They had all gathered around the fire, the children on the rug sucking their peppermints, while he had obliged.

Kawani had heard the story of the birth of Jesus before, from her father's lips. But this time, somehow, it had been different. Maybe it was the knowledge of life in her own womb, or maybe it was her husband's stirring baritone. Most Cherokee found many gods in animals, the heavens, water, earth and fire. Yet she now admitted to herself that there was something moving about the simple story of one god who sent his only son to earth as a babe.

As if in response to her thoughts, a very distinct movement occurred a couple of inches left of her belly button. It felt as if someone were sticking a spoon into her, only from the inside out. When Kawani realized the "spoon" was actually a tiny arm or leg, she gasped, straightened and placed a hand on the spot. There had been no flutterings before — only this.

"You'll be a strong one, you will," she said to the child inside, as the bond between them went a little deeper still.

She waited, but the baby had apparently stretched the once and that was all it intended for now. She couldn't wait to tell Michael.

Thought of him made her stir the fire under the stew. She checked the wood box and realized another trip to the wood pile would be needed to keep dinner simmering. Kawani was reaching for her shawl when a knock on the door stopped her.

A prickle of fear crawled up her spine. She never had unexpected visitors. Michael was on the other side of the property, most likely ten feet down in a four-foot tunnel. His only rifle was with him.

She thought fast, opting to stay inside the house even though the trail of smoke from the chimney announced the house was occupied. If it was anyone she knew, they would call out to her. If it was not, they'd be on their way — or at worst, she would buy some time. The closer it got for the hour for Michael to come in for dinner, the better.

Kawani jumped when the door rattled again under a heavy knocking and a man's voice called out, "Hello!" She covered her mouth with her hand and stood as rigid and silent as a deer sensing danger.

Then ... the snapping of the fire was the only sound. She went back and sat beside it, trembling, the corn husking abandoned. She prayed to the clouds above the near mountain that day, to come down and envelop her, hiding her if this man was her enemy — and to the God above the cloud, Nancy's God, just in case He was there and could help her, too.

She had not heard horse hooves so she assumed the man was on foot. At first she thought she heard some noises from the stable, and she feared the visitor might take Michael's horse. But when there was no sound of retreating hooves she began to relax. He must have given up and gone on his way. She was being silly. It was probably just a harmless drifter seeking directions or a meal. Still, she would wait another good half hour, just to be safe.

Finally, with her hearth fire dying, Kawani crept to the door. She opened it just a crack to scan the dirt yard. All appeared normal. She swung on her shawl and stepped through the portal. That was when she saw him: a tall, lanky man of about fifty sitting quietly on her chopping stump. His age did nothing to diminish the strength of the frame which he now unfolded at the sight of her, or the hardened quality of his bearded face.

"Hey, wait!" he cried when she would have retreated back into the cabin. "I didn't mean to scare you ... just been waitin'. I knew you was in there."

"What do you want?" Kawani demanded in a furious, shaking voice.

"Just to know if this be Michael Franklin's place."

Kawani considered, only slightly reassured by the use of her husband's name. Finally, she gave a curt nod.

"He here?"

"Yes — he's out — working. You needed to see him?"

The man sidled up closer to her. "Sure do."

"He — he'll be here any minute," she said, her rising voice telling of her alarm.

"Well then, guess I'll just wait around a bit till he shows up."

Kawani turned away from his crooked grin and rancid breath.

"Red Dawson, that's my name. You Miz Franklin?"

"Yes."

Kawani brushed past him, hoping he would resume his seat as she gathered an armload of wood, but he loomed over her. Before she knew what he was up to he had taken the sticks right out of her arms, saying, "Lemme help you with that."

He followed her into the cabin and deposited his load at the hearth, leaning appreciatively over the pot hung there. "Mmm, mmm, is that rabbit stew?"

"Venison."

"Mmm, even better! The smell makes my mouth just water. Guess I haven't ate a good meal in a few days now. Maybe I could pay ya for a bowl?"

Not sure what else to do, Kawani lifted the pot onto the table and ladled a serving into a spare wooden bowl. Her hands were shaking so badly that she sloshed it. "I — I'd rather you ate outside until my husband comes."

The bushy brows flew upward. "Oh, of course, of course," Red agreed. But Kawani did not miss the way his eyes moved over every possession in the cabin, and over her, as he took his exit. He sat on the bench by the door, and she shut the door firmly behind him. Quietly she also slid the latch.

About five minutes later, she sagged in relief at the sound of Michael's voice. She silently opened the latch but not the door, listening. Michael sounded both alarmed and threatening as he demanded to know who the interloper was and what his business might be.

"I heard tale over in Na-coo-chee there was a man who'd done right well for hisself here on Sautee Creek. They said you was working all alone. Now, I been minin' goin' on five year up Dahlonega way. It's hard work bringin' gold up out of a tunnel by yerself. I got the experience, and the cash for barrels, wheelbarrows, pulleys, whatever — and I know the feller over at the stamp mill. He'd treat us good."

"Sorry, I'm not interested in taking on a partner," Michael replied.

There was silence a minute. Then Red Dawson asked, "Anybody else here around seein' color?"

"Not that I know of. I'm afraid you've wasted your time. Your luck will be better in Nacoochee."

"I see. Well, good evenin', then. Maybe I'll take a tip from you and find me an Indian wife. My woman is too cantankerous. That sure was good stew."

Michael did not warm to the banter. "I don't cotton to strangers hanging around my cabin," he said. "I'm counting on hearing that you treated my wife respectfully or I'll be coming after you. You can let everybody know we value our peace and privacy."

Moments later, presumably once the man was out of sight, Michael opened the door. Kawani fell into his arms.

"Are you all right?" he asked.

She nodded and proceeded to tell him about the events of the afternoon. "I did not trust him, Michael," she said.

"Neither did I. I think he was checking out what we had here. When I think about what could have happened I could kick myself. I'm so sorry, Kawani."

They ate in silence. Michael was engrossed in his thoughts, a frown drawing down his brows. At last he announced, "I'm not putting off the trip to town any longer. Tomorrow morning I'll take you to the Emmitts and see if you can stay a couple of days. I need to take a payment to Rex, and I want to get a will drawn up and buy a gun, one that I'll leave here in the cabin with you. I'll teach you how to shoot it. Also, I'm keeping too much cash here in the house."

Michael jerked his head toward the fireplace where Kawani knew two loose stones concealed a hidey-hole containing gold bags and a strong box with important papers and cash. He continued, "I'll take it to town, too. I have to try to talk to my father again, much as I hate to. I'll tell him and Mama about the baby. They need to know. And I need to know that if anything ever happens to me, you'll be taken care of. That you can just go to them."

Kawani swallowed. The chunk of venison, tender though it was, seemed to lodge in her throat. She found the picture of Michael's parents taking her in impossible to imagine. But she merely said, "Please, Michael, do not speak of such things. Without you, I would have no life."

"You would. You'd have our child."

She repeated, "I would have no life."

Michael made the trip to town in the new little wagon he'd bought in Auraria. He had thought it best to transport Kawani in it, and he had need of supplies. Plus, the wagon would be perfect for farm work.

He arrived in the lobby of his family's hotel to find Cousin Leon at the front desk. The gangly young man swept him with an astonished look before saying, "Michael — what a surprise!" His eyes followed the satchel Michael sat heavily down.

"Likewise." Remembering how Leon had urged him to abandon his wife, Michael found it hard to be civil. He'd never liked his cousin, anyway. He'd always thought Leon was out for himself and himself only, given to childish fits of temper when things did not go his way. He decided to come right to the point. "Where are my parents?"

"Er — Athens. It seems Grandmother took a fall. Oh, nothing too serious," Leon added hastily at Michael's look of alarm. "Just a broken leg, but you know how long people that age take to mend. Aunt Martha would have nothing but to check on her and help out a while. She insisted Uncle Charles go with her."

"I see. And during their absence ..."

"I'm in charge." Leon spread his hands and grinned weakly, showing yellowed teeth. Michael noticed he was wearing what looked to be a new gray wool suit.

"Your father could spare you so long?"

"Oh, my older siblings can help out plenty at the store. Father is always pushing me to find my own niche, anyway, being the youngest and all."

"Mmm-hmm. Looks like you're doing pretty well with that. New suit?"

"Uh, yes," Leon stammered, opening the lapels to show the superior workmanship. "The tailor just completed it. There's the job, of course, but also —" he turned a bit red — "I've been courting the new judge's daughter, Miss Sylvia Cromley, who just arrived in town. She's quite the lady, you know. Things have been going rather well if I do say so myself."

A vision of a buck-toothed old maid flashed into Michael's mind. Did Leon actually expect Michael to congratulate him, when he was honing in on Michael's territory at the hotel? Well, he hadn't wanted the job, but he did resent Leon trying to take his place with Michael's parents. He just knew that would be part of Leon's plan. He obviously had no idea how ridiculous he looked right now, with his self-satisfied smile and beak nose, like a large bird preening itself.

Before Michael decided how to respond, a sudden anxiety seemed to seize his cousin. "You're staying the night?" he questioned.

"Yes. I have some business to take care of."

"Your — wife...?"

"With friends."

"Ah." Leon took a nervous breath, momentarily relieved. But there was more, just as Michael had suspected. He continued, "Well, you see, your parents — they encouraged me to take your old room while they were gone. I can give you the key to the best suite — or you could use their room, of course."

Michael frowned. It galled him to take a room in the hotel like a common guest, but the idea of being in close proximity to the pretentious Leon — even for a night — was more than he could endure. "I'll take the suite," he said, and added sarcastically, "Need advance payment on that?"

"Of course not."

As Leon produced the key, Michael glanced up to see none but Rex Clarke descending the stairs. Dark blonde hair neatly combed, the young man was dressed for riding in a cutaway coat, slim trousers and black knee boots. A dazzling smile broke out across his rugged face upon sight of Michael, who realized this was one of the few times Rex seemed both neat and completely sober.

"Well, what's the luck," Rex called out. "I was just thinking of you this morning!" He swung jauntily down the bottom steps and came toward Michael with hand extended.

Michael shook the hand and replied, "No, I'm the one in luck. I don't have to search you out this time. If you don't mind going back upstairs, we can talk in my 'new room.'"

"Upstairs?"

"Yes. It's a long story," Michael said, glancing at his cousin as he lifted the key from the counter. "Leon, please have Zed take my rig around to the stable."

"Yes, Sir, Mr. Franklin."

Was that sarcasm, or merely more of the eager-to-please front? Michael shot a glance over his shoulder, but seeing his cousin going about his business, decided to let it go. He led Rex to the suite where he was to stay, unlocked the door, and looked around with a resigned sort of satisfaction. Anything here was more elegant than his rustic cabin in Sautee, he told himself — though it would seem cold without Kawani's sweet presence. And cold it was. He'd ask Leon to start a fire in the grate later.

"So, you have something for me?" Rex asked, sitting on a chair and propping his booted legs on the bed, leaning back at an angle that suited his personal rakishness.

"Yes." Michael snapped open his bag and fished out a sack of gold coins, tossing it at his partner.

Rex caught it adroitly and counted the contents greedily on the veneered, straight-legged desk. A smile like a cat's with a cornered mouse came across his features. "Very good. Lady Fortune has smiled on us," he said, then glanced back at Michael's satchel. Suspicion briefly flickered in his eyes. "What else you got in there?"

"Nothing that's yours." Michael brought out a slip of paper and passed it to Rex. "The receipt from the mint, dated in December." He handed him another paper. "Please sign this one. It gives the totals and says you recognize them and have received one-fourth."

Rex looked faintly irritated. "Well, where's a quill, then?" he snapped.

"Right in front of you."

Rex hesitated, glowering. Finally he scratched out his signature with a grumpy flourish. "You cheatin' me? 'Cause nobody gets away with cheatin' Rex Clarke."

Michael's face hardened. "You want that gold or not?" he demanded.

Rex waved the papers in the air, both drying the ink and, when Michael tried to grab them, tantalizing his partner. The sight of Michael's ire had the opposite effect on Rex, bringing back his grin. He laughed when Michael snatched the receipts, turned and put his coins back in their bag. Then he tucked the bag neatly inside his coat.

"I was just ready to ride out to the property and look over the new house," Rex said, standing. "Want to come? We can secure our valuables in the safe before riding out."

Michael considered, knowing that the only reason Rex could have invited him was to have an audience for his boasting. But Michael had to admit, he was curious. He'd heard The Highlands was going to be one of the most impressive homes in the area. And ... it wasn't like he didn't have the time, with his folks away. He could visit the judge before the courthouse closed today and make his purchases at his uncle's store early the following morning before returning home.

"Fine," he agreed at last.

Half an hour later, both men were mounted — Michael on his father's stallion — and riding through town to the Clarkes' hundred acres located on the fringe of Clarkesville along the Tallulah Road. The sunshine, horseback position and lack of strong spirits combined to put Rex at his charming best, waving at everyone they passed and tipping his hat to the ladies. When he was like this, Michael could see why the girls in town would fall under his spell.

"The house should be completed by summer," he told Michael. "Father has ordered all sorts of special flooring and moldings."

Michael knew it was not unusual for a large, elaborate home to take two or even three years under construction. But a question of another nature lingered in his mind. He knew that Dr. Clarke had been a second son, and that his older brother had inherited the family plantation on the Altamaha River. Rex's mother had died in childbirth, and his father had never remarried. Michael asked, "Why did Dr. Clarke decide to build The Highlands now — after all these years of saving his inheritance and what monies he made practicing medicine?"

They turned into a narrow lane hemmed in by trees, now stretching their naked winter branches to the pale blue sky. A stone mason was beginning the second of a set of pillars on either side of the drive.

Rex laughed. "My opinion — that, one, he doesn't want me to gamble away all his hard-earned cash once he's gone, and two, he's hoping that by building this expensive house, he'll entice me to marry, settle down, and produce grandchildren for his twilight years."

"Sounds like good logic," Michael observed. "Will it work?"

In response, Rex swore, the good-natured grin still in place. "You know better than that. Who needs a nagging wife when one can experience all the pleasures he desires as a free man?"

Michael's sour expression clearly showed his reaction to such reasoning —or lack thereof — but before he could speak, Rex swept him a bow, hat in hand, and said mockingly, "Pardon me! I did forget for a moment that you left bachelorhood behind in favor of marital bliss. How's it going with the little Indian wife, anyway?"

"I resent both your tone and your choice of words. You're a rogue, Rex Clarke, and if you knew the least bit about an honorable woman like Kawani, you would speak very differently."

Rex's loud laugh rang out in a frosty puff, mingling with the din of hammers. "I stand corrected. Well, what do you think?" he asked, gesturing with his hat.

When Michael merely sat staring at the edifice before him, he was astonished to hear his companion add, "Rather boring, is it not?"

"Boring?" Michael echoed incredulously. "No, indeed! It's striking — classic."

"Mmm-hmm. Classic equals boring. I tried to get him to do something fresh — maybe the new Greek Revival style, but he'd have none of it. I'm afraid it's a smaller version of the family home in McIntosh County, minus the wings."

"Federal style." Michael admired the square white house with its low-pitched roof, key-stoned windows, and central door flanked by sidelights and crowned with a swan-neck pediment and fanlight with elaborate tracery. Dentil molding decorated the cornice. The simplicity and symmetry of the architecture gave him a satisfied, settled feeling. He thought he could look at this house every day forever and realized he was already a half-step away from envy. Now what was he thinking? Such material things didn't matter, not in the long run.

"Yep. Leave it to the venerable Dr. Clarke to choose tradition over innovation. Come inside. At least there's an oval room."

Rex swung off his horse and tied it at the hitching post. Michael followed suit, trailing his host through downstairs rooms two deep and up a curving staircase into future bedrooms. Garlands bracketed diazes where chandeliers would be hung, and Adamesque urns and swags were being carved onto mantels. Along the way, Rex harassed the craftsmen, saying to Michael, "Father is constantly busy with his calls, as you know, so he counts on me to crack the whip over the workers. Another way to fill my time with worthy employment."

"Do any of the workers live on the property?"

"No, they all come and go. We don't allow any to stay here. All it would take to burn the place down before it's even completed would be one careless man. That's what happened to the cabin that was here before. Fire," Rex commented as they emerged on the back porch.

"Very common. Accounts for the outbuildings already in place."

"Yes," Rex said, pointing. "The springhouse and privy, and the stable, all still standing — though of course we're building a much finer stable."

"Of course." Michael's eye swept the property with a sudden discerning light that his companion failed to notice. An idea was dawning on him. Putting it aside momentarily, he shook his head. "Very impressive. And all this isn't enough to make you want to go to school, pick a wife and settle in?"

"Oh, I'll go to school, all right — in the fall. The good doctor won't let me put that off any longer. I've decided on Harvard Law. He's a bit put out I don't want to follow in his footsteps, but you know, I don't really have that nurturing side a doctor needs. I'm afraid I'd want to kill half his patients rather than listen to them complain."

Rex laughed, but Michael saw nothing humorous. He only saw the emptiness and lack of love. Regardless of the surface charm he could affect, Rex Clarke was a cold, selfish man — with vices that made Michael shiver. Suddenly, despite the appeal of his surroundings, he was ready to go. The less time spent in the company of evil, the better.

He had just one more thing to say. "You're leaving. Sell me the Sautee lot."

Rex turned glittering eyes on him. "Now why would I do that, when things are going so well? You start farming, you won't have time for mining. No, let's just keep things like they are for a while. Maybe we'll talk again before summer and see how it's going then."

Michael bit his lip, angry at feeling so powerless. Thanking Rex for the tour, he bid him a terse good day and cantered back to town to draw up his will. The world was too fragile a place. He wanted Kawani to be secure.

CHAPTER FOUR

April 27, 1838
Nearing the Georgia coast

ongratulations, *Monsieur Randall, pour un voyage triomphal!*" boomed the voice of Louis Rousseau as Richard emerged from checking the engine room below decks.

The brilliant sunshine reflecting off the water made him blink momentarily. He focused on the dapper figure before him. "Thank you, Mr. Rousseau."

"The Beaufort River is only fifteen to eighteen feet deep at low water. I was holding my breath, but — alas! — to no end. We skimmed by smooth as a crane. What's the draft on the *South Land*, ten feet?"

"Eight, actually."

Rousseau gave a low whistle. "Impressive. Light *and* fast."

"Perfect for coastal passenger runs, as intended," Richard remarked. "As my next steamer will be, for Atlantic freight crossings. She'll be much larger, with cargo space for plenty of cotton — or rice." Richard turned a mischievous smile upon his companion. "I hope I have you convinced to let me handle your next shipment to the Caribbean."

Louis laughed expansively, the gold watch chain glistening on his brocade vest. "You made me an offer I can hardly refuse," he said. "Come, let's go portside and toast the deal."

As Richard followed his new client, the satisfaction of conquest swelled within his chest. This was one more *coup de grace* for the firm of Randall and Ellis. Rousseau was one of the foremost rice planters in Chatham County. His family home south of Savannah, The Marshes, commanded 600 acres on Harveys' Island between the Ogeechee and Little Ogeechee Rivers. Rousseau's near neighbors were the Stiles on Green Island and George Jones Kollock with Retreat and Rose Dhu near Coffee Bluff. As immensely gratifying as the business liaison was, even more valuable was the fact that Rousseau seemed inclined to take the Randalls into his social circle. Ever since the two men had met last March at Godfrey Barnsley's "good-bye to Savannah" ball, Rousseau had been increasingly friendly. He seemed to like Richard's no-nonsense manner.

Richard was under no illusions as to why he had been invited to the $20,000 ball at Scarbrough House — which, as it turned out, was not "good-bye to Savannah" after all. Barnsley had been unable to return to England when the depression of '37 pinched even his vast wealth. Richard had been invited solely because of his wife. No one had to explain to him that an invisible line existed between outsiders — especially Northerners — and the native old money landholders. Oh, the Savannah gentry would certainly be cordial, but for them to invite someone like him into their homes, their lives, that was quite another thing entirely ...

Louis seated himself within view of their two families. Their wives were talking by the rail while the children played on deck. Rousseau's wife Henrietta held her seven-month-old son Dylan, a sweet babe with a fuzz of red hair. At the moment he was chortling merrily as Eva waggled his bare pink toes.

Louis gestured for Richard to join him, flipped open a hamper, and produced two wine glasses.

"Hilton Head, Daufuskie, and now Turtle Island," Louis observed with an eye to the greenery floating by. He poured from a long-neck bottle into the glasses. "Soon it will be Jones Island and into the Savannah, safely home. To the successful maiden voyage of *South Land* — and to the soil she's named for."

"Hear, hear!" Richard exclaimed heartily as their glasses met. "To a new business agreement and a prosperous year."

"Amen to that. When cotton sold for ten, eleven cents a pound this past August, I thanked the good Lord I grew rice. And you were probably thankful that your contract with the Central of Georgia helped offset your investment in the company."

"It did, some," Richard admitted, "though it would have been more helpful if they had used Randall iron for the tracks instead of importing from England. The overspeculation and now these torrential spring rains have really set us back. It will take months to repair the bridges and culverts that were washed away, but I do still think the venture will turn a profit."

"I hope you're right. Stocks surely can't go much lower."

"You had a bit of an investment, too."

"I did." Louis nodded, took a drink, then sat up rather abruptly, reaching down into the hamper beside him. He came up with a newspaper — specifically the *Georgian*. "That reminds me — have you seen this ad? 'Twould seem your steamship-building competitor is forging ahead despite the economic current."

"Oh — Gazaway Lamar," Richard murmured, rather annoyed that particular dark cloud should appear on his personal picnic day. "What does it say? It's about the *Pulaski*?"

"Yes." Louis began reading. "'No expense has been spared to have a vessel to answer the purpose she is intended to accomplish. Her engine — one of the best ever made in this country. Of 225 horse power: her boilers are of the best copper, and great strength. Her qualities as a sail vessel for ease, safety and speed are superior to any steamer that ever floated on the American waters.'"

"Ha!" Richard scoffed. "Lofty claims indeed!" It rankled to know how excited Savannah's elite were about Lamar's side-wheel steam packet. Built by the Savannah and Charleston Steam Packet Company, she was slated for the Savannah to Baltimore run.

"She is also said to be uncommonly elegant inside — though I'm sure no more so than *South Land*, and your boat built for short runs and inland waterways instead of sea," Louis said magnanimously.

"Of course. There's nothing Savannah and Charleston Steam Packet can build that Robert Collins can't match," Richard said, and Louis smiled without comment. Richard knew what he was thinking — that Robert Collins, though builder of a ship rather ironically called *South Land*, was a New Yorker. There was that invisible barrier again. Pushing down his frustration, Richard continued, "Despite that, I must say in all honesty that I find Gazaway Lamar a reasonable and decent sort. And my Christian virtue overshadows my competitive nature. So, I propose another toast — to the success of Mr. Lamar and all other decent sorts."

He had charmed his way through the veneer. Louis laughed good-spiritedly, his face again open and accepting as he raised his glass. Richard was mollified.

The men sipped their wine in silence for a moment, watching the children play. The sun was warm and the wind balmy, carrying the peculiar lilac scent of chinaberry trees and the tang of salt. A peregrine falcon soared overhead.

Louis' mind had not strayed far from the topic of ships, for at length he questioned, "Say, didn't they import parts from England for the *Chatham*, even though she was assembled locally?"

Richard looked at his companion — a handsome man with broad, amiable face and curling dark hair. "Yes, I believe so. That was two years ago."

"The only foundry near Savannah is Henry McAlpin's at Hermitage Plantation. Ever thought of giving him some competition?"

"Mmmm ... it does bear consideration," Richard murmured, then laughed aloud. "If I came up with another venture now, I think my poor wife would croak. She already says I have my fingers in too many pots."

"It's the way of men and women."

"True, but still ... I'd better save that particular pot for another day."

He didn't say it, of course, but Richard had a sense his wife was needing more of his attention just now, not less. He stole a look at her. Dark curls and a fetching silk bonnet framed her face. He was glad to see the shadowy smudges gone from under her eyes. The visit with her sister Ruth in Charleston had done her good.

As much as Richard admired Eva's benevolent tendencies, he had begun to wonder about the motivation behind her mission trips into the Yamacraw slums — and their increasing frequency. Not that there wasn't enough to do there, for the needs of the blacks — both free and those that "lived out" from their masters — and the hundreds of Irish that had flooded the city seeking work on the railroad were indeed overwhelming. It was a rough district, given to disease, prostitution and violence. Richard made sure Eva never went there alone, but was always accompanied by a party from her charitable organization. And he frequently reminded her that she did not have to single-handedly cure all the city's ills.

He watched now as Eva bent to adjust Jack's collar. The boy barely reined in his irritation at having his play halted for a cravat to be tied. At almost nine, Jack was growing too independent for Eva's doting. That doting was just another symptom of what Richard suspected was eating his wife: emptiness, a peculiar sort that lingered despite all Eva had and was verbally very grateful for. It had all begun when she had lost the baby she carried in December of 1836. And only Richard knew the full extent of Eva's desperation — still unfulfilled — to conceive again.

I must spend more time with her, he thought to himself. *Not keep letting her go off to that slum.*

His attention was diverted by his son. Ever the adventurer, with a keen imagination, Jack had produced his set of wooden swords and was trying to get two-year-old Devereaux, still in his infant gown, to fence.

"I'm the dread pirate Williams, and I've boarded your ship, Dev! Now you've got to fight me!" Jack declared. "Come on, come at me now! Yes, that's it!"

Jack jumped around while the toddler clumsily swung the play sword in the air with both hands, his ten-year-old sister Collette looking on with pursed lips.

Richard laughed aloud and nudged Louis. "Look at that," he said. "This should be interesting."

The toddler was surprisingly engaged in the game, giggling as he thrust at his fascinating older playmate. Jack parried gently and jumped onto a flat bench, glancing at his mother. Her back was turned. He whipped off the offending cravat and tied it quickly around his forehead, feeling much more the part with that bit of costuming.

"Aha!" he cried. "Fight for your life, Captain Rousseau!"

Jumping down, he came at the little one with a bit too much enthusiasm for Collette, a tall, slender girl with her family's dark hair and brown eyes. She stepped in front of her brother.

"Really, that's enough, Jack. Can't you see he's just a baby?"

"Out of the way, fair maiden! How can your gallant brother defend you from kidnapping when you get in the middle of the fight?"

"I'm not a maiden in need of rescue," she retorted, reaching a hand up to snatch at Jack's cravat, "and take off that silly thing. You look ridiculous."

Jack batted her hand away. "Aw, you're stuffier than my cousin Suzanne." While he was unguarded, little Dev chuckled and poked him in the side with his sword. "Oh, I'm run through!" Jack exclaimed, clutching the supposed wound with both hands. He died a theatrical death on deck.

Dev was amused by his tongue-lolling demise and launched his round, solid weight on top of him.

"Ugh!" said Jack. "You're a heavy little tyke."

He opened his eyes to see a halo of sunlight surrounding Collette's wry face. She hauled her brother up by the back of his shirt and confiscated his weapon.

"That's quite enough," she repeated. "You're going to hurt him."

"*I'm* going to hurt *him*?" Jack retorted incredulously.

"He's too little for such games."

"Like I said — stuffy."

"I am *not*. When he's old enough, he'll learn to ride and shoot and fence and whatever else boys do. But in the meantime I have to help protect him from big boys like *you*."

Jack's chest puffed out at the accolade. He couldn't find fault with her considering him mature, so instead he asked, "Don't you have any imagination?"

Her little pointed chin went up. "I don't need any. I live in the most beautiful place on earth."

"There's nothing better than being on a sailing ship at sea and having grand adventures."

"The Marshes is better. We have 600 acres and 400 slaves. They are finishing the spring planting now. When the trunk minders flood the fields it looks like our house is floating in the midst of the sea. So you see, Dev won't need to get on a ship," she said, pulling her little brother against her. "He has his own little island kingdom, and one day it will all be his."

Jack couldn't think of a single thing to say. It was an altogether novel and unpleasant feeling. A surge of something hot and unfamiliar came up inside him. He grabbed both his swords and turned away from Collette's proud, satisfied little face.

The next day, a bright Saturday, as the carriage bore the Randalls toward the foot of West Broad Street, Richard asked his son, "Jack, what did you think of the Rousseau children?"

Jack shrugged. He clearly knew that response alone would not suffice, for he added a little bit sullenly, "Don't know, Sir."

"You seemed to have fun playing with them."

"The little girl didn't seem much inclined to play, Richard," Eva observed mildly. "I thought Jack did quite well, though, entertaining little Devereaux. What a handsome child."

"A handsome family," Richard agreed. He chose to ignore his son's uncharacteristic silence. He would perk up once they reached the river. Probably just got up on the wrong side of bed. He looked to his wife, patting her hand. "I'm glad they told us about this race. It gave me the perfect opportunity to extend our holiday a bit."

"Me, too, Richard." Eva smiled sweetly at him.

"I like to see you looking so relaxed and pert, my dear. We'll have to take more such outings. I've been too busy at work … left you too often to your own devices."

"Oh, I've passed the hours well."

"And come home gray and troubled from that slum."

"Only because the needs there are so overwhelming. Richard, you aren't saying you wish me to not go there?"

"No — no. Maybe just to pace yourself. There's much you can do at home as well."

"Stitching samplers and arranging flowers? Richard, the servants take care of everything — everything important, that is. Jack is busy with his tutor now. And you know I'm not given to the endless round of balls and tea parties. I need something more fulfilling, something that's not just about me. What I do in Yamacraw actually makes a difference to people. You understand, don't you?"

How could he deny those pleading blue eyes? His Evangeline, how he loved her. He drew her arm through his. "Yes. Yes, Eva. And you must understand that I only mean to protect you. That, and see you happy."

"I *am* happy, Richard."

How he wanted to believe that. He merely nodded and surveyed the crowd gathered before them, coming into view beyond the straight back of their driver, a black man whom nobody knew he had freed and now paid. While his Northern-bred conscience just wouldn't permit holding slaves, neither would it do for the Savannah gentry with whom he was attempting to rub shoulders to get wind of his sympathies.

And there they were — the gentry, gathered in eager anticipation of the first race of first race of Savannah's Lower Creek Boat Club, going up today against the Aquatic Club of Camden. True, all classes were represented here today, including shining black faces mingling with the white of the predominantly upper crust with their silk dresses, natty stocks, elaborate bonnets and high-crowned top hats. No evidence here of the secret, pervasive fears that had surfaced many times in the past few years — fears of insurrection and mayhem.

But Richard would not so easily forget the tensions that had spread in '36 when rumors circulated that blacks were joining with the Florida Indians to attack whites, prompting the organization of a city guard. Then there were the incidents with the two young men, strangers to the city: a Presbyterian minister charged with secret meetings with Negroes who had to flee the town, and more recently, the son of a Quaker abolitionist who was not so lucky. A native of New York, he had arrived from Charleston with literature on slavery. Word had it that a mob had kicked and cursed him in his hotel room before Mayor Nicoll took him into custody. Once Nicoll found the literature to advocate only colonization, and the mob to have been dispersed by a cold rain, he had helped young John Hopper onto a Northern-bound ship. About that same time, the government had been informed that free blacks visiting Savannah planned to kidnap local slaves. As a result, a city ordnance had been passed requiring the arrest of free blacks arriving by sea.

Yes, there were unpleasant undercurrents that Richard feared would one day force everyone to take sides. But for now, business was good, and life was looking up. It was tempting to overlook the darker side of life in this fine city. Besides, didn't his marriage to an Ellis already define his standing in the public eye? No action or statement was required. As long as he satisfied his own conscience in personal matters, there was really no need to disturb the status quo.

Richard tried not to feel like he was shoving something under the rug as he put on a bright smile and helped his wife and child alight from the vehicle. The calling of seagulls overhead and the dank smell of the river greeted them as they neared the race course, which was a mile long, marked by a buoy. Jack was catching the excitement of the crowd.

"Is that the *Star*?" he asked, jumping up and down to get a glimpse of the black, New York-built boat with a gilt stripe purchased by the Lower Creek Boat Club.

"Yes, and there's the *Lizard*." Richard pointed at a green boat being readied farther away by Camden's Aquatic Club. "She's constructed from trees on the Satilla River, heavier, so it will be interesting to see who wins."

Some men in round crown hats were placing bets nearby, and Richard saw a vendor with a box strapped to his chest.

"Would you like a sweet bun, my dear?" he asked Evangeline.

"Oh, Richard, I don't need one —"

"I do! I do!" shouted Jack.

"— but I'll share one with my son," Eva finished with an indulgent smile.

Minutes later, face and fingers covered in sticky sweetness, Jack gestured toward four young oarsmen, members of the gentry, taking their places in the *Star*.

"Oh, aren't they handsome in their loose, bright clothes," Eva observed. "They make one proud to be from Savannah."

The starter gave the signal. The boats shot forward, and the crowd exploded. The sun glinted bright on the water. The race was over in less than seven minutes, with the *Lizard* winning by 105 feet. The people of Savannah let out a collective sigh of disappointment.

Caught up in the camaraderie of the day, Richard commented, "There will be other races. I have a feeling that a tradition has been born."

He was already picturing a tall and strong Jack manning the oars in ten years — or joining a hunt club or military company — whatever he wanted to do, just so long as he belonged. That was what Richard wanted for him. That was what he would have.

CHAPTER FIVE

May 1838
Clarkesville, Georgia

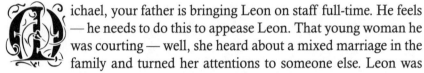ichael, your father is bringing Leon on staff full-time. He feels — he needs to do this to appease Leon. That young woman he was courting — well, she heard about a mixed marriage in the family and turned her attentions to someone else. Leon was very upset. With you gone, your father needs Leon. If he pulls his weight I think Charles might consider passing the hotel to him."

His mother's anguished words, spoken in a stolen aside as Michael left the hotel by the back way, echoed in his ears. His arms and legs felt like dead weight. He would not envy his cousin the management of the hotel if it came to that one day — even his inheritance. But his place in the family, his parents' acceptance and blessing ... that he did covet. Always had. And as much as he told himself he didn't care, he always would.

His father had also hired a maid, a saucy, pretty redhead. Business at the Franklin Hotel progressed as though Michael had never lived there.

Drained from the encounter in which he had finally told his parents about his coming child, Michael now drug himself towards the courthouse. He pulled out his gold pocket watch with his initials on the flip cover — a gift from his parents for his sixteenth birthday — and confirmed the time. Half an hour until his appointment. Now he was thankful for the extra time, for it would allow him to process the morning's events. After the rejection of his parents, he had taken his horse to the livery behind Habersham House. Now he sat numbly on the bench by the main courthouse door and stared unseeingly at the passing traffic, thinking of his father's continued hardness, even in the face of his mother's tears. Since finding his parents in Athens when he had come to town in January, he had procrastinated making another trip. In the back of his mind he had feared the worst — and he had been right. "We can't have Indians as acknowledged family members," his father had insisted. "It would destroy everything I've worked my whole life to build."

By striking out on his own and marrying a woman his parents deemed second class — even though such marriages were fairly common, he thought with a stirring of justice — had he disinherited himself? Now what would Kawani do if something were to happen to him? Where would she go? Now, why did he keep thinking that way? *It's only that I want to make sure she's safe. There's so much trouble brewing right now,* he told himself.

As if to verify his thoughts, a rotund man arrived, nodded, and sat down next to Michael, promptly snapping open his newspaper. The front page facing Michael screamed in banner headline: "General Scott Replaces Wool! Ready to Remove Cherokee by Force! His Speech to the Indian Nation Reprinted Below."

Michael's heart sank to his stomach.

The gentleman saw him craning his neck to read the headlines. "Would you care for the front page, Sir?" he politely inquired.

"Y-yes, thank you," Michael managed. He tried not to tear the section out of his companion's hands. His eyes devoured the article, lingering on the speech that Gen. Winfield Scott had printed in newspapers and distributed as handbills throughout the nearby Cherokee Nation.

"Will you then, by resistance, compel us to resort to arms? God forbid! Or will you, by flight, seek to hide yourselves in the mountains and forests, and thus oblidge us to hunt you down? ... I am an old warrior, but spare me, I beseech you, the horror of witnessing the destruction of the Cherokees."

The article went on to say that Scott had divided the area into three regions, with the middle region encompassing most of the Cherokee lands in Georgia. Stockades to hold the immigrants had already been established and manned with militia. Seven thousand soldiers stood ready to enforce the removal.

Michael swallowed down the bile rising in his throat. So, it was here. No miracle would reverse the course set in place decades before by powerful government leaders. The Cornsilks and all their clan would leave Georgia for lands in the West. The only question remaining was how peacefully they would go.

He folded the paper and handed it back to the man. "Thank you," he said softly.

His companion studied him. "You all right, young man? You look a bit green around the gills."

"I'll be all right."

Minutes passed in which a new, quiet assurance spread. He, Michael Franklin, had saved one. One beautiful, trusting girl with coal-black eyes and hair like a river of ink. She relied on him. Without him, like her family she would be forced into exile from the land rightfully hers, mayhap to die along the way. Michael realized that nothing else mattered now but that they were together, they and their child — Lord granting a safe birth. Right now Kawani was with the Emmitts, who had been grateful to receive her, as Nancy's child had come early only two days before, a tiny girl born blue and lifeless with the cord around her neck. Michael shuddered. Yes, he had chosen his path and now he would follow it with his whole heart.

The appearance of Simon Grant, with his loose clothing hanging on his tall, large frame, and his bulbous red nose and simple smile framed by a wealth of wispy white hair, did much to fortify Michael. After months of Rex Clarke's cat and mouse games, with Michael's latest outrageous offer by letter on the Sautee lot having received no reply, word of Grant's land sale had come as a God-send. The old widower felt he could no longer take the strenuous demands of his farm and had in fact already moved into Clarkesville with his daughter. Ideally, Grant's farm adjoined the Emmitts' to the north. Michael was eager to seal the deal in the office of the property clerk. He had waited long enough for his own piece of land.

Michael stood up and offered his hand with a grin. "Mr. Grant," he said, "let's go do some business."

"What's this?"

A small canvas sack sailed through the air and landed in Michael's potatoes and gravy. He recognized it as the same one he'd left in the safe at the Franklin Hotel, with a note slid under Rex Clarke's door telling him to collect it. Now he gingerly fished the bag out of his dinner and looked up into the blazing green eyes of his one-time friend.

"Your final payment of gold from the stamp mill, as the message said," Michael replied.

"You expect me to believe that's *it*? This is one-tenth of the normal amount, and not even minted."

"You want coins, take it to Dahlonega yourself. I'm done."

"What do you mean, you're done?" Rex loomed threateningly over him. His dark blonde hair was tousled, one end of his cravat hung out over his vest, and Michael could smell whiskey on his breath.

What had ever drawn him to Rex anyway? His reckless abandon of rules? His disregard for what people thought of him? Michael shared some of those same traits, but they had led him in a completely different direction. He had simply wanted his own life. Rex wanted without end.

Calmly he said, "I mean, I'm moving off your property. I got my own now." He patted his breast pocket containing his copy of the bill of sale for the Grant lot.

Rex's pointer finger floated provokingly near Michael's face. "I hired you to mine my gold lot, and I never said you could be done!"

"You didn't hire me. You agreed to one-fourth of what I brought out for one year. It's past one year. Rex, the gold's dried up. Hire somebody else to mine your lot if you must, but you'll find what I'm telling you is true. As for me, I have a family now. I'm settling down to farm. And since you wouldn't sell me your land, I found somebody who would."

Rex's face turned bright red, and he cursed under his breath. Before Michael knew what was happening the dissipated son of gentry came across the table at him, seizing him by the collar and dragging him up until they were eye to eye. "You lying cheat! You tell me where you hid the rest of my gold or I swear I'll come after you and make you pay!"

Michael's anger made him turn deadly quiet. "Take your hands off me."

Everyone in the dining room of the Habersham House had frozen, watching the tableaux unfold. The clink of silverware and the hum of conversation had ceased.

Rex shook Michael like a terrier with a rat. "Not until you tell me what you did with my money!"

Mr. Levy had hurried over, anxious to rebuild his own faltering reputation. "Please, gentlemen, not in the dining room."

Michael didn't move a muscle. He knew the timid innkeeper would have no effect on Rex. The only way to save his own reputation was to initially pretend to play along. "All right, all right," he said.

Rex hesitated. That second was all it took. As soon as Michael felt the other man's muscles slacken, he ducked down and out of Rex's grasp and came up with an undercut that directed all the force he could muster at Rex's jaw. Clarke's head snapped back. Gasps resounded as the big man toppled and fell backwards.

He wasn't exactly unconscious, just dazed enough to give Michael time to toss a bill onto the table and the bag of gold onto Rex's chest before exiting. Michael had no desire to tangle with Clarke. But a man had his dignity to consider. He wouldn't be called a cheat and a liar.

He would ride straight to the cabin without stopping for Kawani so as to get a head start on loading their things into the wagon. Tomorrow he would move his wife into the Grant place. And with all luck he'd never again have dealings with Rex Clarke.

Ben Emmitt had a bad feeling in his gut. That morning it had begun and had slowly intensified as the hours passed without sight of Michael Franklin. He should have arrived at least by the mid-day.

Not that Ben was eager for Kawani to go. No indeed. He had been on the verge of sending for her himself a few days ago when she and Michael had providentially appeared on his doorstep. Nancy had had the aid of a midwife during the birth, but the grieving young mother's care completed, that woman had promptly departed, leaving Ben with an infant to bury and a house full of confused, needy children.

Kawani had them all fed and clean, with those old enough to be helpful set about chores. Meals were prepared in a timely manner while Nancy rested in bed. And in stolen moments the young Indian woman comforted her friend.

Ben sent up a prayer of thankfulness for such friends. Calling to his mule, he decided to take a break from the second plow-over of the cornfield. He wiped the sweat from his forehead and took a swallow from his canteen. As he drank, his eye roved in the direction of the Franklin home. The land was bathed in the amber glow of the sinking sun. But what was that on the horizon? Those black, circling shapes?

Slowly the canteen lowered. Buzzards.

"Oh, God, don't — don't let it be," he said aloud.

He unhitched the mule and, leaving the plow in the field, took the animal into the stable. There he quickly saddled his horse and led the stallion around to the front of the cabin. He must be calm, not let anything show, he thought as he entered.

Kawani looked up at him with a smile. "You're early, Mr. Emmitt. But dinner is almost ready."

"That's all right, Kawani. You all go ahead and eat without me. I was thinking I'd ride over to your place — just to make sure things are all right."

Her smile had faded and the anxiety she had been trying to hide all day became evident. She seemed not to notice as Sam pulled insistently at her apron. "He should have been back by now, no?"

"I would have thought so, but he probably just got stuck in town longer than anticipated closing the land deal. Just the same, with that drifter who'd come around and all, I thought checking on the place might not be a bad idea."

He had not been successful. Kawani's face was pale. "I would like to go with you," she said.

"There's no need. I'll be there and back in a jiffy."

"Please, Mr. Emmitt."

"I've already saddled my horse."

That was the wrong thing to say. With Kawani recognizing premeditated concern, her black eyes became as round as walnuts. And here was Nancy, emerging slowly from the bed chamber, placing a hand at Kawani's elbow.

"I'm hungry!" Sam declared.

"Take her with you, Ben, for her peace of mind," Nancy addressed him, ignoring her son. "I can manage here while you're gone. Like you said, it will only take a short time. Kawani can leave Michael a note asking him to come right away when he returns. It will make her feel better."

"Hungry! Hungry!" piped Sam.

"Oh, all right," Nancy replied, steering him towards the table.

Ben stared at them for a moment, but her back silently announced that the matter was closed. He could only hope his worst fears would prove unfounded. He glanced at Kawani, unable to meet her eyes. "It will take me just a minute to hitch up the wagon."

She ripped off the apron covering her swollen belly, ready to follow him to the stable. It would do no good to remind her of her condition. She was as stubborn as Nancy when her mind was made up. He'd have to go extra slow. It wasn't far, but that would make it nerve-wracking.

During the ride Kawani clung to the wagon seat with white knuckles, perched on the pile of blankets he'd placed under her for cushioning. She spoke not a word, but when she saw the same buzzards that had alerted Ben making lazy circles in the sky, she uttered a single sob. He didn't need to say it could be anything; the possibility of what it was was enough.

Ben pulled into the dirt yard and stopped the rig. Everything was deadly still. The first thing they noticed was that something — probably a panther — had gotten to the cow in the barnyard. What remained of its bloating corpse had attracted the carrion birds. Then Kawani gasped. He followed her gaze to the door of the cabin, which sagged open on its hinges.

"Stay here," he told her, reaching behind the seat for his rifle.

Cautiously he approached the house, his heart hammering. With his back against the logs, he trained his gun on the open doorway and swung abruptly to face the gathering darkness within.

No sound or movement greeted him, but yet there was chaos. Chairs were overturned, the mattress ripped open, and papers scattered over the hard dirt floor. And then he saw the outstretched arm on the other side of the table.

Ben lurched inside. He groaned aloud. Michael lay near the hearth, dried blood caking a wound on the side of his head. The fireplace poker lay nearby. It was clear that he had been dead for some time, probably since the night before.

"Who could have done this?" he moaned.

He heard a movement behind him and whirled. There was no assassin, only Kawani, looking very small and young. Her eyes were wild and questioning. Ben spread his arms, desperately trying to block her view with his stocky body.

"Don't come in here, Kawani! Don't come in here!" he ordered roughly.

If he could only spare her the sight of her murdered husband — spare her brain from the horror that he knew it would replay over and over. Ben tried to push forward, taking her with him out the door, but she caught at his arm, crying out in an anguish that ripped his heart. She had seen.

He dropped his arms, watching helplessly as the young Indian girl launched herself across the room to her fallen husband's side, screaming and sobbing with an agony that turned his blood to ice.

Two hours later, with darkness full upon the land, Kawani stumbled out of the cabin. Her swollen eyes fell upon Ben, sitting numbly on the bench where the drifter had eaten his stew. She started to collapse, and he jumped up to support her. Her hand went to her middle.

"Mr. Emmitt — I think — the baby is coming."

He helped her into the wagon. Then he went back into the cabin, stripped a sheet off the torn mattress, and carefully wrapped up Michael Franklin's body. The man had been smaller than Ben, but his dead weight was another issue. Ben prayed Kawani would not see his awkward struggle to get the shrouded form into the wagon bed. Thankfully, she did not turn around, but remained a small figure on the seat, hunched over her own pain.

Nancy allowed her eyes to close in a brief moment of relief when the midwife finally arrived. It had been a hard labor. In the bed where Nancy had lost her own baby only days before, Kawani had writhed and moaned in the throes of her contractions and sobbed weakly in between. The children were huddled wide-eyed with shock in the corner of the main room, able to hear everything and see far too much despite the curtained partition that separated the bedroom. Ben was unable to remove them to the stable because that was where Michael's body lay, still in the wagon — much to the consternation of the horses.

From the moment Nancy had beheld her husband's glazed eyes as he burst in the door with Kawani in his arms, Nancy had been unable to fathom the depths of the nightmare into which they had been plunged. The loss of their own sweet babe had been devastating enough. Didn't she still feel as though her heart had been ripped out of her body, and didn't her arms still ache with longing to hold a child now slumbering in the ground? But now — no, it was too bad to be true. She felt an oppressive darkness settle around the cabin, like as she never had before, and only then did she think to pray.

Wiping Kawani's brow, sharing her tears, she murmured words of encouragement and comfort — much as the poor girl had done for her so recently. Near dawn, when the time at last came to push, she gave her hand to her friend and urged her to bear down. Kawani hardly had the will. Her grief made her lie abed like a white woman at childbirth, unable to separate one kind of pain from another. Only the repeated orders of the midwife, uttered with the harshness of one concerned for the baby's life, eventually brought the girl's knees up and chin down.

At last a tiny pink head appeared, followed by a perfect body. As the midwife caught the child, Nancy choked on her own tears, joy, grief, amazement and envy all mingling in a confusing miasma of emotion.

"You have a healthy girl," announced the midwife.

Kawani did not smile. She did not strain to see the infant, which was lustily crying out. She hung her head to one side and closed her eyes.

Nancy occupied herself with changing the blanket under Kawani, sneaking glances at the baby receiving her first bath in the wash basin. The midwife's gnarled hands moved gently over the tender pink skin. The baby squalled and flailed. The room spun suddenly and Nancy sat on the edge of the bed. Minutes later, wrapped in the white linen blanket originally intended for an Emmitt child but laid out tonight by Nancy herself, the baby was delivered to Kawani.

The new mother allowed her daughter to be cradled between her side and one arm. She looked down at the babe, examining the fuzz of dark hair. The infant was unusually alert and seemed to focus on her mother.

"She has blue eyes," Nancy said.

"They will darken. Imagine a Cherokee with blue eyes."

"She's only half Cherokee," Nancy reminded Kawani, then wished intensely that she hadn't. She hastened to ask, "What will you name her?"

"My mother should be here to name her. It is our tradition," Kawani said. A tear ran down her cheek. "But since she is not, I will name her Mahala, for her father. It is a name she can also use in English."

"Michaela — Mahala," whispered Nancy. "It's perfect."

Suddenly she realized that with Michael gone, the fate of Kawani and Mahala hung in the balance in more ways than one.

"She should not be bleeding so much," the midwife announced at the close of that day. The woman had taken pity on the weakened Nancy and agreed to linger a while at the Emmitt farm, temporarily forsaking her own. Now she moved with purpose to her big cloth satchel. She removed a packet of something carefully wrapped in tissue paper.

"What's that?" Nancy asked.

"Spanish moss from the coast. I will use it to slow the flow down. If it is not much less by tomorrow, you should send for a doctor."

"My husband has already sent for him. He wanted him to document the — document the death," she said quietly. Nancy glanced across the room to where, after much urging, Kawani had consented to nurse her child. The girl seemed only to want to sleep, and no wonder, thought Nancy. She added, "There had been an injury at the iron works. Dr. Clarke said he would come as soon as he could. The Franklins will come with him. Ben told them about Michael when he was in town."

But it was not until morning, long after the midwife had gone, that Dr. Clarke came. Nancy spent the long night on a pallet her husband fixed for her beside the bed, rising every few hours to check on her two charges. Each time she checked Kawani's dressings she shook her head in disbelief. The bleeding was not slowing.

As the interior of the cabin went from black to gray and Ben went out to milk the cow, Nancy bent over her friend's still form, her normally tidy dark hair spilling around her shoulders. She took Kawani's hands in her own, waking her.

"Kawani," she whispered, "you must try — try to get better. Ben has sent a message to your father. He took it to Edwin Williams, who under the circumstances agreed to deliver it to his brother Charles down at the post office. So your father should be here soon." She did not add that so would Michael's parents, who Nancy was concerned would want to have their son interred in the Methodist burying ground in Clarkesville.

"Just before he left, I told Michael that without him, I would have no life," Kawani said.

Her words shocked Nancy. "But you do! You have a child now."

"No, my friend, *you* have a child."

"What? No! No, Kawani, no, no, no — I won't accept that."

"I am the Cherokee, but you are like the Nancy of my people, the Beloved Woman, who took up her husband's gun when he died in battle against the Creek. You are strong and brave," Kawani whispered. "I see that your God gives you strength. I have been talking with Him as I lie here — " a faint smile came upon her face — "and it will be as I say."

Nancy was aware that tears were issuing out of her eyes. She shook her head in denial. That was when she heard carriage wheels and knew the Franklins and the doctor had arrived.

She sat at the table while he examined Kawani. The children having been instructed to play quietly in the yard, Ben had taken the Franklins into the stable to officially identify and have a moment to grieve over their son. Nancy knew what Dr. Clarke would say before he ever came out. She just prayed that by some miracle the innkeeper and his wife would allow them to bury Michael and Kawani here rather than taking their son's body back to town, where his Indian wife would never be allowed to rest beside him.

"Mama?"

God had been merciful, she had been thinking as she stared into dinner's dying fire. The Franklins had both been amazingly passive about the burial location. Two graves had been dug that very afternoon by the creek that had once seemed to glisten with such golden promise. There, the minister who had accompanied the Franklins as a source of comfort had found himself conducting an impromptu funeral for not one, but two.

After the service, Nancy had invited the couple into the house to see Mahala. Martha had wept and reached out to hold the infant, but Charles had stepped between them with a stony countenance.

"She's better off here," he had told his wife. Turning to Nancy, he had added, "I'm told you just lost a child of your own. You were friends with my son's wife. The solution to the problem seems quite simple, if you will keep her."

"But, she's your granddaughter!" Nancy had burst out. "She needs to be with her family. And — and —." She didn't know how to tell him that she wasn't at all sure if she could even feed the baby.

"I plan to have my son's death fully investigated. If when his affairs are settled you find you still have want of resources, let me know."

Nancy had stood slack-jawed, holding the baby, unable to believe her ears.

"But Charles —" Martha had begun to protest, but had been silenced by a sweep of her domineering husband's hand.

"I will not have that child in my house," he had declared, with his eyes beginning to glisten, "to be every day reminded of the foolish and hurtful course of actions my son chose that led to the loss of his life."

They had warmed up porridge for supper, a normally simple task that had seemed monumental to Nancy. Her every muscle cried out for rest and her mind kept asking how much trauma a person could endure in one week and still retain sanity. She was still pondering this question when eight-year-old Seth demanded her attention.

"The baby's crying," he said. "I think she's hungry."

Nancy's gaze swung to meet her husband's across the room. He read her hesitancy and fear and knew they battled fiercely with something else — hope.

"Why don't you try, Nancy," he urged gently.

On wobbly legs she walked across to the cradle and lifted out the infant. She peered into the tiny face. The baby's warmth felt so good against her. So alive. She even welcomed the crying. Could it be that this was indeed a replacement for the daughter she had lost? It wasn't the same, but it was far more than she had dared to dream of.

It seemed a betrayal of the friendship she had shared with Kawani to desire such a thing.

Still, everything in her strained toward the child.

Please, God, let there be milk.

Nancy took the baby to the privacy of her bed, sat down, and opened her bodice. Then she brought the child born of tragedy to her breast. She prayed for a new beginning, a future of blessing.

Just when she was starting to lose heart, Nancy felt the anticipated response in her body, and a similar surge of an emotional nature swept through her, bonding her for life to the orphan she now held.

CHAPTER SIX

May 30, 1838
Sautee Valley, Georgia

rief — so intense — was difficult to see, even when the echoes of shared emotion rippled within one's own soul, thought Nancy.

When Henry and Sally Cornsilk appeared at their door, their knocking rousing Nancy and Ben from sleep in the hours of the owl, her first selfish thought had been of the child asleep in the cradle. Kawani had given Mahala to her, but would the Cornsilks, the child's natural grandparents, honor that wish?

They explained that they came as fugitives from the Cherokee round-up, thus traveling at night, the words of Ben's note describing Michael's murder speeding their steps. With Benjamin Patton of Clarkesville appointed to the task of removing the Cherokee from Northeast Georgia — and Lieutenant J.B. Magruder acting as his forceful right hand — they could only stay one day. But only when the gazes of the couple searched the cabin for Kawani did it occur to Nancy that the couple was yet unaware of their daughter's death.

Reciting the recent tragic events raked the embers of pain inside Nancy and her husband, and their tears fell again along with the Cornsilks'. For a long time after the telling they sat around the table, heaving shoulders and haggard brown and white faces illuminated by a single candle.

At last Henry asked the same question that had echoed in Nancy's head since the murder: "Who could have done this? For I believe that he killed not only Michael Franklin but my daughter as well."

Ben nodded. "The sheriff investigated the cabin and asked questions around town. It seems witnesses saw Rex Clarke rough Michael up in the Habersham House Hotel — and Michael deck him. It was over the gold. Clarke believed Michael was holding out on him."

"This Clarke, he was the man who owns the land Michael and Kawani lived on?"

"Yes, and not the sort to take a fist in the face without retaliation. So others thought, too. But a young hotel maid swore to the sheriff that she was with Clarke the entire night."

"A generous payment could be ample compensation to a woman with an already shaky reputation," Nancy put in dryly.

Henry looked like he might not comprehend each English word, but he definitely caught her meaning. "Yes, this means nothing," he said.

"Well, it does legally," Ben replied.

Henry blew out a breath. "Legal words, the kind that dry up and blow away in the wind."

"I'm afraid so."

"Then who?" Sally questioned. "This — this miner who you say came by their house?"

"Maybe." Ben shrugged. "Red Dawson is being sought, but I doubt he'll ever be found. But the way everything was overturned and no valuables left — not even Michael's pocket watch — folks are definitely thinking robbery. Lots of people knew Michael kept money at his place. His parents told the sheriff he never gave them any for safekeeping, even though he'd given Kawani the impression that was what he intended. Maybe when Charles Franklin rejected not only Kawani but her and Michael's child as well, Michael decided he'd have nothing further to do with them and brought the cash and gold back home. After all, he'd soon be making many purchases for his new farm he bought from Simon Grant."

Henry looked ready to say something when his wife spoke abruptly, turning towards the window. "Dawn," she said. "How many days since Kawani passed into the spirit world?"

Nancy watched her curiously. "Seven," she replied.

Sally addressed her husband in her native tongue.

Henry looked at Ben, then Nancy. "Much time has been lost, and there is no priest, but the seventh day is the last day of mourning when one of our people dies. My wife would like to mourn Kawani in the native way."

"Of course," Ben said, but from the look he gave Nancy, she was sure he knew no more what that would entail than she did.

"She is buried near?"

Nancy answered, "Outside, by the big oak at the creek."

Henry nodded and helped his wife to rise. "Thank you."

With no more said, the Indian couple walked out of the house. Unable to restrain their curiosity, Nancy and Ben followed, standing in the door frame and watching their guests walk to the creek. A rooster crowed. They reached the grave site, but instead of stopping there as Nancy expected, both of Kawani's parents walked directly into the water! They did not stop until, squatting down, they were totally immersed. Alternately they faced east, where the sun was rising over Lynch Mountain, and then westward, where their people would be exiled, a total of seven times.

Speechless, Nancy nestled in her husband's arm in the chill of the morning.

At last the Cornsilks came up out of Sautee Creek dripping wet. Henry caught his wife's elbow when she would have stumbled. Again Nancy was surprised, for instead of coming in for blankets and dry clothing, Henry led Sally to the third in the set of fresh graves. Before the simple wooden cross that Ben had constructed there, she knelt. With her face to the ground as if she had not another ounce of strength, Sally Cornsilk raised her voice in a high, throaty Cherokee wail. It seemed to echo down the valley — and all the way into eternity, Nancy thought — telling of pain and emptiness, injustice and loss, reaching out to one no longer in the physical world. She shivered. Her heart had made a similar sound, oh, so recently.

Mahala seemed effected by its reverberatation as well, for in her crib she stirred and cried. Nancy was glad to go and get her. But she felt guilty and fearful as she held and fed her, stroking one tiny fist, each dimple of which was already infinitely precious.

Inside the double-crib barn with its gable front and corner-notched logs covered with weathered wood siding, Ben milked the cow. He considered the fact that the colts, yearling and hogs were overdue to be taken to the mountains for foraging season. Recent events had made normal farm duties nigh unto impossible. He had felt right lucky to have set out 150 cabbages during the past two weeks.

Delivering the milk to the cabin, he found Nancy done nursing the baby and preparing to go to the chicken coop. "Seth's too unsettled by that keening," she told him. "He refuses to fetch the eggs for me."

"Seth, you're too old for such nonsense," Ben said to the boy stirring listlessly in the porridge pot. But he didn't have the heart to scold his son overmuch. The children had been through so much lately — things he wished they hadn't been exposed to until they were much older.

He grabbed a hoe out of the barn and set to work on the melon patch. All the while the eerie wailing continued. He was as concerned about it as Seth, though for a different reason. He had heard rumors of soldiers near the old Nacoochee trading post, perhaps there to corral straying Indians. If anyone but his family could hear Sally on this bright, clear day ...

At length, looking up, he spied Henry Cornsilk coming towards him. He stopped in front of Ben.

"You have done what you needed to?" Ben asked.

"We have done what we could under the circumstances. Had we been here sooner, had the family been gathered and a priest present, my wife would have had Kawani fully honored in the Cherokee way. The immersion ritual is part of the purification a family observes when a loved one dies."

"I ... I see," Ben said.

"Do you still have my daughter's belongings in your home?"

Ben nodded briefly. "My wife put everything Kawani brought with her in a bundle, away in a drawer. She thought to save them for Mahala."

It was Henry's turn to nod. "Normally these things would be burned or buried with the deceased. But I see the wisdom of your reasoning. There will come a time when the child will want something of her mother's to see and touch. My wife clings to the old ways, but it is my belief that your family cared for Kawani and gave her sufficient respect in death. I thank you for all you tried to do for her."

"It was our pleasure, for Kawani was a joy to our family and a great help to Nancy."

"There may be one thing more we need to do," stated Henry. "Did Kawani speak of Michael's financial matters before she died?"

"Only when she first arrived, that part of Michael's errand was to speak again with his parents and hopefully entrust them with some cash. There is a safe at the hotel. He was very close-lipped. Not because he was miserly — as you know — but I think because money was only a means to an end, not the end in itself."

Henry said, "I think we need to visit their cabin."

The sick feeling returned to Ben's stomach. "Why? Michael's parents already took anything of value, including his mining equipment and livestock, back to town. Whatever they don't keep will be sold at auction."

"It's just possible they missed something," Henry told him with a gleam in his dark eyes.

"You know something I don't know? 'Cause otherwise, I got no desire to go back to that place."

"Did Michael or Kawani ever mention a hidey hole in the fireplace?"

"No."

"I put it in myself and was the one who told Michael about it. It could be that the Franklins and the sheriff overlooked it. Worth checking, don't you think?"

Wearily Ben nodded. "All right, then. I'll harness up the team."

"And I will change clothes, if I may use your barn."

When they were ready to go, Henry asked Ben to gather kerosene, matches and some blankets. He wished to burn any unneeded possessions. Then he lay down in the wagon bed and covered himself — "in case we should pass anyone on the road," he said.

As he drove with his silent passenger, Ben tried to control his aversion to returning to the site of the murder. When he pulled into the deserted yard, sadness hit him full force. He could hardly make himself get down from the wagon. But get down he did, and enter the cabin — which was almost empty except for a few pieces of broken furniture and pottery. He even showed Henry where Michael had fallen, describing the scene that awful day.

Henry stood a while taking it all in. His face was immobile, as if he were holding back tears. Ben could only imagine the flood of memories that must be rushing over the older man like a mountain waterfall.

At last he knelt quietly near the fireplace and began to work at two stones with his pocket knife. Ben felt hopeful since there was no sign of the hiding place having been recently disturbed. And indeed his hope was satisfied minutes later when Henry pulled out a metal strongbox. He brushed dust and sediment off the top with a wrinkled hand.

"Locked?" asked Ben.

"No," said Henry. "I suppose Michael saw no need. A lock can always be pried off by a thief determined enough to find the box."

"Lucky for us." Ben knelt beside his companion.

Henry opened the lid. On top of a stack of papers was a mere thirty dollars in cash. There was a copy of the property deed to the Grant land tract and a will witnessed in Clarkesville in January.

"It leaves all monies and properties accumulated at the time of Michael's death to Kawani or any living children they may have had," Ben told Henry with excitement. "This along with the deed will be very valuable for Mahala's future."

"Yes. I just don't understand why there is not more cash, or gold coins," Henry replied, frowning. "There should be much more. What could he have done with it?"

"Maybe the sheriff was right and the person who killed him made off with a fortune that night."

Henry shook his head. "It just doesn't make sense."

"Michael's money management didn't exactly make sense, either."

"What is this?" Henry asked, holding up the final stack of papers. They were bound with twine and there was a hand-written note on top.

Ben held it up to the light. "'Receipts from the Dahlonega mint, stamp mill and Aurarian bank, with payments shown to Rex Clarke, Clarkesville,'" he read, "'whose signature shall bear witness along with these papers that one-fourth proceeds were delivered to him. Should the spring of our friendship dry up and hope for future partnership be buried, honesty will at least be proved and my assets found to be in order.'"

"Michael wrote that?" asked Henry. "That does not sound like him — so proper and fancy."

"It's his handwriting." Ben shuffled through the receipts. "This is good — we'll be able to tell how much money he made over the course of the year."

"I have what he left in the Aurarian bank. A month ago I took it out, knowing trouble was about to break. I can tell you it was not much — less than a hundred dollars in cash. But it is yours, for Mahala."

Ben stopped sifting the papers to level his gaze on the Cherokee man. "You mean — you're all right with us keeping her?" He swallowed down the lump in his throat, unaware until that moment how much tension had been tied up in that issue.

"Yes. This very night we will flee to the mountains, Ben Emmitt. I know not how we will live. Much like our ancestors once did, I expect. That is no life for such a small child, even if my wife did find another nursing mother to feed her."

Ben reached out to grasp Henry's arm in a gesture of deep gratefulness. "Thank you," he said. "You have no idea how much that will mean to my wife."

Henry smiled sagely. "We saw the three graves by the creek. And I already see how much Nancy Emmitt loves Mahala. This is as it was intended by the One God."

"Then, with His blessing and ours — and Michael's, I'm sure — take the cash and use it as you have need during your exile."

Back at the cabin, having no way of knowing of the understanding reached between her husband and Henry Cornsilk, Nancy remained in a state of unrelieved anxiety. The death chant by the creek seemed to go on forever, during which time she gave the children breakfast, made up bread batter and put a mess of fresh English peas and potatoes to simmer over the fire. All the while an unnerved Sam clung to her skirts, and Jacob alternately whimpered and created mischief. Nancy fried bacon and drained the grease. She set the table and looked out the door, wondering how long the men would be gone.

It was as she was pulling the wheat loaf out of the bread oven on the side of the fireplace that the wailing finally stopped. She almost dropped the bread on the floor. The silence sounded so strange. Nervously she set the loaf on the table to cool. She looked out the door again. The hunched figure remained at the gravesite.

For another hour Nancy peeked out in between her various duties, wondering what she should say or do — wondering if Sally would stay down there all day. But at last the woman rose and slowly made her way toward the cabin. Nancy had an inspiration.

She grabbed Mahala from the crib and rushed to the door. When Sally reached her, she looked up with a gaunt face and puffy, red-rimmed eyes. Nancy had never seen such desolation. She held the infant out toward the Cherokee woman.

"I thought you might like to hold your granddaughter," she said.

Nancy was rewarded with just a tiny bit of spring thawing the winter of Sally's grief-frozen countenance.

Over dinner Ben and Henry told the women that according to the records found in Michael's strong box, over fifteen months, Michael had mined roughly $9,000 worth of gold out of the creek and the adjacent hillside, an impressive sum for one man alone. One-fourth of that had gone to Rex Clarke, and $1,000 had been paid to Simon Grant for the nearby tract. Even considering expenditures and the cash in hand, that left $5,750 unaccounted for.

They discussed this disturbing fact for some time, putting forward various theories, none of which seemed plausible. The money rightfully belonged to Mahala, and it was distressing to consider the possibility that some unworthy thief was benefiting from the fruits of her father's labors. But, said Nancy, they had to be grateful for what they did have. There was the cash for the Cornsilks in their time of need, Mahala herself, and the Grant tract. Ben said they could easily provide for the child. He thought it best to hold onto the adjoining acreage.

"It may one day be an attractive dowry," he observed.

And, in case of a rainy day, there was always Charles Franklin's offer of financial support.

"I don't want to take a red cent from that man," Nancy declared. "So hard-hearted he wouldn't even let his wife hold the baby. He wants to control all he sees. No wonder Michael ran away from him. It would be unwise to give him any hold over us at all."

"I think you're right," her husband agreed.

"It is good to be beholden to no man, and let none have power over you, if possible," Henry said, taking a generous bite of the pie Nancy had set in front of him. Both Cornsilks had eaten as if starved, informing the Emmitts that they had partaken but little in the past week. Incidentally, that had been in keeping with the first week of mourning a Cherokee loved one — as was breaking the period on the seventh night, when hunters would bring in meat and relatives prepare a community feast for the bereaved family.

"I am sure you have learned that first hand most recently," Ben said.

When the bite was swallowed, Henry nodded and continued, "We have witnessed the degradation of our people, and I am sure it is only the beginning. The soldiers would surround Cherokee families and come upon them without warning. They were supposed to be merciful, but some did not listen. Many were rough and heartless, taking children separated from their parents and wives from their husbands. The families were not allowed to keep their animals, even for milk. Then there were bad white men — not in the army — following the soldiers to take what was left behind. What we witnessed was shameful, and we had several close calls before we came to your cabin."

"The Lord's hand was upon you," Ben said with certainty. "Before you go we will pray it will continue to be."

"It breaks our hearts to see your undeserved suffering," Nancy added. "And does indeed make us ashamed."

"We are sad we will soon be two of very few Cherokee left in Georgia. Our family will be so far away. We probably never see them again," Sally said, tears again welling in her dark eyes.

Nancy laid a hand on her arm and looked lovingly at the tiny head nestled there. The baby's grandmother had not given her up all evening, but now Nancy noticed the dark smudges under Sally's eyes and realized how exhausted both she and Henry must be. Pity swept over her. She rose and gently said, "Mrs. Cornsilk, your husband tells us you must travel tonight to avoid any trouble and make it to the mountains as quickly as possible — but I can imagine how tired you must be. You've both been through so much. You need a few hours' sleep. Why don't you both go rest on our bed while I clean up dinner?"

"Oh, no, no, we not take your bed!" Sally protested, eyes now wide at the thought.

"It might be the last time for a long time that you sleep on a feather mattress," Ben pointed out gently, regretfully. "You should do as my wife suggests. We will wake you before midnight."

The Cornsilks agreed and rose from the table, Sally reluctantly relinquishing Mahala to Nancy's arms. A small sob broke from her lips.

"Oh, you will take care of her, will you not, Mrs. Emmitt?" she asked, anguished.

"I promise," Nancy said emphatically. "Already I love her as my own. We will tell her of her parents and grandparents as soon as she is old enough to understand, and we will make sure she never feels abandoned."

"And *we* promise," Henry responded, "to return to this area as soon as we feel it is safe — not to take her from you, but to live near, and love her as *ulisi* and *ududu* should. Tell her that, please. Tell her we will come back to the land of our ancestors, and not give it up forever."

CHAPTER SEVEN

Early July 1838
Newport, Rhode Island

itting by the seashore Evangeline was in the midst of telling her sisters-in-law about her latest endeavors in the Yamacraw slum — teaching reformed prostitutes skills to sew for middle and upper class ladies — when a huge yawn caught her unawares. In its throes her copy of Thomas Walker's *Art of Dining ... With a Few Hints on Suppers*, just borrowed from the Redwood Library and Athenaeum, fell to the ground.

"Oh, excuse me!" Eva cried. "Too late a night — or should I say morning — at Mrs. Bloomington's ball."

Richard's sister Laura gave a little laugh. "I don't need balls any more to make me sleepless. I have little Sarah." She spent a fond glance on her youngest. On wobbly legs the child was investigating a pile of shells collected that morning by the older children. "I already feel like the little old lady who lived in the shoe. I don't know what I'll do when there are more of them."

A small silence fell. Brown-haired Anne, Houston's wife, sat holding Eva's library volume which she had picked up. She deftly deflected Laura's unintentionally hurtful remarks by saying breezily, "Thank goodness for servants. *Art of Dining*, Eva? Planning a party?"

Eva took the book back, blushing a little. "I need to. Richard says I should turn my attentions more to Savannah society and less to my charitable work."

"Oh, he can't mean it. It sounds like what you are doing is wonderful. I can't imagine he isn't proud."

"He is — he just thinks I overdo it. But it is so rewarding. I've formed relationships with some of the women. Sometimes all they need is a bit of help to make a major change in their lives."

"Oh, no, no, no!" burst in Laura unexpectedly. She upset her stool under their seashore awning in her haste to reach her toddler. "Not in your mouth! No —" she insisted, gathering up the shells as Sarah began to cry loudly — "we must take them away. No touch."

Eva watched silently as Laura put the shells in her basket atop the small table. The young mother gave her child a doll and sat down again with a big sigh. It seemed such interruptions were constant, making fluent conversation impossible. Right now Laura's older two, four-year-old Nelson Jr. and three-year-old Maria, were occupied watching their cousins fly kites. But it wouldn't be long before someone trotted over in a pout, hungry, or with some sort of injury. Even Anne's youngest, perhaps, for Grace Anne was still only five.

Despite the inconveniences the babies caused, this visit to Newport had served as a constant reminder of her barrenness — not the encouraging vacation Richard had intended. Eva was surrounded by adorably dressed, cuddly, tiny people, none of whom belonged to her. She was beginning to believe that her doctor's suspicions were correct — that the miscarriages had done so much damage that she would never again carry a child to term.

Watching the kites tugging against their restraints in the strong, salty wind off the Atlantic, Eva tried to tamp down the spiraling, all-too-familiar despair. Would she never grow resigned? How was it Richard was content with his one son, but *her* heart still longed for more?

She smiled faintly, watching Jack run with his brilliantly-colored high flier while his Grandfather Randall looked on, smiling and clapping. At newly nine, her boy already possessed the height and proportions that promised to make women's heads turn in a decade. He was strong, healthy and smart. The same could be said of both her and Richard's parents, who showed no signs of having declined since they left New York. She should count her blessings.

"It's a shame Houston couldn't join us this summer," Eva said to Anne, resolved to be cheerful.

"Yes, but I think everyone rests easier with him at the iron works," Anne replied. "Skilled labor is at a premium now, and he's putting forth every effort to solicit the emigration of several new workmen from England. He did not want those negotiations to fall through in his absence. He's offering them the moon and stars. I think they will come."

"That's good," Eva said. She also knew that while this might be true, and the Ellises were benevolent, patriarchal employers, they would not hesitate to cut wages if labor became abundant. It was the way successful business was done.

"Still, you must miss him. This is supposed to be your time of rest and refreshing," Laura observed.

"I do, but it's still been a nice time, don't you agree, with all of us together in the house on the hill?"

Eva agreed, apart from her preoccupation with babies. Jack had certainly enjoyed the time with his Northern cousins and grandparents. Although there had been an initial period of awkward reserve, it now appeared he still had much in common with George and Geoffrey. It was good to see him playing. It disturbed Eva that he had not connected more with boys at home.

Though Jack excelled at his studies and took great joy from the hours spent in her father's office, he was something of a loner.

Now the offices of Randall and Ellis were quiet while the rice and cotton ripened in the summer sun. Like their own family, most other factors were away at various resorts.

Yes, it was good they were here. Eva admitted she liked the Colonial charm of the town which had commercially thrived before the Revolution. Nowadays, Newport drew more income from tourists than from trade. The air was cool and fresh, and the summer house the Randalls rented above the port was clean and new. They had enjoyed good society and deep sleep after days of exercise on the shore. She had better enjoy it, Eva told herself, for she would lose Richard's doting attention soon enough with the autumn shipping season.

"Here he comes now," Eva said aloud, spotting her husband descending the steps leading to the beach. He walked with Laura's husband, Nelson Howard. The two men had been to the post office.

"Richard has seemed happy to be with his kin," Laura commented. "How fares he among the Southerners, Eva, truly?"

"Quite well, in fact. He is very aggressive to enter the best society — more so than I, I must admit."

"Well, you would not have to be aggressive, having been born to it," Laura replied.

Unconsciously Eva bristled.

"I would bet Richard's charm goes a long way in helping the gentry there overlook the fact that he is a Northerner," Anne said.

"Yes. Yes, it does."

Eva did not really want to get onto the North-South issue. And presently her attention was distracted by the attitude of her husband's stride. He was approaching fast. As he drew near, she could see the frown upon his face. A letter clasped hard in his hand flapped in the sea breeze like a captured bird.

"Something's wrong," she said, rising, then called out, "Richard, what is it?"

Richard came to her and squeezed her arm before sinking down onto an extra chair, Nelson looking on solemnly. "I'm sick, Eva, sick — horrified."

"What? What is it?" Eva demanded in alarm and suspense.

He looked up, pulled her down. "You need to sit. I had a letter from your father, telling of a tragedy that greatly effects many in Savannah. I'm afraid — Gazaway Lamar's new ship, the *Pulaski*, was lost at sea off the coast of North Carolina. It seems the starboard boiler exploded."

"Oh, Richard!" Eva cried in horror. "When? How many were lost?"

"It happened the night of June 13. Two life boats made for shore, but one capsized within sight of land. Other survivors clung to wreckage and a make-shift raft for days before being rescued. It seems about one hundred did not make it, including Lamar's wife and five of his children. James Hamilton Couper — the master of Hopeton on the Altamaha — was aboard. He was able to save those in his party, his wife's sister and son and a friend with her baby. Also, your father writes of other families you may know."

Richard handed Eva the letter, and she numbly read her father's account of the tragedy.

"Oh, Eva, we're sorry," Anne murmured. "What a shock. Another terrible steamboat tragedy. Wasn't it around a hundred were lost just last year also — when Morgan's flagship *Home* went down, Richard?"

Richard nodded distractedly, his face ashen. It had been that tragedy that had at last catapulted Morgan to the position of managing partner of the company's two remaining ships.

As their companions continued to discuss whether this event would have a positive or negative impact on Randall and Ellis, Eva reached for Richard's hand. Tears eased out of her eyes in sympathy for the horrible losses suffered by their friends and acquaintances back in Savannah. At this moment, neither she or Richard wanted to join the conversation about what this would mean for the troubled steamboat industry. Their Northern relations could afford to be objective and factual. They didn't know these people. Eva did. And their suffering made her count her blessings. She squeezed Richard's hand. Life was too short, loss always imminent.

It seemed to Eva that a gloom hung over the city past the end of summer, long after the public mourning and the funerals were complete. It did not lighten moods that purses still struggled in the continuing depression following the previous year's financial low. Nor was the news about the removal of the Cherokees that filtered down from the mountains to the coast pleasant.

It was this topic which dominated conversation one late October evening around the Ellis' beautifully dressed Chippendale table. Outside, dark had closed its mantle over the coastal city. In the dining room, candlelight gleamed on the best china and silver, set for William's birthday celebration. The children were having their meal in the kitchen, to enter the dining room later for birthday cake.

But for now servants had set out green turtle stew. William had exclaimed much over it before proceeding to share the newspaper's latest account of the Indian removal. Grace did not discourage him, knowing it was his special day and that the opening of gifts would pre-empt the gentlemen's usual time in the parlor after the meal. There was also the fact that the Ellises were quite unique, for when a political subject was raised in mixed company, so long as only family was present, the women shared their opinions as freely as the men.

"They say conditions at the Rattlesnake Springs stockades near Chattanooga are deplorable. The reporters found it unsanitary with whooping cough, measles — and, well, other diseases we will not mention at table," William told them.

"Didn't they try to move some of the Indians out by boat in August?" asked Eugenie's lawyer husband, Stephen Wise. A tall man with heavy brows and sideburns, Stephen's rather dignified demeanor seemed well-suited to his occupation, so Eva had always thought.

"Yes, but the Tennessee River was too low from drought. The Indians didn't much like the boats, anyway. Their leader, Ross, has received permission from the government to manage their own removal."

Grace's sweet face, framed by her lace evening cap, creased in concern. "Autumn is a bad time to be starting a long land journey," she observed.

"Indeed," agreed her husband. "Many more may die along the way."

"It seems such an embarrassment to the government," Eva spoke up. "Hasn't it all been handled rather badly?"

The soup dishes were being cleared. While she had lacked her usual appetite, Eva had managed to spoon down the turtle stew. But the calf's head in white sauce, arriving on a silver tray and being greatly admired by all, made her decidedly queasy. Neither did the veal cutlets look very appealing tonight.

Her mother gently replied, "I agree it has been handled poorly, but there are those who believe that the spread of traditional Christian civilization is ordained by God. That does not justify cruelty or greed ... but the end result may yet be positive."

Eva indicated to the serving maid at her elbow that she would take veal cutlet. She was glad when her husband replied in almost the exact words she would have chosen. "Not to take exception, Ma'am, but there is the fact that the Cherokee did all within their power to emulate our civilization, even to accepting our religion. They are an intelligent, peaceful people — eager to please. Could we not have allowed them to live among us?"

"Well, yes ... until there was gold," Grace replied sadly.

"And the greed of which you spoke," added Eva. She massaged her temple gently, trying to shake the headache that had nagged her all day. "Apparently that vice makes men break promises and conveniently forget the rights of those who have less power than they."

"Are you all right, my dear?" Richard questioned in concern. He looked at her untouched plate. Her heart sank when she saw a flash of hope in his eyes. She could not, would not, herself hope ...

"Yes, yes — just a headache," Eva hastened to tell him, patting his hand.

"Perhaps we should turn the subject," Eugenie said with a mischievousness that was not altogether teasing, "before the philanthropists among us share too much of their controversial sentiment. We might find that their feelings about equal rights extend to all mankind, and then we would have to reveal them as closet abolitionists."

"Eugenie!" Grace scolded sharply. "We would never speak ill of our own, or betray one another, no matter what our beliefs."

"Ignore her," Stephen told everyone. "She's still sulking that the Randalls spent the summer in Newport instead of at White Sulphur Springs with us."

Eugenie tossed her curls. "I am indeed. And I demand that in the name of equality they pass next summer at a locale of my choosing."

Everyone laughed, the tension dispelled. Eva knew Eugenie had always been rather selfish, thinking only of what was convenient and serviceable to her own situation. And though she expressed herself well, she had never dug deeply into the issues of the time — as was customary in well-bred young ladies. Eva realized her own sensitivity was in part due to her selection of a husband with a Northern background. She had missed the South when gone from it, and could never but embrace it whole-heartedly, but she did value the varied perspective Richard and his family provided.

"Perhaps some cake and ice cream would be more to your liking," Eva's father told her with a smile. "I can hear the children clamoring in the kitchen. Shall we call them in?"

"Yes, yes!" Eugenie said, clapping her hands.

Eva smiled when the young people burst through the door moments later, dancing about a white cake decorated with cream-colored icing swags. "Happy birthday, Grandfather!" they all cried, then eagerly asked where the ice cream was.

She did manage to pick at the rare treat, but the cold dessert seemed to make her head hurt worse — or maybe it was the loud voices and laughter of the children. *I have to hold out for father's sake,* she stoutly told herself.

But when they all rose from the table to go into the parlor for gifts, the room spun dangerously. Eva clasped the edge of the table. Her legs and back were weak, and oh, how they ached!

Suddenly there was Richard beside her, his arm going around her. "Are you ill, Eva?" he murmured. "Shall I take you home?"

"No — no. We must stay for presents. I'll be fine." Eva looked at the others who, in their gleeful exit from the room, had thankfully failed to notice her condition. Jack would be so upset if Richard called the carriage now.

Richard felt her cheek. His face went pale, and she saw there that any uncertain hopes he might have harbored were running out of him like the tide.

The morning following his grandfather's birthday celebration, which they had been obliged to leave early due to his mother's illness, Jack was quite worried to look out and see Phineas Miller Kollock's carriage arriving. The doctor — in his mid-thirties and very serious-looking — was ushered quickly into the pink mansion. But Jack's mind was diverted when Meg O'Riley, the Irish maid, urged him to dress promptly, saying, "You're to spend the day at your grandfather's office. He'll pick ye up direct."

It was probably just a cold, anyway, Jack told himself as he downed a second serving of bacon and turnovers. It was an exciting time of year to be at the wharf and in his grandfather's shipping office. He popped out of his seat when William Ellis entered the front door.

The older gentleman's look of worry turned to a smile with an enthusiastic clap of his hands when he saw Jack at table. "Ready to go, my boy?" he called. "The *Queen of Savannah* just docked this morning with iron from the New York foundry. You can help me oversee her unloading."

"Yes, Sir!" Jack responded, tossing down his napkin. *Queen of Savannah* was Randall and Ellis' larger clipper, built after *Eastern Star*. Spending the day on her would be sheer delight.

But Grandfather had spotted someone descending the stairs, for he held up a finger. "Drink up your milk, Son, it will be one minute," he instructed.

When Jack saw his father approach his grandfather, it was all he could do to obey. He wanted to hear the report on his mother. He couldn't see his father's face, but the way Richard clasped William's elbow made his knees suddenly tremble. Straining to hear with all his might, Jack could only make out "chills" and "bleeding gums." Then came two words that fell like stones into his heart: "the fever."

Jack stood frozen, watching his father and grandfather grasp each other in a partial embrace. Then he walked forward, horror overriding obedience, until he stood in the doorway to the foyer. Before they noticed him, he had read their fearful expressions.

"Can you keep Jack for a while?" his father had been asking.

"Of course," William said. Then he saw Jack and, following William's gaze, Richard turned around. As Richard came to kneel before his son, William added, "I'll have the maid get together some of his things."

"I don't want to leave," Jack protested.

"Mother is very sick," Richard explained, looking into his eyes. Father's face appeared sleepless and haunted. "We don't know how sick she might become before she gets better. It would be safer for you to stay at your grandparents' for a time."

"But I *can't* leave! Mother needs me."

"She needs you to stay well."

"But Father, please —"

"Enough! You're going," Richard snapped with a finality that forced Jack to choke back further protest.

How could he tell his father the nameless fear that loomed like a dark shadow in the back of his mind? It was too awful to speak.

Richard ran a hand over his beard-stubbled jaw. "You love it at Grandfather Ellis'," he added with an effort at conciliation.

Jack quietly measured his father, then asked in a slightly squeaky voice, "May I say goodbye to Mama?"

"I'm sorry, Jack, but that would just not be a good idea," Richard replied. "I promise, though, to send word the moment she improves."

Suddenly a picture flashed into Jack's mind. It was the Colonial Cemetery, where drifting Spanish moss kissed the tops of gray tombstones — home to the 700 victims of Savannah's 1820 fever epidemic. His father thought he did not know of such things, but he did. Of those days when the rumble of drays bearing bodies and the stench of burning tar filled the air people still spoke — and not always out of ear shot of curious children. Was this the start of another epidemic, and would his mother soon sleep in Colonial Cemetery, too?

Jack gulped back a sob and flung himself at his father, nearly upsetting Richard's balance. He recovered and wrapped his arms around his son. For an instant Jack felt them tighten convulsively, then Richard stood him away, but not before Jack caught the glint of tears in his father's eyes.

Fighting emotion, Richard straightened Jack's coat, saying, "It will be all right, Son. But for now it's best you're not too close even to me. You must pray for us — for our family."

"Yes, Sir." Jack looked up to see his grandfather approaching with a satchel — his things.

"Let's go, Jack," William said.

Jack was led away, looking back over his shoulder. "Tell Mother I love her," he called before the butler reached out to close the front door.

"I will. She loves you, too, Son."

Those words rang in his ears as his grandfather's carriage made its way to the wharf district. Feeling very alone, Jack scooted closer to the kind older man, away from the cool mists of morning rolling outside the window.

"Is that how Mother got the fever, Grandfather?" he asked. "From the mist bringing fumes from the swamps?" Jack had heard that this was how people got "the black vomit," as it was often called.

"Perhaps. Some do believe the swamp vegetation gives off poisons as it decays. No one is really sure what causes the fever, though, Jack. Personally I think your mother picked it up in the slums. I hear there have been some recent cases there."

Jack's face hardened. He declared, "She should not have gone there. She should have listened to Father."

Grandfather looked down at him compassionately, drawing him a little closer with one arm. "What your father did not forbid Eva's heart insisted upon," he said. "Your mother was forever doing for others, even as a girl. It's a good way to be. You should be proud, not angry with her."

Jack swallowed a painful lump in his throat. He had not missed the fact that William spoke of Evangeline as if she had already died. But because he saw his grandfather surreptitiously brush at his eye, he lacked the courage to point this out. Instead the two huddled miserably together until the carriage stopped.

All joy was gone from the day. Jack felt like he was seeing everything from another person's eyes. All the things that were normally a treat — seeing the sun on the water as it lapped against hulls marked A. Low & Co and Randall & Ellis, observing the cotton and rice being pressed and loaded at the bustling docks, affixing his family's seal in wax to important letters and documents — failed to engage him.

This feeling, or lack thereof, continued for several days. He ate but little and cared nothing for his usual pass-times. Everyone seemed to realize Jack was unable to concentrate, so his tutor was given a holiday which the man thankfully accepted by departing promptly for Augusta. Thus released from his lessons, Jack spent his time at his grandparents' house silently trailing the impassive Saleem, who had ceased to terrify him but still held a certain fascination. Imagining the dark giant had once been a Muslim prince in the wilds of Africa kept his mind off what might be happening at the pink house on Wright Square — at least for a few minutes at a time.

His grandfather did receive reports, and when word came that the fever had gone, Jack eagerly asked if he might go home now.

"No, Jack, you may not," his grandmother told him firmly. "We pray this is the good news we have awaited, but sometimes — sometimes the breaking of the fever is followed by new symptoms."

"Like what?" Jack prodded.

"Don't worry yourself," Grace Ellis replied, a look of great distress crossing her face even as she spoke.

And he could get no more out of her.

He lay awake that night fuming and pondering. If his mother was better, or if she was about to get worse, either way, it appeared to him that now was the time for her only son to come to her. Jack knew what he meant to his mother. She often called him "my only boy" and crushed him to her in a moment of great feeling. Finding such expressions too coddling, Jack had normally been more annoyed than gratified. But now, what wouldn't he do for her loving arms around him once more.

Tears rose in Jack's eyes along with an irrepressible desire in his heart. What right had they to send him away? And with not a word of goodbye. If the fever had broken, she would not be contagious now anyway, would she?

An idea formed slowly in his mind.

Jack crept out of bed and dressed fully in the darkness, then, wrapping himself in a blanket, he lay on the rug atop the drafty floor. Thus sleeping but fitfully, he was sure to stir before dawn.

When that hour came with its faint gray light, Jack threw off his covering. He stuffed his pillows under the bed covers and crept down the servants' stair, letting himself out the back gate onto State Street. He walked briskly toward Wright Square. Along the way sleepy mansions were occasionally illuminated by spluttering whale oil lamps. He passed only a Negro man and a stray goat, thus making his way unhindered to the back gate of his own home. This he climbed with little difficulty, landing two-footed and steady as a cat.

He waited in the cherry laurels a few minutes until he saw a female servant bearing a chamber pot exit the house on her way to the privy. Then he darted in through the door. Mounting the back staircase, Jack's heart beat fast. In a few moments he would be at his mother's side, and once he was there, she would forbid them to send him away again.

Jack made it to the second floor landing and peered about. A light burned in the hall, but no one was around. He was just outside his mother's bedroom door when it opened and Meg O'Riley almost backed right into him! She squawked, steadying the contents of the wash basin she carried which, Jack saw with horror that momentarily glued him to the spot, was a pool of blood floating with rags.

"Mr. Randall!" Meg yelled in consternation. "Mr. Randall — the young master! Master Jack, don't ye go in there —"

The door to the neighboring chamber was opening. The maid had left the portal ajar directly in front of him, and Jack made an unthinking dash for his mother's room. He had just cleared the threshold, a form bending over the rumpled bed in his view, when he was tackled from behind and swept into strong arms.

"Mother!" Jack yelled as frustration ripped through him. He fought his captor even as he was carried from the room and the door closed behind him. "Stop it! Put me down!"

His father bore him down the front stairs and into the foyer, where the butler came running. "Send for the carriage," Richard barked, attempting to stay the flailing arms of his son. He dumped Jack on the hall horsehair sofa, which scraped across the floor as Jack immediately launched himself off it, then was pushed back again in defeat.

"What are you doing, Jack? Are you crazy?"

"I came to see Mother. You can't keep me from her. She's my mother!" Jack cried, fists balled up.

"I can, and I will."

"She's better. Grandfather said so!"

"No, Son, no, she's not. The fever broke, and we thought — hoped — but now — I'm afraid she's very ill. More so than before."

Jack looked into his father's face and saw the anguish there, but all he could feel was angry denial and rebellion. This was not right, not fair — he wouldn't give in to this!

"No, no, no!" he sobbed, tears streaming down his face.

His father tried to embrace him, but Jack fought, squirming and struggling as if he would fly out of Richard's powerful arms and up the stairway again.

"You must stop this, Jack. You can't see her for your own good — and, God forgive me, mine. I can't risk losing you, too."

"The carriage is at the front door, Sir."

Still fighting against forces much stronger than he and wildly calling out for his mother, Jack was carried to the vehicle and deposited inside. Before his father closed the door, Richard said, "Please forgive me, Jack. I love you."

Jack hammered on the window as the carriage pulled away from the curb. He hated the feeling of powerlessness that swept over him. Tears blurred his view of his weeping father standing in front of the pink mansion that was to have been the place of his family's glorious new beginning.

Two weeks later when Jack returned a black funeral wreath hung on the front door.

CHAPTER EIGHT

December 1839
Savannah, Georgia

ichard Randall snapped his book shut and laid it aside. He had thought to relax a while after coming home from his office, but tonight even James Fenimore Cooper's new maritime work, *History of the Navy,* could not hold his attention. He stood up and paced to the window, making the candle flicker with his impatient movements.

He knew what the problem was. It was Eugenie's invitation to dinner. Not just a family dinner, for the Ellises made it clear they still considered him family, but a dinner *party*. Eugenie had been quite insistent that he should come — had in fact nagged him all week. He knew if he didn't show up she would harp for an untold number of meetings afterwards as well.

Richard realized this was his sister-in-law's way of pushing him to again mingle in society, now that his year of official mourning had expired. His guess was that there would be an eligible lady or two among the guests, for the Ellis' desire for his continued entrenchment in Savannah outweighed any sentimental notions that his solitary state best preserved Evangeline's memory. Richard had received a constant flow of affectionate letters from all members of his deceased wife's family while he'd been in New York this past year, and they all had testified to that truth.

He sighed roughly, going to the wash basin. Bracing both hands on its surface, he stared into the mirror there.

"Did I make a mistake? Was this whole past year one big, long mistake?" he asked his reflection.

Without thinking of what he was doing, Richard set out his shaving implements and prepared to remove the shadow which had already appeared on his face. He was careful to work around his neatly trimmed partial beard and mustache.

He had watched his beloved Eva die a slow, painful death, helpless to save her, unable to even communicate with her in the end. After her funeral it was only for Jack's sake that Richard had made himself rise from bed every morning. He knew he had to stay connected to his floundering little boy or they both would be lost. And yet connected they were not.

Richard had been aware that Jack had seemed unable to grieve. He suspected this was at least partly due to the anger his son held against him for keeping him from Eva as she was dying. All Richard's attempts to talk to the boy had failed. Thinking he and Jack both needed a change of scenery, they had left in February when things had settled down at work. In New York, his mother had instantly set about gently chiseling away the icy case that had formed around Jack's young heart — just as Richard had hoped she would. At last, one spring day in his beloved grandmother's arms, Jack had released the torrent of emotions he had been holding inside. Richard had stood outside the room as it happened, listening to the anger and pain pouring out, and had himself slumped to the floor, silently weeping in relief.

After that, Jack had seemed more responsive. But a melancholy hung on both of them, for memories of Eva were even there in New York. Richard had tried to keep busy. He had helped Houston secure two new government contracts at the foundry and had commissioned the building of a large new ocean-going steam ship. He had taken Jack to the shipyard many times, to plays and exhibits, and had closely monitored his son's progress with his tutor. The frequent company of George and Geoffrey had seemed to cheer Jack. But every day, everywhere they went was the feeling that something — *someone* — was missing.

Perhaps it would always be that way, Richard had thought. Unless — the thought had crept into his mind not long ago — unless he took another wife. Richard had rejected the idea as traitorous at first and had told himself what he had been telling Jack all along, "It's just you and me now, Son. But if we stick together it will be all right."

And recently, Jack had been increasingly warm to him, again showing interest in trailing around after Richard instead of having to be urged to leave the house. Jack had really not wanted to return to Savannah, but business here had been waiting, so return they had two months ago. Yet as far as Richard was concerned, the jury was still out on whether they would stay or go back to New York. Not much had been said on that score, but everyone seemed to know it.

Which brought Richard's mind back to the dinner party. Why was he going? Because he felt it fair to give Savannah a chance? Because in his heart he was tired of the pressing sorrow and the loneliness?

Richard surveyed his reflection. At thirty-four, his skin was still firm and his teeth still white and straight. Men his age were expected to marry again.

He changed quickly into evening clothes and hesitated over his glove drawer. He had continued to wear black ones even upon his return to Savannah. But tonight he selected gray and on impulse put a white pair in his pocket. Then, reaching for his hat, he took out a knife and carefully removed its black band.

Richard decided to shun formality and walk the short distance to the Wise home. The exercise would do him good.

Outside, candles burned in windows, greenery and wreaths bedecked doors and sills, and the pungent scent of wood smoke hung over the sandy street. The cool night air did indeed help clear his head. He had to admit it was nice to be able to walk to his destination, rather than worrying about snow drifts and below-freezing temperatures. He arrived at Eugenie's feeling far more optimistic than he had earlier.

"Oh, Richard!" Eugenie cried with pleasure as he handed his wool overcoat to the butler. She rushed out of the parlor to grab his arm. "I'm so glad you came! Do come in and meet everyone. We have two families dining with us tonight, the Brocks and the Calhouns. Mrs. Odelle Calhoun is the older sister of your friend Mrs. Henrietta Rousseau."

"Ah, yes, I've heard her mentioned but never met her," said Richard.

"Well, the Calhoun family is not often in town. Their cotton plantation is in Liberty County not far from Rev. Charles Jones' estate, but please, no business talk tonight, dear Richard."

Patting his arm, Eugenie ushered him into the parlor. As she called for everyone's attention and began introductions, Richard felt a moment of absolute panic. He was used to having Eva at his side, graciously smoothing his social path with her sweet smile and well-timed comments. Now here he stood alone, a rusty old ... *bachelor*. No longer a married man. His whole identity had changed, and with it, his social status.

Trying to conceal his discomfort, he bowed to the Judge Brock family, which appeared to possess an inordinate number of young men. Then he was introduced to James and Odelle Calhoun. Four of their five children were in attendance, ranging in age from the oldest son, Lawrence — in his early twenties and accompanied by his bride, Olivia — to a girl named Ruth who had only just "come out" into society.

It was, however, the radiant oldest daughter named Sunny whom he had been trying not to notice since the moment he entered the parlor and saw her fresh face, gleaming dark hair braided into fashionable loops, and burgundy satin brocade dress. He told himself her resemblance to Eva was not strong enough to merit such attention. But she was so aptly named his eyes kept returning to her despite himself. What a smile! What *joie de vivre* emitted from her person! She seemed so youthful and gay that Richard was taken aback when Eugenie introduced her as "Mrs. Sunny Calhoun Whitaker," adding that Richard would serve as her escort for the evening.

"Your husband — he is unable to join us tonight, then?" Richard asked, bowing over her gloved hand.

The lady, who could surely not be above twenty-one, demurely lowered her lashes. "I'm afraid that like yourself, Mr. Randall, I was bereaved." She glanced up to behold his expression of profound surprise, touched her brilliant gown, and laughed lightly. "Above two years ago," she added.

All Richard could manage was, "*Indeed.*"

When Eugenie indicated it was time for them to enter the dining room, Richard offered Mrs. Whitaker his arm. It was the strangest feeling. He held the chair to the right of his own spot, marked by an elegant name card.

As the soup tureens were set before them, Judge Brock, a heavy-set, dignified gentleman, addressed Mr. Calhoun. "Our hostess mentioned that you have five children. I hope one of them is not ill."

"No, Sir," returned the silver-haired James. "Our son Milton just entered the United States Military Academy."

"An excellent institution, though one can but pray he won't return with his head full of Northern propaganda. Did you not consider the new military school in Lexington, Virginia?"

"We felt the school needed time to establish a worthy reputation."

"Ah, that is understandable."

"So, Mr. Lawrence Calhoun, are you to be the planter of the family after your father's calling?" Richard asked.

"Proudly so," that bright-eyed young man answered.

"We had to convince him receiving his degree first was a necessity," Mrs. Calhoun told the company. "He is already indispensable to us, and loves his work so much that we have to prod him to spend more time in town for his new wife's sake."

Tall, elegant Olivia Calhoun smiled in silent acknowledgement.

"It was a good harvest this year, eh?" Richard asked the young Lawrence, knowing the eighty miles of track between Macon and Savannah had been overrun with freight the autumn just past. He understood it had also been a nice harvest for local planters growing long staple cotton.

"It certainly was! Ten thousand pounds! Six hundred bushels of corn, too."

"I heard that many planters experimented with sugar cane as a possible third crop this past decade or so," said Richard. "Do you still find any profit in it?"

"Not really," replied the older Mr. Calhoun. "It's labor intensive and flourishes better south of the Altamaha. We still maintain a small patch for our own use, though."

"Well, we're glad all that harvesting is behind you so that you can enjoy the holiday season in town," Eugenie said merrily, raising her glass as if in toast.

Richard turned to his dinner companion and asked in a quiet voice, "And you, Mrs. Whitaker? You reside here in Savannah?"

"I do," she replied. "My husband, the late Dr. Thomas Whitaker, left me a small but comfortable house on Habersham and Oglethorpe. He had only just begun to establish his practice when he passed on, but he was an only child. His small inheritance allows me to live independently, though modestly."

"A great boon, I am sure. I am all in favor of independent women," Richard said with a smile.

"Yes, I'm aware your wife was quite active in charity work."

"She was." Turning the subject just a bit, Richard continued, "You know, I heard that this year the state of Mississippi became the first to adopt a property law for married women. What do you think of that?"

Sunny looked faintly surprised. She thought a moment, daintily cutting her roast quail, before replying, "I think that is a wonderful thing. It could be advantageous for women in certain circumstances — and an important step, to be sure — but one would hope that where there is a true union of hearts and minds, a wife should never need fear for her material security or an audience for her desires."

Richard suddenly found himself wanting to touch the small white hand that briefly rested on the table next to his. Of course he resisted, wondering why he found himself so drawn to this girl, but he did exclaim softly, "Still a romantic, Mrs. Whitaker!"

"But of course!" Sunny replied and laughed gently. "I have too much life ahead of me to allow that to be stolen, even by death! — and so do you!" She leaned imperceptibly nearer as if to accent her statement.

Richard was about to make a retort on the subject of his age when Eugenie cleared her throat pointedly. "Pardon me for interrupting, Mr. Randall," she said, "but perhaps you have some knowledge on the subject, having been recently in New York."

"I'm sorry … what subject was that?" Richard asked lamely.

Eugenie looked amused. "We were speaking of the new method of photography developed by Louis Daguerre. We heard Samuel Morse learned at Daguerre's side and brought his technique back to New York.

How long do you think it might be before we can have these daguerreotypes made here in Savannah?"

"Well, Madam, your guess is as good as mine."

"You should have had one made — while you were in New York — to bring back and show to all of us."

"The details of the process only just arrived before I left. A doctor-scientist named Draper was said to be setting to work on the technique, but it would have been premature to seek out a portrait even if I had thought of it."

She made a face. "Too bad. Well, when it comes here, I shall be the first to take my family in for a sitting. Such things can be a great comfort in times of absence or loss. I should dearly love to have such a picture to remember my sister by."

An awkward silence fell momentarily. Realizing her *faux pas*, Eugenie quickly added, "I'm sorry, Mr. Randall. My tongue always gets ahead of my brain."

Seeing her sincerity and reminding himself of Eugenie's simple nature, he replied, "Don't trouble yourself, Mrs. Wise."

He was buoyed when he caught Sunny's eye and the young lady offered him an encouraging, sympathetic smile. Honestly, she lit up the whole room, he thought. She must have a whole bevy of suitors, modest income or no.

Dessert proceeded without further incident. At its conclusion, Eugenie observed, "Since we have so many gay young people among us, I thought we might forgo our separate parlors tonight and have a bit of music and dancing. I am willing to play the pianoforte, and I asked the youngest Mr. Brock to bring his violin. Would that be agreeable?"

There were enthusiastic murmurs of consent. The party filed into the double parlor, which was fully opened and candlelit. While the servants pushed back the furniture and fourteen-year-old Marshall Brock produced his instrument, the company gathered around the piano, where Eugenie rendered "Kathleen Mavourneen."

As they stood slightly apart, Sunny glanced at his hands and whispered, "Did you not bring dancing gloves, Mr. Randall?"

"I — I am not much of a dancer, Mrs. Whitaker. But if you are, I'm certain one of the other gentlemen would be happy to oblige." Richard had noticed the faintly hungry glances the oldest Brock son had been casting upon his dinner companion throughout the evening.

"I can't believe a callow youth could cut a better figure than a polished man such as yourself," she whispered back.

Richard looked at her in astonishment. Was she baiting him, with her dimpled smirk?

"I'll bet you even know how to waltz," Sunny added with a definite challenge.

"Well, I've seen it done, but I've only danced it once or twice," he admitted.

"I've been instructed, but never had the chance to actually try the dance. Here at a party would be so much better a place to start than at a ball, don't you agree?"

Richard laughed in a flustered manner. "I doubt my sister-in-law could be convinced to play a waltz. She'd be among those supporting the view that the dance is too vigorous for women and even faintly scandalous."

As if to illustrate his statement, Eugenie was announcing, "Why don't we form up for a nice quadrille?"

Sunny merely laughed. But before she could say more the enamored Mr. Brock claimed her as a partner. She went away on his arm with a glance thrown back over her shoulder, one eyebrow raised, as if to ask, "What will you do now?"

Richard was highly perplexed. He felt that the young woman had been flirting with him. But surely he had been removed from bachelorhood far too long to accurately interpret such signals. As obvious as she had seemed in her attentions, there must be some other explanation. Someone with Sunny's looks and breeding could have any dashing twenty-something on the marriage market. And plenty of her callers would be rich.

Still, he couldn't keep from watching her graceful movements, the swish of her floor-length skirt as she moved through the quadrille. He fingered the softness of the white kid gloves in his pocket.

When the set was over, Eugenie asked, "What shall we do now?"

"Oh, do let's have a waltz," Sunny suggested.

"I just don't know, Mrs. Whitaker," Eugenie replied. "It's such a new dance — and rather questionable, I think. Does anyone even know it?" She looked around, obviously hoping for shaking heads.

"Mr. Randall does," Sunny said, smiling innocently.

The other young people added that they did, too, and indicated eagerness to practice. Eugenie glanced questioningly at her husband, who silently nodded his approval. With pursed lips she shuffled through her music.

Richard saw another of the Brock brothers about to move on Sunny, who was watching Richard with an expression now surprisingly kind, as if she sensed his dilemma. Making a decision, he pulled out the gloves, stepped forward, and bowed to her.

"Would you honor me with this dance, Mrs. Whitaker?"

She looked into his eyes. "I will indeed." And she placed a hand in his. "Dancing is like laughter — the medicine of life."

As he took her in his arms and swirled her about the room, Sunny never once broke her gaze from his.

"They say to look directly into one's partner's eyes diminishes the dizziness," she murmured as if in explanation.

Richard didn't think it was working so well for him.

At the conclusion of the evening, Richard was still in a confused daze, his senses full of the scent of Sunny's sweet perfume and the feel of her lithe body in his arms. She had already gone but he could still hear her tinkling laughter — so like Eva's — as he donned his overcoat. At least he'd had enough presence of mind remaining to surreptitiously slip young Lawrence Calhoun a business card before he and Olivia got out the door.

Suddenly Eugenie's petite form was at his elbow.

"You should call on her," his sister-in-law said.

"What?"

"Don't 'what' me. You heard me. Why do you think I invited her here tonight?"

Richard stared at Eugenie in amazement. "Are you so eager to get me out of the family, Eugenie?"

"Oh, Richard," Eugenie said tenderly, placing a hand on his arm, "you'll never be out of the family. There's Jack and Randall and Ellis and because of those things, and the fact that we love you, we want you to stay. You will remarry. You're not a man to be alone. So I figure, if you do, it might as well be a good Savannah girl — not some Yankee — and one of my good friends at that."

"But — what makes you think she would have me?"

Eugenie burst into laughter too hearty to be considered proper. "Oh, my, you crazy, crazy man!" was all she would say. "Call on her. She'll have you."

As the new year of 1840 began, Jack gradually became aware of his father's altered state of mind. He could feel Richard's focus slipping from him even before he knew why. Richard could often be caught wearing a distant gaze even in the midst of conversation, and several times Jack heard a certain amount of bustling about after dinner — a time when Jack and Richard normally settled down to books and parlor games in front of the fire — only to learn upon inquiry that "your father's going out tonight, lad."

When he first heard the name "Mrs. Whitaker" it was in conjunction to an order his father was placing for a nosegay. Alarm bells went off in Jack's head. Soon thereafter Aunt Eugenie was heard to refer to this unknown person as "the Widow Whitaker." Jack's concern became even more focused.

So on a bright Saturday in February when his father told him they would take Mrs. Whitaker and Aunt Eugenie for an outing in the park, Jack had already prepared a wall of resistance.

"Who is this Mrs. Whitaker?" he asked.

"A friend of mine. I'd like you to meet her."

"Why?"

Richard gave him a quelling look as they settled in the carriage. "Because your Aunt Eugenie and I like her very much and I think you will, too. I expect you to be on your best behavior."

Jack said nothing more for the moment, but he could think of only one reason his father would seek out a female "friend." And it didn't end with friendship.

When they picked up Aunt Eugenie she squeezed in next to him, leaving the spot vacant beside his father. They backtracked to Habersham Street and finally pulled up before a square brick home with black shutters. Jack watched as his father went to the door, bowing gallantly when it opened. Jack got a sick feeling in his stomach.

He was astonished by the woman his father escorted back to the carriage. She was so beautiful. And so young. The silk flowers of her bonnet framed an exquisite face with a rather nervous smile. When Richard introduced them, handing Sunny Whitaker up into the vehicle, Jack remembered what his father expected. He rose to offer the lady his hand and bowed over her, helping her find her seat.

In response, she laughed in delight. "Oh, Richard, what a little gentleman!" she exclaimed. "I'm so glad to meet you, Jack."

Since he couldn't return the sentiment, he merely said, "Mrs. Whitaker."

That made her giggle. Then she caught sight of the family's Irish footman securing her easel and satchel at the rear of the carriage. She glanced at the black driver, then at Richard. "You keep Irish servants?" she inquired.

"Some."

"Don't you find that a drain on your purse?"

"Not particularly. They came down from New York with us and are very good workers."

Sunny's eyebrows went up. "How unusual. But I do understand loyalty. My three servants have been my protectors and friends since Dr. Whitaker passed away. Two of them were his — the butler and the cook — but my maid was my wedding present from Mama and Papa. I have promised them I will never sell them away."

It seemed to Jack that Sunny said this last bit with particular emphasis, casting another look at his father.

"Of course," Richard replied.

"Like any good mistress," Eugenie murmured.

Jack frowned.

As the carriage started forward the ladies exclaimed over the fair day.

"I can't wait to do some painting even though not much is blooming now," Sunny said. "Perhaps we could set up near the center."

"Whatever you wish," Richard told her. "Should we start with our picnic lunch?"

"That will be fine. I brought a fresh chocolate cake," she told them, turning to Jack with widening eyes. "I made it myself, hoping Jack would like it."

"Oh, you love chocolate cake, do you not, Jack?" Eugenie prodded when Jack was silent.

"Yes, Ma'am."

When they arrived, Sunny picked a spot for lunch in a grassy clearing under some huge live oaks draped with Spanish moss. The footman hurried to spread a blanket and bring the baskets. While this was being accomplished, Jack had to escort his aunt on a stroll, trailing behind his father and Mrs. Whitaker. He saw some boys he knew playing near by and waved.

"After lunch," his father said.

Annoyed by the way Sunny clung to Richard's arm, Jack followed them back to the picnic spot. Sunny still seemed nervous, though Jack couldn't imagine why. His father was obviously enchanted with her every word and movement. He laughed far too often and did silly things like spreading jam on her bread.

Sunny tried to ask Jack about his life — his studies, friends and ambitions — but Jack was not disposed to share any of those details. He offered the minimum response dictated by politeness and made it clear that he was starving, putting away Eugenie's sandwiches — which he thought lacking in both size and quantity — with great relish. But when it came time for cake, though the dessert was both moist and rich, he found he could hardly choke any down. Because they were all watching, he forced himself to. But it seemed to stick in his throat and required an inordinate consumption of water.

"May I go play now?" he asked his father.

"Yes, Jack. Stay near by."

"Yes, Sir."

Jack grabbed his sticks and wooden hoop, which he was beginning to feel he had outgrown although the game was too fun to give it up yet, and his set of battledores and shuttlecock, and raced to join the other boys. They were in the midst of an improvised game of shinny using tree branches and a ball of yarn. Known to be fast and strong, Jack was quickly added to a team.

Once that was done they took turns keeping the shuttlecock in the air and the hoop rolling. It felt good to give vent to his emotions. He tried to ignore the trio not far away, though he could not fail to be aware of his father setting up Mrs. Whitaker's easel facing out from the center of the square. Her laughter kept carrying to Jack's ears.

An hour passed in that manner. Then the parents and mammies of the other boys gradually spirited them away. At last Jack's final playmate handed back his racket, calling a cheerful goodbye.

Jack put the set on the ground and listlessly guided his hoop round and round, not wanting to rejoin his family. It rolled against a tree. He bent to pick it up. As he went down on one knee, he happened to look up and spy his father leaning over Mrs. Whitaker's shoulder, smiling at her canvas. Then Richard came around her stool and picked up her hand, the one still clutching the paintbrush, to place a gentle kiss on the knuckles. She laughed and pretended that she would swipe his vest with her brush.

The little scene sent an arrow straight to Jack's heart. His father was acting the fool, making over a woman like a love-struck boy, making as though Sunny Whitaker could mean to him what Jack's mother had! Jack hated her flirtatious glances and honeyed tones. Who did she think she was? Did she think she could just waltz in and steal his father from him?

Acting out of pure emotion, Jack righted the hoop, fixed his aim with a glaring eye, and sent it flying straight for the pair. It bounced across the distance between them and slammed into the widow's easel. As Sunny stood in alarm, the canvas tipped and hit her skirt before landing face down on the ground.

"Oh!" she cried, staring at the brown and blue paint now streaking her pastel skirt. "Oh!" She looked as if she would burst into tears.

At last someone felt like Jack did.

Any feeling of satisfaction instantly fled when Jack's gaze shifted to Richard. His father looked like a bulging ship's boiler about to explode. Jack could practically see the steam coming out his ears.

Anger and fear coalesced into tears as Jack jumped up, shouting, "I'm sorry!" even as Richard strode toward him.

Richard grabbed him by the collar. "You did that on purpose!" he grated in Jack's ear. "I could shake you within an inch of your life. What are you, a little mongrel? Some orphan child with no raising? You're going to apologize to Mrs. Whitaker, we're going to take her home, then I'm going to get out the switch and make sure you *never* do such a thing again!"

Richard swept up Jack's toys with one awkward arm while managing to keep an iron hold on him with the other. Jack was propelled forward.

"I'm sorry, Mrs. Whitaker," he managed.

Eugenie, having seen the whole incident, had hurried to swipe at Sunny's frock with her useless lace-trimmed handkerchief.

"It's all right," Sunny said to both Jack and Eugenie, trying to still her friend's ministrations. She tried to sound lighthearted but was clearly swallowing her own tears as she added, "It's only a dress."

"I'll buy you a new one," Richard said. "Sunny, I'm so sorry. I can't imagine what got into him. I promise he's not normally like this."

"I think we can imagine," Eugenie put in.

Jack felt his aunt's gaze on him even though he kept his eyes on the ground. Surprisingly, he sensed the matchmaker had taken a step towards becoming an ally.

"Don't be too hard on him, Richard. We can all guess how he must be feeling," she added.

Only Jack's pride kept him from burying his face in her skirts. *Mother*, he thought, *why did you leave us? Why did you put us in this terrible position?*

Richard's voice softened just a little. "I realize that," he said, "but he *will* be punished. This sort of behavior will not be condoned, under any circumstances. I'll take you home now, Sunny. Let me help you with your things. Go get in the carriage, Jack."

"Oh, your picture, is it ruined?" Jack heard his aunt say as he obeyed his father's command.

He got in and looked back, seeing his father carefully lifting Sunny's canvas from the grass. They all looked at it, shaking their heads with a strange sadness. Richard put an arm briefly around the widow's shoulders. He bent and spoke something softly in her ear. Whatever it was, Jack was sure Richard was saying her name, her given name, in that particular, endearing manner: "Sunny ... Sunny..."

Jack turned his face away, choking on tears and bitterness.

The hateful rod of correction was applied four times atop Jack's drawers. With that padding in place the result was more humiliation than pain, but the outcome was the same. Jack regretted the whole scene. He had acted like a spoiled five-year-old. But that didn't change his basic feelings about Sunny Whitaker.

"You're too old to act this way, too old for a switch," his father declared when the job was done, tossing the said object across the room in disgust. Pleadingly he asked, "Why did you do it, Jack?"

Jack bit his lip, shook his head.

Richard knelt down in front of him. "You didn't give Mrs. Whitaker a chance."

"A chance to what, Father?" Jack asked, tears rising again. Stupid, childish tears that he hated. "To marry you?"

"I have not asked Mrs. Whitaker to marry me."

"But you will, won't you? That's why you wanted her to meet me. Well, I don't like her, and now she doesn't like me, either. It was embarrassing, that's why I did it." Jack's voice was gaining momentum and volume as his already precarious emotions spiraled out of control. "The way you two were acting embarrassed me and it was an embarrassment to Mother, too — to her memory!"

Richard's hand slammed down on the bed next to him. "No, Jack," he said with deadly emphasis, "*you* were the one who shamed your mother today. There was nothing silly or untoward in my behavior with Mrs. Whitaker, but what you did flew in the face of all your mother ever taught you and makes me think you must still need a woman's influence in your life."

Disgraced at the thought of being a disappointment to his mother, Jack felt a sob bubble up in his throat. "I won't ever do anything like that again, Father, but please — please — can't we just leave things like they are? Just the two of us? I don't need a mother!"

"Oh, Son." Richard pulled Jack's wavy brown head against his chest. "I love you, and I love the two of us together. We'll always be together. I know you'll soon be a man. You might not need a mother to dote on you any more — and God forbid that you ever think I would try to replace Eva — for that would be impossible — do you hear me? — but Jack, a woman's gentle influence in the home is invaluable. She brings a stability and grace to a family that is otherwise lacking. And for reasons I can only hope you'll understand when you get older, even if you don't think you need a mother, *I* might still need a *wife*."

Richard stood in Sunny's parlor the following afternoon trying to make amends for his son's behavior. "If you will give me the name of your seamstress, I will place a credit to your account to cover the cost of a comparable gown," he said.

"And what would she think of that?"

"That I was replacing a dress damaged by my son, as I would explain to her," Richard retorted. "What does it matter what she would think? She'd sew another dress and be happy for the business."

Sunny slowly shook her head. "That's not the way it works, Richard."

"Then how does it work, Madam, so that I might fix it?" He was getting a little snappy.

She clicked her tongue against her teeth and poured out a cup of tea. "Come sit down and quit pacing," she instructed.

Richard sighed and did as she said, taking the delicate cup in his big hands. "The picture is ruined, too, then?"

"I think with some work it can be salvaged."

"Though why you would want to, I can't imagine — wild heathen boy that he is. He's truly sorry, Sunny, he's just — floundering. He thinks, well, he feels ..." Richard stopped, hoping she would help him out, but she merely looked at him with her wide dark eyes. "Maybe we should have shown him the portrait. He thought you were painting the square."

"And so he wrecked my efforts?" Sunny laughed. "Hardly, Richard. He thought ... of his mother."

"Yes. That's what I meant." Richard paused again, listening to the ticking of the mantel clock. Then his teacup rattled as he threw up his other hand in a gesture of frustration. "Ah, Sunny, I don't know what to do. I don't want to alienate him, but I care for you, and if I give this too much time, one of those young moonstruck bucks will be kicking your door down ... which brings me to another question, something I've been wanting to ask you. Why me, Sunny? Why have you let this old man call on you but put them off?"

"You are hardly old."

"Older than they — and you."

She chuckled. "Well, in any case, your sister-in-law keeps you well-informed."

Richard shoved the teacup onto a side table. "She's right, then," he declared hopefully.

Sunny stood up, walked thoughtfully to the window and stared out unseeingly. "She's right. How do I express it without saying too much? Without indiscretion or — disrespect? You see ... these past few years, both being married and being widowed, have allowed me to learn exactly what I want — what I need. I used to believe that because I was opinionated I needed to be in charge. I liked being married, and I find I prefer it to being alone, but I now know I need a man who is stronger than I am. Someone decisive and confident. Someone older."

Richard stood up. His first inclination, to be sure of her feelings, was to ask her how to fix this emotional conundrum they were in, to ask her if she, and society, would smile on a dress commissioned by a fiancé rather than a friend. Instead, being decisive, he said, "No one would take issue with a gentleman buying a dress for his fiancée."

Sunny turned around, her face lit with the golden afternoon glow — and something else. "No — I don't suppose they would," she said rather breathlessly. "But would a little boy take issue with a finacée?"

"The boy will be all right." Richard nodded.

"Are you sure? I admit I'm at a loss myself. I mean, he's no longer a small child, and not yet a man. He's bound to resent me, and I don't really know how to treat him."

Touched by the unveiling of her insecurities, Richard gathered Sunny in his arms. "I told him I needed you," he whispered. "We'll try again with the two of you. If you're willing ..."

"I'm willing."

"Then Sunny Calhoun Whitaker, I know you are an independent woman, but may I speak to your father about you becoming my bride?"

"Yes, Richard — yes."

With love shining from her eyes Sunny cupped his face in her small hands. Then Richard pulled her close and kissed her. Her response was all he had hoped for — and more.

The wedding was set for November. It was to be held in the recently consecrated new building of Grace Church, which James Hamilton Couper had designed like a Greek temple perched atop a basement. Between the engagement and the nuptials, Jack had plenty of time to get acquainted with Sunny Whitaker ... but not with the idea that she was to be his stepmother. On several occasions during this period he could tell she was trying to connect with him. First she would try talking with him like he was a small child, then like an adult, but nothing really worked because he could not seem to open up to her past a surface politeness. To this point Jack could go — because he saw his father's happiness — but no further. This façade of politeness became their meeting place ... and Jack's trademark. He discovered that so long as he was polite, most people did not press for more.

This rule left off where girls were concerned. Taken with the uncomfortable sensation of becoming aware of them in a disturbing new way, and not wanting to be aware of them, Jack much preferred to pick on them. When he was younger he had been able to do this in a limited physical sense, just for the fun of it — untying their hair bows and scaring them with beetles and worms and such. But now that a certain decorum was expected he had to keep his chafing of the opposite sex to the verbal realm.

The fact that these changes were occurring just as his father was taking a new bride did not help his desire or ability to relate to Sunny. He was only faintly aware of this. Mostly he just knew he wanted to avoid any person wearing skirts or cloying perfume.

If only it were easily done. Jack could feel Sunny's insidious influence creeping like tentacles of ivy into his home before she even took up residence there. The most obvious change occurred when Sunny decided Jack was now of the age when he needed a man servant. Since his mother had died, it had been Meg who had laid out Jack's clothes every morning and set the fire in the grate in his room ... who had bandaged his cuts and brought his medicine when he was sick. Now she was to be sent packing — with excellent references, his father apologetically assured Jack — and in her place was offered Randy, a tall, droop-lipped, rather drab Negro of about thirty. Randy had proven too weak a field worker on the Calhoun plantation, the doctor believing he had a heart condition. So now he was to be given a chance as a man servant.

Jack quickly discovered the slave to have no sense of humor and not much of a temper, either. Swapping out his own suit of clothes with the set on Randy's peg in the middle of the night and placing a garden snake in Randy's bed got absolutely no rise out of the man. Jack didn't let that discourage him. If there was one non-phlegmatic bone in Randy's body he was determined to find it. The task offered an outlet for all the emotional energy that built up inside him lately.

There was something to look forward to, at least. Richard had announced that two weeks after the wedding he would take his bride on a six-month European tour. Passage would be booked in the elegant stateroom of Randall and Ellis' newest ocean-going steamer, christened *Sunny Days*. And Jack would be going, too. Richard explained that he was loath to leave his son for so long, especially during a time when family bonds needed to be strengthening. If Sunny objected much, Jack didn't hear of it, and he certainly didn't ask.

Then it happened. Just three days after the wedding while out riding with his grandfather, Jack was thrown from a skittish young stallion. Raving with pain in his lower leg, he was borne back to the Ellis house where he was staying until time to leave for the trip to Europe. The doctor proclaimed that the leg was broken. It was a clean break and should heal nicely if Jack stayed off it.

The interval between the accident and the trip gave his father opportunity to determine that Jack's health was not enough in danger to prevent Richard and Sunny from leaving, but that Jack should not be able to accompany them. The announcement, rendered with great compassion, nevertheless sank Jack into despair. He felt his father was choosing Sunny over him — and he wasn't surprised. And though he kept this notion to himself, no amount of inner logic could reason it away. Even his grandparents' loving attentions failed to lift the sadness initiated by the disappointment and prolonged confinement.

With the exception of some workmen coming for minor repairs, the pink mansion would be closed up while the new Mr. and Mrs. Richard Randall were away. The bride had objected to occupying the same chamber in which the former Mrs. Randall had died. That room would now be a guest room. Sunny would have Jack's room, with a passage being made into Richard's chamber, and Jack would move across the hall. Richard's Irish butler would oversee these changes, then he, too, would be let go. When the bride and groom returned from Europe, Sunny's servants would take up positions in the pink mansion. They had, after all, received their mistress' promise of lifelong provision. Their former abode would be sold and its proceeds added to the lady's purse. And Jack's father, who had once clung to his convictions against holding slaves, would have slaves in his house.

Jack could not tell himself that these would prove the extent of alteration in his life. He knew better. When he shared with his grandfather how lost he felt, how lost it seemed his mother was becoming, sympathy shown in William's blue eyes.

"I know, Son," William said. "But she's not really gone, is she? We know she's in a better place, and we know she's in *here*." William pointed to Jack's chest, then his own.

"You know, each person has their own way of dealing with grief and the hurts of life," he went on. "Your father's may be different from yours, but that doesn't mean he's forgotten your mother. When it all comes down to it, though, Jack, there's only one thing you can control in your life — and that's how you're going to respond to what life deals you. You've got to find a way to face the future without anger or bitterness — to become a man who will honor your mother's memory."

"Yes, Grandfather," Jack whispered, fighting back tears. He still felt like his father had abdicated that role and it now fell to him alone, though he couldn't bring himself to tell his grandfather that.

Suddenly Jack realized that all William said echoed the conversation Jack had had with his mother in this very room the first day they had come to Savannah. She had urged him to be strong and not hide from his troubles. She had assured him that her love, like that of their Heavenly Father, would never end.

Jack put his chin up. He would do as they both suggested. No matter what the future held he would become a man his mother would have been proud of. One day soon he could make his own decisions. He wouldn't be powerless forever. Soon he could chart his own course, no longer letting the winds of fate drive him this way and that. No longer allowing people, except for a chosen few he could trust, to get so close they could hurt him. And never letting a woman have the kind of power over him that Sunny had over his father.

CHAPTER NINE

February 1842
Savannah, Georgia

light rain had begun to fall, beating down on the white cherry laurel buds, when Sunny's first scream echoed through the pink mansion on Wright Square. Richard, who had brought home some work from the office, nearly jumped out of his chair.

Jack looked up from the ship's model he was building. As a door slammed and running feet sounded on the upstairs landing, his father barreled into the foyer.

"What? What is it, Maum Ethel?" he called up to Sunny's maid.

Jack could hear her full-throated voice piping down from above, full of excitement. "Don't you wahrry none, Mist' Richard. De doctah got everything under control. It just be almos' time."

Richard re-appeared, looking wild-eyed. He paced a few times then darted back out into the foyer, calling for the butler. "Send a message to the Calhouns. Mrs. Randall will want her parents to come right away," he directed.

"Yes, Sah."

Jack thought an inspection of his model might calm his father's nerves. "Father, come look. I just got the sails on my Spanish galleon," he urged.

Richard drew near enough for a cursory examination. "Ah, yes, that's nice, Jack, very nice," he said. "I'm sorry, Son, my mind is with your stepmother right now. Until the baby comes — there are so many things that can go wrong ..."

"It will be all right, Father," Jack tried to comfort him.

But Richard didn't seem to hear. His gaze was distant, and he rubbed one hand over the knuckles of the other. "If something happened to her, I don't know what I'd do ..." he murmured to himself.

Jack pushed down the swell of jealousy and the thoughts of his own mother. He had almost, almost come to accept his father's devotion to Sunny — despite the temperamental side that she only showed when

Richard was not around — but Richard's display of such vulnerable emotion left Jack uncomfortable.

Another sobbing scream from the bedchamber made Jack cringe and Richard start pacing again. His father ran a hand through his hair. If this kept up much longer, he'd look like a hedgehog, thought Jack.

Then another cry rent the air — small and high-pitched.

Richard lowered his hands, holding them out in front of him with an incredulous laugh, then a clap of triumph. Had he feared another dead baby — like the ones Jack's mother had only seemed able to deliver?

The next moment Richard was out of the room, mounting the stairs in the hall. Jack hesitated only a second before following.

"Jest a minute, Mist' Richard," Maum Ethel said, trying to push the door to on Richard's attempts to enter.

"Wh-what is it? A boy or a girl?" he demanded breathlessly. "And is everything all right?"

Ethel spared him a toothy smile. "It be fine. De missus done gib you a healthy baby boy. You jus' wait, though, till we get dem both fixed up."

Richard laughed in happy relief and turning, saw Jack. He tousled Jack's hair and drew Jack's head briefly against his side, saying, "Do you hear that, Jack? A boy! You have a baby brother!"

Rather than answer directly, Jack muttered, "Hey, stop, or I'll look like a hedgehog, too."

His humor was lost on his father.

Jack was contemplating how he would act toward a *half* brother — and one twelve and a half years his junior — when the door to the bedchamber opened. Maum Ethel stood there grinning. Richard didn't wait for her to speak but bolted inside.

Jack felt like he would intrude on his stepmother's private abode if he entered without invitation. The sight of the bloody sheets a chamber maid carried past him did not further encourage him. In fact, it brought back a very painful memory. But today there was life — not death. Yet as his father shook the doctor's hand and bent to inspect a tiny bundle Sunny radiantly displayed for him, Jack hung back in the doorway.

"A son," she said joyfully. Though Sunny's black hair had been combed, her face looked wan against its wavy masses. But her voice was strong as she continued, "You remember how jealous I was last year when Olivia had Carolyn, and Josephine Habersham had Joseph? Then she wrote that poem about him and it was published in the book for the Episcopal Orphan's Home? I just cried when I read it, I wanted to have a baby so bad. I know you have Jack, but I couldn't help it, I wanted one of *ours*. And now … just look … wasn't he worth the wait?"

"Oh, Sunny," Richard said, and with shock Jack realized he was crying. "You don't know — you just don't know. That wasn't a wait. But yes, he's perfect."

Sunny reached up to touch Richard's cheek, and in that moment, Jack felt perfectly shut out. They shared something he could never be part of. The marital bond had been reassuring instead of threatening when his mother had been alive and the recipient of his father's love, but now — now with this new baby — it was another matter entirely. He drew back a step.

The motion caused his father to remember him. "Oh, Jack," he called, clearing his throat. "Come meet the new baby. What's his name, dear?"

"Bryson, remember?"

"Oh, yes — Bryson."

When Jack hesitated, Richard motioned him forward with eager impatience. Sunny was glancing in his direction, putting on a smile. He walked forward, feeling infinitely awkward — like his arms hung down to his knees.

"You might as well learn to hold a baby, Jack. If my prayers are answered Bryson will be the first of many," Sunny said.

Jack wasn't sure why the Almighty would honor Sunny's request when He had ignored his mother's, but he had a guess that, like everything else, this, too, would be just as she wished. Dutifully he held out his arms to receive his baby brother.

May 1844
Sautee Valley, Georgia

She looked for all the world like one of the fabled Little People, Henry thought, as she danced along the creek with her long black hair flying. Clad in her shift, his granddaughter plunged fearlessly into the water. He paused his plowing a minute to watch her, more from admiration than fear — for he knew Mahala had memorized every rock, every current and every pool full of water bugs and tadpoles. Still, she was a wee thing, though tall for her age at newly six.

"*Osdv advdasdodi,*" he called, reminding her to use caution in what she was doing. He had been teaching Mahala Cherokee ever since his return the autumn before.

Yes, it had taken five years of suffering and hiding like a hunted animal in the hills, but at last Henry Cornsilk had returned to the valley of his ancestors. During his time as a fugitive, which he now preferred not to speak of, he had heard of a band of Cherokee in North Carolina who traced their ties to their land back to an 1819 treaty. This group maintained that treaty allotted them American citizenship and guaranteed them the land which was not part of the Cherokee Nation. Some of these Indians had raided the U.S. soldiers who tried to drive them to stockades in 1838. The responsible Indians had been punished, but finally, in 1842, the Army had given up on trying to capture the renegades and the many refugees who had made their way to North Carolina to join them.

Henry and Sally had never left the mountains of Georgia, intent on keeping their promise to the Emmitt family. But when they had heard this news, hope had dawned. Sadly, Sally had not lived to see the hope fulfilled. The years of rough living and frequent exposure had taken their toll on her health. When the fever came, it had been more than her body could bear.

Now his comfort was in the child. How clearly Henry recalled their first meeting! What a sight he must have looked to her, to all of them, knocking on the cabin door that October night, hairy, dirty, and wrapped in a bear pelt! Nancy had rushed to set food before him, and while he had eaten Mahala had stared at him from across the cabin.

He had instantly thought her beautiful — slim and straight in her cotton dress — with clear features and two braids carefully tied with ribbons. Most remarkable of all: her eyes had remained that mysterious smoky blue, strikingly bespeaking her English ancestry in rich contrast with the light tawny skin and shiny black hair.

Ben and Nancy explained to the child that here was the grandfather of whom she had long been told. He would now live on the nearby land that Mahala's father had left to her. Nothing brought a response from the child.

"It is all right," Henry had said. "It will take time."

While he had filled in the Emmitts on the missing years and Sally's death, and they had told him of the girl's accomplishments and schooling, Mahala had listened silently. She obediently helped Nancy with the kitchen duties, all the while sneaking glances at Henry.

It was not until Henry got up to make a pallet in the barn that she had approached him. Taking his hand in hers, Mahala had stroked his skin, then laid his knuckles against her cheek.

"I'm your grandfather ... *Ududu*," he had told her past a suddenly swollen throat. "Can you say '*Ududu*'?"

The bright, dark eyes had fastened on his. "*Ududu* ... you are the same color as me."

Henry had wrapped her in a bear hug and emotionally never let her go. Oh, Mahala stayed with her adoptive family. She was still Nancy's treasured only daughter, doted on by all. For all her boldness and tomboy ways, Nancy had

116

taught her the manners of a proper English girl, and Henry knew the woman's influence to be invaluable. He would never dream of taking Mahala away from the family to whom they both owed so much. But Henry often joined them for dinner, and Mahala did come to him most weekends, when Henry would keep her until Sunday morning when they met the Emmitts at church.

She came trotting across the field now, her wet, bare feet squishing in the red Georgia clay. Henry winced. Ooh, what would Nancy say at the sight of her? And what was she carrying?

"*Ududu*," she called brightly, "what's the word for turtle?" She thrust the creature out at him.

Henry's smile quickly faded when he caught sight of the pointed snout poking out of the shell. "Eeh, Mahala! *Ulinawi* – snapping turtle! Put that thing down!"

"But why, Grandfather? He can't get me! See how far out I hold him?"

"Mahala, *gohiyudiyi*! Do as I say."

With a crestfallen expression the girl obeyed.

Hoping to cheer her, Henry inquired, "*Uyosi?*"

She nodded. "Yes, Grandfather. *A-gi-yo-si* ... I'm hungry."

"Why don't you run up to the cabin and fetch your mama's picnic basket? We can eat at our favorite spot."

"Oh, yes, let's!" Mahala cried, jumping up and down. "Just wait until you see what she packed this time!"

Nancy usually eased the requirement of weekend cooking by preparing a hamper and sending it over with Mahala. It was always filled with enough goodies to not only feed the pair through Sunday morning but also satisfy Henry's hunger for a couple of days into the week. Oftentimes Mahala had prepared some of the food herself and enjoyed bragging on this to her grandfather.

"Put on your dress!" Henry called out after her hopping form.

"Oh, do I have to?"

"Yes."

While she was gone, Henry unhitched his mule and sent her to graze along the banks of the Sautee. He was waiting in their special glade near some rapids when Mahala returned with the blanket and basket. Wet spots from the damp shift already spotted her dress, but she had suddenly become a princess at court, distributing tea and dainties to her admirers. With great finesse she set out their fried chicken, biscuits and pickles.

"And guess what's for dessert, Grandfather?" she asked with sparkling eyes. "Ginger snaps! I made them myself, but you can't have any unless you clean your plate."

"Yes, Ma'am," Henry replied seriously.

Mahala chattered nonstop while they ate. Henry listened to the music of her little voice and thought there was nothing more precious in the whole world. Oh, how she looked like her mother. It took him back some years. Actually there was the promise of great beauty in the child's delicate but proud features – even more beauty than Kawani had possessed, though he would never feed the child's vanity by telling her so.

Finally, the ginger cookies exclaimed over and consumed, Mahala sat back on the heels of her palms, legs extended and crossed before her, and pronounced what was becoming her favorite request. "Grandfather, tell me about our people."

A sad smile settled over Henry's features. "And what shall I tell you, little one?" he asked.

He knew he would have to go back to the olden days to answer her question, for the Cherokees' recent history was an unhappy one. Arriving in Indian Territory in 1839, members of the Ross faction who had long resisted removal had caused contention by reportedly refusing to adopt the laws and constitution of the Old Settlers. Ross had postured for peace and integration, and a council between the factions had been called. However, when the Old Settlers did not immediately move to accept the Late Immigrants' constitution, the convention had broken down in mistrust and intrigue. Unknown to Ross, a secret conclave had called for the murder of the Treaty party leaders. The result had been the brutal killings of John Ridge, Elias Boudinot and Major Ridge. Stand Watie, Boudinot's brother and Major Ridge's nephew, had been warned just in time to escape with his life.

As if that were not bad enough, now the Eastern and Western factions of the Nation spent their time feuding. The Western chiefs and Treaty Party remnants failed to recognize the government Ross had established.

Not that Henry would tell any of that to his sweet, naïve granddaughter. He expected her to ask about the six festivals, or how the braves had once played stickball or performed the Stomp Dance while the women served as shell shakers — or perhaps the story of Dragging Canoe, fierce defender of Cherokee lands. But he was surprised, for today Mahala's request had a more personal angle.

"Tell me about my mother," she said.

That Henry could do. But before he could proceed with a description of Kawani's playful and devoted nature and point out its parallels to Mahala's own, his granddaughter changed her mind.

"No," she said, "I know about my mother. You and Mama talk about her all the time. But nobody ever talks about my papa. Can you tell me about him?"

Henry hesitated. Ben and Nancy had thought it best to tell Mahala that her father had been a miner who had come from outside the valley, but no more — not a last name or details of his background. Friends and neighbors had been asked to honor this wish as well. Nancy had thought it would hurt and confuse the small girl to realize she had a grandfather so close whose rejection kept her from her father's family. For the time being, Henry tended to agree. But as Mahala grew, so would her curiosity. Soon — already, it appeared — such tidbits of information would prove too lean a fare for a hungry mind.

An idea came to him. "Would you like to hear how your mother and father met? I was there that day and can tell you all about it."

"Oh, yes, please!"

Henry proceeded, warming to his subject. Here there was plenty of fodder. He related his daughter's romance with great detail, bringing a dreamy smile to Mahala's face.

"Was he very handsome, Grandfather?" she asked at length.

"Your mother certainly thought so."

"How did he die? Did somebody kill him?"

Henry tried to conceal his surprise. What had led her to that conclusion? Gently he tiptoed up to the truth. "Well, yes, Mahala," he said. "We aren't really sure what happened, but your father found a lot of gold in the stream. Some people believe a greedy man killed him so he could steal the gold."

"That person will go to hell," she said unexpectedly. "It was very bad for him to take my papa away."

"Yes, it was. Maybe he will one day admit that and ask forgiveness. We should hope that will happen."

"Mama says we have to love our enemies."

"Your mama is very wise."

"Yes. The Cherokee and the white man don't love each other. Sam says before the Indians had to go west they used to fight with the white people."

"That is true, too, Mahala. We did not want to give up our land to the Chickamauga or the Creek or the white men."

"Papa bought *this* land," Mahala said, turning the subject a bit and looking around with satisfaction.

"Yes, he bought it to have his own farm with your mother. He loved her very much and did not want her to have to go west. He thought she should stay here, where she belonged — where I once lived with your grandmother. And now, this land is yours. One day you'll find a husband to help you take care of it."

Mahala screwed up her face. "Maybe I'll just let you do it, *Ududu*."

"All right, Mahala." Henry laughed and reached for her hand. He pulled her into a hug, murmuring, "Though the wind tells me you will change your mind."

"*Gv-ge-yu-hi*, Grandfather."

"*Gv-ge-yu-hi*, Mahala."

Their love thus spoken, Henry went back to work. After packing up their picnic, Mahala went to forage near the creek. Henry knew she was looking for patches of six-petal, star-like blue hyacinths and pink and yellow lady slippers. A true daughter of the land, she loved all the little flowers and knew just where to find them. She'd be sure to put them on the table for dinner. Henry smiled. His beloved Sally and daughter Kawani had both been taken from him, but his life was far from devoid of love. The One God had left him Mahala.

The following Saturday, Mahala awoke before dawn when she heard Mama stirring in the kitchen. She was instantly flooded with a great sense of excitement. Today she would not go to see *Ududu*. Normally this would make her very sad — and she did worry that he might be lonely without her — but the adventure at hand was too wonderful to allow lingering regret. Today she would go into Clarkesville for the first time.

Late spring on the farm was a busy season and not normally one when Papa would make the trip to Clarkesville. But there were some goods needed that Mama said just could not wait, and could not be had at the stores in Nacoochee, so going Ben was. On past trips he had always taken Seth with him. Now thirteen, Seth could be counted on to help with the supplies and in case of emergency along the way. Whether he went to Clarkesville or Nacoochee, Ben often also took along one of the younger boys. Mahala had gone into Nacoochee, of course, but never to Clarkesville, which was frequented much more by people from outside Northeast Georgia. She guessed it was because of her age, or maybe because she was a girl. But wasn't six old enough for a trip to Clarkesville? And couldn't Mama do without her for just one day? These were the arguments she had offered her parents from the first minute she had heard them discussing the outing.

At first the looks they gave each other had been strangely worried, and they had put her off. But at last Mahala's persistence had paid off.

"We can't keep her hidden away in the valley forever, Ben," Mama had said. "Just go to Fraser's and all should be well."

And so it was that as the sun touched the horizon Mahala was lifted up into the wagon behind the horses, Checkers and Chess, a food hamper was set in the bed, and her papa and Seth climbed onto the bench on either of her sides. She was so excited the seat springs creaked beneath her bouncing.

"How does she have so much energy?" Seth, who recently found great value in his time abed, moaned.

"Keep your sun bonnet on!" Mama directed.

"Yes, Ma'am!" Mahala smoothed her ribbons and glanced down at her Sunday best dress with the full sleeves and double-flounced skirt.

"Watch out for snakes," Mama added. "And don't leave town without new boots for Mahala."

"Yes, Ma'am!' Papa called cheerfully. He leaned down to kiss Mama's upturned lips. Instructing Sam and Jacob to be good for their mother, he clicked his tongue and gently snapped the horses' reins.

"Goodbye! Goodbye!" Mahala called, waving until the cabin and family were out of view.

They were soon entering the old toll road originally known as the "Unaka Turnpike."

"Mahala, can you tell Seth where we get the word 'Unicoi'?" Papa asked.

Mahala was glad she could answer and proudly did so. "From the Cherokee word *unegv* that means 'white.'"

"That's right, Mahala. I think this is a good time for a little history lesson," Papa continued, not able to see Seth's pained expression. Mahala didn't mind the lesson. She was sitting next to her dear papa on their wagon seat, bound for town. He could tell her anything and find her an eager audience. He went on, "This was once an Indian trail that ran between settlements. The first Europeans to travel it were traders from Charleston who wanted to bring goods to the Cherokee Overhill towns. Did you know that during the French and Indian War the British brought tools and supplies over Unicoi Road to build Fort Loudoun? Even twelve cannon!"

"Really?" That had Seth's interest.

"Yep. As steep and dangerous as parts of the trail were, I heard they lost only one horse. Seth, do you know where the road begins and ends?"

"Does it go from Augusta to East Tennessee?"

"Yes, it does. The original charter of the turnpike company ran out in the late '30s, so now the state keeps up the parts here in Georgia. That's why we have commissioners like Mr. England and Mr. Pitner."

Seth nodded dutifully. Mahala smiled and pointed out, "Look, an orange butterfly!"

"Why don't we see how many animals we can spot along our journey?" Ben suggested.

"Will we see a bear?" Mahala inquired with great excitement and no small bit of fear.

"We might — but don't worry. We'd probably see no more of him than his tail as he ran off into the bushes." Noticing that Mahala was not fully satisfied, he added, "And I've got my rifle, of course, just in case."

She nodded then and slipped her hand onto his arm. It felt so big and hard with muscles. Briefly she wondered about her real father. Had he been big and strong? Had he been as kind as Papa was? Was it wrong to wish she could have had both of them?

A hedgehog, a rabbit, multiple birds, and five deer later, they were nearing Clarkesville. They had crossed Amy's Creek and Beaver Dam Creek and Alec Mountain, which ran between them, then finally, Sutton Mill Creek. The sun was strong in the sky and the air sweet and warm.

As they approached a slow, muddy river, Papa said, "Very near here, Mahala, the Cherokee once had a town they called *Sakwi-yi* — or Suki to the whites. This river, the Soquee, is named for that town."

"Yeah, and they used to meet southeast of Clarkesville at a big tree to plan their attacks on us," Seth put in with relish. "Every time they took a scalp they cut a notch in the tree. That's why it's called Chopped Oak."

"Scalp?" Mahala asked in a strangled voice.

"Seth," Papa said, giving his oldest a warning look and a shake of the head. He turned back to Mahala. "That was a long time ago. Don't worry about it."

Even though Mahala was glad the Cherokee and whites were no longer fighting, it seemed sad, she thought, that the Indians were all gone, leaving only their names — and a few stragglers like her and *Ududu* — behind. She wondered what it was like in Indian Territory. *Ududu* said they had many relatives there. Would she go there one day?

Self-consciously she pulled the edges of her bonnet forward around her face.

Soon her mind was diverted as the traffic picked up and they began to pass big, fine houses. Mahala couldn't imagine living in such a place. Papa said more and more rich people from the coast were building summer homes here. They liked the cool mountain air that was free of disease. A man named Jarvis Van Buren was helping with some of the building. He had come to town to run the Stroop Iron Works but had soon turned his hand to architecture instead.

She couldn't believe all the people in town, and all the buildings — fancy churches and stores and the brick courthouse. Lots of folks were dressed like they were, but there were some men in dark coats and top hats and ladies in flounced muslin dresses who looked like they must certainly be rich.

"It's so busy," Mahala observed with awe.

"Busy enough that a few years back the Episcopal Church held their annual convention here," Papa said, "and now they have a new church building."

"Maybe we'll see Mrs. Nancy Harshaw," Seth said unexpectedly. "I heard Mama say she wondered how she was doing."

Papa frowned, easing the team past a small black buggy. "I doubt we'll see her, but if we do, all you are to say is a simple 'hello.' No more."

"Yes, Sir."

Mahala knew all about "Mean Moses Harshaw." Everybody did. Their Sautee Valley neighbor, who had built a house to rival those here in town, was always getting into fights with someone. Mama said she wouldn't give a chicken she liked to the man. Rumor had it that he made his old, sick slaves jump off the cliffs of Lynch Mountain. He was so mean that his wife Nancy had left him last year and moved into their town house. Mahala thought she would have done the same.

They were pulling up in front of a building whose sign proclaimed "Fraser's General Store." Papa put the brake on the wagon, looped up the reins, and helped Mahala down. Seth had already scampered up to the big glass window and stood gazing at the many items displayed there.

"Seth, keep hold of your sister's hand," Papa directed.

Seth looked annoyed but did as he was told.

Papa spoke to a young man coming out of the store. "Good afternoon, Mr. Sutton."

"Why did you call him 'Mister?'" Seth wanted to know. "He's not much older than I am."

"Yet he's a lawyer here. While it's true he's not much past twenty, he's earned the right to respect," Papa answered. "You may look around while I place my order."

Inside, Papa cheerfully greeted the balding, bespectacled owner, John Fraser, and pulled out his list. They started going over it at a long counter. Mahala looked around, wide-eyed. Seth led her down one of the two long rows of merchandise. She took in big jars of candy, bolts of material, bottles of medicine, soaps and creams for ladies, pots and pans and barrels of food supplies. Seth passed a shelf of books, then paused and pulled one out.

Mahala stood dutifully by. It took a few minutes before she realized she was being watched. Feeling eyes on her back, she turned and caught sight of a little boy peeking through a glass cabinet that displayed jewelry and eyeglasses. He whisked out of sight as soon as their eyes met. But not quickly enough for Mahala to have missed the fact that he was not just any little boy.

She tugged at Seth's sleeve. "Who's that, Seth?" she whispered.

123

"Who?" Seth looked around and, seeing no one, shrugged and flipped the page of a book.

Mahala tugged again. "Behind that counter."

Seth craned his neck. Sure enough, a face the tawny shade of Mahala's was again visible. "Oh, that's Clay Fraser. Mr. Fraser found him abandoned when the Cherokee were rounded up, back when he and Mrs. Fraser ran a store in Dahlonega."

"So he's — like me?" she gasped, feeling her heart start to beat fast with excitement. Besides her grandfather, she had never seen another Indian.

"No, he's full-blooded. But the Frasers adopted him because they couldn't have any children of their own."

Fascinated, Mahala turned back to offer the boy a shy smile. After a second, he returned it, displaying one missing front tooth. Then he disappeared again.

But before Mahala's disappointment could flower, he reappeared from behind the counter. He approached and held out one sticky hand. On the palm Mahala saw a piece of yellow hard candy.

"Would you like a lemon drop?" Clay asked.

Mahala nodded, eyes big. Before Seth could protest, she grabbed the treat and popped it into her mouth. Tangy explosions on her tongue caused her cheeks to pucker in surprise.

"Sour, huh?" Clay said with a grin.

Mahala nodded again. "Thank you," she managed.

"I'm seven. I work here with Father. How old are you?"

"Six."

"This your brother?"

"Yes."

"He don't look nothin' like you."

Having overheard, Seth put in rather hotly, "Well, she's my sister, just the same."

When he went back to reading, Mahala whispered, "My real parents were killed, so now I'm an Emmitt." She was proud that Seth claimed her, but something made her want to share secrets with this new acquaintance.

"Nobody knows who my parents were. They're either dead or gone west," Clay offered matter-of-factly. "But I have a good father and mother anyway. And I get lots of candy."

"That must be nice."

"It is. You don't live around here."

"We live in the valley. This is my first time to town."

"Next time you come, I'll give you a peppermint."

Mahala smiled. They stood staring at each other for a minute. Mahala wasn't sure what to say next, but she didn't really want him to go away, either. Papa settled her dilemma when he approached.

"Seth, you can help me load the wagon," he said. Glancing at Mahala, he added in an unhappy tone, "I'm afraid Mr. Fraser is out of small boots. We'll have to go to Clarkesville Dry Goods. Hello, there, Clay. I see you met Mahala."

"Yes, Sir," Clay answered.

"Goodbye," Mahala said as Papa took her hand.

The boy saluted like he was in the army and called, "Remember — next time a peppermint!"

She smiled over her shoulder. His inky black hair was so shiny, his features so familiar somehow that she didn't want to stop looking at him.

"I've never known a boy who looked like me, Papa," Mahala murmured as they left the store, Papa and Seth carrying boxes of supplies.

Papa smiled somewhat sadly. "I'm glad you made a friend," was all he said.

Once the goods were in the wagon, they drove to the other side of the courthouse to a similar-looking store. They left Seth in the wagon holding the reins. Strangely, Papa seemed uneasy this time as he entered and greeted the merchant, who looked surprised. The tall man's eyes flickered down to Mahala.

"Mr. Franklin, I need a pair of boots for my little girl," Papa said.

"Of course. Come sit down and we'll measure her foot. I think I have a pair that might do."

Mr. Franklin reached up on the wall for a wooden shoe plate with markings on it. As he brought it down, he spoke softly to a little Negro boy who had been dusting behind the counter. The boy scampered out the back door.

Showing them to a bench, Mr. Franklin had Mahala extend her foot. Then he gently eased off the old, worn boot. "My, these were definitely getting tight," he commented, smiling at her. He measured Mahala's foot and exclaimed, "Just as I thought! I have a pair that will be perfect for such a pretty little girl."

While Mr. Franklin was behind the counter, Papa jiggled the bench with an anxious leg. Why he seemed in such a hurry Mahala couldn't fathom. Mr. Franklin was certainly very nice.

That gentleman returned with the shiniest pair of little black boots Mahala had ever seen.

"Uh, we just need everyday boots," Papa told him uncomfortably.

"This is the only pair I have near her size," Mr. Franklin said, stooping to remove Mahala's other shoe. "But I can assure you, you'll be satisfied with the price. Thomas Franklin always aims to please."

Mahala tried out the new boots. They did fit perfectly. She felt so fancy she gave a little twirl, causing the shopkeeper to laugh.

"She must be quite a blessing," Mr. Franklin said to Papa.

"She is," Papa replied tightly.

As he paid, Mahala went to stand at the end of the counter near the front door, drawn by a large china-head doll on a stand. The doll had realistic dark ringlets and a dress out of shiny plaid material. Mahala continued to gaze upon her even when the bell on the door jingled.

She was just becoming aware of a plump older woman standing behind her when the lady spoke. "She's quite lovely, isn't she?" The voice was soft, a little choked, sounding as awestruck as Mahala felt.

Mahala turned and looked up at the woman. The reaction this caused was startling. The lady's hand flew to her breast and tears filled her eyes. "Oh!" she cried. "Look at those blue eyes!"

The lady knelt down, reaching out to touch Mahala's sleeve. Mahala started to back away when, with relief, she felt her papa's solid frame contact her from behind. Papa put both hands on her shoulders.

"So this is she, then," said the woman. "This is Michael's daughter."

"This is Mahala, Mrs. Franklin — *my* daughter."

The lady glanced up. "Of course, of course," she said, flustered. "Please forgive me, Mr. Emmitt. It's just that I have so often wondered …" Her voice trailed off.

Mahala could feel the strong emotions in the stranger, and they frightened her. She was confused. But she also felt sorry for the woman. She seemed so sad, dabbing an eye with a lace-trimmed handkerchief. So when Mrs. Franklin started to speak again, Mahala held in her fear and met the lady's gaze.

"That doll's name is Molly, and she's been here ever so long waiting for just the right little girl to come along. Do you think you could take good care of her, Mahala?"

"Oh, yes, Ma'am," Mahala breathed.

"Mrs. Franklin," Papa began, but the lady rose and motioned to the Mr. Franklin who was younger than herself. "Box her up, Thomas. It seems our Molly has found a new home."

"Oh, no, Mrs. Franklin," Papa protested. "That would not be fitting. What would my wife say?"

Mrs. Franklin shook her head, holding up a hand to stop him while she collected her emotions again. "What could she say, Mr. Emmitt, except to allow the one indulgence a lonely old woman can provide? My girls have all married away, and I find my thoughts turn more and more toward your valley and what might have been. Please let me do this. And if there is anything else you need … you remember my husband did say — financially —"

"No, Mrs. Franklin, we want for nothing. I'm well able to provide for my family."

"I'm sure you are. I didn't mean to imply …. I hear your farm is quite productive. Yes, I do make my inquiries. That way I can at least ease my mind." The woman gave a faint smile, then turned her attention back to Mahala. "And if you, Mahala, will think of old Mrs. Franklin when you hold your dolly, it would make me quite happy."

Not understanding but thinking what was requested was simple enough, Mahala nodded. She glanced at her father, searching for his approval. Reluctantly he nodded, looking pained.

"For such a big gift," he said, "you really should give Mrs. Franklin a hug."

Thinking to quickly embrace the woman's stiff skirts, Mahala moved forward. But Mrs. Franklin knelt again and drew her quickly into her arms.

"Thank you," Mahala said against the lady's soft curls.

"You are welcome, child." Mrs. Franklin finally released her, but placed a wrinkled hand on the side of Mahala's face, looking searchingly into it as if to memorize every feature. "Come back to see me again," she said.

Papa did not respond. He took the doll box and quickly ushered Mahala out of the store. The doll was too precious for Mahala to hold on the bouncy wagon seat, but as they left town she kept glancing back at the box tucked in amongst their supplies. She was overcome with wonder.

"I cannot believe she gave me that doll, Papa," Mahala kept saying. "Why did that lady do that?"

A muscle worked in Papa's jaw. He stared straight ahead. "Because, Mahala," he answered at length, "that lady was your grandmother."

CHAPTER TEN

Summer 1847
Northern Habersham County, Georgia

In 1846 the Louis Rousseau family fell in love with a land which the fabled Spanish explorer Hernando de Soto reportedly had discovered some three hundred years before.

The notion of Habersham County first entered Henrietta's mind at a party when the topic of summer destinations came up. It seemed the Johnstons and Kollocks and many other good families had found the North Georgia mountains the perfect escape from coastal heat and disease. Some of them had even built beautiful summer homes there. Not to be left behind, Hennie had convinced her husband that their family should pass the season there as well.

And so a house in Clarkesville had been rented. In mid-summer the Rousseaus had taken Richard Randall's steam packet up river to Augusta, where they had boarded the Georgia Railroad west, and then north at Union Point. From Athens, home of Franklin College, a coach had been engaged to bear them to Clarkesville.

As the land began to swell into ever-larger hills, Henrietta had brimmed with optimism and praise. Clarkesville had seemed small and rather rustic to ten-year-old Devereaux, though the rest of his family seemed determined to embrace it. Dev thought the rented house drafty and dirty. But again, the others did not seem to mind. They had quickly fallen in with their coastal contemporaries. Nine-year-old Dylan had been captivated with Indian tales and had spent many an hour reading about North Georgia and its history. Louis passed days hunting in the thick green forests. Henrietta and Collette, now eighteen, called on the women in their social circle. Collette had been giddy with the thought of actually dancing outside all night at full moon parties, for here there were no windows shuttered against the fever-laden air from the swamps. There had been a supper at the Phineas Miller Kollock home, Sleepy Hollow, given by his sister-in-law, Mrs. George Jones Kollock. The young ladies Collette's age whom she met at these parties all had ponies that they liked to ride, even to church. It was a gay society — for all except Dev, who found he missed the sea breezes and the comforts of The Marshes. He especially missed Little Joe, son of the plantation's carpenter and his closest playmate.

Dev had to wait until late autumn to return home. But he had to admit the countryside was beautiful in September and October. Goldenrod, red sourwood and tiny clouds of white and lavender wildflowers colored the brush beneath yellow poplars and red and yellow maples. His mother called it "an enchanted country."

It didn't come as a surprise when Dev heard his parents discussing a parcel of land for sale on the Tallulah Falls Road north of town. According to his research, Louis said, the best lands in Habersham lay along the rivers and sold for ten dollars an acre, while oak and hickory lands went for three an acre. All the land was fertile, producing on average fifteen bushels of corn an acre and five of wheat. Even cotton could be grown. There was even a local horticulturalist organization. Before Dev knew it, the acreage had been secured and his mother was brimming with plans for a house. She sent Louis to Gloaming Cottage, home of the favored architect Jarvis Van Buren who had been the builder of Grace Episcopal Church. Van Buren owned two sawmills, one on the Soquee for building materials and the other at the base of Minis Hill for cabinetwork and interior detail. Louis returned with a bag of apples from Van Buren's nursery but no contract. It seemed the gentleman was already much engaged constructing the Presbyterian Church and a Gothic Revival cottage for George Jones Kollock. Of course the Rousseaus had known Van Buren was involved with the church. As members they themselves strongly supported it and were eager to have their own building, though the Methodists had been generous in sharing theirs. Henrietta was a member of The Presbterian Ladies Working Society, which planned to raise money for the new church bell. But hearing these engagements would prevent the architect from assisting their own family was quite a blow to the lady of the house.

"But it must be Van Buren," Henrietta had raged at breakfast the next morning. "Only he has experience with the designs of Mr. Downing. I want something unique, romantic — something Gothic or European manor-ish."

"Well, we'll just have to adjust our sights a bit, my dear. I hear there is a good Welsh builder in the region. And you know, there is nothing more classic than Greek Revival. Imagine how grand massive white columns would look against the forests of green."

Henrietta's lip had poked out, but Collette had paused in buttering her biscuit. She had punctuated the air with her knife. "That is quite catchy, Father — 'forests of green.' Perhaps that could be the name of the place."

"Oh, for heaven's sake!' Henrietta had declared.

"Well, Hennie, you wanted something romantic," Louis had pointed out a bit mischievously.

Ultimately, the name — and the architectural style — had stuck. Before the family headed east in November, the builder had been secured and plans drawn up. Henrietta had insisted on the inclusion of a widow's walk atop the house, so that she could enjoy a bird's eye view of the patchwork quilt of autumn's colors when the leaves changed.

The following year, the idea of another season in Habersham County was made more palatable by the fact that Little Joe and his father would accompany the family. Joe could keep Dev occupied while Joseph's skills were put to use at Forests of Green. He would be ever so much more fun than Dylan, who tended to be more studious than adventurous. And he also did all that Dev told him.

So it was when the family embarked on an outing to Tallulah Falls, Dev thought the day might prove passably interesting. They took two carriages, for the Lambert family of Charleston was to accompany them, to Collette's great delight. She was making quite a joke of herself in Dev's opinion — the way she carried on with the son, Fred. Dev hadn't missed how she had provided tantalizing glimpses of her striped stockings last summer whenever she had been on horseback in Fred's company. Now he was the one on horseback, but she kept calling him over to the carriage for one reason or another, asking him a question or making some pert comment, batting her eyelashes under her big straw hat. She hardly noticed anybody else was around. There had been a time Collette had been Dev's biggest advocate. Now she had other pursuits. Of course, many of her friends had already married. She had to drag a catch in pretty soon or she'd be overlooked in favor of younger debutantes.

"Do tell us about the gorge, Mr. Lambert," she urged now. "You know so much about local history."

"Not nearly as much as your youngest brother, Miss Rousseau," he returned with a grin, turning his gaze upon red-haired Dylan. "I've seen him reading up on the area since last summer. He must know as much as the locals now."

Dylan smiled in an embarrassed sort of way.

"How deep is the chasm, then, young man?" Louis asked his son.

"Nearly one thousand feet, Sir, with a half dozen major waterfalls."

"We know, we saw it last year," Dev put in impatiently.

"Well, did *you* know those facts?" Henrietta asked him.

"No, Ma'am."

"All right, then. Besides, it's *my* first trip. Remember I was ill the day the rest of you went last summer."

"Yes, Ma'am," Dev said resignedly.

Dylan was bright-eyed with eagerness to share more from his precious store of local lore. "All the land once belonged to the Cherokee Indians, but they were afraid to go down into the gorge," he said. "They believed a race of little people lived there and that they would kidnap you, and you'd disappear forever."

"Isn't there something about a Lover's Leap, too?" Collette asked.

"I hear a white hunter was captured once, and an Indian girl fell in love with him. Her name was Tallulah ——of course. When her father sentenced the man to be thrown off the cliffs, she jumped after him," Dylan told her. He was clearly enjoying his role as tour guide.

"Do you think that's true?" Mrs. Lambert asked. She was a thin, tall woman with aristocratic features. "It seems like every ravine or gorge has some such tale."

"Even if it's not, it's a romantic story," Collette proclaimed. She sighed wistfully. "That we could all find such a love!"

Fred smiled at her a bit uncertainly.

Discontent with the limelight lingering on his younger brother, Dev said, "I think that's silly. Nobody would really jump to their death just because another person did."

"You're too young to understand," Collette said.

"We're getting near. Can you hear the river?" Fred asked.

Over the rumbling of the carriages it was a strain to do so, but Dev thought he made out a faint roaring. It grew louder as they drew near the edge of the gorge. Fred directed their drivers to a spot to park near the head of the best trail. As the carriages were unloaded, Devereaux scrambled to the edge of the precipice and gazed down in awe. It was truly an amazing sight, the green of the trees dropping straight away to rock-strewn cliffs, and far below, the Tallulah River cascading downward in a series of mighty falls and blue-green pools.

"Can we swim? Can we swim?" he wanted to know.

"Not today, dear," his mother said.

Dev drew up one corner of his mouth in disappointment. The water looked so inviting, and would even more so after hiking down that long, steep trail.

"Twelve years ago a preacher came here with a group from Athens," Dylan said, edging cautiously up behind him. "When he was alone after a day of sightseeing he decided to take a swim in a beautiful pool between two waterfalls. When his companions returned, Rev. Hawthorne had vanished, never to be seen again. Only his clothes and pocket watch were found, neatly left on a small pine sapling."

Dev turned to give his brother a disgusted look.

131

"Now, we wouldn't want that to happen to you, would we, my dear?" Henrietta asked Dev.

Dev did not reply but his look remained wry. His father added a comment about surprisingly strong currents in the placid-looking pools. If they thought to scare him, they hadn't. He knew he was strong and fast. And smart enough to stay out of currents. But arguing would do no good.

Nothing needed to be said to scare Little Joe, however. The Negro boy had timorously crept up to the precipice and was quaking beside Devereaux.

"What's wrong, Little Joe?" Dev asked teasingly, turning his frustration on the likeliest victim. Joe was a year older than he was, but the boy was small for his age.

"Ah be skeered ob heights, Mastah Devereaux," he replied. "Ain't nothin' like dis in Sabannah."

Henrietta laughed and laid a hand on the boy's shoulder. "That's the truth, Little Joe. But that's what makes it so appealing. It's like a whole 'nother world — so wild and untamed. One can easily imagine Indians and even Little People."

"Oh, don't say det, Ma'am!"

Laughing, they started down the trail. Dev thought it a rather funny procession. Going first, the gentlemen cleared the path of any obstacles or briars. Next came the ladies. Dev didn't know how they made it in their puffy skirts. Collette certainly did her share of squealing and grabbing onto Fred's arm. He was sure glad he was a boy. Not that he wanted any prissy girl clinging to him. Dylan walked quietly in front of him, communing with nature, he supposed, and behind came Little Joe with mincing steps, frequently grabbing at tree limbs and saplings for support. He was followed by the Negro men carrying the oversized picnic baskets and folding stools and tables. The August heat was formidable, even in the mountains. After twenty minutes' time the slaves' dark faces were glistening with exertion.

At last they reached the bottom. Everyone was ready for food and drink. The picnic area was rapidly prepared in some shade near one of those inviting, deep pools at the base of a falls. Dev and Dylan were hungry, but when Dev tried to raid one of the hampers his mother rapped his knuckles with her fan.

"Mother, I'm like to die," he moaned.

She gave in as he'd expected. "Oh, all right. There's an apple on top."

"Thank you, dearest Mother," he exclaimed with a flourishing bow, and dug in the hamper for the piece of fruit.

"Hey, what about me?" Dylan asked incredulously.

Dev said, "Get it yourself, but I guess you'd better ask first."

Munching contentedly, he left his little brother to see to his own needs and went to throw sticks in the water, watching their progress over a series of rapids, until finally he was called for lunch. The children and servants sat on blankets while the adults perched on the little stools. Not surprisingly, the topic of conversation was Forests of Green.

"I do so want it to turn out well. I'm taking notes from the Clinches on what not to do," his mother said.

"Yes," replied Mrs. Lambert. "It's a shame that they are so disappointed in LaMont. Mrs. Clinch tells me that it is not at all well-proportioned and the approach of the road passes near the outbuildings before reaching the house!"

"What a first impression," Collette laughed.

"Indeed. Mrs. Eliza Clinch Anderson is staying with them this season," Mrs. Lambert continued. "You know her husband, General Robert Anderson, is in the thick of things with the Mexicans. It is said that she makes herself ill with worry."

"Her time would be best spent in prayer," Henrietta said piously. "No matter how we felt about the war, our troops are committed now, and it is our duty to pray for them. All of us should do so. God will continue to smile on the efforts of our army and protect our men if we continue to come before Him."

Louis patted her hand. "You speak the truth, my wife. Ah, the wisdom of women and how we men need support from hearth and home for our brave exploits! With such prayers General Taylor will succeed on the battlefield where President Polk failed at the bargaining table — hopefully with as little loss of life as possible."

"As a good Whig I'll still be ashamed of the way we went about acquiring Mexico," Mr. Lambert sighed.

Dev had wolfed down his ham and biscuits. Bored with such conversation and inactivity, he said to Dylan and Little Joe, "Come on, let's build a boat!"

"How shall we do that?" his brother asked.

"We get the biggest leaf we can find, a skinny little stick, and another leaf for the sail. We can see if she'll make it upright to the foot of those rapids."

"All right," Dylan agreed.

Soon the boys were hard at work scouting the nearby woods and constructing their vessel. Once launched, she promptly filled with water and capsized. Then Dev managed to procure some string from one of the servants. Putting that to use, Dylan lashed together a number of small, even sticks, and they again used a leaf for the sail. Dev made sure to get a leaf off the tree that sheltered the intimately conversing Collette and Fred.

Removing his shoes, Dev told his brother and servant, "I'll wade in a bit to launch her. Then let's run up on that hillside so we get a view of the bottom of the rapids."

"Det's pretty steep, Massuh Dev," Little Joe observed.

"What are you, a boy or a girl?"

"Dev, he's afraid of heights."

"What, that little bitty slope? C'mon!"

Giving no further time for debate, Devereaux slid his feet into the cold water. He glanced at his mother. She had seen him but pretended that she hadn't. She didn't want to mar the day with confrontation. He figured as long as he stayed where the water didn't go above his shins she would ignore him. That meant he couldn't go far because the ground dropped off abruptly. But shin-deep was all he needed. He leaned over and gave the little boat a push. Then quick as a flash he was out of the water and running up the embankment, urging Little Joe ahead of him. Dylan came less adroitly behind.

"Look! Look at 'er go!" he shouted.

The rustic little vessel swirled down toward the rocks where the branch of river descended. Once she hit the top she'd go quickly. Little Joe was making his way by bracing himself with his hands. Dev gave him a push onward and upward — but at a moment the black boy was unbalanced. Joe pitched sideways and toppled down the hill, his momentum sending him rolling down a spit of land and bouncing onto an uprooted pine tree which straddled the rushing water below. Just before being dumped into the river Joe caught hold of the trunk, his one foot flailing for a hanging branch.

It wasn't a far drop to the water, and the water was not deep, though it was fast. But the boy was terrorized. "Help! I cain't swim! Help!"

His yelling attracted the attention of the adults, who came rushing over.

"Just pull yourself up," Dev called. Watching the boy, he had lost sight of the boat. He quickly scanned the water. It was nowhere to be seen.

"I cain't! I cain't!" sobbed Joe.

Henrietta did not help matters by exclaiming, "He'll be swept away!"

One of the big slaves moved to go to Little Joe's aid, but Louis put a restraining hand on his arm. "You can't go out on that rotted log," he said. "One of the boys should do it."

"All he has to do is push himself up off that branch," Dev pointed out in exasperation.

"Can't you see he's paralyzed with fear?" Collette said.

"I – I'll go," Dylan said, edging forward with a pale face.

Dev rolled his eyes, irritated both with Little Joe's theatrics and his brother's lily-livered martyrdom. What a big deal they were all making over nothing! But he could hardly let Dylan scale the log and become the hero of the day. He darted forward, scrambled down onto the spit of ground, and straddled the log. He couldn't reach Little Joe without edging forward a foot or so. This he did, instructing the panicked youth to grab his hands and at the same time hoist his weight off the branch below.

"I cain't do it, Massuh Dev! I'm gwanna fall!"

"No you won't. Just grab my hands. I'll hold you."

"I cain't —"

"You will or I'll send you to the rice fields."

The very next second black hands grabbed for white ones. Hugging the tree with his legs, Dev leaned back and pulled up with all his might as Joe scrambled onto the trunk. Dev scooted backwards, Joe crying and clinging to Dev's clothes until Dev thought he'd reach land half naked.

Finally Little Joe collapsed on safe ground, shaking, as the assembled adults broke into applause.

"You wouldn't really, would you?" Little Joe asked him. "You wouldn't send me to de rice fields?"

"No. You wouldn't last there a week," Dev said, speaking more cruelly than he intended. He wouldn't do that to Little Joe, anyway. He was bred to be a house servant. And he would miss Joe's company about The Marshes too much if Joe became a field hand. He just couldn't bring himself to say as much right now.

Dev climbed up to the adults, where they surrounded him with hugs and praise. Slowly Joe came after him, limping and brushing away tears.

"That's my son — positively fearless," Louis said.

"You clumsy boy," Henrietta scolded Little Joe. "What were you doing? You could have been the end of both of you. You're supposed to take care of Master Dev, not the other way around."

Joe hung his head. "I'm sorry, Ma'am."

Dev shot a look at his little brother. Dylan caught his eye — and the warning. And the younger boy remained silent.

Yet it was Dylan who fell in with Little Joe on the hike back up the trail, looping an arm under his shoulders to assist a gate made uneven by a twisted ankle, and quietly speaking words of encouragement.

Early September 1847
Savannah, Georgia

Swelling organ notes filled the air as the Sunday worshipers filed out of the sanctuary of Christ Church. Jack felt a small hand slip into this. He looked down to see the upturned face of his four-year-old half-sister Sylvie. She smiled beautifully. Jack smiled back. Unlike her brothers, Bryson and two-year-old

Alan, who hardly took notice of him, Sylvie adored Jack. Due to the fact that Sylvie was a china doll copy of her mother, Jack found demonstrations of her affection to provoke in him an unsettling combination of surprise and puzzlement. To be fair, Jack had to admit he had never sought out his younger half brothers. But his little sister had, with sweet determination, bored like a hornet right past his armor and straight to his heart.

"Were not the ladies' dresses beautiful, Jack?" she questioned dreamily.

"Like *Godey's* fashion plates."

"And the music heavenly?"

"Like choirs of angels."

Sylvie sighed.

Sunny came up behind them and said, "We attend church to learn about and worship God, not to indulge our senses. You'll understand as you grow older. But, you did sit quietly, and for that I'm appreciative."

Jack found his stepmother's comments on sensory indulgence to hold a faint humorous irony, since she was always dressed among the best, especially at church.

Sylvie held up her china doll. "I talk to her in my head," she offered by way of explanation.

"Oh," Jack said.

"I expect you to try to listen and glean what you can, even at your tender age," Sunny admonished.

"Yes, Ma'am."

"Oh, here is the Wise family. Good morning," Sunny greeted Jack's aunt and uncle.

Stephen bowed slightly. "A good morning to you, Mrs. Randall. Hello, Jack."

"Good morning, Uncle. Aunt."

"Is it not hard to believe that we'll be without Jack's presence next Sunday morning?" Sunny asked.

"Finally away to Princeton," Stephen commented. "When is it that you leave, my boy? We'd all like to come out for your departure — your grandparents, too, of course."

"The ship steams out on Thursday," Richard said, stepping up behind Sunny and offering a hand in greeting. "Ten a.m."

"We'll be there. I hear Charles Jones Jr. favors Princeton for next fall."

Jack nodded. He had met the dark-haired young man, son of the prominent Presbyterian minister and Liberty County plantation owner, though he did not know him well.

Stephen continued, "Well, I hope when you arrive you can find a group of good young men with whom to surround yourself."

Jack knew when his uncle said "good young men" he really meant "southern young men." "I'll be rooming with my cousin George," he said. "He's definitely a good man."

"I'm sure he is."

"I still don't understand why you won't let him go to the new naval academy in Annapolis, Richard," Aunt Eugenie chimed in, typically unafraid to speak her mind. "If ever there was a young man destined to captain a ship, it's Jack. Remember how he was forever playing pirates and buccaneers? He has such a heart for action and adventure."

"And a head for business — which would be utterly wasted at a ship's helm," Richard replied somewhat stiffly.

Eugenie knew full well she had hit upon a sensitive subject, for Richard had pretty well announced that unless Jack followed in his footsteps to Princeton, educational funding would be unavailable. Jack had shared with his aunt how this limitation burned. Eugenie saw herself as Jack's advocate in the absence of his mother.

"Not utterly, Richard. It's not as if being a ship's captain is disrespectable. There are plenty of gentlemen of our acquaintance who have honorably followed the profession, and even risen to the rank of admiral or commodore."

Through tight lips Richard said, "We've been over this ground before, Eugenie, and now is not the time or place to retrace the path."

Jack unobtrusively placed a hand on his aunt's arm, hoping to communicate both that he appreciated her efforts and it was acceptable to drop the subject. Her gaze flickered briefly up to his, then away.

"I'm afraid we egocentric men all want to see our sons follow in our footsteps," Stephen said. "And Jack sealed his fate by already having proven himself invaluable to Randall and Ellis. He'll have to content himself with transacting business with the captains of ships — his ships, which I might add, guarantees a much more substantial income."

"Right you are," Richard agreed.

"I suppose you, too, will be satisfied, Mr. Wise," Sunny put in.

"Eh? How so, Madam?"

"Well, with young Carl bound for Harvard Law next year."

"Oh, yes! Indeed!" Stephen grinned and proudly clapped his son on the shoulder. Carl smiled, his round cheeks turning pink.

"And Miss Ella Beth, how grown up you look this morning," Sunny continued, favoring Jack's sixteen-year-old cousin with her notice.

Ella Beth glowed in response. She was a sweet, serious girl, so unlike her older sister, who was as imperious as ever ... only now ruling over her own household. "My coming out is this season," Ella Beth told them shyly. "I do so hope my cousin will be able to attend my ball while he's on holiday." Her eyes rose to Jack's before she demurely lowered her lashes.

Jack was well aware that Ella Beth's youthful adoration had turned into a full-blown crush. Why did he always have that effect on young women? It seemed the more politely distant he was, the more they swooned over him. Yet, Ella Beth had always been kind, and that was more than he could say for most of the people from his childhood. He wanted to spare her feelings.

He bowed slightly. "I'll do my best to honor your gracious request, dear cousin."

She went from glowing to shining. Oh, dear. That had been as noncommital as he could be without rudely refusing an important family invitation. What had he said or done wrong?

Jack took a step back and bowed again. "If you would all excuse me for just a minute, I have a few goodbyes I'd like to make."

"Of course," said his father. "But hurry. We'll meet you out front."

Eager to extricate himself from Ella Beth's appraising gaze, Jack moved away. The church was emptying fast. He shook a few hands while his eyes scanned the crowd. To his relief he spied the tall form and rather weathered face for which he searched. Captain Hans Johansen was talking with a cotton merchant to one side of the church. Jack selected a quiet corner nearby and waited.

Within a couple minutes, Johansen approached and shook his hand, slipping a ticket into Jack's palm.

"All set," he said. "Tuesday morning at seven. Don't be late."

"I won't."

"Are you sure about this? Seems rather cold, sneaking off and cheating your family of goodbye."

"My family will survive," Jack said calmly.

Wispy tendrils of fog brushed Bull Street as Jack left the house on Wright Square. It was just after 6:00 a.m. on Tuesday morning. He was fairly certain he'd gotten out unnoticed.

Faintly remorseful, he thought about the note he'd left on his pillow. Had it been too short? Was he really, as Johansen had said, cold?

No, for a cold person would not have agonized over each word as Jack had — only a determined one. His reason for an early and stealthy departure might seem silly to many, but he felt strongly enough to refuse to back down, just as his stepmother had refused. He'd tried to frame his parting words in a manner that would both honor his conviction and assure them of his devotion. He remembered every one:

Dearest Father, Stepmother, and children — By now you will have realized I have gone ahead to New Jersey. I found a captain of a different steam line willing to book my passage. I regret I will leave without you waving me off, and without your final embraces, but I think you know the reason. I will not take Randy with me. Please trust, Stepmother, that I have sufficient knowledge of the North and my relatives there to realize being accompanied by an enslaved manservant would hinder my university experience. I know others may take their valets, but I am not others. In all other areas I defer to your judgment and heed your advice. Please accept my final decision in this. Hug the boys and give Sylvie a kiss for me. I will write you when I arrive and let you know how I find things there. With love, Jack

Satchel slung over his shoulder, Jack made his way toward the spire of the City Exchange. He was surprised to sense within himself that he would miss Savannah. As his mother had predicted so long ago, the live oaks and palm trees, the wide sandy streets, and the genteel murmur of voices had all grown familiar — and somewhat comfortable. He did thrive on the hours he got to spend at Randall and Ellis and on the docks. The partners, other factors and planters he knew by name and background. Too, there were those who were dear, especially Grandfather and Grandmother Ellis. It was chiefly because of them that he was able to digest the idea of Princeton over the Naval Academy.

When Jack heard the jingling of metal and the rotation of wheels behind him, he didn't think much of it. In fact, he didn't even turn around — until a couple of minutes elapsed and the vehicle failed to pass him. Then he glanced back with mingled curiosity and trepidation. He immediately recognized Aunt Eugenie's small enclosed calling buggy.

He stopped and waited to discover who had discovered *him*. The buggy drew alongside, halted, and the door opened. The sweet face of Ella Beth appeared in the opening. She merely stared at him without speaking for a moment, her expression mingled affection and disappointment.

"Get in," she said finally.

"So you can forcibly return me to my home?" Jack asked with a tinge of humor.

"I'll take you to the docks. And you can explain to me why you're leaving town at dawn two days early."

"How did you know?"

"I heard you talking to Captain Johansen at church. We're wasting time. Of course, if you miss your ship, that would be exactly what you deserve."

"I cannot get into an enclosed carriage alone with you," Jack said.

Ella Beth smiled faintly, realizing his words reflected on his desire to protect her reputation. Jack was not normally one to quibble over society's lesser rules. She leaned back to reveal a stoic-faced black woman who was circumspectly looking away. "My maid," she said. "If that's not good enough I'll simply have my driver follow you all the way to the riverfront."

Hesitating only a moment more, Jack pulled himself up into the vehicle, depositing himself and his bag on the seat opposite his cousin. Ella Beth spoke to the Negro on front and the buggy moved slowly forward. "Is that all you're taking?" she asked with wide eyes.

"I had the foresight to convince my father to ship my books and clothing ahead in care of my cousin George."

"I see. Jack, why are you staring at me like that?"

"Pardon me, Miss Ella Beth, I was wondering when you became such a determined young lady."

She hesitated briefly. He could see a thought flicker through her mind before her expression smoothed. "Perhaps it comes from the same source your determination does," she said. "Remember we have the same roots."

"*Half* the same roots."

"Yes — most definitely." She smiled as though that idea pleased her. Then she added, "And along those lines, what are you thinking, Jack? Haven't you considered how hurt Grandmother and Grandfather will be when they discover you've already left Savannah?"

Jack looked down guiltily. "I have, and for that I'm sorry."

"Then why?"

Briefly he told Ella Beth about Sunny's insistence he take Randy with him to university ... and his equally firm stand that he would leave the valet here. "I know you probably can't understand, Ella Beth, but I won't have my time at Princeton colored from day one with assumptions about me," he said.

"What assumptions? That you are from the South? That you are wealthy? Because those things would be true."

"No ... that I'm a spoiled son of a slave owner who can't do anything for himself — including think."

Ella Beth regarded him gravely, catching her lower lip between her small, even teeth, as was her habit. "You're a strange bird, Jack," she announced at last. "But I don't love you less for it."

This declaration made Jack decidedly uncomfortable. Exactly what sort of love was she speaking of? He decided to assume the familial sort and replied, "Uh, thank you, Cousin."

"There may come a time when my love and support mean more to you than they do now," Ella Beth told him with a calmness that was even more unsettling.

Was she speaking of coming trouble of a political nature — when because of his unique views he might covet an ally? Or did she mean she hoped for an emotional attachment to unfold with time? Either way, it was strange for a girl so young and normally so self-effacing to be so assured. Jack found he had no reply.

"Did you at least leave them a note?" Ella Beth inquired at length.

Jack nodded. "Regardless of what you might think, I'm not cruel."

"I know that," she murmured.

The buggy stopped. Jack met Ella Beth's eyes, then opened the door and jumped down. They were within easy distance of Johansen's ship. Her decks were bustling with activity, and the gang plank was down. Jack turned to bid his cousin farewell but found her pressing forward to alight. Baffled, he offered a hand.

Ella Beth pulled up the hood of the silk cloak she wore. "Will you write to me from Princeton?" she asked.

Jack studied her large eyes, rosebud lips and the dark blonde hair neatly parted under the hood. She was an attractive girl, but they were both so young and inexperienced of life. And he held fast to his principle of avoiding romantic entanglements. Thus he carefully answered, "I will write to your family just as often as my studies allow, and I'll tell you everything amusing I can think of."

He tried to put a sparkle in his eyes, but he didn't miss the disappointment in hers. Well, better now than later. But what was this? Ella Beth was leaning towards him, perhaps seeking to bury her emotion in his frock coat.

Awkwardly he embraced her and found it not so bad to hold her. She was the soft and familiar on the verge of his uncharted territory. Suddenly he was very glad she had come, that he did not have to face it all alone. His arms tightened briefly. He heard a sniffle and released her.

"You are very brave, Jack," Ella Beth said, fishing out a dainty handkerchief. "Just don't forget us all here."

"No chance of that. Thank you — for coming to wave me off. And not scolding me."

"I meant to, but hadn't the heart."

"You'd best get home before you're missed."

"No, I'll wait."

And indeed, when the boatswain's whistle announced the heaving up of the anchor, she was still there, fluttering her white handkerchief. He waved back until she and the city that had been home for the past twelve years were out of view.

CHAPTER ELEVEN

Early October 1847
Princeton, New Jersey

truggling to concentrate, Jack tried to tune out the faint, rhythmic thumping. In such a small room in Nassau Hall, that was very difficult to do. He turned a page, sighed. It continued. At last he looked up and demanded of George Randall, "You going to keep that up all day?"

"Only as long as you persist in studying."

"I've just got to finish this chapter in philosophy."

"Come on, now, Jack, can't that wait? The post office is going to close, and see, I have my two letters ready, complete with the clever new adhesive stamp." George grinned, holding up his envelopes. "Five cents for Benjamin Franklin and ten for honorable Washington."

"You can go on."

"Honestly, Jack, you've become an old stick in the mud. You didn't used to be this way. No study monitors checking in on us — we ought to be out having a bit of fun."

Jack thought to himself that George, too, had altered. Once happy-go-lucky, he was now much quicker to find fault when things did not go his way. But he merely said, "I've only been here two weeks. I don't want to relax 'til I know my pace. I did come to learn, after all, not make friends."

"Just be careful your competitive streak doesn't scare everyone off. You might end up regretting it. The world is bigger now than you and your tutor."

Jack bit the inside of his lip. "I'm aware of that. Anyway, if you're not studying, what is that book?"

George hesitated, then replied, "Whittier. His meter's heavy — thus, the tapping — but his message is at times rather inspired."

"A gift from your abolitionist roommate from last year?"

"A loaner."

Jack shook his head.

"Hey, at least I'm not afraid to consider different views. Seems like you've bought everything they've fed you for the past ten years," George said defensively. His green eyes, trademark of the Randall men, flashed.

Jack thought it was uncannily like looking at a different — curly-haired and more temperamental — version of himself. "You didn't even know what was going on with the Wilmont Proviso."

No, but Jack certainly did now. Two days ago a spirited debate had broken out in class, with the Northerners and Southerners taking wildly different views of the amendment to the bill that appropriated two million dollars for President Polk to negotiate a settlement with Mexico. The proviso stipulated that none of the territory acquired during the war should be open to slavery. The House and Senate had been at loggerheads, with Northern Democrats tired of domination by and concessions to Southerners, and senators like John Calhoun of South Carolina arguing that territories were the common property of all the states. As such he believed Congress could not prevent people from taking any property they owned into that territory.

During the class discussion, George's Massachusetts roommate from the year prior, Jake Gershwin, had declared the war had been designed to spread an evil institution and that Southerners were now merely afraid of having their balance of power upset. He had been both vehement and eloquent. No one but the professor had even raised a question to any of his arguments — and the professor's response, Jack had guessed, had been merely rhetorical, to test Gershwin's powers of debate. Afterwards, George had told Jack that Gershwin came from a highly intellectual family of free thinkers. Some of the changes in George started to make sense.

"Maybe that is true," Jack said now. "Maybe the politics I've heard discussed have been somewhat lopsided, and maybe I did come with the view that all abolitionists are raving mad lunatics. But don't make the same mistake you're warning me about. Don't judge people you don't even know."

"I know the South is filled with people who think Negroes are stupid and inferior, fit only for servitude."

"And thousands — millions — of Northerners don't share that view? Let's be realistic. How would they respond if waves of freed blacks started pouring north, stealing their jobs?"

"I'm not saying that's not true," George said, raising both hands. "Let's just agree that we've got a problem."

"I don't think anybody would argue that point."

"And that education and opportunity could change the face of the Negro community."

"All right. What then? Free them? Send them where, Liberia?"

"That's not proving such a bad option. Joseph Jenkins Roberts has shown himself to be a capable leader and a good example of exactly what I'm saying. But we both know plantation owners aren't going to let that happen. For free blacks to go? Yes. They don't want an insurrection. Free their slaves? No. There is no easy answer, man. I just hope when this house of cards collapses you know what to do."

Jack frowned. "*You* don't know what to do."

"Not to fix it, perhaps. But I do know which path to follow if trouble comes. But then again, I'm not the one with a Northern heart and a Southern home."

"How can you be so sure of my heart?" Jack asked, a feeling of dread blossoming inside his chest at his cousin's words.

"Because I know you — even though your dear stepmother deprived us of your summer visits these past few years. And even though your father's thrown his convictions to the four winds to please her."

Saying something like that himself was one thing, but having someone else say it, even George, was quite another. Jack rose out of his chair, shaking his head menacingly as words temporarily deserted him.

"Whoa, now," George said, rising, too, and placing a hand on Jack's chest. "I'm sorry. I shouldn't have said that. It's just that I can read between the lines, Jack — and I know what you've gone through since Aunt Eva died."

"No," Jack said, "you don't."

"All right, I don't. But I'm furiously waving the white flag here. What I meant was — I feel for you. You're my little cuz. I don't want to fight. I'm just trying to open your eyes."

"I don't want to fight, either. Just don't think you know them, George."

"Who?"

"Southerners. Georgians. Don't lump them all together and think for a minute that they're not individuals, good people, Christians. Some of them are among the finest and most honorable people I've ever met," Jack said, thinking of his grandfather, and many others. It was true. Among the native Georgians, he'd suffered the sting of condescension from some, but certainly not all.

"I understand that, Jack, but slavery is still a sin."

"They don't see it that way. Many treat their people like family, far better than Northern factory workers and freed blacks."

"Maybe. But they are still not free."

Jack sighed, shook his head. "I don't have a problem refusing to own slaves myself — or with gradual emancipation. But many will. Without slavery, the South's whole economic structure would crumble."

"I know."

"What are you doing?"

George was rummaging in his desk. He produced a small box and smiled. "We smoke peace pipe together," he announced suddenly in falsely halting English. "Family no fight."

144

Despite himself, Jack laughed. "No, no," he protested. "You're not getting me started on that."

"Good Cuban cigar from Vuelta Abajo. Smells like tropical flower." George waved a fat cigar under Jack's nose. "See? You feel better already."

George removed the plain band used to protect the white gloves of smokers in social settings and took out a match. He held the expensive cigar out to Jack.

Still speaking with a fake Indian accent, he urged, "To refuse to smoke peace pipe means no good will."

Jack was faintly irritated at the coercion, but he had always cared what George thought. Some things never changed. He rolled his eyes, jerking the cigar from his cousin's fingers and extending it to the match. After several bouts of Jack coughing, the cousins settled down to the smoke.

"Take a walk with me," George said at length.

"Why? The post office is closed now."

George nodded slowly, conceding that, and saying, "Yes, but the girls from Miss Hanna's Boarding School for young women 'take the air' —" this rendered loftily — "this time of day. A bit of air would do us good, too, don't you suppose?"

"Yes, but not a gaggle of girls."

"How about just one girl?" George asked rather apologetically.

"For you?"

"I'm hoping."

"Well, you're crazy, but somehow philosophy has lost its luster. You've won." Jack stood up, grabbing his morning coat — a shade of green that brought out his eyes — and together the cousins exited their room.

Nassau Hall, designed by Robert Smith of Philadelphia and constructed of light brown sandstone, had provided inspiration for college buildings across the nation. Its twenty-six-inch-thick walls had stood it in good stead during the Battle of Princeton, when an American cannonball had scarred the west wing and another had come through the window of the two-story prayer hall, destroying a portrait of George II. It was in that same room that the Continental Congress had met in 1783. The building had also survived a devastating fire in 1802 and the disturbances of many a raucous student.

Now, Joseph Henry Latrobe's post-fire restoration was evident in the brick flooring and stone stairs with iron railings. A raised sheet-iron roof gave the hall a Federal air, with the recast bell hanging in the cupola. It struck the hour as Jack and George came through the east wing door.

The town of Princeton stretched out before them, bathed in golden light and autumn foliage. A stagecoach stop between New York and Philadelphia, the hamlet had enjoyed growth and prosperity in the last decade with the building of a nearby canal and railroad. Canal Street was now a lively commercial center with factories, a hotel and pattern book houses constructed by a local architect.

Jack guessed it might be the sight of graceful steeples that prodded his cousin to ask, "You coming to church with me again tomorrow?"

"Maybe."

"Maybe? Do I need to write your father that your morals are already slipping?" George asked jokingly.

"No, I was thinking of trying the new Methodist Episcopal Church." Jack didn't like to say that the very Yankee atmosphere of Nassau Presbyterian made him slightly uncomfortable. Ninety members, mostly African-American, had recently branched off from the congregation to form Witherspoon Street Presbyterian, which was already rumored to be connected with the Underground Railroad. Jack guessed things might feel more familiar among the Episcopalians. Some preservation of his personal status quo was surely understandable, wasn't it?

Of course George didn't think so. In the spirit of upholding their newly established peace, the older boy didn't say anything further, merely clicked his tongue against his teeth. Jack sent him a scowl. George pretended not to notice and started cheerfully whistling "Jim Crack Corn."

Surrounded by the Georgian-styled homes so popular in Princeton, they proceeded down Nassau Street toward the girl's school. On Jack's initial tour of the town, George had told him that the house had been built in 1780 for the local tavern owner. The Marquis de Lafayette was said to have stayed there on his 1825 visit to The United States. Now, just as George had predicted, a number of young ladies were strolling the lawn. Some were chatting, and a few were engaged in games.

"So who's the girl?" Jack asked, interrupting the whistling.

George looked sheepish. "Miss Anna Gershwin."

"You're kidding, right?"

George shook his head.

"What, the old roommate's little sister?"

"That would be her. But just wait 'til you meet her, Jack. She's funny, good-looking and brilliant."

"I wouldn't have guessed."

"Wait, what am I thinking bringing you with me?" George asked, hitting his own forehead with the heel of his hand. "With the effect you have on women? I must have taken leave of my senses. Just act dull and a

146

bit slow and that should make certain she doesn't bother with you after a first look."

"Oh, thanks. Play the dolt, no way, but I'll try not to spread my charm too liberally," Jack told him.

"Look, there she is. Let's draw alongside the fence over here."

"Did you prearrange this meeting?"

"We have an agreement. I try to come by every Saturday at this time if I can."

"Oh, please," Jack moaned.

George jostled Jack with his elbow, for the said lady approached. Jack could instantly see the attraction. Miss Anna was clad in a fine woolen dress of sage green which brought out her milky complexion. Dark brown eyes and tendrils of curling red hair were fetchingly framed by a brown silk bonnet.

George took her hand and bowed over it. He, too, cut a nice figure in his gray morning coat and black trousers.

"What a pleasure, as always, Miss Gershwin," he said, all spit and polish. "May I introduce my cousin, Jack Randall of Savannah."

Jack had to suppress a strong temptation to cross his eyes and let his mouth fall open like the village idiot's. Instead he took the small gloved hand and bowed over it, too.

"Savannah?" she asked, arching a brow.

"Yes, Ma'am."

"Bring your slaves with you?"

Now really, that was too much. But when he thought of how narrowly he had escaped Randy, Jack couldn't muster up much anger. Sarcasm would have to do. "All two hundred," he replied pertly.

"Oh, ho, ho," Anna laughed, glancing back at George. "I see the apple doesn't fall far from the tree, even on the Southern branches."

"Yes, he's a tease. Don't pay him a bit of attention. His father is in the import-export business. The only slaves are house servants owned by his stepmother." Before Anna could pursue that subject, George quickly continued, "So, what's new? How was your week?"

"Brilliant. I recited another passage of Shakespeare and had a botany lesson. It seems to me we ought to be discussing the latest happenings in politics and literature. If it weren't for Jake being at Princeton, I'd have gotten to attend a much more progressive school."

Jack thought that Anna's assessment of the school probably was not an accurate gauge of its curriculum. She seemed the sort to always be reaching beyond what she had.

"But then we never would have met," George pointed out, sweetly bringing Anna's fingers to his lips.

She had the grace to blush becomingly. "That's true," she admitted. "And there is a musical evening tonight at Mrs. Smith's house. Can you come?"

George smiled. "Eight o'clock?"

"Yes, exactly. I'll be playing my latest arrangement on the harp. Oh, I almost forgot. I brought you this. I'd be pleased if you'd read it and tell me your views." Anna handed George a book she had been clutching inside her cloak. Jack glimpsed the title, *The Rights and Conditions of Women*. She added, "It's the first open defense of women's right to vote by an American clergyman."

"I see you get in some extracurricular reading between classes," George joked, a bit uncomfortably. Was it due to the stack of books already awaiting him in their room at Nassau Hall, or the subject of the text just presented?

"My aunt," said Anna. "She sends me all sorts of things in my care packages."

She glanced at Jack, as if to search for protest. He merely raised his eyebrows and remained silent. Thus unprovoked, she returned her gaze to her beau, expectantly.

He bowed. "I will be glad to look this over and render my opinion."

"I look forward to our conversation."

From the porch of the school, a woman in a black dress had appeared and begun to ring a tinkling brass bell.

"I must go dress for dinner," Anna told them. "It was nice to meet you, Mr. Randall. I'll see you tonight then?" she asked George.

"Indeed."

With a parting look and smile, Anna Gershwin flitted gracefully across the leaf-strewn lawn.

"My, my, my," Jack murmured. He received a certain amount of satisfaction that he now had something to harangue George over.

George grew defensive. "What?" he said. "I'm not afraid of a woman with a brain. Are you?"

"I'm afraid of all women."

As they turned away from the school, George got a dazed look on his face. "Although," he continued, "sometimes I think she must be descended from a Salem witch or something, the way she seems to have put her spell over me."

"I'm glad you said that and not I."

"But you agree! Did you see the way she looks at me? Yow!"

Laughing, Jack clapped his cousin sympathetically on the back.

Later that night, after George had gone out clad in his nicest black frock coat and silk cravat, Jack found himself pondering the day. As difficult as things might be between them, he still liked his cousin and valued his good opinion. He was glad peace had been restored.

Setting aside his philosophy text, Jack glanced up and noticed the book of John Greenleaf Whittier's poems still lying open on George's desk. He moved across the room and sat down. Before him was "Massachusetts to Virginia," a response to Virginia's attack on the Bay State for refusing to enforce the fugitive slave law. It was a long poem. Jack scanned it briefly. Several stanzas stood out:

What asks the Old Dominion? If now her sons have proved
False to their fathers' memory, false to the faith they loved;
If she can scoff at Freedom, and its great charter spurn,
Must we of Massachusetts from truth and duty turn? ...

Hold, while ye may, your struggling slaves, and burden God's free air
With woman's shriek beneath the lash, and manhood's wild despair;
Cling closer to the 'cleaving curse' that writes upon your plains
The blasting of Almighty wrath against a land of chains ...

The voice of Massachusetts! Of her free sons and daughters,
Deep calling unto deep aloud, the sound of many waters!
Against the burden of that voice what tyrant power shall stand?
No fetters in the Bay State! No slave upon her land!

These lines he could not dismiss as mere rhetoric. They were too impassioned and hit too close to home. He had to admit that what political discussion he had been exposed to at home had been decreasingly about the state — its financial struggles and economic development — and increasingly national in nature. Was George right? How many other Northerners truly felt like Whittier? Was there a time coming when the country's issues could only be settled by war? And if that time came, what would *he* do?

Feeling rather nauseous, Jack decided to retire for the night. He undressed and lay in bed listening to the whistling autumn wind and telling himself that it wasn't like the world was about to end. But he kept hearing in his mind: "No fetters in the Bay State! No slave upon her land!"

149

CHAPTER TWELVE

February 1850
Clarkesville, Georgia

artha Franklin burrowed deeper into the warm quilts, trying to shut out the noise. *Not again*, she thought. But the hacking cough continued, and it a good hour still before day break.

"Will you never get over that cold?" she murmured in exasperation.

Her husband was stirring, getting out of bed.

"What are you doing?" she asked. She reached out and caught the tail of his night shirt, which she discovered to be soaked with sweat. Martha rolled over. "Not the fever again, too, Charles! You should send for the doctor today."

"No, no," Charles grumbled. "There's nothing he can do. Another sleepless night. I might as well get dressed."

He sounded breathless and wheezy this morning. Martha lay thinking as her husband put on his clothes. She had noticed Charles' increasing lethargy these past few weeks. He had given more and more responsibility to Leon while barely seeming to make it through each day, eyes bloodshot from lack of sleep and gait dragging. Martha had begun to suspect something was seriously wrong.

Just then another fit of coughing overcame him. As he leaned over the bureau, hacking into a handkerchief, Martha slid her bare feet to the cold floor and padded silently up behind him. So when Charles drew the handkerchief away, she had a clear view of the yellow sputum there — lightly streaked with blood.

"Oh, Charles," she gasped.

He met her eyes, unable to veil his own apprehension.

"You stay here. I'll send Zed for Dr. Clarke."

Dressing quickly in the gray predawn, Martha did not bother to look outside. It wasn't until she opened the door for Zed to fetch a horse from the livery that she realized the town was covered in a peaceful blanket of soft white snow. Flakes were still silently descending from the dull sky. But all she could see in her head was the blood-streaked handkerchief.

Charles had not been the husband she had expected, Martha had to admit. She had been aware of the hard side of his nature from the first, but he had won her with his ardent, persistent declarations of passionate love and promises of a prosperous future. She had told herself that over time and under the influence of a woman he would soften. She had been wrong about that. But he had never abused her, and he had fulfilled his promises to provide. She had to content herself that for a poor girl that was something.

Also, there was the fact that while he may have left her wanting for tenderness, his devotion and fidelity had never been in question. And except where Charles' coldness had deprived her of the love of her son and granddaughter, she hadn't really minded that he made the decisions. He had been a rock, a shield between Martha and the world, which was full of insecurities for a woman alone. And so it was that the prospect of life without him initially terrified her.

For it was exactly this realization that Martha was faced with when Dr. Clarke exited the bedroom and told her the news that Charles had tuberculosis.

"Tuberculosis?" Martha questioned blankly, standing in the middle of the parlor rug like a plant that had taken root.

"Consumption," Dr. Clarke further clarified. He closed his black bag.

That Martha understood. For centuries the disease had been so named because it appeared to consume its victims from within, leaving them gaunt, spectral versions of their former selves. It was only fairly recently, Dr. Clarke told her, that a man named Schönlein had renamed the sickness.

"This man, this doctor, whoever he is — did he come up with new research? A cure?" Martha asked hopefully.

Dr. Clarke shook his head, compassion in his eyes. "I'm afraid not. In the past decade the owner of Mammoth Cave in Kentucky brought many tuberculosis sufferers there hoping its pure air and constant temperature would help them … to no avail. We don't really know what causes the disease, or how it is spread. We only know that in most cases the lungs become infected, leading, inevitably, to death. It may be a matter of weeks or perhaps a few months, but, Mrs. Franklin, you should prepare for this eventuality."

Wordlessly Martha let the doctor out, then went into the bedroom. Charles was sitting on the edge of the bed with his fists on the mattress, head hanging. Martha drew near and pulled him close to her. They stood that way for some time.

"He gave me some medicine but I don't expect it will help much," Charles said at last. "I'll move my things into the guest room so I won't keep you up at night."

"No, Charles, that's not necessary —" she began, but he cut her off.

"Yes, it is. You're going to need to be strong, Martha. We can't have you becoming exhausted and ill, too. Besides, what do they even know? I could be contagious."

Martha gave a sob. "I don't think I can be strong, Charles, not about this."

"You *are* strong, or you couldn't have put up with me all this time."

She laughed faintly, realizing he was right. "That's true."

"I've been a hard man, Martha, and done some things I regret."

"Have you, Charles?" she asked distantly, tapping into buried hurt, afraid to hope he might be willing to at last confront it. But instead of lingering on that topic, he went on, not noticing the mental shutters that came down over his wife's eyes. "At least I'll leave you with a sound estate. My will is in order. I leave everything to you, Martha, except the expected token gift to my brother and his youngest son. Leon's done a lot to help us. I don't like him much, but he's been dependable. When I'm gone, he should manage the hotel well for you."

Charles was stopped by a fit of coughing. Martha brought him a glass of water. "There, now," she murmured. "Don't talk that way. You're not dead yet."

"Might as well get used to the idea," Charles gasped.

She stood silently, watching him drink. Slowly, above her initial grief, there rose an awareness. A realization that she could and would make it. Already she knew she would not allow herself to fall on the mercy of her pompous, self-serving nephew. *She* would hold the purse strings. She would make the decisions. No longer would she need suffer a man to dictate how she must live her life.

There came, too, the guilty knowledge that ironically, with the death of her spouse, there might finally come the opportunity for love, a love for which she had been longing for twelve years.

Martha turned, and as she washed her hands at the basin, her gaze ascended to the snowy mountain slopes to the west.

For the past six years, every Christmas and every birthday, Mahala had received a package from Clarkesville. At first there had been toys, slates and candies. Then beautifully bound books and crisp writing paper. Once a year she received neatly folded material for Nancy to make her a new Sunday dress — and a matching, store-bought bonnet trimmed with flowers. Mama explained that this was the only way Mahala's grandmother was allowed to express her affection, due to her prejudiced and cold-hearted grandfather, owner of the Franklin Hotel.

Mahala had not been overcome with rejection upon learning the whole tragic story. She was well accustomed to the way many white people treated Indians. Her grandfather's actions were just what she would have expected. Instead, it was a relief to learn her father's identity. She felt like a lifelong question mark had at last been removed. And when the first package came, then another and another, she was touched by Martha Franklin's care. Suddenly there was someone else in her life besides the Emmitts and *Ududu* — wonderful as they were — but someone else of her own blood, her *white* blood, who loved her.

After that initial meeting, Papa allowed Mahala to accompany him to town at least once a year. The routine with these visits became a stop in Thomas Franklin's store, where, like the first time, Mahala's uncle would quietly dispatch his little Negro servant. Soon enough Martha would appear, eyes in her round face alight with anticipation, and they would have a visit. At first Mahala was shy, but Martha's obvious interest in her every word and action soon won her over. Sometimes they walked by the Soquee, Mahala throwing in sticks and leaves and watching them drift slowly in the muddy water. On other occasions they went to the Habersham House, where Martha would treat Mahala to milk or tea and apple pie. Mahala would try to mind her manners and not gobble the delicious dessert. One time they even went to the Episcopal Church, where they sat in the boxed pew and chatted for an hour.

During these meetings, Mahala would reveal things about herself such as how her brothers picked on her but would stick up for her any day, how she had a pet rabbit she'd raised from a baby, and how her favorite subject in school was grammar. She then proceeded to proudly pour forth a string of Cherokee, just to illustrate her fluency in both languages. Martha looked rather shocked at that.

Life was pleasant and full for Mahala. Most people in the valley knew her story and treated her well. She received excellent marks in school, where she was Mr. Johnson's prize pupil. Besides that, there were church socials and occasional weddings and harvest parties. She also enjoyed the perfect balance between Mama's increased efforts to instill ladylike behavior and being able to run wild at *Ududu's*, where she basked in the tales of her native people. All of these tales seemed magical to Mahala, for the fact that the Cherokees were gone lent a mystique to that side of her ancestry. She never felt she had a reason to be ashamed of who she was.

Then the pace of life was irretrievably altered one morning just after school let out for spring. It was a beautiful day, blue and cloudless. The countryside was a pastel rainbow of buds and blooms – yellow forsythia, purple plum, white pear and pink cherry. Mahala was helping Mama set out the garden. She kept straightening to stretch the muscles in her back, sniffing the tang and watching the column of smoke in the air where Papa and the boys were burning off the lower field. Suddenly she noticed a nice black carriage trundling up the road toward the house.

"Look, Mama, a visitor!" she cried.

Nancy wasn't concerned. "Oh, probably someone going up to the Harshaw place," she said, dropping in a pumpkin seed and covering it with earth.

But the carriage turned into their drive.

"Oh, dear," Mama said now, jerking off her apron and Mahala's and balling them up. She darted into the house, which was now two stories because Ben had expanded it when Mahala was eight. In a second, Nancy ran back out, smoothing her hair and face as though she had dirt streaks everywhere. "Who could it be?"

Mahala was too excited to express her amusement at her adoptive mother's flusterment. The vehicle was stopping, and an old black man climbed down from the driver's seat. Mahala recognized him.

"Zed!" she exclaimed as the slave opened the door and Martha Franklin stepped out. "Grandmother!"

Martha was all in black, with no ornament to break the severity of her dress. Nancy stared in astonishment. "Mrs. Franklin," she said, "what a surprise! You're in mourning!"

"I buried my husband day before yesterday." For such an announcement she displayed little emotion, which was rather strange — although Mahala and Nancy both guessed why. Martha's eyes sought Mahala and hungrily roved over her from head to toe. With unconditional affection, she took in the gangly new height of early adolescence and the muddy boots before continuing. "No doubt my trip here will stir up the gossips, but I simply couldn't wait another day. Not another day. I had to see my Mahala."

Mahala hurried forward into her grandmother's arms. "I'm sorry you lost your husband," she murmured.

"Me, too, child, though to be truthful I'm glad there is no longer an impediment between us." Martha glanced briefly up to heaven as if afraid a lightning bolt might be dealt down from above.

"Well, won't you come in?" Nancy offered. "Let me get you some refreshment. Will you be staying the night?"

"Oh, no, I wouldn't heap a surprise like that on you," Martha said as she followed Nancy inside, one arm about Mahala's shoulders.

"It would be no trouble at all, and would give you more time with Mahala."

"I hope to have much more time with her already."

The reply stopped Nancy short. A look of suspicion passed over her features. But she remembered her manners and pulled out a chair for Mrs. Franklin. "I'm afraid all I can offer you is water, but I'll put some coffee on for lunch."

Mahala knew Mama had been planning to send the men a hamper out to the field so that they could eat quickly and continue with their work. Dinner was the main meal of the day. Now all that had changed, but Mama gave no indication of the inconvenience. Instead, she began the messy task of frying up some chicken, encouraging Grandmother to sit and chat with Mahala. Mahala felt guilty doing so while Mama worked, but she obeyed. Grandmother shared the story of Charles' illness and death and all the latest happenings from town. Mahala listened politely, not interrupting as Mama had taught. That was not difficult because although she called Mrs. Franklin "Grandmother" — it seeming to please her so — the lady was still virtually a stranger.

Finally Mama said, "Mahala, please run out and tell your father and the boys who is here and to come in for lunch."

"Yes, Ma'am." Mahala scrambled for the door.

When she returned, the male Emmitts washing off at the well, she found the table neatly set with the good dishes from North Carolina and Mama's face a stiff mask. Mama was trying to act like everything was normal, but she held her bottom lip funny. When Papa's eyes met Mama's after he greeted Mrs. Franklin, she looked like she would cry.

"What's wrong, Mama?" Mahala asked.

"Nothing," Nancy said, setting the bowl of peas on the table.

Mrs. Franklin looked sad. But of course that was not unusual, Mahala thought, her just having lost her husband and all. After the prayer, she dug into her chicken with relish.

Following a few minutes of chit-chat among the adults, Papa asked a little gruffly, "So, Mrs. Franklin, if you do not plan to spend the night with us, why are you here? Did you truly drive all the way out here just for a few hours' visit?"

Martha did not flinch from Ben's direct gaze. She answered in a steady tone, "Mr. Emmitt, my daughters have all married away. Not one stayed nearby. All these years I have thought of the granddaughter denied to me by my husband. I look at her, and I see my only boy. Now Mr. Franklin is gone, and yes, I came because I couldn't wait any more." She paused and smiled at Mahala, who was watching her closely. "There is so much I want to know about her, and things that she should know about me. Things she *should* know about her father and his family. I was hoping, Mahala, that you might like to spend some time with me in Clarkesville."

Mahala opened her mouth, then closed it. She had seen the Franklin Hotel, and my, it looked grand. Now, to be able to enter it with her grandmother, the owner ... it would feel like she was a princess in a castle. Too, she thought of Clay Fraser. She had seen him several times on her visits to Clarkesville. He had kept his promise of the peppermint; in fact, every time they met he had a small something for her. He liked to ask about her Cherokee grandfather and would grow disappointed when the stories Mahala began to relate were always interrupted. "I wish we had more time," he'd say. "You're the only one like me." So, she already had a friend in town, one eager to pass time with her. Last time she had seen Clay, she'd felt the same way, for he'd grown tall and handsome, with a new air about him — and no more gap-toothed smile.

All this passing through her mind, Mahala nodded and said to her grandmother, "I would like that."

"Just how long of a visit did you have in mind, Mrs. Franklin?" Papa asked in the same reserved tone.

"Why, however long Mahala would like it to be."

"Children, out to your chores," Papa said unexpectedly. "I'll be along in a bit."

"But Pa, I'm not done," Jacob protested loudly.

But Seth, a strapping nineteen now and looking to start his own farm soon, firmly gathered up all his younger brothers and shooed them outside. Mama sat with her hands on either side of her untouched plate, looking as if she'd swallowed a fly. Mahala reluctantly followed her brothers out the door. Yet when they went off to various jobs, she darted silently back to the house and crouched beneath the open window. No way was she going to miss this conversation. She had every right to hear what was said concerning her.

"Let's speak plainly here," came Papa's voice. "You're not talking about a few weeks' stay, are you?"

"It is true I would like Mahala to live with me indefinitely," Martha replied calmly.

Mahala felt like her heart fell down to her toes. *What?* That changed everything. Leave the Emmitts, the only home she had ever known, and her grandfather? She could never do that!

Echoing her very thoughts, Mama said, "Mahala would never do that."

Papa added, "Mrs. Franklin, Mahala is part of our family, given to us by her mother. Besides the love we have for each other, she is indispensable to my wife."

"Your wife has three sons. I have no one." Was that a catch, a pleading, in Grandmother's voice?

"She loves it here," Ben continued. "Not only with us, but with her grandfather, who is also completely alone in life. Mahala is his reason to live. Would you take her away from all of us by force?"

"That would not be my choice. I'd hoped you would consider the benefits I can bring to Mahala. You are but an adoptive family, no matter how loving. I am her flesh and blood. I would give her my name, a place in my life, and a legacy in my will. Think of the opportunities she will have. I could further her education, give her music lessons and the training of a lady, the skills and abilities to be independent in life, to make her own decisions. She would meet influential people. All my daughters married well. Mahala would not have to settle for some obscure farmer and a tiny patch of earth. If you truly love her, you will consider these things."

"Mahala would be happy with a tiny patch of earth," Mama protested tearfully. "You don't know her. She's a child of the streams and mountains. You'd make her into something she's not."

"It's a parent's duty to make sure their children are well-rounded," Martha pointed out.

"She would not go. She would not go," Mama repeated, breaking down into tears completely.

Mahala bit her lip and sat on the ground, her legs too weak to support her any longer. She felt like she was being torn in two. But Mama was still right. This was her home.

"She would," came her grandmother's voice, "because you would tell her to."

"We would never do that," Papa said firmly.

Mahala breathed a quiet sigh of relief.

But then she heard the sound of paper rustling. "I'm afraid you don't have a choice," Martha said. "I'm sorry. I did not want to have to show you this. But as you can see, the judge in Clarkesville recognizes my legal right to Mahala. The word of the girl's deceased Indian mother would never stand up in court. I am Mahala's legal guardian."

It took every ounce of control Mahala possessed to hold steady until her grandmother left, saying to Nancy and Ben, "This time next week."

Papa and Mama each stood with an arm around Mahala as the black carriage drove away. She could feel their own tightly reined emotions.

"This isn't final," Papa said to Mama. "I'll go to the judge."

Nancy nodded.

Then, once Papa quietly called the boys back to the field and Mama went into her bedroom, Mahala ran all the way to her grandfather's. She didn't stop once, but with tears tracking her cheeks, flew all the way into *Ududu's* arms. He dropped the hammer he had been using to repair the fence around the pig sty and embraced her, alarmed, asking what the matter was. Mahala realized he probably thought someone at home was bad hurt or dying, but she couldn't get any words out to answer his questions for several minutes, the sobs were coming so hard.

Henry led her to a bench outside his cabin and made her sit down, offering his handkerchief.

"*Ududu*," she finally gasped, "Grandmother Franklin came today. She — wants me to come live with her. I heard her tell Mama and Papa she has papers — papers to make me. But I don't want to, *Ududu*! I don't want to go!"

Fresh tears overtook her, but not before she saw her grandfather's tanned face turn white with shock. *Ududu* said nothing for a while, only wrapped his strong arms around her and let her soak his cotton shirt.

"She says she can give me things, a better life than Mama and Papa. But I don't care. I won't leave you! Tell me what we can do to stop her. Papa said to Mama that he will go see the judge. You'll go with him, won't you? You won't let her take me, will you, Grandfather?"

Henry looked pained. "I must be honest with you, Mahala. I have long feared if your white grandfather died, this very thing could occur — and truly, I do not know how we can stop it."

"We could run away — go join the Indians in North Carolina! They would welcome us!" Mahala suggested desperately, frightened at her grandfather's uncertainty.

"And how would that help your poor mama and papa? They would *never* see you again, then."

Mahala hiccupped and loudly blew her nose into the little checked cloth. "That's true, but you're not just going to let her take me, are you?" she again demanded angrily.

"If your grandmother has a document stating her right to you, there may not be much we can do. A judge who is probably her personal friend would never honor the wishes of an adoptive family and an old Indian man over that of a reputable white grandmother."

"I thought you would fight for me, *Ududu*! You always talk about the bravery of our ancestors and how fiercely they fought for what was theirs!"

Henry looked ashamed at her words. He sighed. "Perhaps this time the bravery will be in your heart, Mahala, and not in our actions. I know Ben will do all he can to keep you, but I don't want to give you false hope.

That was what kept John Ross pushing and fighting when the fate of our people was already decided — and his quest caused even greater disunion and disappointment. Try to see the whole picture, little one. Nothing happens without a reason. Perhaps this is the path your life was meant to take."

"I don't choose this path!" Mahala cried.

"Many times we cannot choose the direction we walk, but we can always choose the manner of our stride. If you must go, do not go angry at your grandmother. She has been lonely a long time, and from what you have told me of her, she does love you. She may only know how to grab for love, but you, little Mahala, can show her how to give it willingly."

"I don't think I can, *Ududu*," Mahala whimpered. Surrender did not come easily to her nature.

"The One God can help you to do so."

"How can you be so sure? Aren't you mad at Him? Didn't He give me to you and now He's taking me away?"

"The Lord giveth and the Lord taketh away, blessed be the name of the Lord, as the Good Book says."

"That doesn't seem fair."

"Much in life is not fair. Again, how we respond to what we are given shows who we are. You are strong, Mahala. And you may find many treasures await in your new life, if you are open to finding them."

"But you *will* make sure Papa goes to the judge?"

"I will, though I won't go with him. A Cherokee grandfather living here in the county would only harm his chances."

Mahala sighed, feeling her heart was torn from her chest. "All right. I'll go home and do as I'm told, but you'd best be asking the One God for all that help, because I'm too mad to be nice to Him or Grandmother Franklin right now."

Ududu nodded with understanding and took her inside for bread and milk. Then, holding her small hand in his big, calloused one, he walked her home to her very worried mama. Mahala watched him leave in the cool twilight. She saw him pause just before he was out of sight, leaning his weight on an old sycamore tree, his shoulders shaking with grief.

CHAPTER THIRTEEN

Spring 1850
Clarkesville, Georgia

The carriage rolled along in the deepening twilight, lurching over ruts in the road. In the gathering darkness Mahala could spy bright splashes of blooming dogwoods and wood azaleas. Once she heard the haunting cry of a bobcat, and the sound seemed to echo eerily in her heart.

She had been over this road before, but always in the company of Seth and Papa, with the promise of returning to her cozy home after a short outing. Now no such return trip awaited.

Mahala turned to the woman opposite her and broke the silence by asking, "May I visit my family soon?"

Grandmother looked sympathetic, but Mahala reminded herself not to be fooled by the sweet countenance. She had seen just how harshly Martha Franklin could act in her own interest. "Of course you may, once you get settled in," she replied. "But I think if you give it a chance, you may find you like it in Clarkesville. There must be a hundred questions going through your head right now. Come sit beside me and I can answer some of them."

Martha patted the seat beside her but Mahala didn't move. As disobedient as it was, she just couldn't. She could only look at her grandmother levelly.

"It would not have been your choice to come with me," Martha said quietly.

"No, Ma'am."

Martha looked pained. "I thought you wanted to visit Clarkesville."

"Visit, not stay."

Martha bit her lip. "I hope that will change. If only you knew how much I need a companion — an ally. I'd like the two of us to be a team. I'd like you to help me run the hotel. As you get older, of course ..." When Mahala still did not speak, she continued. "For now, there are some things I can teach you — about the business — and becoming a proper young lady. I've also arranged for you to sit in on some private lessons with some other girls your age."

"Private lessons?" Mahala inquired with an uncertain quaver.

"Yes, French, music, manners — how to be a good hostess — things like that. Miss Pettigrew was an instructor at a fine girls' boarding school

160

before she retired and moved in with her widowed sister. Judge Mason and one of our attorneys, Mr. Wilkinson, send their daughters to her, mornings, rather than away to school or to Mr. Ketchum's school on College Hill outside town. Old College isn't a big success from all I hear, and I do not approve of a man overseeing the education of young women. For that, a woman of breeding is needed. We are very lucky Miss Pettigrew agreed to take you."

"But Grandmother, I don't need to know those things," Mahala objected over the growing lump in her throat. "I already can read and write, and Mama taught me plenty of manners."

Martha's countenance and voice grew suddenly stern. "Mahala Franklin, you will be a credit to me — not an embarrassment. I mix with the best people in town. Our hotel attracts wealthy and influential guests. Never will I have it said that my granddaughter is an uneducated half breed. Do you understand me?"

"Yes, Ma'am," Mahala squeaked. She couldn't decide if her grandmother's tone, the term "half breed," or the use of the name "Mahala *Franklin*" took her aback more. She had always been Mahala Emmitt. Now even that had changed. Mahala felt like she was sinking in a whirlpool of confusion, with no familiar, solid ground to grab.

Her grandmother's expression softened again. "I know you're bright, Mahala, and you will do well with a bit of finishing. In the afternoons, you can help me about my duties. You will be indispensable to me. I fully intend that your cousin Leon will be nothing but a token male in my establishment. You and I will be independent, respected ladies if it takes everything I've got to make it so."

Mahala blinked. She hardly knew what to say in the face of such determination. She was about to inquire about this cousin Leon when they passed an imposing edifice. The huge columns across the front were under construction. Noticing Mahala's interest, Martha sat forward and looked out.

"Ridiculous," she said. "Pretentious. Our newest competition, 'The Palace.'"

"It is amazing," Mahala murmured.

"If you like that sort of thing. Me, I prefer solid and traditional."

A moment later the carriage drew to a stop and Zed opened the door. Mahala followed her grandmother, stepping to the ground. The three-story hotel rose before her, golden lights glowing in most of its curtained windows, with some guests placidly rocking on its encircling porches. A delicious smell of food cooking made her stomach rumble. Mahala had to admit it was a welcoming scene — not intimidating like The Palace Hotel.

"We'll go in the front way," Martha directed. "Our living quarters will be to the left. Leon has been staying in a downstairs suite since Charles fell ill. I have asked him to move back home next week. No matter how he acts, Mahala, always remember I view this as his job, not his inheritance. Do not let him intimidate you."

"Yes, Ma'am," Mahala murmured. She marveled that her grandmother seemed so sure of their future relationship. Did she not fear Mahala's lack of cooperation — or the possibility that the Emmitts might eventually win her back? For now, Mahala decided it was best to just play along.

Inside the gracious entrance hall, a tall, slender man in his thirties hurried to greet them — or rather, to greet Martha, for except for the barest of glances as Martha introduced her granddaughter, he appeared not to even notice Mahala. So this was Leon, realized Mahala with instant dislike. She silently seethed at the way his disregard reduced her to the importance of a fly on the wall. He ran through an update of the day's business and concluded with an announcement that dinner would be sent into the family dining room just as soon as they were ready. Mahala thought he looked faintly hopeful that he might be invited to join them.

"Have Maddie deliver it right away," Martha responded. "I want to get Mahala settled into bed early. She starts with Miss Pettigrew at eight a.m."

"Miss Pettigrew?" Leon gasped.

"Is there a problem?"

"Only — I — do you think that's wise?"

"Obviously I must." Martha placed an arm around Mahala's shoulders. "If you think I have any intention of hiding this child away, Leon, dismiss that notion at once. And from now on, mind your own business ... or I can find someone else to mind mine."

Offended, Leon clamped his mouth shut in obvious irritation. But he said no more. He turned on his heel, face red, as Martha led Mahala into a private parlor.

"You see what I mean," Martha murmured as she untied Mahala's bonnet strings. She gazed at Mahala, then, in a sudden paroxysm of emotion, cradled her face adoringly. "Dear child! How can anyone look at you and not love you? Such a beauty — with those blue eyes. Of course, not everyone looks for beauty. We must be prepared that many will find fault regardless of my efforts on your behalf, or what a sweet girl you might be. You will try for me, won't you, Mahala — try and be happy? For know that all these years it has been my dearest wish to have you here with me. And now, you really *are* here."

Mahala gazed back at her grandmother, sensing her sincerity yet still battling anger. She wanted to point out that she was only here because she had been forced to be. How could she give her love to this woman when the bonds she felt to her family in Sautee pulled at her so painfully? And that pain was her grandmother's doing!

Yet her grandfather's words came back to her even now — his encouragement that she should attempt to also love this place and this woman. She could start with the kernel of pity she felt over Grandmother's lonely life.

"I'll try," she whispered.

"Thank you, Mahala. You won't be sorry. This will soon feel like home — you'll see."

Later that night, after Mahala managed to choke down most of her chicken dinner, her grandmother showed her into a bedroom. It was quite lovely, with a high bed covered with a white candle-wicked spread, a small writing desk, a marble-topped dresser and lace curtains at the window.

"This was your father's room," Martha said. "I've made a few changes to make it more feminine and comfortable for you. I hope you like it."

"Oh, I do. Thank you," Mahala said. She saw her circumstances in a slightly different light, realizing her father had once lived here. Curiosity stirred. What sort of things might she learn about him, living in his world?

"Shall I help you do up your hair?" Martha asked unexpectedly.

Mahala turned to her in confusion. "Do up my hair? If you mean braid it, I can do that myself."

"Oh, no, my dear, I mean in rag strips. You're a young lady now. You'll find the stylish girls your age wear ringlets. Have you no strips?"

Mahala shook her head.

"Just a minute. I have some extra."

Before Mahala could protest, Martha had disappeared. But she was back almost as quickly with a handful of narrow sections of torn sheeting. "Here, let's turn back the bed and sit down. Take your boots off. That's it."

Martha took up a silver-handled comb that had been lying on the dresser. Mahala sat stiffly as her grandmother brushed her long black hair. Mahala's lip wobbled. She tried hard not to think of Mama as Martha divided her hair into sections, carefully wound each one up around her finger, and tied it off with a strip.

"I've had plenty of practice doing this, though it's been a long time," Martha said. "It's nice to have a young girl back in the house. I'll tell you a secret, though, if you promise never to repeat it."

"What?" Mahala asked softly.

"Your father — he was always my favorite." With that, Martha tied off the last curl and lightly kissed Mahala's cheek. Her reward was a brief, uncertain smile. "There you go. Now get into your gown and get some sleep.

Tomorrow after breakfast I'll walk you over to Miss Pettigrew's. Would you like me to say prayers with you?"

"No, thank you. I can do it."

"Very well, then. Good night."

It was awful enough feeling like a woman one minute and a child the next, Mahala thought as her grandmother closed the bedroom door. Why did her whole life have to turn upside down, too? Mahala looked in the mirror at her rag-tied head and felt like a stranger stared back at her. She was in the grand hotel, with its foreign sounds of people walking about and lantern light flickering outside on the street, but she didn't feel like a princess in a palace. She was small and alone.

A knock startled her. Had her grandmother come back for something?

But upon opening the door just a crack, Mahala beheld the smiling black face of a woman in her forties. She had never given any thought to the fact that her grandmother might own slaves besides Zed.

"I'm Maddie, Zed's wife. Work in de kitchen. Ah heerd Miz Martha's brung you to live here. Got some oatmeal cookies." Maddie waggled her eyebrows and waved the tray she held in an enticing manner. "Thought you might like a little snack before bed."

The cookies did smell good. Mahala opened the door wider to admit the plump servant, who still had an apron tied about her waist. She entered and placed the tray on the bedside table.

"Thank you. They look delicious," Mahala said.

"Well, didn't turn out so good as last time. Ah be thinkin' they needed a pinch more brown sugar."

Wondering if the woman always spoke in half-sentences, Mahala bit into a cookie. She couldn't find a thing wrong with it and said as much.

Maddie looked doubtful. "You jus' eat 'em all up, honey, and drink det milk down, too. Looks like you need a bit of fattenin' up." She reached out unexpectedly to encircle Mahala's slender wrist. "Lak a chicken bone," she commented. "Drink de milk. Didn't you get nothin' to eat on det farm?"

"I got plenty to eat," Mahala answered indignantly.

But Maddie didn't pay any attention, for she had turned to Mahala's bed and was engrossed in smoothing the wrinkles out. This was rather confusing since Mahala anticipated lying down on it as soon as the woman left. But she watched in silence as Maddie patted and pressed until the surface was perfectly flat, with the covers turned back below Mahala's pillow in an exact V.

"Do you make all the beds in the hotel, too?" Mahala asked.

"Sometime, when your granny need me an' Ah be done in de kitchen. But mostly Ah cook. Ah make biscuits every mornin'."

"Are you the only — servant?" Mahala asked, dutifully taking two swallows of milk.

"Jus' me an' my man, Zed. We got no chilluns. So Ah be glad you here now. We need a chile in dis place, to cheer things up. Ah seen your granny cry one too many times 'bout how far away you was, what when Mister Charles was alive. Ah be glad now, too. Got someone to appreciate my cookies. Det Mister Leon, he look lak a grasshopper. Always too busy to eat."

Maddie turned to survey Mahala, who was popping the last bite of cookie into her mouth.

"Feel better now, don't you?" she asked. "Nothin' lak a cookie an' milk to soothe a body. Now you sleep good, Miz Mahala. We take good care of you. You be happy here, you see."

With a pat on Mahala's arm, Maddie took the tray and made for the door, her errand of mercy complete.

"Thank you," Mahala said, a bit bemused.

She closed the door behind Maddie. As much as she appreciated the servant's gesture of kindness, she hoped no one else would bother her tonight. All she wanted was to wrap up in a ball of misery, close her eyes, and pretend she was back home.

Mahala opened her trunk and dressed in her nightgown. Then she wound herself up in the quilt Mama had sent from her bed at home. Thus fortified, she settled tentatively onto the feather mattress. There she lay, like a butterfly in a cocoon, awaiting the mysteries of her future.

The next morning, Mahala had eggs, biscuits and bacon at the dining room table. Then Martha led her out into the hotel lobby. After a brief consultation with Leon, who had an unattractive friend Mahala heard her grandmother call Abel leaning on the desk visiting with him, they were about to exit when an elegantly dressed woman called her grandmother over. Obviously this was not a person to be ignored.

Mahala stood where her grandmother bid her, but it was uncomfortably near Cousin Leon's post. He looked her over with an expression of disgust.

"My, we're all decked out today," he observed sourly.

Abel grinned and snickered. "Still a half breed," she heard him mutter.

In response, Mahala raised her chin but kept her eyes averted. Her reserve only seemed to irritate Leon more.

"Don't you be turning your little nose up at us, you insolent chimp," he hissed under his breath, leaning close enough that his voice would carry to her ears alone. Mahala stared at him, shocked at the grown man's hateful words and tone. He continued, "Your grandmother may have taken you in and treated you like a white girl, but don't for one minute think that same acceptance will ever extend from me. You should be shipped out West with the rest of them, where you belong."

Mahala had encountered prejudice before, but never so vehement, and never directed so personally at her. Her lips rounded to speak, but Leon raised his eyebrows and put a finger over his lips. "Shh. Not a word — about me — or to me — or you'll be sorry. Never forget that."

The boy named Abel winked at her.

An expression of consternation settled over Mahala's features, but she remained silent. She believed him. Cousin Leon was creepy.

Grandmother turned from her conversation and took Mahala's hand. As they left the hotel, she looked down and asked, "Is something wrong, child?"

"No, Ma'am." Then, a moment later: "Grandmother, why did Cousin Leon never marry?"

Martha shot her a suspicious glance. "Why do you ask?"

"Oh, just wondering."

"Many years back, Judge Cromley's daughter broke his heart," Martha told her. "Since then Leon claims none other can interest him."

"Why did she break his heart?"

"None of your business, child. Don't worry about it," Martha replied sharply.

Her grandmother's evasiveness made Mahala more curious than ever, and certain that there was much more to the story. But it was clear no more information would be forthcoming. Right then and there she decided her best method of defense where Leon was concerned was to make herself as scarce as possible. Hopefully if she didn't get in his path he would leave her alone.

Martha changed the subject. "Are you nervous about your classes? Don't be. You'll be the star pupil in no time," she said.

But that first day at Miss Pettigrew's was an absolute nightmare.

When Mahala arrived, feeling stiff and unnatural in her best dress, with her hair in the proper little side curls, the spinster looked her over in a resigned sort of way, as though Martha's excessive gratitude had forced her into accepting a second class student. Mahala was led past a parlor into a small classroom. A desk had been prepared for her behind those of two other girls. These young ladies looked down their noses until introductions were complete, then proceeded to turn their backs and apparently forget her for the rest of the day.

"*Parlez-vous français, Mademoiselle?*" Miss Pettigrew inquired.

"No, Ma'am," Mahala responded, with absolutely no temptation to demonstrate her fluent Cherokee as she once had for her grandmother.

"Well, you will very soon," the school mistress replied, handing her a text book. "Page three, please."

As Mahala opened the book, Miss Pettigrew explained that they would have lessons in literature, etiquette, letter writing, piano, and the art of home management. At times they would make use of the parlor, such as when they practiced their music or served tea. She made no claims to being a dance mistress, but considering the lack of one "in these rustic climes," as she put it, she would also endeavor to render some basic instruction in that area. This excited Latilda Mason and Star Wilkinson very much, but only added to Mahala's dismay. When would she ever have an opportunity to attend a dance, anyway?

By the end of the week Mahala was conjugating "*je parle, tu parles, vous parlez, nous parlons*" but was no closer to having meaningful interaction with her classmates. She was good at French, much to Miss Pettigrew's eyebrow-raising surprise. And she understood these were to be "finishing lessons," but she missed the spelling bees, math and geography and especially the easy camaraderie of her school back in the valley. She also missed her brothers, more than ever at the close of each session when Latilda's fifteen-year-old brother Greg arrived to escort the other two girls home. There was no one to escort Mahala. Not that she would want to have Greg as an escort, much less as a brother. Indeed, she could only wish desperately that the boy shared his sister's preference for ignoring her. Instead, he had a smart mouth and no compunction about using it on those younger or more vulnerable than he.

"My, my, what have we here?" he had said when he had first spotted Mahala. "An Indian maiden who missed the round-up. What would *you* need finishing classes for?"

Mahala had not dignified his comments with a reply, though the ensuing giggles of the girls had burned her retreating ears. After that she had made every effort to be away before Greg arrived.

On Friday, though, he came early. When she heard his swinging step on the front porch, Mahala's eyes filled with tears. It had been a long, strained week. Every morning had been filled with lessons in the foreign new subjects and every afternoon she had worked with her grandmother. All day long, Mahala always had the feeling she was one step behind where she needed to be. Then there was the relationship with her grandmother. Mahala enjoyed working with her — and she had to admit she found the duties at the hotel interesting — but Martha still seemed like a stranger. Mahala didn't think she was ready to change that yet, even though she desperately needed an ally against Leon. Whenever she chanced to pass her father's cousin in the hall, he brushed past her as though she were a dirty alley cat someone had let in off the street. That was plenty enough for a girl to endure, wasn't it? As for

Greg, who could stand him? One more insult and she'd either fly to pieces or fly to boxing his ears.

She gathered up her books and dashed into the parlor in hopes that Greg would enter the classroom from the hall. The girls giggled at her frantic escape, but she was in luck. She made it out the front door unmolested.

Mahala breathed a sigh of relief and, closing the door behind her, looked up to see none but Clay Fraser, for whose very face she had longed this whole week. He was driving a wagon and looked so grown-up there on the seat. He caught sight of her and, with an expression of surprise, drew the team to the side of the road before Miss Pettigrew's gate.

"Mahala," he called. "I heard you were in town."

Inexplicably Mahala found herself blushing. "Yes," she said. "I spend mornings here — at Miss Pettigrew's."

"Um, that's something."

"Yes, silly, isn't it?"

"Not at all. Hey, I'm taking some meat and supplies out to some of the estates. The houses are real pretty. Might give you a chance to see around, if you want to ride along."

Mahala's heart leapt. But tempted as she was by the offer and Clay's engaging grin, she thought her grandmother might worry if she didn't return home soon. She was still contemplating this when an unwelcome voice sounded behind her.

"Well, if it isn't Red Clay Fraser!"

Mahala turned to glare at Greg and, realizing he had interrupted a conversation, he added loudly, "Oh, it makes sense now — the lessons! Takes a lot of polish to be a grocer's wife!"

Latilda had the grace to gasp her brother's name and give his arm a little shove. He just grinned wickedly as Mahala's face turned bright red.

Clay had raised himself up off the wagon seat. "You ignorant bumpkin, this time I'll thrash you hard enough to shut you up for good!"

"Come on then. I'm not scared of a meat wagon Indian!"

But before Clay could loop his reins and climb down, Mahala made a split decision and clambered up onto the seat. Clay looked at her in astonishment.

"He's not worth it. Let's just get away," she urged. When he did not move to obey her, she burst out frantically, "Just drive! Drive! Let's go."

He did as she said, glaring back over his shoulder at the youth on the porch.

"I knew it!" Greg yelled after them. "Coward!"

Responding to the insult, Clay started to pull back on the reins to stop the team, but Mahala reached across and boldly shook the lines, giving the horses the signal to trot. Clay looked amazed and a little incensed, but she placed an apologetic hand on his arm and said, "I'm sorry. I just don't want you to get into a fight on my account, not minutes after we met up. You can blame me for forcing you to rescue me."

"I still won't live this down until I settle it, Mahala."

"Some other time then, please. I can't stand to look at Greg Mason's face another second."

"He's been bothering you?"

"A little." Mahala shrugged. She didn't want to add any fuel to Clay's fire by letting him see how much Greg had upset her. "Doesn't matter. He's just ignorant. Where are we going?"

Clay hesitated, obviously reluctant to let the subject go. "My first stop is Pomona Hall," he told her. "I pull up to the servants' entrance of the big houses, and they buy fresh cuts of meat supplied by the butcher, Mr. Love. I keep a stock of seasonings and staples from father's store in the wagon, too. Just makes it easier, especially for those who live farther out."

"You go every day?" Mahala asked incredulously.

"No. Just twice a week." Clay paused and glanced over at her. "I guess I ought to thank *you* for rescuing *me*. I've been in one too many scraps lately. Another one today and there'd be sure trouble at home."

Mahala smiled. "You're welcome, then."

Clay glanced at her again thoughtfully. "You look different."

Self-consciously Mahala touched her curls. "Must be the hair," she murmured. She pressed her skirts down over the top of the shiny black boots the shoemaker, Willis Thompson, had made especially for her, thinking Clay, too, had changed. He was still open and friendly, but his voice was deeper, and his tanned forearms, exposed by rolled-up shirt sleeves, promised hard muscles. He wore his hair short and neat. She tried to imagine him with it long like their ancestors'.

"Somethin' wrong?"

"No, nothing," Mahala said quickly.

"You must really be missing your grandfather and the Emmitts."

"Oh, yes, very much," Mahala breathed, relieved to have someone who understood and cared. "It all feels so strange here — like a dream. I keep thinking I'll wake up and be back home in the valley."

Clay studied her sympathetically. "I think you are home now, from what I hear."

"What do you hear?" Mahala asked sharply.

"Only that Mrs. Franklin's dead set on keeping you."

"Well, my papa and grandfather have something to say about that," she snapped.

"The wishes of white kin—"

"I don't want to hear about that." Dreadfully close to tears again, Mahala cast her eyes about looking for a way of escape. But the wagon was still moving down a busy street.

"All right. I'm sorry. Just settle down," Clay said, putting a hand on her arm to calm her.

Startled at his touch, Mahala drew back. She glanced into Clay's black eyes. His gentle smile did steady her a bit. "How bad could it be, living here, if you get to see me every day?" he teased.

Mahala smiled weakly. "I guess I *could* use a friend," she replied honestly.

"Me, too. Look, here are the gates to Pomona Hall."

"Who lives here?"

"Mr. John Stanford. He named the place for his grandfather's home in England. They brought all the hardware and workmen from there. Folks say it's the nicest place in town. He throws lots of parties."

Mahala was charmed by the queenly white beauty of the house, which was set among the fir trees and flowering shrubs. The foundation walls were of local stone. Clay told her that he had once peeked inside the front door and seen grand double stairways that joined on the second floor landing. As he had indicated he would, Clay now pulled to the rear of the residence. Mahala waited in the wagon, admiring the tall balustrade and sniffing the boxwoods, while he dealt with a portly black woman wearing a turban and white apron. She liked the privacy the acreage provided the house. Birds and squirrels darted among the trees. One would never know town was so close.

She said as much to Clay when he swung back up into the vehicle.

"Just wait 'til you see The Highlands. I personally think the house is even nicer, though what a person would do with all that room I can't imagine. Give me a cabin and some land, and I'll be a happy guy."

Mahala looked at Clay with surprise.

"What?" he asked.

"Just — that's exactly what my father always said, according to my grandfather."

A shadow seemed to pass across Clay's features. "Mahala, make sure you stay in the wagon at The Highlands, all right?"

"Well, of course, but why?"

"I don't expect we'll see anybody but the cook, but just the same … don't go running off anywhere."

"Is the owner mean or something?" Mahala pressed, thoroughly curious now at Clay's evasion of her question.

"You could say that. He's a lawyer who's made his name by carefully picking his cases. He only takes those that are hard to defend. His clients are always able to pay well and, some say, are always guilty. But he seems to always get them off using some legal loophole."

Mahala shivered. "He must be very smart."

"Guess so ... when he's not in his cups. And gambling. Folks say he loses more money than ever since his father passed away. At least the old doctor tried to rein him in some."

Clay was right about the house. It looked so stately and welcoming with its balanced proportions and black shutters that Mahala thought it sad that it should not have a benevolent owner. A house should reflect its master.

Clay went up onto the porch to talk with a servant. Mahala was watching a red bird flit through the fresh green leaves and enjoying the warm spring sun on her back when a twig snapped nearby. Emerging from the woods Mahala saw a man with dark blonde hair, carrying a rifle in one hand and a limp, upside-down turkey in the other. With each step the dead bird's feathers bounced and separated. The man's eyes fixed on her. He might have been considered handsome were there not a hard look of wear about him.

"So, the Indian boy has a sister," the man commented, drawing near.

"I — I'm not his sister," Mahala said.

"Well, who are you, then?"

"I'm — Mahala Franklin."

The man's eyes widened, then he raked her with a sharp gaze that missed nothing, coming at last to rest on her blue eyes. "Franklin," he repeated slowly. "And so you are."

He shifted the gun under the arm carrying the turkey and reached out toward her. Mahala did not want to give him her hand, but she could find no polite words to protest his attentions or the proximity to the dead fowl. Her hesitation was well-founded. When he grasped her hand, instead of shaking it, he brought it to his lips and placed a lingering kiss on her fingers. Highly unsettled, Mahala jerked back, resisting the urge to wipe her knuckles on her skirt.

The man laughed loudly at her reaction, attracting Clay's notice, and said, "Well, it's not as if I'm a complete stranger. Rex Clarke. Your father and I were once friends ... a long time ago."

Rex Clarke! Hadn't he been a suspect in her father's murder? Mahala's mind reeled as Clay hurried over.

Clay said hastily, "Mr. Clarke, your cook was about to buy a roast, but perhaps you want her to hold off since you had some success hunting."

Rex grinned. "Looks like you did, too."

Clay's complexion darkened, but he pretended not to know what Clarke was talking about. "The roast?" he prompted.

"Naw. Come back another day. And bring your little friend with you." Rex held up the turkey in a gesture of farewell. Its skinny head on the long red neck wobbled wildly. "'Bye now."

"What did he say to you?" Clay asked as they rumbled away in the wagon.

"Not much. I just didn't like him. He kissed my hand." Mahala stuck out her tongue in a girlish grimace of disgust and then liberally wiped her hand on her skirt.

"That was a liberty he had no business taking — and you only twelve! Of course, he probably thought you were older. I'm sorry I brought you here, Mahala. The less Rex Clarke knows about you or sees you, the better."

"Why? Do you think he killed my father?" Mahala stared at her companion with wide, innocent eyes.

Clay stared back a minute without replying, looking faintly surprised. "I don't know," he said at last. "But it is a well-known fact that your grandmother will go a whole block around to avoid meeting him. He's just — not a good person, Mahala, especially to women."

Mahala pondered that, gratified that Clay would put her in that category. Clay certainly seemed wise in the ways of the world, considering he was only a year older than she was. Well, maybe that was the difference of growing up in the town versus in the country.

"Come to think on it," he continued, "maybe I ought to take you home. The other estates are out Tallulah Road and Stonepile. It will take a while to visit them."

"All right," Mahala agreed. But she was wondering when she'd see Clay again. The little bit of time she'd spent in his company had been the brightest of her week.

When Clay drew the wagon up in front of the hotel, Mahala smiled and thanked him for the outing. She was very surprised when he came around to hand her down. Her feet were just touching the ground when Martha barreled out the front door and straight toward them.

"So it's true!" she cried. Mahala quickly let go of Clay's hand. "I couldn't believe it when Latilda Mason came by here and told me you'd taken off in a wagon with this hooligan. What were you thinking, boy? Have you no concern for my granddaughter's safety or reputation?"

Clay's mouth had opened but no sound was coming out. Martha was drawing Mahala away from him as if he had an infectious disease. Mahala intervened. "Clay only rescued me from Latilda's mean brother. He was just taking me to see the houses on a couple of his deliveries."

"You are both of an age where you ought to know better. You are no longer little children. And it would suit me well if you left my granddaughter alone, Clay Fraser."

"I'm sorry, Ma'am. I meant no harm."

While his expression was defensive, Clay's words sounded fairly contrite. But Mahala rounded on her grandmother. "Why do you say that, Grandmother? Because he's a Cherokee?" she burst out, clutching her books to her chest as tears sprang into her eyes. "Well, he's the only friend I've got in this awful place, and you can't send him away. You're not being fair."

"Mahala, you are making a scene," Martha said in a low tone. "Now, you will go into the house and you, young man, will ask my permission before you even think of seeing her again. I will have to give great consideration to my answer."

Mahala fled the street, tears blurring her vision. Embarrassed and angry, she threw down her books as her grandmother followed her into the parlor and closed the door. "You didn't have to treat him like that!" Mahala cried. "Everybody looks down on us and tells us what to do because we're Cherokee. I'm tired of it! I hate it here. I want to go home!"

"You are home, and you will obey my rules. You are not to go driving around outside town with young men. You are not to go anywhere without asking me first."

"But we didn't mean anything by it. He was just being nice." Mahala swiped at her tears.

Martha looked at her and drew in one corner of her mouth. "Come here," she said. She placed her hands on Mahala's shoulders and guided her to the fancy inlaid mirror. "Do you see what I see?"

Mahala pouted. "I see an unhappy girl."

"Maybe today, but I also see the promise of great beauty tomorrow. And also great strength, if you will accept guidance. There is much we need to discuss about you becoming a young woman, Mahala — and also the ways of men."

Mahala's mind flashed to the dark blonde man kissing her hand. "I met Rex Clarke today," she blurted out.

She didn't have to be curious long about what Martha's reaction would be. Her grandmother whirled her around and demanded, "Where?"

"We made a delivery to his estate."

"See what I mean! That Fraser boy has no sense! Who would take a young girl to The Highlands? You stay away from Rex Clarke, Mahala."

"Clay said you didn't like Mr. Clarke. Is it because you think he killed my father? Didn't he have an alibi?"

Martha sighed and looked down, taking Mahala's hands in hers. "I'm sad to say his alibi was one of our own maids," she said. "Rex was living here at the time. After the incident I immediately dismissed the girl, and it was said she went on to the gold camps in California. I still don't know whether I believed her or not. Rex certainly had motive. It's true that Rex had threatened your father, and Michael had left him knocked out in the dining room of The Habersham House."

"Why?" Mahala asked eagerly. She liked the way her grandmother was talking to her, like she was a grown-up.

"Rex said Michael was cheating him, not paying the full portion of gold agreed to. Of course I never believed that. But nothing about what happened that night could be proved. The investigation was closed and everyone assumed a drifter robbed and murdered your father. For whomever did it to get away with it … it just kills me. Come, sit down. There's something I want to show you."

Mahala obeyed, sitting on the sofa while Martha opened a drawer in a side table. When she came back, Mahala saw that she held a daguerreotype.

"We had this made the year before your father went to Sautee, when we were all at the fair in Athens. It was the last time we were all together," Martha said. "It's one of the few things I have left to remember him by. Whomever killed him took everything of value in the cabin — even the pocket watch your grandfather and I had given him, engraved with his initials."

Glancing at her tearful grandmother, Mahala took the picture, which captured a younger and happier Franklin family. Her eyes skimmed past the daughters in their full-skirted dresses and settled on a handsome young man striking a confident pose. For the first time she was looking at her father. For some reason she could not explain — probably the stress of the past week — an indefinable longing rose up within her and she began to cry.

If Michael Franklin had lived, how different her life would be today. How she wished he were here to put his arms around her.

Instead, it was her grandmother who embraced her, gently resting Mahala's dark head on her shoulder.

"Don't you see, Mahala? You're all I have left."

CHAPTER FOURTEEN

Christmas 1850
New York, New York

now was falling outside the Houston Randall mansion, adding a soft layer of white to a previous crusty accumulation. Sleigh bells jingled merrily as holiday party-goers made their Christmas Eve rounds.

The inside of the home was trimmed with holly, ivy and mistletoe. Fires burned at every downstairs hearth. Maids scurried about clearing the dessert dishes from the massive dining room table, and "I Saw Three Ships Come Sailing" sounded merrily from the parlor piano, where the ladies were gathered.

The song ended, and Jack heard Anna Gershwin's half-joking, half-pouty voice. "Where is my George? Minutes after announcing our engagement over dinner, he disappears into the gentlemen's parlor. Is this a harbinger of things to come?"

The women's patience would soon expire, and they would seek out dance partners, Jack thought as he entered the gentlemen's salon. He'd better hurry if he wished an audience with his uncle. A cloud of smoke greeted him as he entered the room. A quick assessment of the black-garbed assemblage told him Houston was indeed present, but judging from the intensity of the discussion, it was unlikely that Jack would be able to immediately spirit him away.

The Gershwins were house guests of the Randalls, and Jake had not hesitated to make himself the center of attention. Jack was again reminded of the great difference between Northern and Southern Whigs as the young man, his upstanding white collar and voluminous four-in-hand necktie making him appear as though a black bird had just crash landed at his throat, expounded the shortcomings of the Compromise of 1850. His father, Collin, looked on, nodding in agreement at his son's words. While more reserved than Jake in sharing his views, he was no less ardent in his beliefs. He seemed proud that his son served as a mouthpiece for his causes.

"The admission of California as a free state in no way makes up for the abandonment of the Wilmont Proviso," Jake was saying. "The Proviso would have ensured that no future slave-holding states be admitted to the Union. Here we already have New Mexico being allowed to decide for themselves. 'Popular sovereignty,' bah!"

"Most people feel the climate and soil in the newly acquired territories will not prove conducive to slavery," Houston pointed out calmly.

Jack edged his way toward his uncle as unobtrusively as possible. His younger cousin Geoffrey caught his eye and smiled.

"Whether it will or not, a door has been left open that should have been firmly closed. When will Congress stop trying to appease the slave owners?"

"Perhaps only once they've left the Union," George added. Everyone looked at him. "Well, it's what they're talking about, is it not, Jack?"

Jack froze, unwillingly caught in the limelight as all eyes turned to him. He knew George referred to the meeting earlier that month of Georgia delegates in Milledgeville, where a response to the Compromise had been determined. The Compromise would be accepted — but only as a final conciliation. Next time it was offended, Georgia would secede — and likely initiate the removal of other states as well.

His cousin explained, "Jack's father just wrote him a letter stating that many supported the platform Georgia recently adopted — to love the Union second to the rights it was designed to perpetuate. We all know that hothead Robert Toombs would jump at the chance to help lead his state to secession. In the envelope containing his letter, Uncle Richard had enclosed a newspaper clipping from Fayetteville that he said was causing some interesting discussion."

"What did it say, Jack?" Grandfather Randall asked quietly, leaning forward with both hands braced on his cane. His green eyes had faded with the years but still held the gleam of sharp mental faculties.

"Yes, do tell us," Stephen Wise urged.

Jack hesitated. His father had sent the piece for his own consideration. He didn't really want to share it with the Gershwins. "It — included a portion of James Madison's letter to Alexander Hamilton at the time the convention was meeting in Richmond to ratify the Constitution. He spoke of conditional ratification — that compacts must be reciprocal."

"So some Southerners are taking that as permission to withdraw?" Collin Gershwin asked.

"What does your father think?" inquired Grandfather Randall. His face looked pained.

"Some do feel the government has failed to uphold their end of the contract," Jack admitted slowly, "but, my father believes, not seriously enough to endorse secession. He loves the Union. So do many other moderates, as seen in the results of the Georgia convention."

"Of course, Son," Grandfather Randall said, seeing Jack's discomfiture.

Jake continued with no such sensitivity. "What do they possibly have to whine about? They got their precious Fugitive Slave Law — an abomination and a shame to our country. The fugitives now have no right to trial, and we all know how these special commissioners appointed to their cases will decide … five dollars if the slave is released and ten if they are sent away in chains! And not just fugitives, either. The free blacks within our borders are terrified of being rounded up and sent South."

"I hear many are moving up to Canada," George put in.

"That's true. But I think what the South will find is that holy causes flourish in adversity. Threats of fines and imprisonment will not stop freedom-minded Northerners from aiding fugitives. I believe movements like the Underground Railroad will only grow stronger."

"I'm sure you are right, Jake," Houston observed, "and each man must do as his conscience bids him. But what I think we would all do well to remember is that we should not rush headlong into a divorce from our Southern states. Like a marriage—" he paused to smile at George — "God has united our country. Tearing it apart would prove more painful than we can imagine. We should not give up early on solving our differences in a peaceful, logical manner."

Jake shook his head. "Such words sound fine, Mr. Randall, but I must respectfully disagree. The compromises of politicians will only delay the inevitable. An evil like slavery will not die out on its own, as some hope. It must be forcefully expunged."

Jack's stomach quaked at Gershwin's choice of words, for they conjured up bloody images he wished to avoid. They also aroused all his personal uncertainties. Jake's manner could be off-putting, making Jack wonder if he really wanted anything to do with such a man. But Jack could not deny the truth in some of what he said. Maybe some causes were worth breathing fire about.

Jack's last visits home had been painful, for he had looked at things through a different light. He had never seen a slave mistreated, though he knew it did sometimes happen. But he had found himself looking into the faces of the house servants around him, even those who appeared happy and content with their owners, searching for a flicker of hopelessness in an unguarded moment, wondering what they might become if they had education and freedom to choose. Yet, too, he had seen such goodness and love from slave owners, an unwavering acceptance that slavery had existed since Bible times, that was just how it was. Jack truly believed many of his Southern friends and family to be blinded to the evil among them. And many others turned their backs on the horrors and abuses that occurred rather than stand against them and stir up trouble.

Friends and family. Now there was an irony. For of the first he had precious few, and from the other he still felt alienated — more so than ever now. That weighed heavily in the decision he had made. Where the connections of his heart had failed, he could but follow his head. And logic told Jack where to cast his lot.

Still, he was forever seeing both sides of issues, much as he hated it. Jack found himself saying, "Slavery is not the only issue, even if it were a topic the North had the right to decide ... which is debatable due to many historical precedents of state sovereignty. Speaking from experience as a shipper's son, Southerners greatly resent the past decades of Northerners swooping down on their cotton to bear it away in Yankee ships to Yankee mills, charging outlandish export fees and discouraging independent Southern commerce."

Jake laughed dismissively. "I can't imagine why! The South is too lazy to industrialize. They'd rather rest on their laurels and brag about King Cotton."

Jack felt his face grow red. His uncle put a restraining hand on his arm, saying, "Now young men, we can't solve all the country's problems tonight. We're supposed to be celebrating an engagement, remember?"

Jack gave his shoulders a tiny shake to cause his frock coat — and his muscles — to relax back into place. "Yes," he agreed, turning to George. "And the women grow restless. Just before I came in I heard your lady love lamenting your easy abandonment of her."

George jumped up. "Well, then, I'd better go smooth her ruffled feathers."

"We should all adjourn," Houston agreed.

With murmurs of acquiescence glasses were set down and cigars extinguished. Before Houston moved away, it was Jack's turn to touch his uncle's arm.

"Could I speak with you a moment?" he asked.

"Of course, Jack."

Before exiting, Geoffrey, who knew of Jack's plan, gave his cousin an encouraging grin and a discreet thumbs up. Jack nodded. When the room was emptied, he turned to Houston. He took a breath.

"As you know, Sir, after this term I will complete my studies at Princeton," he said.

"Yes, Jack, we are all very proud of you and George."

"My time in New Jersey and in the company of your sons has changed the way I look at many things. I never wanted to move South to begin with, and never felt I found my place there growing up. I am ... uncomfortable with the practice of slavery. And while my father may have altered his principles to accommodate those around him, I find I cannot."

Houston nodded but did not speak, waiting for his nephew to go on.

Jack's nervousness was betrayed only by a slight shifting of his jaw. "Geoffrey has apprised me that you are good friends with the owner of a prominent shipping firm. He seems to think you might put in a good word for me if I wished to stay in New York after graduation."

Houston lifted his tumbler and rolled the amber liquid around in the bottom of the glass before taking a swallow. He did not meet Jack's eyes as he asked, "And is that what you wish to do, then, Jack? Stay in New York?"

"Yes, Uncle Houston. It is." Jack waited, wondering why the older man did not look at him, smile or shake his hand with hearty welcome into the Northern branch — all of which he had expected. In fact, Houston turned and walked toward the window, where Jack could see that the snow continued to quietly fall outside. He hastened to add, "If you think that I should be loath to exchange partnership in Randall and Ellis for a lowly clerk's position in a stranger's firm, don't. I don't mind working hard, working my way up ... just so long as I have not sacrificed my convictions."

Jack also knew that it would be a fascinating time to work for a New York shipping firm. Randall iron was being ordered to strap over the frames and on the sides of the inner keels of fast new extreme clipper ships. Some of these ships sailed for foreign ports at speeds of up to twenty nautical miles per hour.

Looking out the window, Houston gave a half laugh and slowly shook his head. Then he turned to face Jack. "You are quite a young man and we have always missed you ... wanted you close. We were so hopeful your father might return after your mother died. But now, he has put down roots in the Southern soil that I think will never be torn loose. I'm not in a position to tell you what to do, Jack, but as a father myself, I find I wonder how I would feel should one of my sons choose to move to Georgia. Would I think I had failed him in some way? Would our relations even be able to survive the break that such a move would imply?"

"Begging your forgiveness, Sir, but my father would survive. He has a full house with his second wife. This is not about him, but me."

Houston set down his glass. "I know, Jack. And oh, how I admire your courage. But did you consider the ramifications of the discussion just held in this room? There is a fault line running between North and South only waiting for a strong enough tremor to cause a permanent break. I have to wonder if you've considered the distant future, or just the current circumstances. You staying in New York could mean a permanent separation between yourself and your father, your Ellis grandparents and everyone else who was part of your life there. Are you truly ready to turn your back on your family and home state?"

His uncle's perceived rejection made Jack grind his teeth in an attempt to control his emotions, to keep the moisture from his eyes. "I have family here, too, and *New York* is my home state," he replied roughly. Then he spoke from the heart. "I've never felt at home since I left here as a boy. As painful as it is to cut my ties to Georgia, this is where I belong."

"Oh, my poor boy, what a quandary you are in," Houston responded, reaching out to embrace Jack. Jack remained stiff in his arms. Sensing this, Houston added, "I don't say these things to put you away from us, Jack, only to request your very careful consideration. If you make this decision do not do so rashly."

Jack pulled back. "A few minutes ago you said each man should do as his conscience dictates."

Houston nodded. "So I did. But conscience is a matter of mind *and* heart. Do you love them, Jack? Are your convictions truly stronger than your love?"

When Jack did not reply, Houston clapped his arm with a firm grip. "Pray and consider. If you still feel the same at the end of your holiday, we'll talk again — and you'll be welcome here. All right?"

"All right."

"Coming out to the parlor?"

"In a minute. I need a minute."

"Fine." Houston smiled wistfully, patted Jack's shoulder, and left the room, closing the door behind him.

Jack covered his face with his hands, roughly wiping the tears from his eyes as he made his way to an armchair by the crackling fire. Elbows on his knees, he sprawled there, watching the flames for some time. With the unexpected nature of the conversation with his uncle, all the certainty he had finally thought he grasped was dissipating as quickly as the smoke spiraling up the chimney. *I thought I belonged here. Now my own uncle doesn't agree,* Jack thought as the hurt sliced through him. *To go back — I can't! Oh, God, what will I do?*

Late May 1851
Clarkesville, Georgia

On a Friday evening Mahala slipped out the back entrance of the Franklin Hotel and skimmed down the street, her head covered by a silk scarf. She hoped the veil and her oldest dress would work together to discourage curiosity. As her grandmother had predicted, she had bloomed early, her body preceding her spirit into maturity. She had not yet become accustomed to the stares of grown men, though now she understood why Martha required her to have an escort about town.

Mahala was breaking that rule now, as she did every chance she got to sneak away to her secret place. Sometimes Clay was allowed to walk her to her lessons, or to a church function, especially if Martha was busy or could not spare Zed to tag along. Mahala rather wished Clay was at her side now. He had grown quite tall and made a formidable protector. But, he could hardly be her escort when she was *en route* to meet him secretly. Mahala was also not allowed to leave town without Martha's permission. And seeing as how her special retreat was on its periphery — and she was sure her grandmother would not approve Mahala teaching Clay Cherokee — this was just one plan she would have to keep to herself.

Head down, Mahala walked north until she neared the bridge that crossed the Soquee. Seeing no one immediately in sight, she scrambled down the bank and to a large weeping willow. She ducked under its fresh spring canopy of trailing green and breathed a sigh of contentment. Here, on a patch of grass that joined a sand bar, she could watch the river's slow progress and the activity of surrounding wildlife. She also had a good view of the bridge. Currently a buggy was crossing. She recognized it as belonging to John Stovall's son John, owner of the impressive new white mansion on Blue Creek.

The fact that the Stovalls were friends with the Emmitts brought her adoptive family to mind and caused her to become reflective. She was several minutes early — on purpose. Settling down with her back to the willow's trunk, Mahala opened her journal and began to write. As a precaution, and to keep her second language fresh, she recorded her thoughts in Cherokee. She curled her toes in her boots with the pleasure of aloneness and self-expression.

It was not long before she heard his voice. Parting the tendrils of growth that curtained her, Mahala peeked out. Clay was talking to a black servant also bound out of town, back to his home at Farm Hill. He worked for Dr. George Duval Phillips, a man who had been instrumental in establishing both the Presbyterian and Episcopalian churches in Clarkesville. Dr. Phillips now served in the state legislature.

"The wedding went off all right, I expect," Clay said, his voice carrying down to Mahala's nook.

"Yes, Sir."

"I guess we won't be seeing much of Mr. William in these parts any more."

"No, Sir. Not wid Miss Catharine bein' from near Atlanta way. Ah spec Mist' William set up practicing law down dere in Marietta."

"Ah, well, we wish them happy. Good night, now," Clay said.

The Negro man waved in return, carrying on his way and not seeming to think it strange that Clay stopped at the bridge, looking out over the water. His back to her, the Cherokee boy skimmed stones across the water until the path was clear. Then he vaulted around the edge of the embankment and scrambled under the tree next to her, his face bright with mischief.

"Here I am," he announced.

"I can see that."

"Did you bring my slate?"

Mahala handed it to him. She smiled. "Did you bring me any newspaper clippings?" Clay was forever cutting out any references he found to the Cherokee Nation in newspapers or journals.

"Not this time." He scooted back next to her. Drawing one knee up, he propped the slate on it and grinned. "What shall I learn to write today?"

His shoulder was touching hers. Mahala moved over, frowning that his encroachment had forced her to relinquish her own comfortable position. "I was thinking about verbs today. You've done pretty well with the alphabet and nouns. Let's try some simple actions — like walk, *aisv*. Walks, *anigia*. Walking, *aisvi*. Walked, *aisvgi*."

Clay stared at her blankly.

"Give me the slate."

His fingers brushed hers as he did as she asked. With the stub of chalk, Mahala wrote out each conjugation in small, neat print, and angled the board so that Clay could see. Then she wiped it clean.

"Now, one at a time. You write them out."

After he spelled each form, Mahala quizzed him. She made sure he remembered all the words before moving onto another.

"It would surely help if we had some proper teaching tools — like books in our own language," she said.

"Maybe you should write one," Clay suggested. His gaze fell on her journal. "Well, I guess you already are."

"That will never be published."

A wicked gleam came to his dark eyes. "No, but think how much it would aid my learning process if you'd share it with *me*."

Mahala laughed. "I suppose you'll have to limp along unaided!"

"Oh, cruel girl! Does this mean there are some interesting tidbits in there? Perhaps something about the handsome and intelligent Clay Fraser?"

Mahala couldn't help herself; she picked up the journal and held it against her. "Certainly not."

"Oh, come on, not even a mention? Who doesn't mention their friends?"

Her face softened some at that. "Well, maybe a word here or there, but nothing interesting as you put it, so don't get a big head."

Clay grinned.

"I still wish I had some better way to teach you — other than writing one word at a time on a slate."

Clay shook his head. "Don't worry about it, Mahala. You are doing a great job. I'd want to learn even if we had to scratch letters in the sand. This is very important to me."

"I know, and I admire that."

Their eyes met. His held a faint longing. "Don't you ever want to go, Mahala?"

"Go where?"

"Tahlequah, the Cherokee capital. To be with others like us. To no longer be the odd man out, the one people put down. Don't you feel you would *belong* there?"

"The only place I want to be is at my family's farm," Mahala replied. "That's where I belong."

"You still feel that way? I thought things were better with your grandmother. She lets you go to them at Christmas, and allows the Emmitts and your grandfather to stay in the hotel at no charge when they come to town."

Mahala drew her knees up under her skirt and looked at the tips of her boots. It was true that her grandmother had been less heavy-handed than she had expected. Her concessions had won some ground in Mahala's heart. "That's true, but Nancy Emmitt raised me. No one can replace her."

"I understand."

"Wouldn't you feel bad to leave the Frasers?"

Clay nodded. "Yes, I would miss them. But the time is coming when I'll be a man, able to make my own decisions. Father expects me to take over the store, but Mahala, I just can't imagine that being the sum total of my life. I've got to see some of the world, have some adventure ... more than just this little town. Don't you want that, too?"

Mahala shrugged. "I don't know. Maybe. I guess it depends on who gets me. The Emmitts are still waiting to hear the judge's decision from the state court. Where I live will determine the course of my life, at least in part."

"You mean it will determine who you marry."

"I'd like to think girls have more to decide than that."

Clay was about to say more when Mahala held up her hand, hearing the rumble of a wagon. She leaned forward. "Oh, it's Mr. Blythe bringing the mail in from the valley! I was hoping he'd come by this evening!" And she darted out from under the tree toward the road. She was hailing the postal carrier when Clay came up beside her.

"Oh, Miss Mahala, good evenin' to ya," the old man said, lifting his hat off his head as he stopped his wagon.

"And to you. Do you happen to bring any mail for me?" she asked hopefully.

"As a matter of fact, I believe I do. Let's see, it's in this packet here from the Nacoochee post. Just a minute."

As the man leaned arthritically back to dig in a sack behind him, Mahala smiled at Clay, bounding on her toes and clasping her hands in barely contained excitement. Her joy was not missed by a passing ruffian of a man astride a tired-looking mare. He actually slowed his nag to take in the sight of her, his face breaking into a yellow-toothed smile.

Clay drew himself up threateningly. "Move on," he said. "You got no cause to be ogling the young lady."

The man guffawed. "Hey, if you don't want folksa lookin', you'd best keep your sister at home."

It wasn't the first time they had been taken for siblings. Mahala rather liked it. She did look upon Clay as a sort of big brother. She moved closer to him, and he clasped her arm, glowering. Even old Mr. Blythe had straightened. "Go on with ye now," he said in a rheumy voice, wiggling his whip in the air.

Thankfully the traveler was doing just that, though certainly not out of fear of the postal carrier, Mahala thought with a smile of gratitude at the old man.

"White trash," Mr. Blythe mumbled. Then he leaned down toward Mahala, an envelope in his hand. "Here ye go, Miss Mahala. From yer Mama Emmitt. Why don't ye take it home to read?" He looked and sounded faintly pleading.

"Thank you, Mr. Blythe," Mahala said.

The old man gave her and Clay an uncertain glance before he clicked his tongue to his team. Mahala smiled brightly and waved as he drove off toward town.

"Oh, dear," she said, "I hope he doesn't tell Grandmother that he saw us out here together."

"I don't think so. He's a good sort. For all he knows we were just taking a walk — and where's the crime in that?"

Mahala looked at Clay wryly. "Come on. You can practice 'eat' while I read my letter. What was it again?"

"*Agisdi, unigisdi, alisdayvhsgv, ugvgi,*" Clay said faithfully, scrambling down the bank behind her.

"Very good!"

"I'm getting hungry just thinking on it."

Mahala gave him a playful shove. Under the willow, she sat cross-legged and tore open the letter while Clay stretched out with the slate. Her eyes skimmed Nancy's opening lines eagerly, then settled on what she sought at the beginning of the second paragraph. A moment later a sob bubbled from her lips.

Clay looked up. "What? What is it, Mahala?" he asked in alarm.

She covered her mouth with a trembling hand, unable to get an answer out. She felt numb with shock.

"Mahala?"

She shook her head. Clay's hand touched her back. His face was close, worried. "The judge has denied my parents' plea," she finally told him. "They have no other recourse. I am to live with my grandmother until I marry or come of age."

Clay moved to embrace her gently. He patted her back. "Oh, Mahala — I'm sorry. No — no, I'm not."

Quickly she pulled back to look at him, her lips parting.

Clay's mouth worked, rose into half a smile, then fell. "I can't lie to you," he said. "I'm sorry for your feelings, I truly am, but sorry that you have to stay in Clarkesville? No."

Mahala could not hide her astonishment at what she saw in Clay's eyes. Neither could she speak. When he lifted a hand to cup her cheek, she pushed it away. Mahala grabbed up her things and scrambled to her feet.

"Mahala, wait!" Clay called, but she was already running, running back toward town, her silk scarf trailing out behind her. She ran all the way to the rear door of the hotel, never minding the now very curious stares of passers-by. Twilight was falling when she closed her door on the world and collapsed weeping onto her bed.

There had been a second when she had been tempted to flee on the bridge leading out of town and not stop come dark or danger until she reached the sheltering roof for which she longed. Of course that had been an absurd notion. Of course she had no choice but to return to her grandmother's, bitter though it was. And it was not long before Martha was knocking on her door, having heard her sobs. But Mahala had turned the lock and would not rise at her grandmother's pleading. Neither would she answer.

A few minutes later the door opened via skeleton key and Martha strode inside. Mahala raised a ravaged face from the coverlet. At the sight of her, Martha rushed over.

"What is it? What's happened?" she demanded.

Mahala fought her off. She couldn't stand the touch of the woman who had brought her such pain. This seemed to alarm her grandmother even more.

"Tell me what happened. Did someone hurt you?"

"Yes! You did!" Mahala bellowed in a voice so raw with tears she hardly recognized it as her own. She threw the crumpled letter at the older woman and buried her head under her pillow, willing her grandmother to take the paper and just go away.

But she did no such thing. She sat quietly for a moment — reading, Mahala assumed, though her own eyes were childishly squeezed shut — then she laid the letter aside and murmured, "I see. And now you hate me. Would it do any good for me to tell you I did not try in any way to influence the judge's decision?"

Mahala raised her head again. "No. No, it won't, because you started this whole thing by taking me away from them, and you could have stopped it at any point."

"By giving you back?"

"Yes."

"You love them an awful lot," Martha observed suddenly. Mahala was silent, watching her warily. "I guess that will never change. But I want you to love me, too, Mahala. And while I have no intention of giving you back, neither do I plan to hold you prisoner. I don't see why we cannot work out some sort of arrangement. What time of year did you like best in the valley, Mahala? Now, mind you, it can't be summer and early fall, because I need you here too much then."

Mahala slowly raised herself and scooted back on the heels of her hands, gazing at her grandmother with wide eyes as she realized what was happening. "Spring," she said a little breathlessly. "I liked spring, when I could help Mama put in the garden and watch everything grow."

"It was beautiful in the country then, eh, everything budding out?" Martha asked.

"Yes. Very beautiful."

"Say, March through May?"

Mahala nodded.

Martha rose and walked to Mahala's little desk, where she got a paper and envelope from a drawer. She set it beside the ink stand and turned to face her granddaughter. "You have a letter to write," she said. "See that you do it quickly and get ready for bed. I'll have Maddie warm your supper and bring it in."

Mahala remained frozen, watching Martha walk to her door. When her hand was on the knob, she turned. "Oh, and next time I find out you've been outside town alone with that Fraser boy, I'll tan your hide."

"Yes, Ma'am," Mahala gasped.

"Hop to it now."

As Mahala scrambled to the edge of the bed, she thought she saw a smile on her grandmother's departing face. She sat at the desk a long time, despite Martha's urging for her to hurry, trying to process what had just occurred. With three months a year to be anticipated in Sautee, life took on a decidedly different outlook.

What she didn't know how to write to Nancy, and couldn't expect Martha to fix, was why she herself would be reluctant to be alone in private again with Clay Fraser. And how was she to deal with a boy she loved as a brother but who, she now realized, thought of himself as anything but?

CHAPTER FIFTEEN

Early July 1851
Savannah, Georgia

hen the spires of the city of Savannah came into view, Jack asked the Almighty if He was sure He knew what He was about. He wasn't much in the practice of conversing with God. He preferred to make his own decisions. Then there was also the fact that whenever pressed by crisis into contacting the Creator, he came away shaken when he actually got a response.

Jack had taken his uncle's advice at Christmas. His search for direction had taken him into the spiritual realm. Every night after his conversation with Houston, he had dreamed of his family here in Savannah. First he had dreamed that his grandparents searched their house for him in a childhood game of hide and seek, becoming alarmed when they could not find him. Jack was hiding in the butler's pantry, stifling mischievous laughter. Another night Sunny had stood in his mind before a stack of Eva's belongings which she had consigned to the attic. Her skirts hid a portrait of Jack's mother. "I'm sorry," she had said, "but it just must go." Ella Beth's face had risen before him, her soulful brown eyes pleading as she reminded him, "Just don't forget about all of us here." And finally, he had dreamed of his mother's grave, peaceful and quiet among the live oaks and Spanish moss. Her voice had whispered on a breeze, "Do you love me, Jack? Then you've got to love the South."

The morning he dreamed of Eva, he had known he had to go back, or his life would always lack closure. He would have run away from what frightened him the most — not finding himself and his place among those who did mean the most to him. He could never have despised what he did not also love. There were wounds which could only be healed here, in Savannah.

His cousins had been disappointed when they learned he would not be returning to New York with them. But Jack thought they had understood. Houston certainly had. In his parting moments he had said, "Take your convictions with you, Jack. They can guide you wherever you are."

Now, gripping the ship's railing, Jack truly hoped so. The salty smell of the waterfront on the balmy air took him back to his first arrival at this port, when his parents had promised the beginning of a wonderful new phase of life. The parallels of past and present were not lost on him, most especially the sense of trepidation pervading both times. The one difference was, he was older now, educated, and well-informed — able to stand on his own. No longer wholly susceptible to the barbs and whims of others.

He fought down a rising lump of emotion at the sight of his grandfather's slight form beside his father's tall one, waiting there on the dock. *God*, he thought, *I do love them*. They were the reason he was coming back. Richard and Sunny had been with him at graduation last week but had returned ahead of Jack. William Ellis had been ill and unable to travel then. So it was all the more pleasing to see him now.

The men caught sight of him and began to wave. Jack lifted a hand to return the greeting.

The steamer jockeyed for space alongside coastal sailing sloops bringing sea-island cotton, lumber and turpentine from local plantations, and clippers from the West Indies and northern ports loaded with imported ale, tea, fruit and coffee. A much larger number of steam boats than Jack remembered from before also were in port. The local ship yards had been busy.

Neither could Jack fail to notice the new rows of commission houses being constructed along the city's forty-foot-high bluff. Some of these were five or six stories on the waterfront side, with warehouses on bottom and upper level offices fronting Bay Street. The smell of timber and the roar of machinery filled the air. From all evidences, financial depression was but a memory and Savannah was headed toward becoming a boom town.

Jack had to wait until anchor was lowered and the gang plank secured. He took that time to gather his thoughts and his baggage. Then he walked toward Richard and William with a smile.

Apparently they could not decide who should be first to hug him, for both men did so at once. Their welcome was so enthusiastic Jack was a little surprised.

"Son, look at you!" William exclaimed, flicking Jack's silk cravat. "How natty you look — and how mature."

"He has an air that will slay the ladies," Richard agreed.

"I'm not here for the ladies," Jack replied, still smiling. "I'm here for you ... and ready to get to work."

"Spoken like a true partner of Randall and Ellis," his grandfather exclaimed, brown eyes twinkling. "Come, we have something to show you."

The silent black coachman picked up Jack's valise as William turned his grandson with a hand at his back. But they did not get into the waiting vehicle. Instead, Jack was led along Bay Street. His parent and grandparent smirked like mischievous boys as they motioned him across a cast iron bridge and up the steps of a newly built mercantile house. Jack stopped at the door, reading a bronze plaque that proclaimed "Randall and Ellis Shipping."

"You've relocated?" Jack asked in wonder.

"Surprise," said William.

And Richard added, "Had to be at the heart of the action. Come inside."

They entered a handsomely appointed reception room. A young man behind a desk greeted them respectfully and tried to look very busy even though it was relatively quiet. However, Jack supposed that the firm's northern imports and passenger schedules would be enough to promote industry even when factor's row was a summer ghost town.

"Clerks on this floor … partners upstairs," his father said, leading the way to the next story. He stopped before a door at the top and stepped aside so that Jack could see the name plate that read "William Jackson Randall, Esq."

Feeling overwhelmed, Jack laughed and rubbed his jaw.

"Well, go on in," his grandfather urged.

Jack turned the handle and walked into a sunlit, spacious room. Leather armchairs faced a large desk. A wide bookshelf to one side had already been stocked with maps and leather-bound volumes, one section given entirely to pigeon holes and small drawers. Ship models constructed by Jack himself as a boy decorated the upper shelves, and a large globe on a pedestal stood nearby. The desk was ready with ink, wax, seals and other office supplies. Best of all, a view out the window behind it assured Jack that he was on a level with the tallest ships' masts in port. He could hear the slap of water on the hulls, the shouts of sailors and the clatter of drays below.

While he stood looking out, his grandfather came up behind him and touched his arm. "Next best thing to being on a ship, I hope," he murmured for Jack's ears alone. "Welcome home, Jack."

Jack turned to embrace the smaller man. "Thank you, Grandfather. I'll do my best to make you proud."

"You already have, Son. And happy — because now that you're here I can spend more time at home enjoying my old age with your grandmother."

"But not full retirement yet, I hope," Jack said.

"No, not yet."

Richard stood back grinning at the two of them. As Jack ran a hand over his new desk, Richard said, "I hate to hurry this moment, but there's a house full of people waiting to greet our young man. We don't want to make them too impatient, do we?"

"I don't know," Jack declared, teasingly sprawling in his chair and interlacing his fingers behind his head. "I think I could stay here a while and just savor the atmosphere."

He grinned and ducked as his father reached out to give him a knuckle hair cut.

"Oh, no, you don't," Richard laughed. "Get up."

For a moment Jack felt the years fall away with the warm camaraderie. He was seven again, full of admiration and adoration for his father. He could almost forget that the house full of people waiting to greet him included Richard's second wife and three children. Ah, real life always intruded.

It had been decided that Jack would live with his grandparents. This only made sense since Sunny and his father already had a house full, and the Ellises claimed theirs rang with emptiness. Jack's hope was that not only would the peace and privacy benefit his outlook, but his relationship with his father and stepmother as well.

So it was to the Ellis mansion on St. James Square that the carriage bore them. The air was sweet with flowering trees and shrubs, the sound of children playing and the chirping of birds. A new Methodist Episcopal church had gone up on the square during Jack's absence, joining several houses that had been built in the last decade.

Upon their arrival, they were admitted to the house by Saleem. Jack was attempting to tell the servant that he had not aged a year in the last ten when the hall overflowed with smiling family members calling greetings and jostling to embrace him. Again, he was taken aback by the warmth of the welcome, and said as much when they gave him space to draw a breath.

"We're just so overjoyed that you came back to us, and didn't stay up North," Grandmother Ellis declared with perfect honesty.

Jack stood with her hand tucked into his arm and surveyed those assembled. Sunny was there, with Bryson, Sylvie and Alan. His mother's sister Eugenie had brought her grown children as well, except for Suzanne. Carl was home from Harvard, looking fat and satisfied with life, as different as could be from his sixteen-year-old firecracker of a brother, Joseph, who had been just a baby when Jack had first come to Savannah. Jack's gaze fell on Ella Beth, standing between them. She wore a yellow silk dress with fresh yellow roses in her hair. She was watching him and smiled very faintly. He was reminded of her coming out, when she had been gowned in the pure white of a debutante, and he realized maturity had made her even more attractive than she had been then.

191

Before they could speak or move toward each other, Jack felt a tug on his sleeve. His eight-year-old half-sister stood at his elbow wearing a perturbed expression. He bent down to hear her complaint in the noisy hall.

"I'm very, very upset with you, Jack."

"When I've only just come home?" he asked in amazement. He pulled on a corkscrew ringlet. "I haven't even had a chance to harass you yet."

"But you have. You've harassed me terribly. You've decided to live here instead of at home, with us."

Jack was dismayed to see tears actually filling the little girl's eyes. He knelt down, faintly aware Ella Beth was still watching. "Dearest, please don't be sad," he said quickly, pulling Sylvie into his arms.

"Don't you love me, Jack?" she sniffled against his shoulder.

He patted the soft, shiny dark hair. "Of course I do. I only have one little sister. But I've grown up now and will be working a lot. I've got to keep my grandparents company. But that doesn't mean I can't come see you very often. And just think, I can take you out with me, riding and driving, and to concerts in the park — all kinds of things!"

Sylvie pulled back and wiped her eyes. "Will you really?" she asked hopefully.

"Yes! Most definitely. There's no other young lady I'd rather squire about."

A beautific smile broke out on the child's face. Then she grew serious. "When will you come?"

"What?"

"I said, when will you come?"

"Uh, how about Saturday?"

"What time?" Sylvie demanded.

Oh, dear, this girl was going to mean trouble for the opposite sex. "How about two?" Jack suggested.

The smile returned, and she raised a brow. "I'll be waiting."

With a flourish, Jack placed a noisy kiss on his sister's hand. He stood up, laughing, and shared a glance and a shake of the head with his grandmother.

"You are very popular today, dear boy," she said, "for now I want you to escort me into dinner."

"With pleasure."

Conversation over the long dinner table flowed freely. Jack got the impression that there had been a previous agreement to avoid politics, for everyone seemed to concentrate on updating him on local happenings: the rash of fires that had plagued the city, the paving of some sidewalks, the multitude of locomotives and ships used to transport the recent tide of cotton, the purchase of lamps and posts by Savannah Gas Light to replace inadequate private whale oil lamps, and the stint Bishop Elliott had taken in the pulpit of Christ Church following the death of the rector, Rev. Neufville. Much was also made over Jack's graduation with honors. And Eugenie wanted to know what the New York ladies were wearing the winter past. Jack's complete ignorance on the subject drew hearty laughter.

After dessert, Jack excused himself, needing a moment of solace. He stepped out into the back garden, where the scent of roses hung heavy on the late spring air. The soft call of a mockingbird mingled with the distant hum of conversation. As he took out a Cuban cigar, he thought of George, and his stomach twisted. His cousin — his constant companion for the past four years — now a world away. Jack stood with one boot propped on a low stone bench, smoking, his mind back in his Princeton dorm room.

The rustle of petticoats on the pebbles of the walkway caused him to turn.

"I see your father's displeasure was not enough to curb your habit," Ella Beth said, smirking.

Jack moved to extinguish the cigar, but she added, "No, never mind me. It would be a shame to waste such an expensive indulgence. I say if that's the only vice you brought back from Princeton you're doing pretty well."

He removed from the bench and went to stand across from it so she could sit down. She did so. "Are you a gambler?"

Jack gave a dismissive half-laugh. "No."

"A drinker?"

He shook his head. Ella Beth nodded. "Have you broken any hearts?"

"Not that I know of."

To this reply she merely stared, her mouth drawn into a flat line. He didn't like her look, or her silence.

"I hear felicitations are in order," Jack said.

She nodded again. "Lieutenant Draper is a very good sort. I met him at a dinner at Mrs. Mary Marshall's. She has always entertained the gentlemen of the Savannah Volunteer Guards."

"Yes. She was a widow of its captain, I believe."

"She was. Well, she introduced us a couple of years ago. Lieutenant Draper — Frank is also a lawyer. He met with my father's approval. So ... the wedding is set for this November."

"A long courtship ... and a long engagement. Surprising." Jack put out his cigar, grinding it under his heel.

Ella Beth rose and came to stand in front of him. Her brown eyes searched his. "Is it?" she murmured.

Jack began to feel put on the spot. Heat rose to his face. Rather than answer directly he said, "You deserve someone steady and devoted, Ella Beth. I wish you happy."

His reply seemed to anger her. "What makes you qualified to judge what I deserve, Jack? You, who have been gone these past years? You came to my coming out ball, and home again that next summer, and I thought — I hoped ... So don't act like you wondered at my delayed attachment. I would have waited longer — would still wait, but when you stayed in New York the past two holidays, I could only think something or someone you had found up there had secured your allegiance."

"Ella Beth ..." Jack gently touched her ruffled sleeve. "There is no one I care for up North, but neither did I think I had ever done anything to give rise to your affections."

She shook her head. "You didn't have to *do* anything, Jack. Just being you was enough."

He frowned in confusion. "Sarcastic? Independent? Or stubborn? Which quality did you find most appealing?"

"Oh, shut up. Yes, you were all those things, but there is also a tender vulnerability that — breaks my heart. Because I wanted to — to help that ..."

Her voice trailed off. What she had said had him off-center. Was she actually leaning toward him? He would have to be dead not to be tempted by those soft rosy lips, but the temporary gratification would not be worth the permanent commitment such an action would precipitate.

His hand tightened on her arm. Taking a steadying breath, Jack said, "There are too many reasons I'm not ready to marry, Ella Beth. In fact, I don't think I ever will — at least not until I'm an old stone past feeling but too tired of myself to continue on alone."

At his words, Ella Beth's brown eyes shot amazing sparks. "Oh, you'll marry all right, some girl you'll be crazy about, someone who moves you in ways I apparently can't. But don't worry, I won't notice. I'll be absorbed as the very deserving wife of Lieutenant Draper." She turned and, grabbing her skirts, hurried toward the house. Then, hand on the door, she glanced back over her shoulder and added in a choked voice, "And don't think I'll ever mention it again."

Then Jack was staring at nothing, dazed and confused by the unexpected encounter. It had hit him head on like a dray full of cotton. He had just graduated — was still so young — and still completely convinced no woman would ever coerce him the way Sunny had his father. Love or not, he never intended to be anyone's lap dog. So love was best avoided. There were too many more important things to do with his life than become bogged down in a debilitating romantic morass. Still, he did care for Ella Beth, as a cousin and a friend. And she *had* set him back a step with the intensity of her feelings. Was he making a mistake in letting her go? One he might one day regret?

He thought he would probably only know the answer to that well after the date of her wedding.

In mid-1851 the fleet of Randall and Ellis Shipping consisted of a coastal passenger packet, two three-masted schooners that typically ran New York to Savannah, and two large steamers for Atlantic crossings. The captain of *Fortitude*, the newer cotton and rice steamer, was preparing to retire. And Jack could think of only one man he wanted for the job.

Jack knew that after leaving his father's employ, Jeremy Northrup had passed several years in the China trade. Following that had been a gap during which the man had been unaccounted for. Now word had it that Northrup was running packets on the Clyde River in Scotland with no intention of ever returning to the States. Despite the bit of a mystery about where the man had gone and why he had left America, Jack felt certain enough of Northrup's record and personality to want to hire him. He figured he had the best chance of doing so in person. So immediately upon arriving home he set out on a steam ship for Scotland.

Needless to say, Jeremy was very surprised to see him. No longer a sun-kissed, strawberry blonde first officer, Northrup had aged. He wore a captain's uniform, but his happy-go-lucky outlook on life had sobered. Silver shone in his hair, and there were shadows about his eyes. But he laughed when Jack introduced himself and easily recalled the voyage on *Eastern Star* when he had helped deliver six-year-old Jack to his new home. Yet a certain reserve characterized their meeting over dinner in a local hotel. So it was that Jack was not unprepared when Northrup failed to be enticed by the handsome salary Jack offered.

"You are not married?" Jack asked.

"My wife of one year died in childbirth four years ago," Jeremy replied.

"I am sorry. You have no family in this area, then?"

"No."

"And the pay you receive, is it significantly more than what I offered you?"

"Well ... no."

"Then, may I ask what keeps you here?" Jack cut a bite of his roast beef and looked up to see Jeremy hesitating again.

Finally he replied, "The environment is to my liking."

Jack raised a brow, aware that his companion had danced around his question. "You've grown vague since our last meeting," he observed.

"And you've grown into a man, but one just as determined as I would have expected." Jeremy grinned.

"Perhaps you'll satisfy my curiosity in another area — how you passed '45 and '46, the years between your routes to the Far East and your time here."

Jeremy smiled again, lamely this time, shaking his head. "You've pegged me, young Jack. I can see there's no evading you. You're like a pit bull that gets a mouthful and won't let go. Before I give you your answer, though, you tell *me* one thing. Why me? Why come all the way to Scotland to recruit me?"

Jack shrugged, leaning back. "I like you. You once did excellent work for my family. Since that time, I've followed your career. You have the experience I need."

"There are many experienced seamen in Savannah."

"All right." Jack pretended to surrender, throwing up his hands. "You gave me an excuse to hear a bit of brogue first hand."

Jeremy laughed. "You rich gentry amaze me."

"Let's just say I have a sense about you. I said I like you, and when I like someone, I'm loyal."

"That may change when you hear how I passed the years you *didn't* know about. Then again, maybe not. I'm not sure where you stand on the issue of slavery."

"Slavery?"

"While in port one night in Nassau, a tough old bird convinced me that I'd make a fortune as his first mate. His ship, as it turns out, was a slaver. I don't talk about the things I saw during those two years." Jeremy shuddered and stared at his tin cup. "I call them my black sheep years. I told myself I was indifferent to the suffering I saw and that the short stint would be well worth the money I made. It wasn't. Money isn't everything. I ended up trying to drown my guilt in strong drink. That's why I don't touch the stuff now. And why I never want to see another slave ship again."

Jack sat for a moment contemplating his companion's words. Then he said simply, "I am more convinced than ever that you're the man I need. If you decide to face your demons, here's my card." Jack slid it across the table. Then he rose to leave. "I'll be sailing out in two days."

The two men shook hands.

Two days later, Jeremy met him at the dock twenty minutes before Jack's ship raised anchor.

Early August 1851
Savannah, Georgia

The afternoon after arriving back in Savannah, Jack and Jeremy set out from the Ellis mansion, where Jack had provided the captain a room, to the shipping office. There Jeremy met with Richard and was familiarized with the firm's duties.

"Is the *Fortitude* back in port, Father?" Jack asked. He turned to Jeremy with a smile. "She'll do you proud. Two hundred horsepower, long and low — much like the packets you ran on the Clyde."

"No, she hasn't arrived yet," Richard said. "Although I just received the manifest for *Eastern Star*. Everything is in order. She's been cleared to sail to New York in the morning."

"Not the same *Eastern Star* your family first took to Savannah," commented Jeremy confidently. They all knew well that clippers could not tolerate the twisting and wracking leverage of their immense spars for more than a few years.

"The *Eastern Star II*, actually," replied Richard. "But built to her exact specifications."

"Her captain isn't also retiring, per chance?" Jeremy asked with a hopeful smile.

Jack stared at him, aghast. "Captain Northrup, even *Star II* is an old tub by anyone's standards. I would not insult a man of your experience by asking you to take her to sea."

Richard added, "Her freight is turpentine, lumber, timber, and fruits and vegetables — nothing glamorous."

"Just the sort of freight I like." Jeremy pinned Jack with a meaningful gaze.

"Captain Polk has been belly aching about how his wife is set to deliver their next child," Richard remarked thoughtfully. "He thinks she'll go early."

"If he'd not be upset, I'd like to volunteer for the trip," Jeremy told him. "You know how old seamen are — don't like to lose their sea legs. Can't be too long on the dry ground. Sailing *Eastern Star* would bring back good memories. Then, young Jack, if you need me for your *Fortitude*, or whatever else, I'm your man."

Jack shook his head. He threw his hands up in the air. "All right — have it your way."

Richard smiled. "I'll contact Polk. Why don't the two of you give the ship a final going-over? Here's a listing of her cargo." He slid a paper across the desk.

Jack took it and stood up.

"You are a strange man, Jeremy Northrup," he said as they made their way to the dock. "I should pay you less for your foolishness."

"But you won't." Jeremy grinned at him.

It was fairly quiet along Plank Road. That would change soon enough when the cotton came in. More than a half dozen locomotives would arrive daily, pulling twenty to thirty cars of the state's "white gold," which would then be transported by dray to the riverfront warehouses. Once sold, the cotton was compressed by one of five steam-powered presses before being loaded onto ships. In the process, even the Negro dray drivers and stevedores got rich.

"Your cargo on the return trip will include some sugar, tea and coffee, but will mainly consist of iron from my family's foundry," Jack told his companion. "The Central of Georgia is constructing a whole new complex, including a $500,000 depot. There will be a round house, an engine house, a warehouse, and a boiler and patten room. Iron is to be used in much of the building — roofs and columns and such."

"That must be very gratifying," Jeremy commented.

"Indeed."

"You know, there are some who believe a developed railroad system in the South is an incongruous concept."

"Some in the North?" Jack lifted a brow.

"And some in the South. Factors, for instance. Granted there's plenty of cotton going out, but what is going in? The South is agricultural. Plantations and farms are mostly self-sufficient. And those who have money for high end purchases let their factors handle them."

"A man named Hammond from South Carolina believes just that," Jack agreed. "He's published his views in Charleston. But I believe they are not to his credit. The railroad brings jobs. It makes a backwater crossroads a town. It brings industry. Railroads will bring the South into the modern era."

Jeremy smiled. "You sound just like your father. And obviously, the Central of Georgia is flourishing."

Jack nodded. "The Central compliments the Mississippi River. Planters there find it cheaper to bring goods in over the railroad than to ship upriver."

Coming back around to the original topic, Jeremy said, "I'll need to look over all the papers tonight."

"You can take them home with you."

"Good. Whew, I'm already missing the Scottish climate." Jeremy pulled out a handkerchief to mop his brow. "The humidity here hits you like a tidal wave."

Jack smiled and pointed. "There she is, being readied for her voyage. Come let me introduce you to your crew. The first mate is an easy-going sort who should prove very helpful."

"Ah, this does take fifteen years right off me," Jeremy said appreciatively as they walked up the gang plank. "She is the spitting image of the first schooner."

After Jack presented Northrup to the crew, he gave the older man a tour of the vessel, pointing out any changes that had been made in recent years.

"When you were a wee lad, did you ever imagine being aboard as part owner?" Jeremy asked.

Jack smiled. "On the voyage when we met, in truth I envied the captain more than anyone — even my father."

"Well, you're welcome to sail with me any time. Won't ruffle my feathers a bit, *Sir.*" Jeremy chuckled as they descended the ladder into the hold, raising his lantern high. "I'm sorry, it's just hard for me to get the image of you as a wide-eyed little boy out of my head."

The smell of ripening fruit and freshly planed lumber filled the room. Jack moved among the piles and crates, consulting his papers, checking that everything was fastened down securely. As his father had said, everything appeared to be in order. He was just about to suggest they return above decks when something caught his eye.

"What's this?" he asked, bending over a pallet of lumber. A splatter of dark liquid glistened in the lantern light. Jack swiped his finger through it and held his hand aloft.

Squinting, Jeremy drew near to help investigate. He cursed softly. "It's blood!" he exclaimed.

Their eyes met. Then Jeremy drew a pistol from his belt and bolted up the stack of lumber, pointing the weapon down into the darkness of the narrow space between it and the hull. Jack heard a gasp and a plea.

"Please don't shoot me, Suh!"

He followed Jeremy to the top of the pile. There in the crevice was a muscular black man, the whites of his eyes shining up at them. He wore tattered clothing and held out a pleading hand as if to protect himself.

"Get out of there," Jack demanded. "Into the light and tell us what you're doing here."

The man tried to acquiesce, but winced in apparent pain and fell back. Jeremy had to give him a hand. When the intruder finally collapsed in the middle of the hold, everything was explained without a word being spoken — by the bloody whip lashes across the man's back, snaking even across his arms.

"How did you run with these fresh wounds?" Jack asked quietly.

"The minute they leave me alone, I feel nothin' except knowin' it never gonna happen again. I run all night an' sneak aboard your ship before de dawn. Please, Suh, please don't turn me in. Dey kill me if you do."

Jeremy looked sick and angry at being again forced to confront the evil he abhorred. "Who is your master?" he asked, but before the man could answer, Jack sliced his hand through the air in a silencing gesture.

"I don't want to know," he said. "But you can tell us the reason for your beating, and your name."

"Ah put my hands on a white man, tryin' to stop 'im from usin' a black gal. Dey call me Jim."

Jack nodded and gestured for Jeremy to step away from the slave, who hung his head, knowing his fate lay in their hands.

"Do you believe him?" Jeremy asked.

"His wounds dare me not to," Jack whispered. "Captain Northrup, how would you feel about a chance for redemption?"

"Redemption?"

"Don't you find it ironic that on your first voyage out of Southern waters a runaway chooses *Eastern Star* as his transportation to freedom?" Jack asked. "You could take this man to my cousin in New York, should I simply provide his address, and he would be more than happy to take him in."

"What is one man, when I was party to the enslavement of thousands?" Jeremy asked quietly.

"To this one man, I'd guess, the world."

"Jack, you're young. You don't know what you're getting yourself into. Should you be discovered ..."

"I know at best we'd lose every client we have, and Randall and Ellis would be ruined forever. At worst I'd have my neck stretched by a lynch mob."

"Good heavens. Doesn't that prospect frighten you?"

"Yes. But doing nothing about what I came to believe while I was at Princeton frightens me more. I could spend my whole life in comfort and ease should I deny my convictions, but I don't want to have to explain my cowardice one day to the Almighty. I believe we're all here for a reason. Don't you?"

Jeremy stared at him in amazement. "All right, forget what I said about the wide-eyed little boy. You are a man I'll be proud to work for. And I'm in. I'll do it. But first off, his back needs medical attention."

Jack raised his voice to a normal level while he replied, "You'll find a first aid kit in the surgeon's cabinet. But you'll have to tend to him yourself, and bring some clothes and food tonight as well. We don't want to expose ourselves on account of missing oranges and apples when you arrive in New York."

Understanding their decision, Jim began to sob unashamedly in relief, muttering, "Thank de Lord. Thank you, Suhs."

Jack returned to him. "Your danger is not yet passed. You'll have to keep hidden from the crew. And you're not to tell anyone about us aiding you — not when you get to New York, not five years from now. You understand?"

"Yes, Suh."

"There's one more requirement." Jack waited until the man's eyes flickered up, not quite looking at his face, as slaves were taught, but clearly giving him full attention. "When you get to New York, make something of yourself."

"Ah will, Suh," Jim said. He wiped tears from his eyes and placed his hands on Jack's boots in an unsettling gesture of gratitude. Jack quickly stepped back.

"Return to your hiding place until this gentleman comes back. And try not to bleed all over the cargo this time."

Jeremy shook his head at Jack's wit before following him up the ladder to the deck above. "I think we're both fools, young Jack," he said as they straightened. "But for the first time in seven years, I feel alive again."

Jack knew what he meant.

CHAPTER SIXTEEN

January 1854
Savannah, Georgia

A month shy of her thirteenth birthday, Carolyn Calhoun stood on the steps of St. Andrews Hall and bit her lip, overcome with nervousness. It was the beginning of her second week at Madame Granet's dancing school. If last week had been any indication, she was destined to become one with the *potiers* at any future *fête* her parents forced her to attend.

Oh why, oh why couldn't she be back at home on the plantation, snug in her room overlooking the formal gardens? She would be curled up like a cat in the window seat with a good book. Mamsie would bring her tea with a sugar lump and a slice of pound cake, which she would eat quickly so that her skinny little sister Eliza would not barge in, catch her in the act, and tattle to Mother. Mother thought Carolyn needed more exercise and less cake. Mamsie said Carolyn was just a baby and should enjoy her cake. She would soon enough grow tall and thin like her mother, and could worry about her figure after her growth spurt.

Olivia gave her a gentle push, bringing her daughter unwillingly back to the present. "Go on, now," she urged. "You'll be late."

The family carriage waited behind her. Olivia would shop while Carolyn danced … or tried to.

"Mother, please don't make me. Last Friday when Madame Granet brought in the dance master I stepped on his feet. Rachel Hall said I waltzed like a walrus."

"Oh, darling. Girls this age can be cruel. But don't mind them. They're just jealous. Rachel Hall only wishes her family had half the standing yours does."

Olivia fussed with the bow at Carolyn's neck. Carolyn wore a black and red wool fitted coat with matching hat and carried a rather unnecessary fur muff. Her blonde hair was neatly parted and curled. The flounced skirt of her dress stood out at the bottom on stiff horsehair braid, showing shiny black boots. Carolyn carried her silk dancing slippers.

But no matter how finely she was dressed, or how supple her slippers, or what her last name was, she felt like a toad beside the girls in her class. They

202

were slender and lithe, some of them already experiencing the changes of womanhood. In contrast, Carolyn was short, round and childish. Those other girls also knew just what to say and when to use their wit to greatest advantage, while Carolyn became tongue-tied and red when addressed by strangers. Some of the young ladies had already been to boarding school. Carolyn had spent most of her years quietly ensconced at Brightwell, and wishing for nothing else. Now, she was beginning to regret her sheltered existence.

"You're just learning, anyway," her mother continued. "No one expects perfection. Now, I will walk behind you up the steps and on to your class. I think you'd prefer that to me dragging you in by the arm."

Carolyn gulped and started forward. Her consternation only intensified when she realized her procrastinations had made her late, for the youths were already gathered in their chairs, girls on one side and boys on the other. Eruptions of giggles swelled from the crowd. At first Carolyn froze, thinking she was their object, but then she saw not Madame Granet standing before them, but one of the local dance masters of public and charity balls — the same whose feet she had trodden last week, Monsieur Robert. He was explaining that Madame Granet had a personal conflict, so he had agreed to take her class — but with a change to the week's anticipated subject, which had been quadrilles.

"I shall introduce to you that most comic, most vigorous, most entertaining dance ... the polka."

The girls gave a smattering of tittering applause while the robust young men cheered. They all knew anything Monsieur Robert did would be highly entertaining.

Carolyn's mother patted her arm in farewell. Carolyn proceeded to slip as unobtrusively as possible into the back row, where she divested of her coat.

Monsieur Robert stood before them beside a podium, his graying dark hair and mustache gleaming with pomade, his eyes twinkling. Behind him was the commodious dance floor, which Carolyn tried not to focus on. "Now I know that last week Madame Granet taught you to waltz circumspectly, gracefully, as proper young people should. We want that same propriety to extend to the polka. I shall teach you to avoid the vulgarisms of hopping or kicking out the heels — much to the endangerment of passing shins." More giggles. "You shall see that in the dance the feet shall be scarcely lifted off the ground, with small, neat, gliding steps. We shall do it correctly, but in my opinion, one should never take a delightful activity like dancing too seriously. In that spirit, I would like to share with you an excerpt from 'A Canon for Mr. Polka,' published almost a decade ago in London by a mischievous Captain Knox. He directs his comments to the gentlemen."

Carolyn began to feel more at ease. The other pupils were more focused on Monsieur Robert than her. That was good. The teacher cleared his throat and began reading.

"'Every ballroom was like a whirlpool; dancing more resembled the driving home from Derby than anything else; the collisions rivaled in frequency and severity, those of the iron railways ... The price of fans rose frightfully, partly from the pressing necessity of them, and partly from the enormous destruction of them in the melée. A mystical sign like that of the free-masons became established among the fraternity and sorority of the Polka, whereby they recognized one another, viz. the standing significantly upon one leg. We may here be allowed to present to our readers, a most valuable code of rules, to be observed by all aspiring youths who wish to shine in Polka...'"

Carolyn glanced around at the smiling young faces that would, in a few years' time, grace the ballrooms of Savannah. She felt hopelessly plain by compare. What poor boy would moan and roll his eyes when paired with her this week? Carefully she snuck a glance at the assemblage of hapless males. Most of them were her age, not yet interested in females *or* dancing. But on the back row were a few taller young men who sat more like gentlemen and resisted whispering among themselves.

To Carolyn's amazement, one of these was looking straight at her! She immediately turned red as a beet — redder even than the young man's hair. He smiled and she looked away.

"'At the concluding note of the bar before you begin, throw back your left foot. If there is such a thing as a pewter Mercury, or a plaster Cupid in any of the gardens in your neighborhood, you may practice standing in the attitude the figure is in, the being able to stand like a goose on one leg.'"

Rolls of laughter ensued.

Goodness gracious, what could this mean? He must be sixteen. Despite his boyish air, he had the promise of broad shoulders and a neatly squared jaw. She peeked again. He winked.

How dare he? Even Carolyn knew such impudence was not to be tolerated.

It was then, on the verge of allowing indignation to take the upper hand, that she recognized him: Dylan Rousseau, younger son of the wealthy rice planter Louis Rousseau. And more importantly, her grandmother Odelle was the older sister of his mother, Henrietta, thus making Carolyn and Dylan first cousins once removed. Despite this, the branches of the family lived very separate lives in Chatham and Liberty counties, one planting rice, the other, long-staple cotton. Carolyn had not seen Dylan in years. She managed a faltering smile and studied her fingers, trying to focus on the humorous rules being highlighted by Monsieur Robert.

"'Stop when you hear your partner sobbing very painfully, or when you observe her gown is coming off.'"

Gasps went up from the girls. They looked at each other, certain Madame Granet would not approve of such discourse.

Monsieur Robert continued blithely. "'Nothing marks a chivalrous mind, more than consideration for women; for which reason also, you will not fail to carry a small pincushion in your pocket to repair damages, for their dresses are everlastingly coming to pieces, and the 12 to 14 spare pins they generally carry, are seldom sufficient to keep them together for more than two, or at most, three Polkas.

"'Recollect that utter disregard of time, common at present in Waltzing, is not safe in Polka, as it can be more easily detected. If you *cannot* dance in time, dance with nobody under nine or ten stone. At that weight, if she has any ear, she will probably keep you tolerably steady; if she has none, everyone will think it is her fault.'"

Carolyn colored again, half expecting all eyes to turn to her. She felt sure such common references would not be welcomed by the higher families. She began to wonder over Monsieur Robert's background.

"'If you can dance, impress upon your partner that she must trust herself implicitly and unresistingly to your guidance — Faith being the only virtue that saves in Polka.

"'If you have a taste for going round the room on the wrong side, against the stream ... take care to push your partner *before* you. Everybody that can *must* get out of *her* way. In case of casualties, go on never minding ...; and now, if you cannot distinguish yourself in Polka ... don't blame me.'"

Monsieur Robert concluded with a flourishing bow to the enthusiastic applause of mostly boys. Some of the girls pushed out their lips disapprovingly, but many were smiling and shaking their heads at such naughtiness.

"And now, I would like to ask my lovely daughter Miss Sarah Robert for the honor of an exhibition polka."

A young lady with her hair elegantly atop her head rose gracefully from the front row and curtsied to her father. Her attractive appearance elicited murmurs of admiration.

"Miss Robert had her coming out last season, so gentlemen, I regret to inform you that she is your superior in maturity," the dance director said teasingly, taking Sarah's hand and bowing. "If our pianist will favor us with the lovely new 'Jenny Lind Polka,' we shall demonstrate the dance."

Carolyn watched in awe as the father-daughter couple stepped into position and, after a short intro, went flying away over the dance floor. She had never seen anything so wonderful. It was as if they were one, a cloud skimming the ground but scarcely touching. Oh, how she longed to be that graceful.

The music ended, and the young people applauded. This time Carolyn was among the most enthusiastic. Next the teacher had them all stand in the clearing while he broke down the steps and had them repeat them. He and Sarah walked among the pupils, making a gentle correction here, giving a compliment there.

Then, the awful moment came ... the moment when Monsieur Robert had the students pair up. Carolyn froze. She was thinking of making a dash for the facilities when a tall form appeared before her. She looked up into the smiling brown eyes of Dylan Rousseau. He actually clicked his heels and bowed.

"Cousin Carolyn," he said warmly. "It's been a long time. I didn't expect to see such a familiar face."

"N-neither did I. But aren't you rather old to be here?" she blurted.

Dylan laughed. "I managed to avoid dance classes up to this point, but this year my mother was adamant."

"Oh, I see."

"Would you do me the honor of practicing the polka with me?"

"I — I'd be most delighted. But I must warn you," she added in a rush of honesty, "I'm a terrible dancer."

"Then we'll be a perfect pair."

Dylan's openness helped put Carolyn at ease. She had to reach up a bit to rest her hand on his shoulder. He clasped her other hand in his. The music was playing, and the room was rather chaotic with people talking and hopping around in the awkward throes of the learning process. Carolyn breathed more deeply when she realized no one was watching them. Dylan leaned one way, then another, with the music.

"You have to feel the rhythm, as my older brother says — and not think too much. He's perfect at dancing ... well, at everything. Let's try little steps. One-two-three-and-"

Carolyn moved with him, swaying back and forth. She stared at her feet at first, still almost stepping on Dylan's toes, until in a quick gesture he gently raised her chin.

"Eyes," he said, continuing his counting. Suddenly his shoe brushed the side of hers. He stopped. "Oops! You see how bad I am. I can't dance unless I count. I'll be a brilliant ballroom conversationalist, won't I?"

Carolyn dissolved into giggles. She wanted to thank him for keeping her from being the only dunderhead in the room — for at least *acting* like he was the problem. But she couldn't find the words.

"All right," he said, taking a breath and getting back into position. "Let's try again. We can do this, Cousin Carolyn. Remember, faith is the only virtue that saves in the polka."

She gave a decisive nod, willed all her powers of concentration to their sharpest, and looked into Dylan's brown eyes. Two measures later, a miracle occurred. They were dancing. No, they were flying — just like the Roberts! She couldn't think on it, or she'd mess up. She could only give herself to the music and the dream. Dylan laughed triumphantly and whirled her around the room.

Then, the music ended. Dylan bowed with a flourish and Carolyn remembered to curtsy.

"Bravo!" shouted Monsieur Robert.

Everyone began clapping, and Carolyn realized the floor had cleared. They were all applauding *her*. She turned redder than Dylan's hair a second time that day, but oh, what a feeling! To be the object of admiration rather than scorn! Carolyn sensed a turning point in her life, a crystal moment of clarity, of realization that change was possible — even for her.

"Well, let's give them a bow, Cousin," Dylan said, and still holding hands, they turned and honored the crowd.

That was when she saw him. The most handsome boy she had ever laid eyes on had come in through the door and was watching, his dark wavy hair gleaming above a tiered overcoat that accentuated his broad shoulders. But he wasn't grinning or clapping. He was looking at Dylan with something like surprise.

Dylan followed her gaze. Monsieur Robert was announcing luncheon break as Dylan said with an emotion she could not read, "That's my brother Dev. Come over and meet him."

Carolyn's feet suddenly felt like lead, but Dylan was tucking her hand on his arm just like she was a beautiful debutante, leading her toward the young man at the door.

"Dev, this is Cousin Carolyn Calhoun — you know, Aunt Odelle's granddaughter, of Brightwell Plantation. Carolyn, my brother, Devereaux Rousseau."

Carolyn curtsied stiffly but did not remove her hand from Dylan's arm. She felt as if her hand touched Devereaux's it might go up in flames. There just ought to be a law against looking that good. But Devereaux seemed hardly to notice her discomfiture — or her at all, for that matter. He gave a perfunctory half bow in her direction, but his eyes quickly shifted back to his brother.

"What are you doing here? I'm surprised," Dylan said.

"Me, too. I didn't know you had the energy for a polka."

"Were you impressed?" Dylan grinned and made a show of preening.

"Yes, actually."

"Maybe your style's rubbing off on me. Or perhaps it was the sensitivity of my partner." He turned to smile at Carolyn, who nearly choked.

"Indeed," Dev said dryly, looking as unconvinced as Carolyn felt. "I was in the vicinity and thought we'd go to lunch."

"Oh." Dylan's eyebrows rose again in surprise. "Sporting. Cousin Carolyn, would you like to come along?"

Carolyn forced herself to relax her grip on his arm, lest she cut off the circulation. Dylan could surely read her petrification in the presence of his suave older brother. As much as she longed for Devereaux to gaze at her with Dylan's easy warmth, she knew that was no more likely to happen than her being able to choke down a morsel in his presence.

"Um, no, thank you," she managed. "I brought my lunch."

"Too bad. Well, I'll see you later ... and for every polka from here on out," he joked.

"Y-yes. Thank you."

"May we walk you to your seat?"

"No. Thank you." Oh, goodness, could she say nothing else, nothing even faintly clever? Devereaux was looking at her. One more moment in his presence and she thought she would combust with embarrassment. "I — I'll manage."

Taking her arm out of his, Carolyn nodded to Dylan as he gave her a little bow and headed off to get his greatcoat. She turned and started across the length of the room. The pupils who were staying had begun to break into little circles, producing their box lunches and chattering. She was mentally preparing herself to go off to a corner and eat alone when several girls caught sight of her, rose, and hurried over.

"Carolyn, who *was* that handsome boy?" an attractive red head demanded.

Carolyn was sure the girl hadn't known her name last week. "M-my cousin," she stammered. "They are both my cousins." With the words, a flood of warm gratefulness spread through her. As long as she lived, she would be thankful to Dylan Rousseau for the prestige he had unknowingly bestowed upon her — for the rescue, for that was what it had been.

"Your cousins? Pray introduce *me!*" crowed another.

"*Where* did you learn to polka like that?" asked none but Rachel Hall. "Maybe you could teach us."

Bemused, Carolyn was drawn into their circle, barely getting out one answer before she was forced to give another. She found her dress complimented and her family praised as she dazedly unwrapped her lunch.

"Mmm, those sugar cookies look good," exclaimed the red head.

"You can have them," Carolyn replied. She handed them over without a moment's hesitation. "I don't need them, anyway."

Early June 1854
Chatham County, Georgia

Devereaux Rousseau spurred his black stallion past neat sections of lush, flourishing rice fields, his eyes taking in the drainage ditches, canals, gates, and river beyond. The "stretch flow," the last flooding of the fields before the "harvest flow," was being slowly drained off. He rode past the raised white winnowing house with the steam-powered mill behind, a tall, wooden structure with its adjacent brick chimney. A little closer to the main house, two-room brick slave quarters radiated out in three directions. Bathed in the early evening light, the scene looked tranquil. Black women working in their gardens paused to respectfully nod at the "young master" as he rode past. Children playing in the street scattered to make a clear path for his powerful stallion.

Dev took in the mule-powered cane mill and syrup boiler and the cluster of functional buildings surrounding the house — carriage house, stable, chicken coop, corn crib, privy, ice house, smoke house, hospital and plantation office. These were the sights that had been so familiar for eighteen years, soon to be so far away.

He purposefully made a large semi-circle across the property so that he could approach The Marshes from the main drive, thus fixing the house in his memory. It was a handsome, two-and-a-half-story brick structure, Georgian in architecture, with paired chimneys, side-gabled roof, and a decorative crown over the front door. Its façade was currently marred by scaffolding, for at his mother's insistence massive Ionic columns were being added "to bring it up to date."

Dev knew he didn't have to ride around back to the stables. As soon as he dismounted by the porch steps a young Negro boy came running to take the reins. Dev hardly paid him any heed, bounding into the front hall and sweeping off his straw hat.

He was hungry and had no mind to wait until dinner. He checked the dining room. Maids were busy arranging flowers and setting places on the table, but on the sideboard he found a covered tray of biscuits and strawberry jam. The cook knew to leave such snacks about for "the boys."

Dev sliced and slathered a biscuit and bit into it as he jogged up the stairs. On the second story maids and valets hurried to and fro, lugging trunks and valises. Henrietta's voice could be heard calling orders and summoning servants. Tomorrow the family would leave for Savannah, and thence on to Forests of Green in Habersham County for the last summer together before Dev went away to college. Even Collette and her husband Fred Lambert would join them from Charleston.

As Devereaux entered his bedroom, Little Joe — now a tall and gangly nineteen — looked up with relief. "Oh, thank goodness, Massah Dev," he cried. He held a stack of books, and another stack sat at his feet. "Ah cain't decide which ob these you wish to take wid you."

Dev quickly looked through the volumes and set several aside: Major William Gilman's *Manual of Instruction for the Volunteers and Militia of the United States*, *History of Alexander the Great*, *Life of Francis Marion*, Sir Walter Scott's Waverly novels, and a set of Greek works from Herodotus, Plato and Aristotle.

"There," he said, "that should be fitting. Have you got my wardrobe packed?"

"Mostly everythin', Sir."

Dev poked around in the open trunk, approving the selection of coats, shirts, trousers and waistcoats. "Very good. And your things?"

"Ready, too. Ah's also ready, Massah Dev. Ah cain' wait to see Virginia."

"You mean you can't wait for all that free time you'll have while I'm in classes."

"Det, too." Little Joe grinned unabashedly. Dev clapped him on the arm. The servant was handsome and intelligent and fairly efficient now, too, having been trained as a manservant by Louis' valet.

"See, another benefit of attending school in the South," Dev commented.

As if summoned by his son's words, Louis Rousseau entered the room. He made clear the fact that he had heard what Dev said by stating, "Perhaps you can expound on those benefits one more time, for my sake. Why VMI, Devereaux? You're not going to have a military career. You're coming home to The Marshes."

Devereaux sighed. He knew the prescribed educational pattern for young men in his position. Most would attend Princeton, Harvard or even

Franklin College in Athens. Then they would return to Savannah for a brief stint in law, politics or medicine before retiring to their plantation to take over a first son's duties as heir. Once again Devereaux found himself explaining to his father that he found a degree in law or medicine pointless when he had no desire to pursue these occupations.

"It makes just as much sense to receive military training — serve a bit in the militia units when I get back — or maybe take a temporary assignment somewhere," Dev told his father. "Besides, you've said yourself that trouble is coming. If it does, won't the South need able leaders?"

Louis nodded thoughtfully. He could not deny that sectional conflict continued to slowly escalate. The latest trouble was over the Kansas-Nebraska Act, which Democratic Senator Stephen A. Douglas of Illinois had just seen signed at the end of May. An avid supporter of railroad expansion, Douglas had desired tracks to be laid through his home city of Chicago to the West. Many Southerners wanted a transcontinental railroad to pass through New Orleans. In exchange for his northern route, Douglas had pushed through the act that would allow Kansas and Nebraska to choose whether to be admitted as slave states or free. The problem was, this nullified the 1820 Missouri Compromise, which had stated that no slavery would be allowed north of 36°30. Already a grassroots opposition in the North was moving to form a new Republican Party. More trouble was sure to come.

"All right," Louis sighed. "We just want to make sure you've made the right decision. It's not too late to change your mind."

"I won't change my mind," Devereaux said.

"And you're sure about VMI over our own military academy?" Louis asked, turning back at Dev's door. "It's common now for boys to attend the institute in their own state —— not go so far away."

"VMI is the best," Dev maintained.

Later, once Louis and Little Joe had left him alone in his luggage-strewn chamber, Dev walked slowly to the window and looked out over The Marshes, pondering the one thing he couldn't explain to his father — didn't even fully understand himself. All his life, he had sailed along. Everything had come easy. Nothing had been a challenge. He had possessed everything a young man could desire. Consequently, nothing had much meaning. Dev had the sense he walked in a dream, a silken cocoon of sorts, cushioned from the world outside. He knew that this was no justification for complaint, and indeed lethargy had so far taken over that it was an effort to even rouse his discontent. But he had seen other people express a puzzling intensity of emotions which he had never experienced. Maybe if he had to reach for something, if the course of his life should alter just enough to bring some form of newness or excitement, he would break through the silent barrier of his own complacency. Maybe he would wake up and connect to the world around him.

Savannah was growing, her burgeoning population spreading south into newly created wards. Shipping magnate Andrew Low, commonly known as the richest man in the city, had experienced tragedy while his new home was under construction. His wife, four-year-old son and uncle had all died, leaving him with two daughters. But this year, 1854, he would bring his new bride Mary Cowper Stiles, daughter of the minister to Austria, to live on Lafayette Square.

One square west, Low's partner, Charles Green, had hired John Norris, architect of the U.S. Custom House on Bay Street, to construct a Neo-Gothic mansion that many people said was the most costly private building in Savannah. It featured amazing oriels, battlements, protruding bays and even molded drip stones. The home sat beside the new St. John's Episcopal Church. Within view of this grandeur, Carolyn stood in her bedroom of her family's town house on Bull Street. Her home, too, had been designed by John Norris, the Italian villa façade proudly fronting Madison Square.

Today, she *was* interested in impressing. In a couple of hours, her great aunt Henrietta would bring her family to dinner. The Louis Rousseaus were currently in town at their house on Oglethorpe Square. Carolyn's grandparents would also be in attendance tonight. The only person she could seem to think about, though, was Devereaux. She hoped he would like her house, but even more, she hoped he might notice the changes in *her*.

Looking into the mirror, she took her sandalwood fan and rested its closed sticks on her right ear, raising one eyebrow.

"When may I be allowed to see you?" she murmured, speaking the secret language of the fan aloud. Then she plopped it down. "Oh, it's no use. I look ridiculous. He won't even notice me for a good two years yet."

Carolyn turned to one side and assessingly ran her hands down her bodice. The last six months' dedication to exercise and restraint from sweets had indeed melted the pounds away, but she was still short — and straight. Hopelessly girlish. An idea dawned. She darted to her door and peeked out. No one was in sight. She closed the door and ran back to her bureau, digging two silk stockings out of a drawer. She'd have to change dresses before dinner, but if she could just stuff these in her chemise before Mamsie helped with the toilette …

Carolyn was so absorbed in her task she didn't observe the door crack open and a wisened black face peering inside. She jumped a mountain mile when Mamsie's voice rang out and the old woman barreled into her room.

"Jus' what you think you doin', Missy? Get det sock outa dere! What your mama think if I let you go out all plumped up like det?" With absolutely no compunction, Mamsie reached into Carolyn's neckline, pinched one end of the stocking, and pulled. Then she removed the other. Carolyn stood shame-faced before her. "You always was a sensible gal, Miss Carolyn. What done come over you?"

Carolyn merely stared back at her, not quite sure herself. She *was* acting feather-brained. But then she thought of Dev, and her face softened. Anything, *anything*, would be worth his notice. Even resorting to cheap female tricks.

"Ahhh," said Mamsie, smiling knowingly. She patted Carolyn's cheek with a leathery hand. "Love. Love's what put det look on your face and all de sense outta your head. Who done catch your fancy, Mastah Dev or Mastah Dylan?"

Before Carolyn could reply, she caught sight of her younger sister Eliza standing in the doorway. As it was she didn't think Eliza had heard anything, but she quickly shushed the servant with a look of pleading distress. Mamsie turned around, saw the girl waiting there, and mumbled, "Ah'll jus' put dese away, Miss Carolyn, an' Ah'll lay out your dress. You be sure to come up in an hour to change."

"Yes, Mamsie."

Mamsie caught her arm. "An' always jus' be yourself, Miss Carolyn; det's pretty enough," she apparently couldn't resist adding.

Carolyn shot her a look of gratitude but couldn't help thinking "herself" was too dull to attract a fly, much less Devereaux Rousseau. She turned to her sister. "What is it, Eliza?"

"I'm bored. And sick of this old house. Let's play graces."

Carolyn wrinkled her nose. As much as she liked the game, it must be ninety-five degrees outside. "It's too hot," she replied. "We'll be a sweaty mess before dinner."

"It's not that bad in the shade on the front lawn, near the pond. Oh, please, Carolyn. Just for a little while?"

Carolyn felt herself caving. Eliza was an energetic, almost tomboyish sort, still very childish. She had been rather neglected lately as Carolyn had focused on more ladylike pursuits. Eliza was the one person who had always unconditionally adored her, despite her tattling ways. There wouldn't be many more years that Eliza would need her like she did now.

"Oh, all right," she agreed. "But just for a few minutes."

"Yea! I'll get the sticks and hoop!"

A few minutes later, they stood on the lawn in their linen dresses and wide-brimmed straw hats under the shade of the live oaks and a towering magnolia. Carolyn attempted to get close enough to her sister that they could exchange the beribboned hoop without exerting too much effort. Still, the breezeless late afternoon took its effect. Carolyn was about to comment on her stickiness when Eliza, sticks crossed to pull and deliver the ring, declared, "What a handsome family they are."

"Who?" Carolyn turned. Just as her rounding eyes fixed upon the four Rousseaus disembarking at their gate, the ring whooshed through the air and hit her — *thump!* — right on the temple.

"Ooh! Are you all right?" Dylan called, hurrying up the walk.

Carolyn bent to pick up the hoop to hide her embarrassment. "I'm fine," she said when she straightened, though she couldn't resist shooting her sister a furious glare.

"What?" Eliza innocently spread her hands. "Point it, shoot it, catch it — that's the game!"

Dylan's family gathered behind him, and he made the introductions. By avoiding looking at Devereaux, Carolyn made the appropriate responses.

"I hope we're not too early," Henrietta said. "Your mother invited us to chat and have some lemonade before dinner."

"Oh, no — I'm sure she'll be delighted that you are here," Carolyn replied.

"She just — failed to tell *us*," Eliza blurted.

"All the better. We can join your game," Dylan said. "Come on, Dev. You know you prefer something active to sitting around sipping lemonade."

"Maybe, but since when do *you*?"

Dylan shrugged. "I'm actually pretty good at graces. All the times you refused to play a sissy game, as you called it, with Collette, she was forced to seek me out."

Devereaux quirked an eyebrow. "Well then," he said. "Have you two extra sets of sticks?"

"Um — yes." Carolyn motioned for Eliza to run get them from under the magnolia tree, perplexed and uneasy at the way the afternoon was unfolding. She pretended to check that Mr. and Mrs. Rousseau had been admitted to the house while out of the corner of her eye she sized up the brothers. Both were dressed in linen summer suits and straw hats, and both were neatly groomed. They had some gestures and expressions in common, and their voices had a similar sound. But there the similarities left off. Besides the differences in hair color, Devereaux was taller than

Dylan and bore himself like a young Apollo. In fact, it was simply hard to look at *anyone* else when Dev was in the vicinity. But Carolyn promised herself that this time she *would* keep her eyes on the hoop.

Eliza ran back and distributed the sticks. Devereaux decided they should be on teams and directed Carolyn and himself to stand before the gold fish pond with its statue of a girl pouring water from a pitcher. No one questioned this, and the game began with Eliza keeping track of points. "Swish" went the sticks, and "whoosh" went the hoop, streamers flying. At first Carolyn was so distracted by Devereaux's nearness that she missed several times, her arms and legs feeling like jelly.

Gradually her attention shifted to the competitive undercurrent humming between the brothers. It began with Dylan's playful antics. He would turn around backwards to make a shot or catch the hoop on his hat, eliciting riotous giggles from the girls. Devereaux then began doing things of a similar nature. The game became more physical as the young men shot the hoop farther and higher, almost more than the girls could manage. But in their exchange Carolyn found freedom. She determined Dev would not catch every one of Dylan's shots while she stood there like an unmotivated lump. This was her chance to impress her skill and agility on the boys' minds. So she ran this way and that, her skirts bouncing as she jumped, laughing as she almost collided with her team mate, heedless of the heat.

"The polka queen returns!" shouted Dylan as she triumphantly pointed her stick in the air, having thrust it through the ring.

"Shoot it with your eyes closed!" Dev urged.

Grinning, she did so, shutting out the sight of a pouting Eliza, who was having trouble keeping up. Dylan caught her projectile and launched it back. Dev stepped farther away from his brother, extending his arm to show that Carolyn should make their line parallel with the fountain. She did so just as Dylan sent the hoop sailing in her direction. Carolyn ran, reaching.

"Stop, Carolyn!" yelled Eliza.

But it was too late. Carolyn's boot caught on the edge of the pond's pavement, and she felt herself falling — falling. With a terrific splash, she landed in the water, goldfish scattering in alarm. Her skirt inflated around her like a great blowfish, and she raised dripping arms in horror. This couldn't have happened.

"Are you all right?" Dylan called for the second time in less than an hour. He was rushing toward her, but Dev was closer, and it was his hand that extended out to Carolyn first. She pulled on it and raised herself, a sodden mess oozing green algae.

Carolyn's woeful gaze met Dev's. His eyes were twinkling. "You have jolly bad luck, don't you?" he said.

Had she another year of maturity and confidence, she might have laughed, and they would have made a big joke of the situation — had maybe even bonded over it. But the mortification was simply too great for her thirteen-year-old soul. Carolyn's eyes filled with tears. Dev didn't notice, as he had produced his handkerchief with a flourish and was attempting to remove slime from ivory linen. Dylan now stood over them, full of sympathy and concern. Eliza was still open-mouthed.

Suddenly she couldn't stand there another minute. "I — I must go change!" she cried. And pushing away her hero's ministrations, Carolyn fled the scene. As she went she heard Dylan say to his brother, "Now see what you've done. That was a dumb thing to say to her."

"What?" demanded Dev. "She *does* have bad luck."

Upstairs, Carolyn ran straight into Mamsie's arms, where she sobbed out her distress. The old woman patted her and made shushing sounds, graciously oblivious to the dress-to-dress transfer of liquid. Then, hiccupping, Carolyn explained what had happened as the servant gently removed her garment, toweled her off, and helped her into a rose taffeta dinner dress.

"It be all right, Miss Carolyn," said Mamsie. "Now what you gonna jus' do is go on down dere as regal as you kin be an' act like nothin' ever happened. Dem boys be gennelmuns enough to not mention it. You show 'em poise now an' dey be more impressed den if you neber did fall into det fountain. Look how pretty you be."

Mamsie turned her toward the mirror. She stared at herself with vacant eyes as Mamsie quickly reworked her hair. She was convinced a pretty dress could never hide the truth of what she was — a blundering idiot who had not once but twice completely humiliated herself in Devereaux Rousseau's presence. Her falling into that fountain was all he'd remember of her in his years at school, no matter how poised she acted now — if, that was, he remembered her at all.

216

CHAPTER SEVENTEEN

Jack whistled as he trotted on horseback down the sandy street, Sylvie's favorite pony in tow. He was feeling good. He had closed the purchase on the warehouses he'd had his eye on for some time, had stopped in at the livery stable with time to spare, and was now ready for a ride with the only young lady he called on.

Thought of young ladies swung his mind briefly to Ella Beth. One afternoon last week he had happened home early to find her at tea with his grandmother. Since her wedding three years ago she had done her utmost to avoid him. Their first few chance encounters after that particular conversation in the garden had been decidedly awkward. Ella Beth had maintained a cool reserve. But last week Jack was sure he had sensed a thawing. She had actually laughed at his jokes. Well, goodness, how long could she maintain her role of ice queen? They were, after all, cousins, their paths bound to cross. Jack was relieved that they might at last return to a semblance of familial affection. He liked Ella Beth. Liked her, but time had indeed proven he did not love her.

The wind was picking up and clouds scuttling in as he tied the animals to the hitching post. They'd better hurry if they wished to avoid a drenching. Jack bounded up the steps and knocked on the door of the pink mansion.

When the butler opened the door, he swept a bow for the sake of his half sister, whom he saw approaching, and said, "I am here to escort Miss Sylvie on her ride."

"Oh, Jack, we can't go," she moaned, reaching for his hand.

Jack stepped inside so the servant could close the door. "What? Why not? It's not so bad yet. So long as you've got your hat pinned securely we'll be all right."

The face of the eleven-year-old girl crumpled. "No, it's not that," she said. "Mother says two new cases of the fever have been discovered today. She and father are closeted now, discussing what to do. They are thinking of leaving the city."

"Oh, dear. Who told your mother about the fever?" Jack asked. He wanted to make sure the news was accurate. People, including his father, were so prone to panic where the dread illness was concerned.

"Mrs. Sarah Kollock, the doctor's wife ... our new neighbors. They just moved into the brown three-story in June."

"Ah, yes, then that would indeed be accurate," Jack murmured to himself. "Well, I'm here in any case. You can put down my name on your list of callers."

"What list?" Sylvie asked with false innocence.

"The one all young ladies keep of the beaux who call. Don't think we don't know of such things. The girl with the longest list gets a feather in her cap, right?"

Sylvie laughed and play-punched his arm. "I'm too young for list-keeping and beaux. And you wouldn't count, anyway. You're my brother."

"Oh, that's right!" Jack declared, hitting his forehead and pretending enlightenment had dawned.

"Silly Jack. Leave it to you to make me laugh in the face of an epidemic."

"Maybe it's not so bad as that. Let's go in and see what they're saying," Jack suggested.

His curiosity was satisfied the moment he opened the door.

"Oh, Jack, I'm so glad you're here," Sunny cried, rushing over to him and drawing him into the room. She was clad in *a dress à la disposition*, the fabric a small print with an elaborate coordinating border print down one selvage and on the sleeves and skirt flounces. Wryly he noticed she had cast aside a linen basque to which she had been adding buttons and military-style braid. Always at the height of fashion was his stepmother.

"Yes, we have just made a decision," Richard added. "In view of the outbreak of illness I think it best to remove the family from Savannah."

"So it's to be New York then?" Jack asked a little hopefully. Many of the elite set had vacationed in that city last year. He remembered the women's tales of the wonderful shopping at places like Stuarts had tempted Sunny. Jack felt that a stint in his native environs, and among his family, would be of great value to Richard.

But it was not to be. "No," his father replied, "nothing that far away. We thought how much simpler it would be to pass a couple of months in North Georgia."

"North Georgia," Jack echoed.

Sylvie poked out her lip. Jack knew she had hoped for the museums and amusements of the big city.

"Yes," said Sunny, "we hear how lovely the mountains are. The Rousseaus are there even now." Henrietta Rousseau, a good deal younger than her sister Odelle, was Sunny's aunt.

"Have they invited you?" Jack asked.

"Well — no. We will check into one of the hotels in Clarkesville until we can secure a suitable cottage to rent — or perhaps there would be an invitation once they know we have arrived."

"I see."

"We want you to go with us, Jack," Richard said.

"What?" Jack turned to him in amazement.

"Yes. I have every reason to believe the outbreak will not be confined to the slums — though heaven knows you'd still suffer exposure, due to your association with the sailors and Captain Northrup."

Jack knew his father referred to the fact that Jeremy had taken rooms on the fringes of the Trustees' Garden, now a seedy section where he had found contact was more easily maintained with the African-American population. Ever since he had first experienced success in helping the runaway Jim to freedom, a passion for aiding others in similar plights had overtaken the captain. Providence had established both men in a perfect position for this sort of enterprise. Unbeknownst to any save Jack — and even he was not always apprised of the details of his employee's plans — Northrup had contrived to spirit blacks in trouble to freedom as occasion permitted. Once it had been a young house servant falsely accused of theft, another time a husband, wife and babe facing separation on the auction block.

Jeremy was in port now, though the next voyage would deliver rice to the Caribbean instead of more gratifying cargo to the North.

Jack had no thoughts of leaving Savannah himself. "This is hardly the time for a long absence! Who would oversee the operations of the firm should all of the managers skedaddle to the mountains?" he demanded.

"Your grandfather, or, should they wish to accompany us, the head clerk. I care not, Jack! You don't seem to understand. Everyone with the means to leave is leaving. Nothing is more important than the safety of the family."

"Then by all means remove them, but I'm staying," Jack replied.

Richard jumped up. "By the blazes, you are *still* the most stubborn boy!" he declared.

"Jack's not a boy, Papa," Sylvie observed sweetly.

Richard turned to her, having forgotten her presence. "Sunny, would you take her upstairs?" he requested of his wife, who rather unwillingly obliged.

"I'll come again for our ride," Jack called out after his half sister. She was looking back dolefully over her shoulder as she was led away. He turned to his father. "Neither Grandfather or the head clerk are adequate for what needs to be done this time of year. You know that. I'm young and strong. Take the little ones, and I'll see to the business."

"No."

"Yes, begging your pardon," Jack said tersely.

"Well, I don't pardon you. You think all there is to life is work, and it's just not so, Jack. Why do you always have an excuse when Sunny asks you to dinner? And when have you ever attended a social or one of those Bachelor's Balls?"

Not following his father's reasoning, Jack looked to the ceiling in exasperation. "Never. Bachelors are those eligible for and interested in marriage, and I don't count myself among that number."

"Exactly! You live like an old widower."

"And going to the mountains is going to change that?"

"It might help reintroduce you to the pleasures of family life. Sylvie adores you, and I admit you are good to her, but the boys hardly know you. We should take this opportunity to spend time together."

Jack paused, considering, surveying Richard's gently lined face. Finally he asked softly, "Why are you so intent on this? I am no longer a boy. While I value your opinion, I can and will make my own decision."

Richard grasped his arm. He looked into Jack's eyes. "I'm intent because while you may no longer be a boy, you're still *my* boy. I love you, Son, and to be quite honest, the thought of you dying in the same manner your mother did terrifies me beyond reason. You, Jack, are all I have left of her."

If Richard had sought the one hole in Jack's armor, he had found it. Jack couldn't remember the last time his father had spoken of Eva — and to do it now with such tender conviction and passion brought tears to Jack's eyes. That coupled with the declaration of love moved Jack more than any pleas or threats could have. He turned away so his father would not see his emotion, nodded abruptly, and quickly left the room.

August 1854
Clarkesville, Georgia

A rather humid darkness was falling outside the Franklin Hotel as Mahala bent over the bed, leaning down with her wooden key to tighten the ropes supporting the mattress. She held it taut and slipped in a peg while Patience Blake tightened the other side. Fourteen-year-old Patience, the baker's daughter, came by to help out during busy times, and Mahala was sure glad she did. Otherwise Mahala would be running back and forth from one side of the bed — and, ultimately, the hotel — to the other.

Mahala shook open a fresh sheet and said, "I can finish up here. Just empty the basin and bring up some water, then see if Maddie needs you to help serve the latecomers their supper."

"All right, Mahala." Patience took the basin and flashed her shy smile.

Mahala smiled back. "Thank you."

She was not accustomed to anyone of the same sex liking her, much less looking up to her, but apparently Patience did. Mahala told herself she had gotten past the point of caring what anyone thought of her. Most girls seemed to feel she was beneath their friendship, and boys, well, they were best steered clear of.

She supposed she could say she was still friends with Clay Fraser, but ever since his infatuation had become clear, Mahala had been forced to impose a certain cautious restraint on the relationship. She obeyed her grandmother's order to never see him alone. As a result, Clay had backed off, but Mahala still frequently sensed his emotions simmering just below the placid surface. She was careful not to lead him on.

As Patience went out, closing the door behind her, Mahala plumped the mattress and smoothed out the sheet. She inhaled appreciatively. Fresh from drying in the outdoors, the linens smelled like fresh air and sunshine.

Maybe, she thought, she would see if Patience wanted to eat a slice of Maddie's apple pie with her after their duties were done. It would be nice to talk with someone near her own age. No matter how busy she tried to stay, attempting to content herself with work and a few choice relationships with adults, the truth was that at only sixteen, Mahala still wished for companionship.

Mahala put the pillows on the bed and looked around with an assessing eye. Once she had determined everything was indeed ready for the next guest, she lowered the wick in the oil lamp until the flame extinguished. Taking up the armload of dirty linens, she left the room.

The hall was lit by a series of lamps mounted on the wall, with small mirrors behind each to increase illumination. She had almost made it to the head of the stairs when the door of their best suite opened behind her and a man called out, "Miss? Excuse me, miss?"

Mahala turned. The gentleman seemed taken aback. She was accustomed to that. Most people were shocked to see blue eyes combined with Cherokee skin and hair. The reaction was a bit gratifying on this occasion, though, for the man was young, well-built and handsome, with wavy brown hair.

"Yes?" she asked.

"Um — do you happen to keep any Brown Windsor soap? Mrs. Randall has apparently left hers behind in our haste to leave Savannah."

Mahala knew about the fever outbreak. She only hoped these people weren't carrying the disease. "I'm afraid not," she replied, "but our soaps are handmade with the finest ingredients. Lavender gives the fragrance, and the shea butter makes it much more moisturizing than straight lye."

"Oh. I see. Well, can we have a tub, and some hot water sent up?"

"Jack?" called a woman's voice. Mahala also heard the piping of children in the room.

"Of course," she said levelly.

The door pushed open farther and a very attractive brunette appeared beside the man — though Mahala thought she seemed older than he. Oh, well, it was none of her business. Plenty of young men married older women for money and standing. Mrs. Randall made eye contact with her. She held out a hand towel.

"Are these your best linens?" she asked.

"Yes, Ma'am, the same that all the guests receive." Mahala was getting a little perturbed. These people from the coast expected to be treated like royalty.

"Scratchy," the woman declared. She looked at the man and added disdainfully, "I certainly hope Richard finds us a house soon." Then back at Mahala: "I thought the mountains were supposed to be cool. After two days of travel by rail and coach, this stickiness is really too much. At least can we have a tub sent up?"

"Right away," Mahala said. She glanced at the man called Jack and was surprised to see that he was suppressing a smile, his eyes twinkling. She turned on her heel and headed for the stairs.

As the door closed behind her she heard Mrs. Randall say, "Rather sassy for a maid, wasn't she?"

Early on the morning after his arrival in Clarkesville, Jack took a walk through town. The red clay roads were a bit muddy following a recent rain — possibly from that same storm front that had caused so much damage in Savannah just prior to their departure — but the natives were all smiles and cheer. Business and industry appeared to be flourishing, and the homes and churches were really quite lovely, surrounded by the lush green of hardwoods and evergreens. Jack recalled his mother telling him of the autumnal beauty of the North Georgia mountains, and he could just imagine the area bathed in fall's bright color parade. It would indeed be breathtaking.

Research and inquiry had revealed that a rail line to Franklin, North Carolina had been proposed as early as 1835, with the General Assembly in January of this very year approving the laying of tracks from Athens to Clayton. The railway was to be known as the Northeastern Railroad of Georgia. He'd heard that in Atlanta Jonathan Norcross was also stirring up interest in an Air Line Railroad — a direct route that took little heed for towns or obstacles — proposed to run from that city to Charlotte, North Carolina, and on to Richmond. Such a rail line would surely pass through Habersham County. The entrepreneur in Jack was stirring at the idea. He understood that visitors came not only to escape the coastal diseases but to take in sites like Tallulah Gorge, Toccoa Falls and Tray Mountain. If a railroad did come, how much more the already thriving town would boom!

So it was that a particular structure had already attracted his notice: the white-washed, Greek Revival-style Palace Hotel, a bit garish for the setting but with just the pizzaz to lure certain wealthy, pretentious customers. As luck would have it, a "for sale" sign was posted on one of its Corinthian columns.

He sat down to breakfast in the Franklin Hotel's dining room, surveying his surroundings. The sight of biscuits and gravy with sausage made his empty stomach rumble. While he was waiting for someone to arrive with his serving, he leaned toward a man who appeared to be a local.

"Excuse me, but would you happen to know who I should see about The Palace Hotel?" he asked.

The man in the bowler hat looked blank. "I'm sorry?" he replied.

"The Palace. It's for sale."

"Oh, no, I don't know anything about it. I'm from Tennessee."

"Oh, I'm sorry."

A plate landed with a '*thunk*' in front of him. Tiny bits of gravy splattered on the tablecloth.

"You don't want to buy The Palace Hotel."

Jack looked up to see the girl from the hallway the night before, an apron covering a blue dress that matched her unusual eyes. Her shining black hair was braided and wound into a bun at the back of her slender neck. Despite the hairdo, the womanly proportions of her figure, and her bearing — which Jack considered capable, even regal — she was quite young. As before, his curiosity stirred.

"You're not a maid, are you?" he asked.

She lifted a shoulder. "I suppose it depends how you look at it. Maid, waitress, and granddaughter of the owner."

"Am I to know your name?"

The young woman hesitated. "Mahala Franklin."

Jack folded his napkin, stood, and bowed. "Jack Randall. A pleasure to meet you. Now why don't you sit down here and tell me why I don't want to buy The Palace."

"I can't sit down. I have five other guests waiting for their breakfast."

"Of course," Jack said, glancing around. "Perhaps, when they are satisfied, you might return?"

She looked thoughtful. "I suppose I could spare you a minute."

"I'm honored," Jack declared mockingly. This had the effect of drawing down her arching brows. He ignored her reaction and sat back down, glancing at a white pot she had set on his table. "That coffee?"

Wordlessly she flipped over his cup and poured a stream of steaming black liquid into it. She turned and hurried back to the kitchen.

Jack was faintly perplexed. She was one of the first females to fail to swoon in his presence. It was rather refreshing.

He watched her as she moved among the tables, noticing that the other customers received their meal with a lighter hand than he had. She must have still been perturbed by Sunny's snobbery of the previous evening. Now she glided about with a natural grace, back straight and head up. He wondered how much of her confidence was innate, and how much was a well-seasoned front to deflect the prejudice she must surely encounter due to her mixed blood.

Jack realized with a start that the strange girl had completely distracted him from his musings about the hotel.

He had almost finished a second cup of coffee by the time she returned to his table. The dining room was emptying, the lull in conversation creating a more pleasant atmosphere.

"Would you care for another serving?" she inquired.

"No, thank you, I'd just like to have our conversation now."

"Won't your wife and children be joining you, or would biscuits and gravy be too rustic for their taste?"

"My wife?" Jack questioned, then laughed aloud.

She looked rather startled. "*Mrs.* Randall?" she prompted.

"*Mrs. Randall* is my stepmother. And the children my half siblings," Jack explained. "My father was out last night when we met. Mrs. Randall likes to sleep late. The children are snacking on biscuits and grapes until she is dressed to come down. It will be another good half hour, I expect."

"Oh," Mahala said, taking this in. Her hand rested on the back of the chair opposite him. She looked as if she had been given more information than she cared to possess.

Jack chuckled. "Do sit down — please."

She did so, folding her hands on the table before her and coming straight to the point in an almost childlike manner. "You don't want to buy The Palace because a man fell through the balcony outside his room last year. He won't ever walk again."

"This man, was he excessively large?" Jack couldn't resist asking, trying not to laugh.

Mahala was indignant. "No. Of course not. What does that matter? The place is shoddily built, and the locals despise it."

"I see ... and before the accident, which I assume sealed the fate of the owner, did the hotel enjoy a thriving clientele?"

She hesitated, steepling her long, graceful fingers. At last she replied, "Yes."

Jack suppressed a smirk. "And this wouldn't have anything to do with your warning me off?"

The brows winged downward for the second time that morning. "Of course not. Somebody is destined to buy it; why should I care if it's you?" she asked.

"Exactly so." Jack thought to himself that if she knew of his determination and success in the transportation and travel industry, she might feel otherwise.

In any case, Mahala Franklin was rising, still frowning, and sliding her chair back under the table. "Look, I was merely trying to warn you off a bad investment. But if you have enough money to sink into that bottomless pit, and you think you can get people to actually stay there again, go ahead! Be my guest."

As usual, Jack couldn't resist rising to the bait — and the challenge. "I believe I am. And I think I will, thank you," he announced cheerfully.

The young woman actually huffed. "Good day, Mr. Randall," she retorted. And grabbing up his plate and saucer, she strode away.

CHAPTER EIGHTEEN

Just before dinnertime at the very end of August Mahala and Patience Blake trotted on horseback towards Clarkesville, concluding a most enjoyable ride.

"Thank you for asking me to come with you," Patience said, drawing widely on her dappled mare's reins to avoid a man driving two cows before him. "I'm not very good on horseback, as you've seen. Certainly not as good as you. But then I've never had much practice."

Mahala glanced at the girl and smiled. Patience did still look nervous atop the hotel's livery mare, but her fortitude was impressive for one so young. And her immaturity was of the innocent, not the silly, variety. She was a thoughtful companion. Mahala had enjoyed the outing.

"I can assure you," Mahala said, "what practice I had before I got Unagina was rather inadequate — seeing as how it came on the back of Papa's old team horse. You should have seen my brothers trying to keep me up on his back!"

The girls laughed, then Patience said, "Well, then, you must be a natural. You look ever so confident now. You are so lucky. I can't imagine receiving such a fine present for my sixteenth birthday."

"She is wonderful." Mahala patted the horse beneath her. The spirited little mare was named in Cherokee for her shining chestnut color. "But you already are lucky, to have such a lovely family."

"Yes, I am. But truly your grandmother must adore you, Mahala. The horse *and* the riding habit. You look like such a lady."

Mahala ducked her head, unaccustomed to such verbal praise. "*That's* something, isn't it?" she replied wryly.

Patience was not daunted by her sarcasm. Her russet hair gleamed in the waning sun as she firmly shook her head, her round face sweet and serious. "My mother has always taught us that gentility arises from the heart and mind, not one's outward circumstances. Coming from a gentlewoman who married for love rather than advancement, her words have extra weight, don't you think?"

"A lady is as a lady does, hm? Well, I'm sure she is right. You would not be so kind otherwise."

As they drew near the entrance to the hotel's stable, Mahala saw a familiar figure leaning against the building. Clay Fraser was sitting on a pile of straw, knees drawn up before him. At his side was a metal tackle box and a fishing pole. He smiled when he caught sight of her.

"Uh, oh," Patience murmured. "See you inside."

Mahala drew up before the young man. Clay gave a low whistle.

"What are you doing, Clay?" she asked.

"Waiting on you, hoping to convince you to come fishing with me. Looks like I'll be waiting some more, 'cause you'll have to go change those fancy duds. But that's all right."

"You know I can't go to the river with you, Clay," Mahala said reprovingly.

"So I asked a few friends to come along. Surely your grandmother can't find fault with that," he said, rising. With a boyish grin he opened his tackle box. "Grasshoppers and worms, see? We're sure to get several fat trout. You can take them home for Maddie to fry up."

"I don't know. Like you said, I'm not dressed for fishing, and Grandmother is probably already ready to eat dinner." Mahala looped her reins around in one hand and gave Unagina a command in Cherokee to stand still. Clay instantly held out a hand to assist her as she dismounted, but to her surprise, when she went to pull back, he did not let go.

His eyes had narrowed. "Sounds like a string of excuses to me," he said in a low tone.

Immediate indignation flowed through Mahala, and she snapped, "Let go of me, Clay Fraser."

"Maybe I should," Clay replied thoughtfully, with an edge to his voice.

Someone cleared his throat at that moment. Both of them turned to see Jack Randall standing at the corner of the stable, dressed as immaculately as ever. Clay dropped Mahala's hand.

"Excuse me, I don't mean to interrupt anything, but I require a word with you, Miss Franklin," Jack said. His hands were behind his back in what appeared to be a relaxed posture, but his eyes were fixed on Clay, and there was a certain expectation there. Rather like the expectation in the word "require," thought Mahala irritably. They were both annoying, just in different ways.

She looked back at Clay. "Another time, perhaps," she told him quietly.

He nodded, biting his lip. "I see how it is," he said. Then he grabbed up his pole and stalked away.

Mahala watched him go, regretting the fact that she had been the cause of his boyish appeal turning sour.

Jack Randall interrupted her thoughts. "He'll be back another day," he said cheerfully.

Throwing him an annoyed glance, Mahala led Gina into the stable, leaving Jack to follow her. He did so, easily falling into step beside her. As they passed the stall where Patience rubbed the nose of her mount, the girl's eyes widened.

"What is it you wished to speak with me about?" Mahala asked.

"My family has accepted an invitation to the Rousseaus' summer home. We will be leaving in the morning. But I wished to inform you that I plan to only be gone two weeks, and would like you to hold my room."

Mahala looked at him as she led Unagina into her stall and began to unbuckle the saddle. "That is something best told to my cousin Leon at the front desk," she said.

"I prefer to tell *you*. As you may have heard, my offer on The Palace Hotel has been accepted. I have placed an ad for workers in the *Advertiser*. Should any applicants arrive in my absence, please ask them to return two weeks from today for an interview."

"Again, that should be shared with Mr. Leon Franklin," Mahala said through a slightly clenched jaw. Could she not be in this man's company for five minutes without getting angry? His calm, dictatorial manner was just so frustrating. She wanted to remind him that she was not his secretary, but the rule of politeness to hotel guests forbade her to speak her mind on the subject.

"And I will do so," Jack said congenially, with a nod. "But something tells me you are at the heart of all that goes on within the Franklin Hotel. I will pay in advance. Please retain the whole suite. I am expecting a foreman from Savannah, an accomplished gentleman who will oversee the renovations. He can stay in the adjoining room."

Suddenly it became clear to Mahala ... Jack Randall was not telling her these things because he felt her to be in charge at the hotel. He was letting her know he was now her competitor, and the game was on. And enjoying it all very much.

"Very well, Sir," Mahala said with deadly calm. She did not look at him as she gently removed the bit from her horse's mouth.

Jack smiled, nodded, and walked away.

On a fine early September morning the Rousseau carriage issued from the gates of Forests of Green, loaded down with luggage. Inside Devereaux breathed a sigh of relief. His mother's leave-taking of her first son, "her fine, handsome boy," had been anything but graceful. Dev imagined she would weep most of the day.

Of course, perhaps the presence of her house guests would help restrain her emotions, once the original upset had passed. The Randalls. Another reason Dev was more than ready to leave for Lexington, Virginia. In all honesty he guessed Richard and Sunny were not so bad. Richard was pleasant and accommodating, and Sunny had found more subtle ways to manipulate her circumstances than Henrietta employed. Sunny, his older cousin and Carolyn Calhoun's aunt, was also refined and easy on the eyes and nerves. But Dev was not used to children and found the interruptions and noise of the two boys tiresome. At first the little girl had tried to follow him around — after her older half brother had returned to town, that was — but once Dev ignored her for a while she had gone on her way. It wasn't that he didn't like the child, mind ... he just didn't have a clue what to do with her.

For Jack Randall, though, he had developed a definite distaste. He was glad Jack was not Sunny's son; therefore, Jack and Dev were no relation. Jack, who was about seven years his senior, had a knack for keeping people at arm's length. They had started out on the right foot, recollecting their occasional childhood meetings. Back then Dev had thought Jack dashing and adventurous. Now he found his aloof confidence demeaning, and it quickly became clear that they held vastly different views on the way the world should function. Princeton — or his Northern cousins — had obviously exerted an influence. Dev had often sensed Jack watching him, observing his interactions with Little Joe and others on the estate, no doubt judging everyone by his own lofty standards. There was nothing worse than a person who thought everyone should be just like himself. Jack's return to Clarkesville last week had come none too soon. It was only after he left that Dev had realized Jack Randall was one of the few individuals to get a rise out of him ... though he had, he hoped, concealed that fact.

Now, Dev found himself actually looking forward to the journey north. It would give him time alone, time to think. He was truly anticipating the challenges the next few years would bring.

He smiled at his father, who was framed against the drying leaves of the changing seasons as he sat in the open carriage. There was a nip in the air. Both men wore light wool coats, Louis' vest straining slightly against his expanded girth as he reclined on the seat.

"Thank you for coming to see me off," Dev said.

"I'd have it no other way."

"You're no longer holding VMI against me?"

Louis waved his hand in the air, dismissing the matter as trifling. "VMI is a good school, and it will all come out the same in the end — just as you pointed out. Just so long as you are happy and you distinguish yourself — as I have no doubt you will."

"I won't let you down," Dev promised.

They were nearing the stagecoach stop along Clarkesville's main thoroughfare. Suddenly Dev spied an interesting entourge proceeding down the sidewalk. A grandly dressed matron, nose in the air, minced along on her husband's arm. The man punctuated each step with a definitive swing of his walking stick. Behind them were a black slave woman and the half-Cherokee Franklin girl, both loaded to their eyebrows with valises, boxes and parcels of various size. The slave was actually carrying less than the hotel owner's granddaughter. Dev had seen the young woman around town before and had been impressed with her dignity and mature manner. He liked that. He had no use for helpless, frivolous females. And then of course there were her stunning looks, which even at her tender age would turn any man's head. He had never formally met her before, but he had a feeling that was about to change, for as he watched the stack of packages teetered, and the topmost slipped to the ground. Trying to keep the rest secured, Miss Franklin patiently bent to retrieve those she had dropped. There was no sign of vexation or self-pity that most other women in her circumstance would exhibit. But the nature of the scene irritated Dev.

"Stop the carriage," he said to the driver. The man's response was immediate, but Little Joe, also seated above, turned to look at him in confusion.

Dev leapt out of the carriage and was picking up parcels before anyone could question him. His eyes met Miss Franklin's as they were both still in the squatting position.

"Let me be of assistance," he said, freeing a hand to lift his hat. "Devereaux Rousseau."

"I — I know," stammered the girl, momentarily taken off guard. "Mahala Franklin."

"I know that, too."

She looked even more surprised. "Really, Sir, I don't require any help. If you'll just restack those here ..." Standing up, she held out her arms.

"No, I will not. I have an aversion to seeing young ladies such as yourself treated like slaves. Was the hotel manager unavailable, or unable to send some boy on this errand?" Dev asked, standing also.

A faint smile lifted the corners of Mahala's mouth. "The hotel manager thinks me anything but a lady. But really, Mr. Rousseau, I don't mind. It's part of my job to help the guests with whatever they require."

Dev looked down the street. The regal couple whose belongings had caused such inconvenience sailed on ahead, never once looking over their shoulders to check on the progress of those following. Nodding to his carriage driver, he gently prompted Mahala to continue their own walk.

Mahala had noticed his luggage-laden vehicle. "And you, Mr. Rousseau, are you also taking the stage this morning?" she inquired.

"Yes — to South Carolina, and on to Virginia. I'm to start at the military institute there."

"Well, best of luck to you, then."

They had reached the ticketing office, where the stage was waiting. The portly woman turned and saw Dev with an armload of her possessions. She was instantly all concern and contriteness.

"Oh, my goodness, Sir, I would not have had a gentleman such as yourself bothered with my parcels!" she exclaimed, hastening to take them from him.

"Indeed, Madam, it was no trouble. I judged the load to be more than this young woman could adequately bear." Dev gave her a tight smile. "And I was happy to come to her assistance." He turned and gave Mahala a *true* smile as she straightened from setting down her load next to the female servant's.

"Hmm," said the woman. "Well, thank you."

As she turned away, Mahala added softly, "Yes, thank you."

There was a becoming color in her cheeks.

Dev bowed. He started to speak again, but Mahala's eyes had fallen on his approaching father. With a quick smile, she turned on her heel and hurried away. Louis caught his arm.

"What was that about?" his father demanded.

"Just rescuing a maiden in distress," Dev replied lightly, expecting the praise that normally accompanied such exhibitions of his gentility.

"Well, save your gallantry for the drill field — or more worthy maidens," Louis growled. His expression then changed with amazing quickness, and he clapped Dev on the arm. "Aw, I'm just grumpy at my final moments with you being interrupted. A father must convey parting words and all, you know."

Dev doubted his father's judgment of the Franklin girl had been anything less than honestly felt. But he made himself smile and ask, "And what words do you have, then, Father?"

"Nothing very original, I fear. Only study hard and choose your friends wisely. If you do, you might keep them for life. Let nothing sway you from the beliefs you leave home with — love for God, family and state. If you uphold those commitments you will always have honor."

"Thank you, Father, I will, I swear it," Dev said, surprised that he was actually moved by Louis' admonition.

"And write to your mother as soon as you arrive, and often after that, or she will drive me to distraction." Louis chuckled.

"Of course."

His trunks had been loaded. The driver was giving a final going-over to his rig and horses. It was time for goodbyes. Louis and Dev clasped each other in an embrace with murmured "I love yous," then Devereaux stepped up into the coach and found a seat.

Minutes later, the vehicle thundered by the Franklin Hotel. Dev caught a glimpse of the intriguing Mahala Franklin entering its front door and allowed himself to wish for a moment that there had been more time, and circumstances were a little different...

November 1854
Montpelier, Georgia

Carolyn stood at the window of her boarding school room at the Montpelier Female Institute fifteen miles west of Macon and watched the swallows fly into the setting sun. It was this time of day that she was most prone to feel lonely, her thoughts turning to her family at Brightwell. How she missed Eliza and Mamsie. So it was good that she had a letter to answer tonight.

It was also good that most of the girls had gone out to a musical evening. That was something she would have enjoyed attending herself but for the fear of being pressed into performing. She had really devoted herself to the piano since arriving here, practicing two hours each day. As a result, her musical abilities had soared. But she was still shy about playing in front of an assembly. Still shy about everything.

It was painful, this shyness, but almost impossible to shake. Carolyn took great pains to know every star in the night sky when they studied it with a telescope, to roll her *r*'s so eloquently that her French teacher declared she spoke like a Parisian native, and to make perfect marks on her literary recitations. She did this so none could mistake her reticence for slowness. She could hold her own next to the other pupils even if she couldn't connect with them.

Carolyn couldn't fathom the giddy whirlwind in which many of the girls chose to live — especially the newer students her age. Their giggling and games made no sense to her. And while there were certainly those more serious and mature students, they had not yet noticed her. Until — and if — they did, she was too uncertain to reach out to them.

Carolyn wondered if she would feel fat and clumsy her entire life.

She moved to her little desk and with a gentle hand smoothed out the letter just received from Savannah. She smiled as she recalled the riot of attention its arrival had caused. Briefly she had been the focus of both envy and teasing.

"Carolyn got a letter from a *boy!*" one of the girls had cried. Others had quickly gathered around.

She had looked at the return address and her heart had nearly stopped when the last name had practically leapt off the envelope at her. *Rousseau.* But how silly to imagine for one minute that Devereaux would write to her from VMI! It had been Dylan, of course. But she wasn't as disappointed as she might have expected.

"Who is it from, Carolyn, a beau?" the girls had asked.

A warmth of affection had filled her chest. "No — a friend," she had answered, bringing the comfort of the letter to her bosom. How like Dylan to consider that she might be lonely in this new place and in need of a word from home.

He had written that shortly after Dev got off to Virginia their father had returned to The Marshes, where a successful rice harvest had been concluded. Dylan and his mother had only recently returned there themselves after enjoying the company of the Randall family at Forests of Green. The fever epidemic in Savannah was finally abating. They would be staying on at the plantation until January, when his mother was keen to go into the city for the winter social season. But, Dylan wrote, the prospect looked boring to him minus both his brother and his polka partner. In fact, he had addressed the letter to "The Polka Queen." As if Carolyn was old enough to attend any functions with him, anyway! But the accolade brought a smile to her face, and in a bold spirit rather unlike her, she sat down and started writing:

> *To the Grand Polka King of Savannah: Thank you for your letter of November the fourteenth. As you must have guessed, any correspondence from home is dearly anticipated. I am so glad you are all well.*
>
> *I am settled in here at Bishop Elliott's school. As you may know, the complex is situated on an eight hundred-acre site which includes the fourteen health springs, so the location is quite beautiful. I like all my teachers and am enjoying my course of study, which includes French, piano, history, mathematics,*

geography, natural philosophy, literature and drawing. I wish there was some emphasis on theology so that I could hold an intelligent conversation with you once you attend Princeton Seminary. But you shall have to be patient with me. You asked my opinion as to your choice of occupation. I can think of none that would suit better.

I am so glad that at seminary you will be spared the indignities your brother is suffering as a plebe at VMI. To be dunked in water and have your cravat tied in a dozen knots! I am sure the letter you received made your family more anxious rather than less. Hopefully he is right in that once he gets from camp to barracks the bad treatment will stop. It sounds like he will be very busy with reciting algebra at eight, geography at eleven, English at three, and battalion drill at five, and adding French in January! But I, too, hope he will thrive under the challenge. I am sure he will.

Though I am doing well in my studies, if I am to honestly answer your question about the friends I have made, I must say I find myself still much alone. Please do not pity me, for I feel sure as time passes I will find a few kindred spirits and grow up confident enough to enjoy their society. I have only just begun here, after all. I do not look for careless laughter and shallow confidences, but for a deeper and more lasting relationship that surely takes time to discover.

There is an excellent church where I can nurture my spiritual growth, as you so wisely bade me. And as the Psalmist wrote, the Lord is indeed my strength and my song.

I do not forsee any visits home for quite some time. But I do hope that we may meet again before you leave for the North. Yes, I would indeed be happy to receive your letters, as they provide a perspective quite different from my mother's and sister's. I would love to hear of all that transpires in our beloved city.

Your cousin,
Carolyn Calhoun

CHAPTER NINETEEN

Early June 1855
Clarkesville, Georgia

n a warm Sunday evening the Franklin carriage brought Mahala back to the hotel following her spring visit to Sautee. It had been a pleasant three months, but it was hard to believe how things had changed. Of course Seth had long ago married and bought his own farm, and now Sam was gone, too. Only Jacob remained at home, and him not for long. As a result, Nancy had been keener than ever on Mahala's company. She had spoken hopefully of Mahala being able to return to the valley next year after her eighteenth birthday.

Mahala still loved the valley, but after becoming accustomed to the activity of town — and reaching a time in her life where that activity was meaningful — she wondered if Sautee would seem too isolated were she to permanently move back there. Even while she was visiting, a certain restlessness had begun to stir that surprised and even dismayed her. She found herself frequently wondering what was going on in town, what she might be missing. As much as she loved nature and the beauty of the hills and river, she found that she now longed for something more — for growth and adventure, relationships, and the surprise of what each new day might hold. She had the feeling she was standing on the brink of great change.

When she had spoken of these things with her grandfather, he had nodded patiently in understanding, but there had been a sadness in his eyes. Mahala had felt she was betraying him — and Nancy and Ben. Why must it always be this way, she wondered — choosing one thing over another, and hurting someone in the process? If only she could have one normal family like everyone else. But no, she didn't really wish that, for that would be wishing away the sacrificial love of the Emmitts, dear *Ududu*, and the options her grandmother offered her. It was just so hard. She was glad she had one more year to decide.

So it was that Mahala returned to the hotel with conflicting emotions. Her grandmother was waiting on the front steps. She smothered Mahala in an embrace, exclaiming over how healthy she looked — "but did you keep on your bonnet?" — and how lonely the place had been without her.

"I missed you, too, Grandmother," Mahala said truthfully.

They put their arms around each other's waists and turned to go in.

"I have your favorite dinner waiting, and jasmine tea steeping. I got a new coverlet for your bed — wait until you see it! And tonight I will mix up a buttermilk compound while you take your bath."

Mahala made a face. "Still trying to wash the Indian off of me, Grandmother?" she asked wryly.

"Now, Mahala, that was not nice. You know the noblest ladies of society use buttermilk when they've been out in the sun. It's good for the complexion."

Mahala shook her head, not fully convinced. She knew Martha preferred to downplay her Cherokee heritage, but she refused to make an issue of it, choosing to focus instead on the love they now shared. Her grandfather's counsel had been recalled many times since she had come to Clarkesville five years ago — and it had paid generous dividends.

As they passed the hotel dining room, her eyes lit briefly on a dark blonde man sitting near the entrance. His gaze locked on hers. A cat-like smile spread over his face, and he rose from the table where he was dining with another man and gave her a bow.

Martha tugged on her arm, drawing her toward their quarters as she said in a disgusted voice, "That scoundrel! I believe he must come here merely to vex me. Never give him the time of day, Mahala."

"I know, Grandmother. Don't worry."

In the parlor, Mahala sank wearily onto the sofa. "I think every bone must be out of place after that rough road," she commented.

"A hot bath will set you to rights again," Martha said. "I'll have Maddie heat your water just as soon as the dinner dishes are done. For now, tea."

She moved off to retrieve the cups from the china cabinet.

Zed entered bearing Mahala's trunk. "Welcome home, Miss Mahala. You want dis in your room?"

"Hello, Zed — yes. And thank you." Mahala smiled as his grizzled, graying head and bent back disappeared down the hall. She had even missed Zed and Maddie.

"Here we go!" Martha returned with a steaming cup of tea for each of them. Mahala sat up to take hers, appreciatively inhaling the floral aroma. They had just both settled and taken a tentative sip when the door to the hotel burst open.

"Patience!" Mahala cried joyfully. She jumped up to hug the girl, who smiled and returned the embrace, but seemed disturbed. "Patience, what's wrong?" Mahala asked.

The girl's big brown eyes darted from her to Martha. "It's that Rex Clarke. He's asking to see Mahala."

"What?" both Martha and Mahala cried in unison. Martha added, "What does he want?"

"Just to speak with her, he says. I told him she had just returned from a trip. But he's very determined. The other gentleman has gone, and Mr. Clarke says he wishes Mahala to join him while he eats his pie. He insisted I go fetch her."

Martha came indignantly to her feet. "We'll just see about that. If he won't take 'no' for an answer from me, I'll have him and his pie thrown out into the street!" she declared. She placed a hand on Patience's elbow. "You girls both stay here. I'll take care of him — and the dining room. Patience, you may have my tea."

So saying, Martha marched out of the room like a general going to battle.

Looking after her with wide eyes, Mahala murmured, "I wonder what he intended to say to me."

"Whatever it was, it couldn't be good." Patience reached behind herself to untie her apron. "That man has eyes like a snake. And he looks at us young girls like we're the rats." She sat down, considering Martha's cup. "Did she really want me to drink her tea?"

"Go ahead."

"Believe I will. I'm parched. So, how were things in our newly created neighboring county of White?"

"Good. Peaceful." Mahala smiled at Zed as he came out of her room and returned to the hotel. "But I'm glad to be back. Fill me in on everything."

"All right. Let's see ... that awful Latilda Mason got married and moved to Athens, thank goodness. And Clay's been moping around. He's kept on asking if I've gotten a letter from you."

"Oh, dear."

"But I expect what you *really* want to know about is what that Mr. Jack Randall has been up to."

Mahala couldn't help a smile, and she sat forward slightly. Over the winter she and Patience had made a game of "spying" on the progress at The Palace, groaning over how Jack greeted everyone like a politician garnering votes, reporting all the hearsay about the man and his investment to one another, and when they were sure Randall was out and the workers done, peeking in the hotel's lower windows. Now Mahala had to admit to herself that the renovations being conducted by her competitor had occupied more of her thoughts these past weeks than they should have.

"He's just so annoying," she said aloud, without thinking.

"You mean so handsome."

Mahala made a face. "That's beside the point — if I even agree, which I didn't say I did."

Patience rolled her eyes over her teacup.

"Anyway, you were saying ..."

"Oh, yes. He had marble brought in for the foyer — *marble*! And a grand piano shipped from Savannah. And then, just last week, a French chef arrived!"

"No!"

"Yes. Everyone in town was talking. And probably people all over the region, too, considering how he's advertised."

"Advertised?"

Patience nodded. "Glowing reports of his fine hotel in all the papers from Charleston to St. Augustine ... and Athens and Gainesville, Milledgeville, Augusta ..." Her voice trailed off as she took a leisurely sip. Clearly she found the man of more interest than the hotel.

Mahala told herself she herself was afflicted with no such nonsense. "Did you save those ads?" she asked.

"Save them? Whatever for?" Patience wondered aloud. "It's not like I'm going to stay there."

It was Mahala's turn to roll her eyes. "Honestly, Patience, have you no business acumen whatsoever?"

"Acumen?"

"Never mind. Oh, I just wish I could see his ads for myself. How am I to combat him? He'll steal all our customers."

"Oh, he ran the ad in the *Advertiser*, too — just to let all of us know how fine he was, I guess," Patience said.

"Truly?" Mahala cried and hopped up. She ran to the table where her aunt kept periodicals and pulled out a recent edition of the local paper. Snapping it open, she quickly perused the five columns of small print, skimming over the ads of local tradesmen and various legal notices for Habersham, Towns and White counties. At last she said: "Aha!"

She read aloud, "'A Grand New Hotel to Open in Clarkesville: Celebration to Coincide with July 4. All those individuals with friends in the sultry climes may wish to invite them to lodge this year at The Newly Renovated Palace Hotel on the square in Clarkesville. Now under the management of a Savannah Randall, The Palace will offer truly the most royal treatment: elegantly furnished suites with English toiletries, *cuisine de Paris*, livery with suitable thoroughbreds, departing excursions to all the local attractions, large dancing floor, etc., etc. All the elegant amenities. Apply now by letter of reservation to pass the season at The Palace and attend the Grand Opening Ball.' Grand opening ball, indeed," Mahala sniffed. "What airs! What falderal!"

"It does sound rather lovely," Patience said dreamily.

"Well, if it does, we must make the Franklin sound even grander," Mahala replied impatiently, slapping the folded paper against her skirt as she walked back and forth. She had been gone too long. Jack Randall had gotten ahead of her, and now she must head him off. She was ready for the fray. Nothing would be more satisfying than showing that man he could not just waltz in with all his money and connections and put them out of business. They would not bow out that easily. She continued: "And, since we aren't that grand — as in, glitzy and new and fancy — we must play up what we *are*."

"All right," said Patience. She sat up like an attentive pupil, waiting for Mahala's instruction.

"I need a pencil and paper." Mahala sought those in a nearby drawer and beckoned Patience to the table, which was already set for dinner. She pushed aside a place setting, then looked up at her friend. "So, what are we?"

"Old?" Patience offered uncertainly.

"Not old. Established." Mahala wrote hastily on her paper. "We have a long-lasting reputation. People *like* us, don't they?"

Patience nodded. "Oh, yes, and the biscuits!" she exclaimed, catching the idea. "My father always says no one — not even he — can make biscuits as good as Maddie's."

"That's good! Old family recipes. And the welcome of home. What else? Insider tips on local history and attractions. Can you think of anything else?"

Before Patience could answer, the door opened and Martha bustled in, followed by Maddie, both carrying trays with dinner from the inn's kitchen. Mahala jumped up to hug the black woman, who had to hurry back to her work station where supper dishes awaited. Patience and Mahala helped distribute the plates full of steaming chicken and dumplings and English peas and carrots. Then the three women sat down and joined hands to bless the food. Martha prayed, thanking the Lord not only for dinner but Mahala's safe return.

When they raised their heads, Mahala asked, "So did you get rid of Mr. Clarke? What did he say?"

"Yes, and nothing," Martha replied primly, screwing up her round little mouth. "I told him if he came around here again asking for my granddaughter I'd chase him out with the broom for all the town to see. He said 'yes, Ma'am,' lifted his hat, and left."

Patience burst out laughing, but Mahala wanted to know, "What do you think he wanted to say to me? Now we'll never know. What if it was something about my father?"

Martha smacked her hand down on the table. "You just put that right out of your mind, Mahala Franklin. You want to solve the mystery of your father's death? Rex Clarke is not the key. He'd lie to you just as soon as look at you, and no matter how honorable he might make his intentions for getting near you appear in the beginning, I can assure you they aren't."

"But Grandmother, you said yourself you can't stand to see Father's killer go unpunished, and Mr. Clarke is our only lead. Maybe if I pretended to be friendly to him —"

"No, Mahala. The man corrupts all he touches. You are not to speak to him. Ever."

Mahala swallowed. She pushed the peas on her plate. Her grandmother's hand snaked out and grabbed hers. There was a trembling intensity in her grip that caused Mahala to look up, wide-eyed.

"I fear for you, Mahala. Your boldness makes you foolish. At least ... it could in this case. Will you heed what I'm telling you?"

"Yes, Ma'am."

"All right, then." Martha released her wrist. "We'll talk no more of it. I hate the very mention of that man's name. Now, what's this?" she asked with an effort at lightness, lifting Mahala's notes from the table.

"Just some ideas for an ad," Mahala replied.

"An ad?" Martha echoed, then read aloud: "'Well-established, reputable hotel: your second home in the mountains, run by warm, friendly natives. Old family recipes. Reasonable rates with rustic, elegant charm.' Hmm, that's not bad."

"I'm not finished with it. Patience and I were just jotting down our thoughts. I wondered if you had a list of addresses for the coastal papers?" Mahala asked.

Martha nodded, laying the paper down. "I think I still do, though it's been a long while since I advertised."

"Don't you think it's time to start again?"

"Well, people know we have always been here ..."

"And thanks to Jack Randall, they also know The Palace is here now, too," Mahala replied.

"Is that what prompted this?" Martha asked, raking her with an inquisitive eye.

"Of course. Don't you care about him trying to steal our customers?"

"I think we don't have anything to prove. And there's no way we can compete with his money and dash."

"But we can at least hold our own. Please, Grandmother — an ad. I think it will more than pay for itself."

"All right." Martha sat back in her chair, still thoughtfully sizing up her granddaughter. "Write your ad. We'll send it. But watch that you don't get your feelings over-involved in this little competition of yours. That spark in your eye makes me suspect you're enjoying yourself a bit too much. And Mr. Randall is not the sort you have any business provoking."

July 4, 1855
Clarkesville, Georgia

She was seventeen, but it was her first party dress. And Mahala felt as nervous as a thirteen-year-old as she stood in front of her mirror. She anxiously smoothed the bodice of her tiered taffeta gown, which whispered as she moved, and adjusted the red and white roses trimming her neckline and black curls.

The impossible had happened. Not only was she attending a dance; she was *performing* a dance, as one of eight former students of Miss Pettigrew's. Despite the fact that a woman had begun to oversee instruction at Old College the year Mahala had started with Miss Pettigrew, Mahala had completed her tutelage privately. Martha had liked having her close by, with little time lost between her classes and her work. Now, the industrious teacher had taken the town's Fourth of July celebration to heart and had volunteered the young ladies to render a Liberty Quadrille of her own creation set to patriotic music. Unfortunately, there were few former students still unwed and living in the area. Mahala's initial refusal to participate had not been honored. The little lady had called again and again until at last Mahala had capitulated, bowing to her former teacher's determination. And so they were to open the dancing tonight on a platform erected on the courthouse lawn.

Mahala peeked out the open window at the crowds already milling in the streets, which had been temporarily blocked off to traffic. A festival atmosphere prevailed. Lanterns hung in the trees and along hotel porches. Children laughed and frolicked. No one seemed bothered by the lingering heat.

Of course a good part of the festivities centered around the opening of The Palace, which was brilliantly illuminated from top to bottom. It did indeed look elegant now, if rather out of place. Mahala shuddered as she considered how rustic their little dance performance would surely appear to those assembled inside. Maybe they would all stay in Randall's hotel, where he had engaged his own musical ensemble from the coast ... at least, maybe they would all stay put until the fireworks Jack had purchased were set off.

She turned as Patience entered her room, looking sweet in a short-sleeved muslin gown of a pastel hue. Patience paused and put her hand to her bosom. "Oh, my," she gasped. "Don't you look grand! Oh, how I wish my parents had had the money to send me to Miss Pettigrew."

"So do I," Mahala replied. "Then you and not I would be performing the Liberty Quadrille. I feel ridiculous, all trussed up like this. I'll be the town's laughing stock."

"You will *not*."

"I just want to get it over and come home."

"Oh, but you can't do that. Clay will be waiting on you, and you can't miss the ice cream and fireworks," Patience declared.

"I guess you're right," Mahala sighed. "This is probably the only dance I'll ever attend. I might as well make the most of it."

"That's right, Mahala. You're not afraid of anything. And you've never been embarrassed of your heritage before. Don't you start now. I don't care what anyone might say. They'll all *know* you're the most beautiful girl out there."

"Oh, Patience." Mahala bent to embrace her staunch young friend. "Thank you."

Patience gently adjusted a loose rose bud and wrapped her arm through Mahala's. "Let's go."

Martha was waiting in the parlor. Thanks partly to Mahala's ad, they, too, had a full house, but Martha had vowed nothing would make her miss Mahala's performance. She rose as the girls emerged and gave a cry of delight, kissing Mahala.

"What a lady you are," she said.

Martha followed them through the square, glowering at young men who turned to observe their progress, shepherding them safely to the stage where Miss Pettigrew waited on her brood. A band composed of various local string musicians sat in the shade of the nearby oak tree, for it was hot even approaching eight o'clock. They all waited while the mayor welcomed the crowd and introduced the evening of dancing. Then, in twos, the girls climbed the steps to the stage and took their places. Mahala did not really know the girl she was dancing with, but she didn't mind … better it be a girl than a boy at this awkward moment. Thinking of boys, there was Clay Fraser, right in the front row, watching her with adoration.

When the music began, she tried to close out the memory of his face and concentrate on being as graceful as possible. They performed three movements. During the concluding bars of the last, they unfolded and rotated around a large flag until it was facing the crowd, at which point they raised it upright at the edge of the stage. Applause exploded as the band moved into "The Star Spangled Banner."

When it was over, men began to cheer and throw flowers onto the stage, surging around the girls as they descended the steps. Mahala's face burned. She felt like an object on display, totally out of her element. She was relieved when Martha and Patience came on either side of her and led her away from the ruckus.

"My goodness, what ungentlemanly behavior!" Martha exclaimed. "I believe some of the ruffians have already been in their cups. Perhaps you girls should come back inside."

"Oh, Mrs. Franklin, please! It will be all right. My father is nearby with the rest of the family, and here comes Clay Fraser now. See?" Patience pointed to where the tall young man was shouldering his way through the noisy crowd.

"Oh, I feel so much better," Martha murmured sarcastically.

Clay arrived and stood before them. Removing his hat, he bowed. The gesture was for the three of them, but his eyes were only for Mahala. "Good evening," he said. "Miss Mahala, let me be the first to congratulate you."

"Please don't." Mahala shrugged under the sticky weight of her finery, wishing now for nothing more than her cotton work dress and a stack of linens to hide behind.

"Why not? You were wonderful. I'd like to see a bunch of Savannah belles do any better."

"Thank you, Clay."

"I must return to the hotel now," Martha said. "Mahala, are you going to accompany me?"

"Oh, now surely she didn't get all dressed up for that one dance," Clay protested. "With your permission, Mrs. Franklin, I'll escort both ladies to enjoy the rest of the evening's festivities."

Martha looked questioningly at Mahala, who nodded discreetly. "Very well," she murmured, sounding a little disappointed. "Just mind you don't go off anywhere except in company."

"Of course, Mrs. Franklin," Clay replied emphatically.

"Good night, then." Martha kissed Mahala's cheek. "I'll see you right after the fireworks."

"Yes, Grandmother."

As Martha turned and made her way back towards the hotel, Clay tucked the hands of the girls onto his arms. Escorting them back to the square, he muttered, "Does she think to keep you hidden away forever? You're seventeen — the age most girls marry!"

"Now Clay, don't speak ill of her," Mahala replied. "She's only protective — and she needs me."

"I think she'd have you never leave."

"Now that isn't true," Mahala said, but secretly she had wondered about the same thing. Well, until she herself wished to leave, it wasn't an issue.

They stood near The Palace at the edge of the crowd, observing the Grand March. It was a jolly procession, the columns now unwound into a serpentine. Laughing, flushed faces floated past in the deepening twilight. Fiddle, banjo and dulcimer raised gay notes to a purpling sky.

When the dance ended all the participants were standing with hands still joined, facing into a large circle surrounding the band platform. The caller announced a Federal Schottische.

"Oh," said Patience. "This is one that my papa taught me. And there he goes out to dance with Mama."

Mahala knew what any gentleman was required to say next, and Clay responded according to protocol. "Since he is already engaged, would you care to honor me?"

"I would — only — if —" She glanced uncertainly at Mahala.

"No, please, go ahead. I am more than happy to watch," she assured them.

"Will you be all right here alone?" Clay looked at her rather wistfully.

"Yes! I'll stand here near the porch."

"The next dance, then?" he questioned.

"All right, just go ahead! You'll miss your opportunity," Mahala urged, giving them both a little shove.

As they went off, Mahala put her arms around herself, wishing for a shawl — even in the heat — to cover her conspicuous patriotic ensemble. She was thinking about plucking the roses from her neckline when the music started. The dancers step-hopped their way around the circle, bowing and promenading. She grew bored and began to observe that elegantly-clad guests occasionally entered or exited The Palace. Her curiosity stirred. She had heard and read such grand things about the hotel's interior. She could hardly go sacheting in the door all by herself, but what was the harm in a little peek in a window?

Mahala edged her way down the side street where she might look inside unobserved. She found a window and, edging her skirt past some bushes, raised herself on the toes of her slippers. She could see through an open hallway paved in marble tiles into a large room where couples danced gracefully on a polished wood floor. It appeared to her unpracticed eye that they were doing some sort of polka, but the moves were more complex and ever so dainty.

She became so engrossed in following their footwork and straining to hear the tune that she did not see a figure approaching diagonally from within. There was a flash of white and black evening attire as the window flew open and music poured out. Mahala jumped back. Jack Randall's head appeared in the opening.

"Well, if it isn't Miss Mahala Franklin!" he exclaimed.

At that awful moment she was sure her face matched the hue of her roses. To be caught peeping like some six-year-old! How did she get herself in such circumstances? Obviously, her nemesis was enjoying the situation immensely.

He grinned good-naturedly. "You really don't have to resort to peeking in windows, you know. Anyone is welcome to walk through the hotel tonight. Even my arch enemy. The ball is for guests only, but you'd get a much better view from the hall here."

Mahala was so mortified she could think of nothing to say. So she turned without a word and started to hurry away. But her dress caught on the shrubbery and she was obliged to pause and yank it free. As she ran up the street she heard Jack Randall's mocking laughter floating at her back.

Once again she wanted nothing more than to go straight home, but she forced herself to stop, trembling, near the porch. Grandmother would be livid and her friends worried if she went home alone, but what was more, she couldn't beat such an undignified retreat. It was bad enough that she had let Jack scare her off like a frightened rabbit. He couldn't spoil the whole evening. Dismayed to see that the schottische had not yet ended, Mahala forced herself to take a few deep breaths.

Then she felt a touch at her elbow. She whirled and viewed Jack Randall in shocked dismay. At first she thought he had followed her to rub in her embarrassment. But he seemed to take pity on her. "Miss Franklin," he said in a more gentle tone than she'd ever heard him use. "I'm sorry I laughed. I was quite sincere in my invitation for you to come inside."

"That would hardly be proper," she replied, looking away. "My friends are still dancing."

"I see. Then allow me to serve as your escort."

She looked at him, questioning the propriety of *that* even more. But he did seem sincere. And there was a boyish glint in his eye that somehow belied the strong masculine frame so dashingly set off by his black tail coat. Her courage rose. She *did* want to see inside that hotel. Lightly she laid her hand on the arm he offered her. He smiled and led her through the double front doors.

Instantly she felt that she had entered another world, no doubt one to which the Randalls were well-accustomed — but which made the Franklin Hotel appear shabby in comparison. Everything was new and glistening, from the white marble floor to the crystal chandelier. A wide staircase curved up in front of her. The reception desk nestled in its crook. To one side was a parlor area with red velvet settees and armchairs. To the other she glimpsed a dining room. She immediately knew all the furniture was the best quality, as were the paintings and mirrors on the wall. Potted trees and fresh floral arrangements softened the décor.

"It's beautiful," she murmured.

"Thank you. I was hoping you would like it," he said quietly.

She looked quickly up at him. "You were?"

"I couldn't have my competitor truly believing I lacked in taste."

"Of course not," Mahala said a bit sourly, but inside she was wondering. Did he really value her approval?

"Come into the dining room. We've laid out the refreshments there," he said.

As he led her along, guests bowed and nodded to him with obvious admiration and respect. Jack returned their acknowledgement graciously, encouraging them to enjoy themselves.

"Allow me," he murmured, taking up a plate. Going down the lavishly presented table, he selected several items. He returned to her side and handed her the plate, pointing out the various delicacies. "Escalloped oysters, terrapin, a bonbon and in the glass, of course, café mousse."

Mahala raised a brow. "Why did you bring me in here? To see me turn green over your grandeur?"

With a bit of sudden irritation, Jack replied, "Just eat."

She hesitated, as if being offered the poisoned apple.

"Eat," he said again. "Please. Enjoy it."

Slowly she raised the terrapin to her lips. As she nibbled he watched her. The café mousse was the best thing she had ever tasted.

"Like it?" Jack asked when she closed her eyes in delight, momentarily forgetting him.

"Oh, yes." Why did it seem he was measuring her? Her skepticism returned. "Of course one would expect no less from the French chef."

"I'm glad to hear it." Jack handed her empty plate to a passing servant, saying, "Please bring the lady a drink."

"No, no, I'm fine," Mahala hastened to interject.

"Are you sure?"

"Yes."

"Care to watch the dancing?"

Mahala nodded, and Jack led her down the hall she had already glimpsed. Being on his arm had a strange effect, for she knew that so long as she was there none would dare to question her presence or her background — at least not in public. For a moment she felt like a grand lady. It was oddly freeing. She did not have time to ponder this, though, for as they reached the ballroom entrance, Jack said, "Oh, they're doing a waltz next. Would you honor me, Miss Franklin?"

"N-no!" she exclaimed, freezing in fear and pulling back from his grip.

"Why not? Your festive ensemble should be seen in here, where there's light, not out there in the dark. Oh." He paused, a thought dawning. "Surely you know how to waltz. Don't you?"

Indignation suddenly filled her. "Of course I do," she snapped.

"Then — please ..." Jack gestured with one arm toward the open floor.

Mahala saw people begin to turn and stare curiously. Suddenly she knew she could not bow out gracefully, any more than she could stand there and explain to Jack Randall why she didn't want to dance with him. There was the intimidation of being surrounded by wealthy and cultured people. But more than that was the fact that she was inexperienced. She had practiced waltzing with girls and a couple of shy boys, and the idea of whirling around in the arms of this man in particular made her giddy with fear. But if she declined now, it would be worse than running down the alley earlier.

She placed her gloved hand in his and allowed Jack to lead her onto the floor. As they went Mahala heard whispers from the periphery. She held her back straight and her head high, though inside she was trembling. She must have been trembling outside some, too, for he seemed to sense it and took a firm grip on her hand and waist, offering a reassuring smile.

The music of flute, piano and violin lilted into a graceful melody. Jack nudged her waist and she tentatively stepped out between his feet. As they began to swirl to the three-quarter tempo, turning around and around each other, the floor filled. Jack carefully guided her in clockwise turns in the counter-clockwise whirlpool of dancers.

When Mahala felt confident enough of her steps, she whispered, "Did you mean to humiliate me?"

"Good heavens, no. And see, you dance quite well."

"It's taking all my powers of concentration."

Jack laughed aloud. "If you were unsure, you should have told me, Miss Franklin."

"Right. With everyone watching."

"You look quite lovely tonight, by the way."

Mahala couldn't bring herself to thank him, though she felt color steal into her cheeks. She was growing dizzy, but she resisted staring into those green eyes. She hadn't really looked at him fairly before. Patience had been right. "We're still going to be the talk of the town tomorrow," she said instead of lingering on her thoughts.

"That's all right with me. I've never cared much about idle chatter."

"You can afford not to care."

"True," he stated, "but you give a pretty good impression of not caring, either."

Her gaze swung to his. "Impressions are not always very accurate."

"You know you will probably receive several gentlemen callers tomorrow," he added with a smirk.

"I sincerely doubt that."

"I don't." Jack's eyes caressed her face.

As they swirled past the entrance to the room, Mahala suddenly caught sight of Clay with Patience on his arm, both of whose mouths were agape.

"Ah, your friends have arrived. Shall I deliver you to them?" Jack asked.

"Yes, please."

He swung her off the dance floor and bowed over her hand. "I'm immensely thankful you agreed to waltz with me," he said.

"I'm immensely thankful I managed to not tread on your toes," she replied in a rush of honesty.

His responding laughter — delighted rather than sardonic — made her warm all over. And strangely unsettled. She was suddenly eager to return to Clay and Patience. But when she saw the thundercloud that was Clay's face, she hesitated.

"We were worried about you," Clay told her the minute they drew close enough to speak.

"We couldn't think where you'd gone," Patience added. "This was not exactly the first place we would have guessed."

"Apparently it wasn't the last, either," Mahala said, embarrassed by their lack of manners.

"A man saw you going in with Mr. Randall."

"Yes, Mr. Randall offered to show me inside. Have you met before?" Mahala asked.

"Not officially," Jack replied. "Though I've seen Miss Blake at her father's bakery."

Mahala proceeded to make the introductions, only hoping she did so correctly. Now why should she care? But she did. She didn't want to look like a country bumpkin in Jack Randall's eyes. And Clay wasn't helping matters, with his sullen refusal to look Jack in the face.

Patience did what she could to alleviate the discomfort by saying sweetly, "Your hotel is amazing, Mr. Randall." She was clearly in awe of her surroundings.

"Thank you, Miss Blake. My goal was to create an accommodation heretofore unseen in these parts — something on a par with The Pulaski House in Savannah."

Mahala drew back almost unconsciously. How silly of her to think that a few minutes waltzing with Jack Randall would have birthed a friendship. His comment told her how little he truly thought of her home and background. The Franklin Hotel, so fine to her when she had arrived from the valley, was just a backwoods inn to him. He had merely brought her into The Palace to show her the difference, as she had expected in the beginning. And she had been easily bedazzled.

"It would appear you've accomplished what you set out to," she heard herself say coldly.

He turned to her, seeming a bit surprised at the change in her tone. He smiled, but not openly like before. "I'm sure we'll find there's no need for competition, and we can all be friends. There should be more than enough guests to keep us all in business."

"Of course."

"Come, let's not take up any more of Mr. Randall's time," Clay urged, taking Mahala's arm.

"Not at all! I enjoyed our visit," Jack said.

"Good night, Mr. Randall," Mahala replied. She felt his eyes on her back as she walked away.

From the amazed look on Patience's face as they stepped onto the porch, she would have plenty to say when Clay was not around. Clay, too, was silent, but Mahala knew that would not last, either. And indeed as soon as Patience's brother came to claim her for a reel, Clay turned to Mahala and asked, "What were you thinking, going off with Jack Randall? Did the pretty dress go to your head, Mahala?"

"You have no right to speak to me that way, Clay Fraser."

"Maybe I don't, but that's not gonna stop me. I couldn't help wondering what kind of designs he had on you."

"I don't think he had any designs on me, other than to show me his fancy hotel. And I wanted to see it, so I went in."

"But the way he was looking at you ... and you—"

Mahala's eyes snapped up to his face. Clay took her arm and gently led her to a hay bale. "Never mind," he said softly, drawing her down beside him. "It's just that we're not a part of that world, Mahala. We never will be."

"I know that."

"I just don't want to see you get hurt — or embarrassed. You're too proud for that. Too good."

"I won't," Mahala murmured with a sudden surge of tenderness — and gratefulness. "Thank you, Clay."

"All right, then. Will you dance with me?"

She smiled. This was so different than being with Jack Randall. There were no games and no hidden meanings, only honesty and a natural comfort. Clay was right. She didn't belong in there waltzing on a polished floor, no matter how sophisticated and alive she had felt in Jack's arms. She belonged out there under the stars, grabbing Clay's hand as the band tuned up for a Soldier's Joy.

They ran to get into the circle of couples facing couples — a big circle, because this was an old dance everyone knew and loved, from the children to the old people. Under the early summer moon they balancéd and turned each other, the ladies chained, and they passed through to repeat the steps again. All the while, Clay smiled down into her eyes, and she knew that he loved her. She told herself she should begin to get used to the idea. She couldn't keep a good man waiting forever.

So when they stood with the crowd facing The Palace Hotel and the first vivid explosion of yellow stars lit up the night sky — and Clay's hand slipped into hers — she didn't pull away. Instead, she squeezed, her breath taken by the next shower of brilliant red. Mahala allowed Clay to hold her hand the entire time they watched the fireworks display provided by Jack Randall.

End of Book One

Coming Fall 2013—

The Gray Divide:
Book Two of the Georgia Gold Series.

As the country hurtles toward division and civil war seems imminent,
Habersham's "summer people" must choose sides and alliances that
could sustain or destroy them in the coming decade.

ABOUT THE AUTHOR

Denise Weimer

ative Georgia resident Denise Weimer earned her journalism degree with a minor in history from Asbury University. She is the author of romantic novella *Redeeming Grace*, and her magazine articles about Northeast Georgia have appeared in numerous regional publications. She is a wife and mother, a life-long historian, and the director of a mid-1800s dance group, The 1860s Civilian Society of Georgia.

I n *The Gray Divide* - that nebulous chasm between life-changing decisions where the residents of Habersham County and "the summer people" from Savannah find themselves - unexpected friendship unites Mahala Franklin and Carolyn Calhoun. Half-Cherokee orphan Mahala must choose between her peaceful life in the Sautee Valley and helping her grandmother run The Franklin Hotel in Clarkesville, where she is sure to encounter that dreadful competitor Jack Randall, but where clues to her father's murder might also be uncovered. Carolyn Calhoun bows to pressure to select a husband between wealthy rice planter Devereaux Rousseau and his minister brother, Dylan. But what happens if clarity comes too late?

Meanwhile, as head of his family's shipping firm, Jack must decide which course to chart as the country plunges into civil war. Which will prove stronger, inbred principles or love? And while Devereaux's choice to serve Savannah's prestigious Oglethorpe Light Infantry is a simple one, the demands of leadership and the dangers of battle prove far harsher task masters than expected.

Join Jack, Mahala, Clay, Carolyn, Dylan and Dev as they bridge *The Gray Divide* to find love, friendship and integrity on the other side.